Border Crossings
An Aid Worker's Journey into Bosnia

By
~~Aubrey Verboven~~

Al~~~~~

HOPE YOU ENJOY
THE JOURNEY,
AUBREY

First Edition, June 2011

Copyright © Aubrey Verboven 2011

Cover design and photo by Aubrey Verboven

All rights reserved.

ISBN-13:
978-0987744708 (Dajti Press)

ISBN-10:
0987744704

Reader feedback is always welcome and can be directed to
Border-Crossings@bell.net

News and information can also be found at
https://www.facebook.com/BCrossings

To Cynthia.

When a man hath no freedom to fight for at home,
Let him combat for that of his neighbours;
Let him think of the glories of Greece and of Rome,
And get knock'd on the head for his labours.
To do good to mankind is the chivalrous plan,
And is always as nobly requited;
Then battle for freedom wherever you can,
And, if not shot or hang'd, you'll get knighted.

Lord Byron

Tafas: Truly, now, you are a British Officer?
Lawrence: Yes.
Tafas: From Cairo?
Lawrence: Yes.
Tafas: You did not ride from Cairo?
Lawrence: No. Thank Heavens. It's nine hundred miles; I came by boat.
Tafas: And before? From Britain?
Lawrence: Yes.
Tafas: Truly?
Lawrence: From Oxfordshire.
Tafas: Is that a desert country?
Lawrence: No; a fat country; fat people.
Tafas: You are not fat?
Lawrence: No. I'm different...

Lawrence of Arabia

ACRONYMS

APC	Armoured Personnel Carrier
APWB	Autonomous Province of Western Bosnia
BanBat	Bangladeshi Battalion
BiH	*Bosna i Hercegovina* - Bosnia and Herzegovina
BOV	*Borbeno Oklopno Vozilo* – Yugoslav-built wheeled armoured personnel carrier
BRDM	*Bronirovannaya Razvedyvatelnaya Dozornaya Mashina* - Russian armoured reconnaissance vehicle
ECMM	European Community Monitoring Mission
EU	European Union
FBI	Federal Bureau of Investigation
FreBat	French Battalion
GPMG	General purpose machine gun
HV	*Hrvatska Vojska* - Croatian Army
ICL	Internal Confrontation Line
ICRC	International Committee of the Red Cross
JNA	*Jugoslovenska Narodna Armija* - Yugoslav People's/National Army
NATO	North Atlantic Treaty Organisation

NepBat	Nepalese Battalion
NGO	Nongovernmental Organisation
PolBat	Polish Battalion
PX	Post Exchange – duty-free stores for UN peacekeepers and staff
RPG	Rocket Propelled Grenade
RSK	*Republika Srpska Krajina* – Krajina Serb Republic
RS	*Republika Srpska* – Bosnian Serb Republic
RCMP	Royal Canadian Mounted Police
SAM	Sanctions Assistance Mission
UNICEF	United Nations Children's Fund
UNCIVPOL	United Nations Civilian Police
UNHCR	United Nations High Commissioner for Refugees
UNMO	United Nations Military Observer
UNPA	United Nations Protected Area
UNPROFOR	United Nations Protection Force
WHO	World Health Organisation
ZOS	Zone of Separation

Areas of Control - Croatia & Bosnia - September 1994

Areas of Control
- Bosnian Serb Army
- Bosnian Croat Army
- Army - Rep. of Bosnia & Herzegovina

Krajina & Bihać - Boundries & Travel Routes

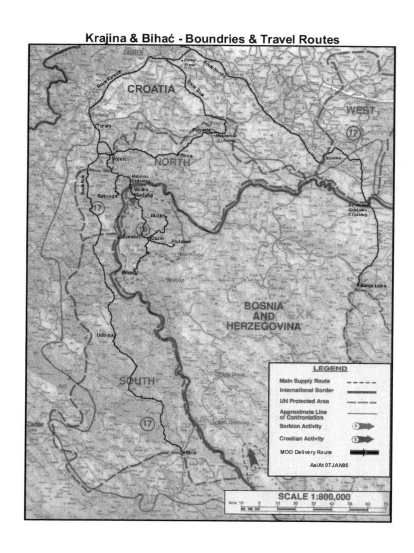

Chapter 1

As the water hit his face, Justin fought to clear his mind and focus. In a haze, he stepped from the shower, anxiously dried-off, dressed and gathered his belongings. A heavy shoulder bag and bulging duffel bag were his worldly possessions for at least the next six months. Justin's watch read 5:30 a.m. Straining to recall, he could have sworn it read 3:30 a.m. last he looked.

By this point Ronald had awoken – the previous night he had promised to help Justin catch his morning train to the airport. As the evening progressed in a drunken eddy, Justin never believed the guy would really follow through.

For two weeks prior, Justin and Ronald had been on a course organised by an emergency aid group named Medical Outreach Overseas or MOO. The training gave new MOO volunteers crash indoctrination in logistical skills they would need on foreign humanitarian missions. The course covered everything from completing inventory, waybills, and supply procurement to keeping medicine cold, rigging generators, and water purification. All normally mundane activities made interesting by the war zone in which they would be performed.

Fresh out of university, Justin had tired of the ceaseless bickering and whining that anchored his tame Toronto universe. Frustrated by a complacent world obsessed with earning money and protecting retirement benefits, he had to get out. He desperately needed something new – something to do just for its own sake.

Yet in such a just and plush society, he was supposed to mark time dutifully amongst the masses. When the period was right and Justin was old, the great meritocracy might anoint him worthy to participate in something interesting. Until then, it would be drudgery and sleep.

So, with a mint diploma in hand, Justin approached the obvious venues that might one-day grant such privilege. It did not take long for his ambition to sap.

For government jobs, the standards were high; they did not hire just anyone straight from school. Desire alone would not suffice. At a minimum, they demanded more education, more language abilities and a proficiency in math and patterns.

With increasing regularity, the army was sending noble soldiers overseas as peacekeepers. But, they did not want restless dreamers. They demanded an extreme capacity to live under regulations and endure yelling and nagging. And down the road, they may hold your hand through six months of standing at a checkpoint or hauling out trash in some contaminated base with a bunch of guys bitching that they would rather be back home.

Humanitarian aid organisations sent people abroad too. But they sought skilled professionals. They were not going to offer adventure to people without work experience.

Justin did not have time to wait for the system. He had to go soon or else complacency would ensure permanent comfortable enslavement to this blasted land.

A half-year after graduation Justin's privileged education gave him the honour of being a security guard at a theatre hall. His main responsibilities – making sure people did not smoke backstage and that unruly fans did not harass the resident opera singers. He faced an enormous climb in this honest culture.

Justin eventually gained promotion to answer phones at a travel agency. There he faced complaints from customers rewarded for their shopping with discounted airfares to worlds far more interesting than his own.

Finally, Justin ended up in a warehouse wrapping giant pallets of toiletries with giant rolls of shrink-wrap. The remuneration was decent but how long could one's mental health endure? He was descending farther with each eight-hour shift spent hunched-over circling cargo skids.

Yet, from this mindless swirl, Justin caught glimpses of darker mindlessness festering elsewhere. People more important than Justin were making sanctimonious oaths promoting a great New World Order. The vast uncomfortable world beyond the borders of Justin's seemed on the verge of retrieving lost self-determination and prosperity. Walls that divided a distant capital came down in brotherly euphoria. Systems of hegemony that had long simmered in notional war ceased their rivalry. Yet, for all that the leaders promised, they instead only seemed to bring betrayal. Justin did not seek inclusion amongst the wishful pontification of the new Order's prophets. His imagination stirred with the bounty of the new unknown. Blood and flesh, love and hate – he needed to find a place for the young of heart and loose of foot.

Normally unmoved by the distant abstractions he saw on the TV news, disgust and rage now welled with each new indignity. Infants crushed to death in the very trucks Justin's world sent for their rescue. Charred hands reached from foreign living room rubble. Villages impaled on toppled minarets.

Why should any of it suddenly make a difference to him? No forces had ever pulled to dislodge Justin from the ease of North American existence. Those around him could not fathom his obsession to be abroad. His birth luck was the envy and aspiration of so many the world over. How could events in some wretched land, so far away, urge him to risk all that? What could he possibly achieve there? He could never make a difference with those savages. And what profit could he possibly gain?

Justin had few answers to these irksome questions posed by the self-absorbed people he knew. Damn them all and their smugness. He just knew where he had to be. As each staid day passed, a parched yearning grew to be where history and humanity reigned rawest.

All the while, letters of rejection piled higher – he could have wallpapered a room with them. Thanks for your interest but…we require more experience…you only have one university degree…you are not of the right profile…your background is not specific enough…we wish you all the best in your future endeavours. It was a vicious circle. No one had much interest in an eager person.

The only hopeful glimmer came from a relatively young aid group, Medical Outreach Overseas. The organisation sent fresh volunteers and still idealistic doctors around the world to help those in need. At the moment, they had no places to offer Justin abroad. Nevertheless, they could use his help in the local office if he had free time and no expectation of pay.

Justin found time and chipped in when he could. He made photocopies, wrote newsletters and organised files. It was not nearly as exciting as the stuff posted on the office walls and bulletin boards – UN maps of snaking tangled frontlines, letters of lonely adventure from projects in distant dusty continents, group photos of expats showing off their euphoric exile from Canada. At least Justin was now a bit closer to the pulse – a few less degrees removed from the action outside.

Twenty-four and impatient, Justin was certain of two things – that he was bulletproof and needed displacement. The reports and letters at MOO convinced him that Eastern lands would be the best test of these assertions.

Justin plugged away for months and, as fortune finally and mercifully had it, a position in the field came open. MOO's management searched their databases and contacts for suitable candidates. Nobody jumped out of the human resource computer. Not handcuffed entirely by bureaucratic methods and transparent process, MOO pragmatically came to consider Justin. Amongst his patchwork of menial employment, Justin had worked summers for a truck company delivering cargo around Toronto. This, coupled with the fact that he had been a low maintenance office volunteer, led MOO to believe the right candidate sat before them.

In June 1994, two painfully slow years out of university, the boom finally inched upward. Justin had a shot at the raw world outside. Holland would be his first step in this direction. It was only a little less docile than Toronto but it was a change and that is what really mattered.

MOO-Toronto sent Justin to the organisation's international headquarters in Amsterdam for training. There he joined a group of some twenty other Dutch volunteers on the verge of being scattered to emergencies around the world – Sierra Leone, Liberia, Sudan, Rwanda, Somalia, there was no shortage of places for groups like MOO to find victims to bandage.

The youthful relaxed manner of the new colleagues was refreshing and Justin quickly befriended many. Liberated and in Europe, he dove headlong into the social habits Amsterdam and his new friends had to offer.

After a fortnight of long days in class and long nights on the town, Justin stumbled out of Ronald's apartment with two heavy bags. Beneath the stairwell, Ronald found his bicycle and balanced the duffel bag across its frame.

Ronald's apartment was only a five-minute walk from the train station. Teetering down Amsterdam's abandoned streets, the pair made it in 15. Panicking through the station, they reached the platform just as the airport train arrived.

Hoisting his bags into the train, Justin swung round and shook Ronald's hand. "Hey, thanks for everything. Too much fun this town."

"No worries, man," Ronald replied smiling. "I'll write when I find out where MOO sends me." Rolling his eyes he added, "Probably Africa."

"Well, keep your head down." Justin replied. Realising how stupid he just sounded and that he clearly had no experience to base this advice on, he corrected, "Or up…screw it, just go with the flow."

Announced by the conductor's whistle, Justin took his next step. A flash of hesitation stabbed and fear of what lay ahead tried to take hold. What was he getting himself into? The panic was not from the jag of danger but more from the murk of unknown.

He had made a commitment, though – on paper and, most of all, in his conscience. He had to keep going and see how far it led. There would be no more time for speculation.

As the doors closed, Ronald grinned and gave a thumbs-up. Justin was finally and truly heading farther east to the mad panacea he lusted. He was on his way to the Balkans.

One foul cup of coffee and a stilted nap later, Justin transferred planes in Austria. His ticket claimed Croatian Airlines would fly the last leg to Zagreb. Wandering the Vienna Airport expanses, Justin dodged businessmen racing through routine and tourists stumbling through confusion. Meandering and asking directions, Justin found his departure gate in a darkened basement nook gutted for renovation. The airport seemed reticent to admit it had flights to the Former Yugoslavia. Justin's boarding pass even bore Austrian Airlines' logo.

Dour brooding faces of passengers festooned in bombastic attire filled the sombre waiting area. The men flaunted bright shiny suits complimented with big gold jewellery. The women flashed frilly costume with still more gold than the men. For all, parading perceptions of wealth was the utmost priority. They appeared a privileged group allowed to travel to and from their warring police state.

Justin found a quiet corner to nurse his growing hangover pangs until a bus came to ferry them to their plane. Driving past terminals and warehouses, there was no sign of aircraft. Tension pervaded amongst the fretful travellers clutching cameras and duty-free bags.

At a secluded apron, commotion erupted as a flurry of bags fell to the ground. Justin ducked from cameras, zoom lenses and video equipment suddenly pointing at head-level. All aimed at a bleak lonely prop plane parked at the tarmac's edge. Excited chatter enveloped the bus as all jockeyed for the best photo positions.

Aboard the vaunted aircraft, an elderly woman sat beside Justin and leafed through a copy of the in-flight magazine – its cover emblazoned with "Croatia." She bore the proud look of a new parent. She turned the pages and held it at arm's length, admiring, wondering how outsiders would view such a mighty tome.

Across the aisle, a man with a copy of the magazine flagged down the stewardess. He enquired about the other aircraft owned by Croatian Airlines.

Theatrically, she held up four fingers, for the other 737's in the airline's fleet. Sighing with feline contentment, the man sat back and crossed himself. He periodically strained forward to look out the window – hoping for a glorious glimpse of one such jet.

When their meals arrived, Justin's aisle-mate pocketed every item on the tray bearing a red-chequered motif – the napkin, drink coaster, stir-stick, plastic glass.

Hoping to arrive with a good overview of the waiting war, Justin flipped through a folder of articles he had photocopied while finishing paperwork at the MOO headquarters. The news media always had a way of oversimplifying things; Justin figured he would have a good grasp of the armies and frontlines by the time he landed.

Croatian refugees were blockading UN peacekeepers in the hope that the starved foreign troops would then return the Croats to their lost homes.

A Bosnian Muslim industrialist and warlord, who cut deals with both Serbs and Croats, had declared independence for his own fiefdom. He in turn, ended up fighting a mini-civil war against his own Muslim brethren.

A brilliant but deranged Bosnian Serb general was bent on revenge against the Muslims after his beloved daughter committed suicide.

Serb jailors had executed a Dutch mercenary in custody for killing two-dozen civilians on behalf of the Croatian Army.

Bosnian Serbs were offering local Muslims bus rides and visas to Sweden in exchange for thousands of Deutsche Marks and the deeds to their homes. The buses were real but only dumped the victims, by the hundred, in no-man's-land.

A Bosnian Serb was arrested in Germany for torturing and murdering Muslims at a concentration camp called Omarska. Former inmates said he had forced prisoners to bite off each other's testicles.

Who was fighting whom in this place? And why? And who were the good guys in this mess?

Touching down in Zagreb an hour later, applause erupted throughout the plane – deliverance at last.

At the sleepy airport's passport control booths, Justin slid his documents to a young slender police officer. She had a peaked cap perched atop locks of long bleached hair. Her exaggerated eye makeup was strangely attractive.

Slender fingers, decorated with long red nails and cheap shiny rings, flipped the pages of Justin's passport.

"Meester Justin frum Kanada," she announced slowly. "You vill need wisa."

Justin's imagination and pulse stirred exponentially.

Still smiling, the officer exited her booth clasping Justin's passport. A holstered automatic pistol bounced against the hips of her tight blue skirt as she graced to the police office across the hall.

She returned minutes later with a bright red-chequered stamp in Justin's passport.

Handing it back, she smiled again, "Velcome to Croacia."

Justin stammered and could only utter a couple of words of drivel. Wiping beads of sweet from his forehead, he slinked over to the luggage carousel.

Retrieving his duffel bag, Justin crossed through sliding doors into the world he had only seen on TV. Outside white jeeps, busses and vans raced by – all stencilled with black "U" and "N" on their sides. A patchwork of foreign soldiers, all with light blue berets, milled about in a camouflage fashion show.

Danes, with powder blue cravats, sported green and brown leopard prints. Swedes, in desperately cool sunglasses, wore fatigues covered in green and black polygons. The French fashioned precise berets and tapered combat pants. Dutch troops in shorts rode by on practical black bicycles. Jordanians sauntered in American fatigues capped with big muffin shaped berets. A gaggle of Russians lingered in shiny tracksuits.

A white MOO Toyota Landcruiser driven by a Dutchman named Rolf Blaat, pulled up. Introducing himself and loading Justin's bags in the back of the car, Rolf mused, "Ah, you made it."

Looking Justin up and down he added, "You look like crap. Why does every Canadian coming from Amsterdam look completely wrecked when they get here? Anyway, we need to stop next-door and pick up one of our trucks."

Rolf had short brown hair and a round face permanently smirking at life's general irony. As a man of average height, he was by Dutch standards, pretty short. He spoke English with no accent. There was really nothing typically Dutch about him.

At the runway's far end, they entered an adjacent military facility – the United Nations Protection Force - Camp Pleso. Originally, an old Yugoslav army base it was now UNPROFOR's main logistical centre for peacekeeping operations in Bosnia and Croatia.

Beyond the main gate's Finnish sentry, Rolf suggested, "How about a coffee? I know a good place."

Warehouses and prefab containers lined Pleso's streets. Row upon row of brand new white Jeeps and Nissans crammed every space in-between. Men in flowing robes and more shiny tracksuits walked by.

Passing a Burger King operated out of a truck-trailer, Justin remarked, "Excellent, you can get burgers here."

Nodding at the fast-food stall, Rolf stated, "Pure salmonella on a bun that. It's funny though, the Croats are pissed off that they don't have a McDonald's in Zagreb. Belgrade has five and Ljubljana even has one. Croats are convinced it's the first step to EU membership. Naturally, they say it's all a Serb conspiracy."

Inside a small building, with a large orange sign reading "*Holland Huis*" they found a bar with a giant-screen TV, shelves of books and board games and a portrait of the Dutch Queen. A few soldiers sat at assorted tables watching Dutch satellite television.

Justin ordered coffee with a plate of croquets and French fries in peanut sauce to quash his lingering hangover spasms. He inhaled the Dutch junk food and pored over a UN situation map with Rolf.

"So, what's MOO doing in Croatia?" Rolf asked rhetorically exhaling from his hand-rolled cigarette.

"Well, basically we're delivering medicine and dressings to hospitals and clinics in the Krajina." Wiping ashes from the Croatian part of the map, Rolf explained, "This big piece of the country is occupied by Serbs – they call themselves Krajina Serbs. They're like Serb hillbillies.

"Right now, they're holding about a third of Croatia but in three separate chunks. The UN arranged a cease-fire between the Croatian and Serb armies and declared these parts as UN Protected Areas - UNPA East, West and North and South. The Serbs proclaimed this territory the Republika Srpska Krajina. It's a pretty shit excuse for a country in my opinion. Their capital is the southern town of Knin – a total dump. The international community don't recognise them though. They say it's still Croatia…but around here, the only thing that matters is the recognition of guns. Whoever has more guns keeps the land.

"Anyway, there's no shortage of trained doctors and nurses in the Former Yugo – just a shortage of medicines. Croatia isn't under embargo and can import whatever it wants. In proclaiming their European nationhood, they told us they don't need our charity. But the Croat authorities also take offence to us giving aid to their enemies – the Krajina Serbs. So for now they take the West's hard currency and throw up just enough bureaucracy to make working in Krajina a pain in the ass."

Unable to find any relevance to the clippings he read on the plane, Justin inquired, "So what's the security situation on the ground?"

"Real combat ceased about a year ago. The Serbs took a lot of territory but their existence is pretty shaky. Croatia blocks all trade with RSK. Knin's cousins to the East, the Bosnian Serbs, aren't giving them much help either. The Bosnian Serbs have there own Republika Srpska and they're still fighting Bosnian Muslims and Croats on all fronts there.

"So in Krajina, we deliver the basics to hospitals in UNPA North and South. We also try to keep an eye on the local hospitals to make sure they're not forwarding the meds on to the army."

"Sounds pretty straightforward," Justin nodded hoping all this info would miraculously sink into his reeling mind.

"The other region that will be of particular interest to you is Bihać. This is where the real fun is."

Pointing to a region beside Krajina on the map, Rolf continued, "Bihać is a pocket in the northwestern corner of Bosnia inhabited by about a quarter million Muslims. The pocket is completely surrounded by Serbs. To the east and south the Bosnian Serb Army hold the surrounding hills. These guys have all the guns and tanks. And they've got General Mladić."

"Yeah, the psycho general who's daughter killed herself right?" Justin asked trying to impress.

"That guy's one crazy fuck. He's threatened to bomb London and Washington if NATO launches air strikes. Sounds unlikely, but what sort of nut makes a threat like that? Maybe he knows something we don't. I'll tell you this…the guy has barely started to murder," Rolf asserted.

"Anyway, to the north and south," Rolf went on, "the Army of Republika Srpska Krajina surrounds the rest of the Pocket. The Bihać Muslim's army, the Fifth Corps, have no heavy weapons and no supplies. All they have are very large balls and Atif Dudaković – their commander. Somehow, he's held out against these odds and he keeps finding new ways to fight a much larger enemy.

"The main town, Bihać, will be one of your delivery points. It's surprisingly close to the Bosnian Serb south-east front-lines, though."

"How close?" Justin asked anxiously.

Exhaling smoke, Rolf shrugged, "I don't know, three maybe four hundred metres at some points. It changes every day."

"Oh yeah, there's one other thing," Rolf added. "The Fifth Corps aren't just surrounded; they're also fighting a civil war against other Muslims. In the far northwestern corner of the pocket is Velika Kladuša. In that town, a Mr. Fikret Abdić owns an enormous agro-commercial empire. In the 1980s, he turned one of Yugoslavia's poorest regions into a pretty prosperous place. He paid his workers well and built them houses. He has businesses in Serbia, Croatia and Bosnia. To the locals he is their protector and provider; they follow him fanatically – even call him "Babo" or Papa. In the late '80s, he got into trouble issuing tonnes of phoney bonds on his company – Agrokomerc. He defrauded the state of something like a billion Marks. When the Communists threw him in jail, his people offered to work, without salary, for the years it would take to pay back the millions he owed.

"After he was released from jail two years later, he became a member of Bosnia's collective presidency. He wheeled and dealed with all sides to keep the living standards high and stop the Serbs from invading his town. The Sarajevo Muslims and President Izetbegovic see Abdić as a renegade. He's even got a medieval castle above Velika Kladuša. When Abdić declared his corner independent, he called it the Autonomous Province of Western Bosnia. Then fighting broke out - Muslim against Muslim - between Abdić's men and the Fifth Corps, which stayed loyal to Sarajevo.

"Naturally, Abdić turned to the Serbs and rented artillery and men for combat. The Serbs took the money and bought new arms to fight Muslims in other parts of the Bihać Pocket and Bosnia.

"At this point, Abdić's APWB is just a small zone around Velika Kladuša and has a good 35,000 supporters at his feet."

Still too excited to believe he was really in the Balkans, Justin remained unable to absorb all he had heard. How could one war be so complicated? Nodding at Rolf's Drum tobacco pouch, he asked, "Hey, could I get one of those?"

"So, what's my job in all of this?" Justin asked as Rolf tossed him a hand-rolled smoke.

"At this point we need you to organise and make regular deliveries from our Zagreb warehouse to clinics in Krajina and Bihać. Best part is that you'll need to get permission to go to these places. There's lots of annoying bureaucracy with the Serbs, Croats, Bosnians and Babo. That will be a good game. You'll figure it out.

"From our experience so far, the Croats will give you token interference – you know, official Croatian state procedures. It's their way of showing that they're civilised Europeans.

"To enter Krajina, the Serb's in Knin will be rather accommodating. They want all the outside stuff they can get their hands on. But at the same time, they need to show their legitimacy. So they'll be slow and incompetent enough to prove they're independent.

"Bihać is an entirely different problem, though. The Croats have no problem with us visiting the Muslims – sometimes they even say they're allies. The Serbs will definitely have objections. The only way to Bihać is through Krajina. On the chance the Serbs let you go through their territory, they won't let you enter the Pocket through the southern section. All traffic to Bihać goes through Velika Kladuša where Abdić will try to take half of your cargo. Of course, this can only happen when there is a cease-fire long enough for your truck to get safely over the internal confrontation line between Abdić and the Fifth Corps. And that's all just getting there; that's only half the trip.

"Oh, and remember these rules change every day, in every place and if you do learn the rules that day, they'll be changed again."

Anxious to get working and learn it all for himself, Justin eagerly inquired, "When can I start?"

"Well, there's a little problem that came up in the last few days. In the cease-fire between the Croats and Serbs, the UN promised to help the displaced Croats get back to their Krajina homes when it was safe. Obviously, it's not very safe. Nobody is very patient here. The Croat refugees decided to force the UN to help them right now. They're blockading all the crossing points so no supplies get to the UN peacekeepers in the Krajina. Since MOO drives white vehicles and is helping the Serbs, these people are having trouble distinguishing between the UN and us. So, they aren't letting us cross either."

"How are we getting into Krajina then?" Justin asked.

"We're not really. The Croat officials give us permission to enter Krajina knowing that it's worthless at the blockades. They're in no hurry to negotiate and get these people back to their homes. In the government's opinion the only time it will be safe to return is when every last Krajina Serb is dead or driven to the hills of Bosnia."

Finishing his beer, Rolf stood up, "Let's get your truck and at least start trying to deliver aid."

At a nearby hangar, three Dutch mechanics tinkered with a MOO truck. Looking out from under the truck, one private waved, "Ten minutes, just finishing the oil."

As Justin gazed curiously at the truck, Rolf explained, "We got the trucks second-hand from the Dutch Army. They keep their trucks in good shape. The Dutch Battalion here services our vehicles as a favour."

Rolf wandered off, poking around the hangar's rows of shelves. Justin climbed aboard the truck to check it out. A DAF four-wheel drive turbo – it blew away the tired old Fords he had driven in Toronto as a student. The truck's dashboard was wired with a Philips stereo, a VHF radio and a Capsat satellite text console.

Rolf reappeared with a big grin and arms full of ration boxes. Loading them into the back of the Landcruiser he explained, "Managed to find some French Army rations. There're worth gold – much better than the shit Dutch rations, or worse, the German ones."

Holding up a box for inspection, he said, "Look at this one. It has Duck Pâté and cheese. And for dinner, '*Muton au Haricots*'…gourmet. If you ever see any of these lying about grab them. Supposedly, older rations had wine and a pack of Gauloises. French generals are smart; they know if they make the men look smart and feed them well, they can send them to any shit-hole they feel like."

Sliding into the driver's seat, Rolf called, "You take the truck. Follow me. I'll show you the way to our warehouse." Waving and shouting thanks to the Dutch mechanics, Rolf drove out of the hangar.

Justin could not stop beaming. His truck started with a blast of dark diesel smoke and a deep melodic roar. After a rough start, this day just kept getting better and better.

Long rows of aging German and French military transport trucks lined the base's roads. Dilapidated Russian jeeps and wide, boat-shaped eight-wheeled armoured personnel carriers filled the parking lots.

From Pleso, they skirted Zagreb on a main highway for three quarters of an hour. Pulling into a vast warehousing complex, they passed storehouse entrances bearing stickers from numerous aid groups and UN agencies. At the complex's far end, Rolf opened a large sliding door covered in MOO stickers and Justin squeezed his truck inside the storage area.

Justin hopped in the Landcruiser and they headed onward to the MOO office downtown. Pointing to a row of 10 diesel tanker trucks in the facility's parking lot, Rolf commented, "See those? They belong to Abdić. He's still doing business with everyone, regardless of the war. He owns half this city already."

In central Zagreb, there were no signs of war damage and the people on the streets appeared to be going about life as normal. The only hint of nearby trouble was the abundance of white UN vehicles racing around. The front lines were only 60 km away, yet billboards screamed colour and consumption. Croatia was almost trying too hard to prove it was just another western country.

Those billboards not promoting capitalism advertised an upcoming visit by the Pope. Complimenting the Pontiff's pious pose were other hoardings of President Franjo Tudjman in patriotic pose. Attempting to exorcise his Communist past, a few posters had President Tudjman sharing billing with the Pope.

A large house in a residential neighbourhood overlooking the downtown core served as the headquarters for MOO's operations in Croatia and Bosnia. The top floors of the house doubled as a residence for the expatriate volunteers.

In the basement office, a lanky Dutchman with long curly locks slouched on a couch. He was smoking a hand-rolled cigarette crowned precariously with a long ember.

"Mik De Groot this is Justin," Rolf introduced. "He's going to be our Krajina and Bihać man. In the mean time, I was wondering if you could take him with you to Banja Luka tomorrow morning?"

Mik tilted his head, took a drag and calmly smiled, "Sure."

A lithe woman in her late twenties with straight dirty blonde hair marched by purposefully with a stack of medical supplies.

Rolf stopped her in mid-step. "Justin, please meet Laura Foster. She's a horrible Canadian like you. She works with Mik in Banja Luka. They're stuck in Zagreb because of the blockades. They actually reopened the Banja Luka office a couple of weeks ago and now can't get back. We'd evacuated the place months earlier because it wasn't safe."

Balancing the boxes, Laura grinned and shook Justin's hand. Winking at Rolf and Mik she said, "Finally another Canadian. I thought the Dutch were taking over."

Rolf gave Justin a bulletproof vest and a white Kevlar helmet – both adorned with MOO's red-cross-like logo. Pulling the vest's ceramic breastplate out of its pocket for inspection, Justin found a manufacturer's sticker guaranteeing the plate would stop bullets up to 7.62 mm calibre.

Reinforcing the point, Laura handed Justin a permanent marker to write his name and blood type on the vest and helmet.

Rolf led Justin upstairs to a large coldly formal room with a long meeting table. An older bald man with drooping jowls and a sloped forehead sat at a desk fiddling on a laptop.

With a sudden air of formality Rolf announced, "Kees 't Hooft, I wish to present to you our newest worker, Justin."

Kees stopped typing and looked up over his half-moon glasses. He smiled and leaned forward to shake hands.

Rolf continued, "Justin, this is Mr. 't Hooft the Balkan Project Manager."

"So, you will be working in our Split office?" Kees asked.

"No, he's covering Krajina-Bihać," Rolf explained quickly.

"Ah. I will compose a job mandate paper for you shortly," Kees explained with paternal aloofness. "Right now, I am completing the new mission statement and policy framework for the Bosnia operations. We'll be able to discuss our regional strategy when I've finished."

Outside Kees' office, Rolf quietly said, "Don't worry about him. You won't see much of him while you're on this mission. He may be in Croatia but he is dealing with a different war."

"Which one is that?"

"Nobody really knows," Rolf replied. Raising a finger for emphasis, he added, "One very important piece of advice. If he ever asks you what you're doing or how things are in you area. Never, never tell him that there is shelling."

"What?"

"He's in a bubble. If he gets the slightest hint of danger, he shuts down the operation and evacuates everyone," Rolf continued. "He's a bit jumpy...every time he suspends our work, people in the hospitals suffer."

A large matronly woman emerged from the dining room down the hall.

"Ah," Rolf said with a large smile, "This is the most important person in the office. Justin meet Branca. She's the cook."

Smiling warmly, she took Justin's hand and guided him into the kitchen area. "*Kava?*" she offered.

Justin pointed questioningly to the empty drip coffeemaker on the counter.

"*Ne, ne,*" Branca asserted and picked up a large Turkish coffee pot bubbling on the stove.

Anticipating a mini cup of the potent brew he had heard much about, Justin nodded eagerly, "Yes, please."

Smiling, Branca instead filled a coffee mug with the steaming murky liquid.

Seeing Justin's eyes bulge in surprise, Branca's smile grew.

"Wow," he gasped.

Branca beamed even more.

Initially, Justin sipped the strong coffee gratefully. But by the time he had consumed half, his heart rate rose violently. For the first time ever, Justin had met a cup of coffee he was physically unable to finish. Branca took this as the ultimate compliment.

There was a considerable air of excitement amongst the office's staff members. That evening, Iggy Pop was scheduled to play a concert at a nearby sports centre. It was a big deal as Iggy was the first foreigner of any consequence to perform in Croatia in over three years.

That evening the sports arena was filled with a few thousand ecstatic young fans. Mik and Justin managed to push their way near the stage. When Iggy and his band hit the stage, a group of four guys jumping up and down hoisted a buddy onto their shoulders. To their left, a dozen other youths, with shaven heads, chanted and made fascist arm salutes toward the stage.

By the second song, three policemen shoved their way through the pulsing crowd. They pressed by the throng of young fascists without a word. Scowling viciously, the cops reached over and punched wildly at the guy propped on his pal's shoulders. The levitating youth fell straight to the ground. Entangled in surrounding arms and legs, the police grabbed at him violently. Standing him on his feet, they yelled a menacing warning. They turned and flailed farther into the crowd, threw a few more punches and uttered yet more threats.

Iggy Pop ground off a couple more tunes before stopping to introduce himself to the adoring crowd.

"Hey you Zagreb fuckers!" he bellowed. "Thanks for stopping your fucking war to hang out with me for a while!"

The crowd grew wilder. The fascists saluted higher and harder. The rest screamed, "Iggy! Iggy! Iggy! We love you…"

Chapter 2

The next morning, Mik, Laura and Justin loaded the Landcruiser with food, medical boxes and their body armour. Mik hopped into the front seat and fought to fold a stack of topographical maps. Ashes from his untapped cigarette speckled the documents. Without gaining any obvious order, he shoved the pile under his seat.

From the passenger side, Laura asked, "You got all our crossing permissions?"

"Uh, no. I forgot," Mik replied sheepishly and went into the office.

He returned clutching a new mess of papers. Patting his pockets for the car keys, he glanced at his colleagues, smirked and ran back inside.

Justin's only real duty on this trip was learning the route from Zagreb to Banja Luka. On top of his responsibilities in Krajina and Bihać, Justin would be delivering cargo to Mik and Laura's warehouse.

The intoxication of events gave Justin no cause for complaint about being a spectator. How often did a person just get to visit infamous places?

One night into the Balkans and Justin still could not fully fathom that he was physically in Croatia. If it was true, it was awesome. There was nothing back across the Atlantic that could rival any of this. The summer of 1994 would be the best ever. Nobody back home had wanted him for jobs of any significance. Why now, should anybody entrust him with being part of history? Justin had to avoid questioning this generous fortune; fate could easily amend such oversight. So, for the time being, he just told himself to go along with it all until he could go no farther.

Crossing the Sava River, the trio headed eastbound out of Zagreb. Officially, maps still listed the four-lane artery, leading eventually to Belgrade in Serbia, as E-70 – the Highway of Brotherhood and Unity. There was little evidence of traffic and even less of fraternity. Barely 80 km from the Croatian capital the freeway crossed into Serb held territory. The group's first stop, Novska, was the last Croatian town before the environs of UNPA West – Republika Srpska Krajina's forgotten appendage.

Vast strips of fertile farmland lined the highway. Although they flew down the abandoned route at a good 150 km/h, the monotonous scenery only inched along.

Leaning forward, Justin asked Mik, "So what did you do before coming here?"

"Me, I studied engineering but actually worked as a journalist in Holland. You know, trying to uncover the truth."

"How'd that go?" Justin asked.

"Not so good," Mik shrugged. "I didn't fit in. Besides, the work was really boring. Not much truth in writing about dog shows and tulips."

"And you Laura?" Justin inquired.

"I was an emergency room nurse in Winnipeg. This isn't much of a stretch really."

"So why did you end up in this business?" Justin pressed.

"Budget cuts in Canada. Got laid off." Leaning around, Laura asked, "But more importantly, what's your story? What are you fleeing?"

"Uh...feelings of impotence I guess."

Glancing at Mik, Laura gave the slightest smirk, "Yeah well be careful, this place will test that...what you find here will be entirely up to you."

Keeping both thumbs on the steering wheel, Mik rolled a cigarette. Shouting over his shoulder, Mik explained that he and Laura had only been working in Banja Luka for a few weeks. Prior to that, the Banja Luka office had been empty for two months. A trio of preceding expats had manned the office for almost half a year but in that time had received continuous death threats from local Bosnian Serb nationalists. Working conditions finally became untenable and the three completely stressed-out foreigners made a break for the Croatian border – never to return.

Banja Luka was the largest town in Republika Srpska. Its resident Serbs had long since expelled or killed most the town's Muslims and Croats. With the Bosnian war's frontlines much farther south, there was never a threat of shelling or gunfire in town.

"This lack of physical danger gives the Serbs the luxury of free time for suspicion and paranoia," Laura chimed in. "The already whacked-out residents mix with Serb fighters returning from the mad frontlines. They see any foreigners in Banja Luka as UNPROFOR spies – there only to direct NATO air strikes.

"Few international organisations have ventured into this region. Aside from the UN High Commissioner for Refugees, International Red Cross and MOO, there aren't many outsiders working in BL. From here, we cover the humanitarian needs of almost all Republika Srpska – that's three-quarters of Bosnia."

"For the UNHCR and ICRC staff, assault, robbery and jail are almost daily events," Mik added. "MOO's been pretty lucky. We're just trying to help anyone we can but the local crazies just see us driving a white car – so we must be spies."

"Why does MOO put up with all that crap? Why don't they just say screw it?" Justin inquired.

Laura nodded, "That's just it. We could do that. But since so few of us work here, it means we're needed that much more. Everyone and their dog is working in Croat and Muslim central Bosnia. There's at least 150 NGO's down there...everything from real aid groups like CARE and Oxfam to a bunch of freaky hippies in a double-decker bus. Believe me, that joint really does need the help. That's why MOO's got a huge project there too.

"But that doesn't mean we can forget Srpska's humanitarian needs. Even if the Bosnian Serbs keep putting up road-blocks and spew venom at the outside world..."

Mik turned off at the Novska exit, just before the highway lanes came to an abrupt end – blocked by a maze of concrete slabs and steel tank barriers. Behind the obstacles, a line of elderly protesters sat in lawn chairs surrounded by Croatian flags and scattered lanterns. Beyond them, stood their target – a white sandbagged bunker and an old M-113 armoured personnel carrier manned by Jordanian peacekeepers.

Entering Novska, Justin strained to find obvious signs of destruction. Serious fighting occurred a couple of kilometres away but it still appeared an unimpressive, liveable town.

Past Novska, they attempted to enter UNPA West via a quiet secondary road. Mik pulled up just short of a new cluster of protesters and furiously scrambled through his papers. Pulling out a document, he scanned the text and stopped abruptly. Plucking at the pile, he produced an identical paper and nodded.

"This one's in Croatian," he muttered to Justin. "The other one was in Serbian. Maybe three words different. It could have been ugly."

The trio stepped casually toward the barricade. Mik reached out to shake the first hand he saw.

Motivated by curiosity and boredom, the crowd of older men and women quickly enveloped the newcomers.

Justin was convinced that his first sight of war damage would finally authenticate his presence in the Balkans. Yet it was this unspectacular gaggle, who had all suffered somehow, that was the war's truest spawn.

After an introductory charade, a man emerged claiming to speak some German. Mik replied with his own limited German and held up the Croatian document. It simply stated that MOO was not part of the United Nations and that it was an independent charity helping all in need on all sides. At its foot, Rolf's signature and a MOO stamp afforded some legitimacy. Hopefully, this scrap was all they needed to allay existing fears.

The five strongest men in the gaggle jockeyed with elbows and shoulders. Unsure what to do next, they hesitantly seized and pored over the paper – all pointed at its stamp and signature.

The German speaker asked Mik where he was going.

"Prijedor," Mik answered.

Laura whispered to Justin, "It's a town that was mostly Muslim and Croat before the war. Mik's gambling on their sentiment."

Justin nodded slightly but was still lost. He was not sure how lying would help.

The group received mention of Prijedor positively and muttered the name amongst themselves. Heads nodded as the word spread. The group seemed tentatively receptive.

Before they could find consensus, a burly man pushed out from the crowd. Pointing at the barricade he yelled, "*Nema šanse, Ne!*"

Wagging a large weathered finger in Mik's face, he affirmed, "*Nema UNPROFOR-a!*"

Mik stepped back startled. Pointing to the Landcruiser he insisted, "*Nije* UNPROFOR…MOO."

A matronly woman came forward balancing a tray of fresh buns smothered in dripping chocolate. She ceremoniously laid the tray before the three visitors and proudly made the first offering to Mik. Once the guests had been cared for, she made the tray available to her fellow protestors.

Justin had barely finished his bun when he was handed a second. Rubbing his belly, he refused politely. Ignoring his effort, the pastry was placed in his hand. Justin raised the second bun in thanks. The crowd pronounced gracious collective acknowledgement and then snapped back to the business at hand.

Fresh baking aside, Justin was having difficulty feeling hostility to the throng barring his way. They looked nothing like the gun-toting goons he had expected in every shadow. These were just people frustrated in the confusion. War had driven them from their homes. All had lost much. They reserved most of their rage for those who had terrorised and forced them here. They left some anger for the Croatian government that had promised them national nirvana but left them unprotected. And they saved a final dram of fury – that deepest rage of dashed expectations – for the United Nations they believed would be their great panacea. Used and manipulated by all parties, these people now struck back in the only way they knew.

Not everyone in this war could be innocent though. Of those before Justin, who were the victims and who the victimisers? What horrors had they witnessed and what horrors had they inflicted? It really did not matter – in the end they were all likely victims of someone else.

Mik continued pleading his case but the group became increasingly unenthusiastic to allow passage. Meanwhile, two protestors had wandered over to the Landcruiser and peered into its windows. Noticing the pile of body armour and helmets under the back seat, they called out wondering why such items were in the vehicle.

The barriers of language and tension gave Mik little chance to explain that he always carried the protective gear as a matter of safety.

The protestors immediately equated such materiel with the nearest worst place in the world.

"Banja Luka!" the accusation erupted.

"*Ne, ne* Prijedor," Mik appealed.

The crowd's mind was set; they were not going to let these aid workers cross their barrier and visit such a Serb-infested bastion of rot.

Sensing the protestors' nervous shift, Mik shook scattered random hands and retreated.

The three tried a number of other checkpoints in the area. Unfortunately, a motorcycle driven by two young machos followed the group to each barricade. At every new crossing, the youths became more aggressive toward the foreigners. After the fifth attempt, the trio headed back to the Zagreb office.

On a hunch, Mik stopped by the UNHCR headquarters in Zagreb. He knew a field officer there who was familiar with Banja Luka and the surrounding region. As luck had it, the UN worker knew of a back road, caught in geographic limbo that was overlooked by the blockaders.

The following morning the trio set out for Banja Luka's backdoor. They broached Novska once more.

Along a straight flat section of road, an elaborate memorial stone bore the etched impressions of two young men's faces and a chiselled lamentation.

Northeast of town, the lush agrarian and wooded terrain became blemished with destroyed houses along the road. With each kilometre, the destruction grew stronger. At some unmarked point, they crossed the plane where people resided together peacefully to the one where they smashed their neighbours' doors and torched their lives.

Arriving at a sleepy UN checkpoint, a pair of Jordanian peacekeepers eyed the white Landcruiser lazily. They barely glanced at the group's ID cards and waved them through.

According to the UN maps, this crossing point marked the beginning of the Zone of Separation established as a buffer between the Croatian and Krajina Serb armies. Under the cease-fire agreement, responsibility fell on the UN to observe and ensure that the area remained demilitarised. The Jordanians were more intent on observing than ensuring.

Following the UNHCR officer's directions, Mik turned onto a narrow, lightly paved road.

"What do we do about landmines?" Justin asked anxiously.

"Yeah, there are probably lots around here. Anyway, this road's paved and the UN drives it regularly. Their engineers should keep these routes clear."

Advancing slowly and avoiding potholes, he added, "You can help by keeping an eye open for anything suspicious – you know, fresh dirt berms, bomb fragments, wires, boxes."

Laura added, "We're heading straight for the old frontlines. The Federal Yugoslav army and local Serb militias made a push from the south but were stopped by the Croats in October 91. The UN's been keeping the Serbs and Croats apart ever since."

Burned shells of plain rural homes lined the narrow road that meandered amongst rolling pastures. A suffocating weight lingered above the bucolic tranquillity. Beneath this smog, hints of past ferocity overwhelmed. Things worse than evil happened here. Unkempt vegetation tried to smother the last signs of this once rustic community. Tempting patches of forest scattered in the distant hills – perfect for long blissful days spent wandering.

For generations, this placid locale would rarely have strayed from its measured daily pace. Now there was no evidence of any life. All individual character, the personality of each home's family, crushed and burned from existence. Bullet-pocked and shrapnel-scarred frames hosted blasted rubble and collapsed beams. The only character remaining was that of the destroyers. Scrawled prominently on surviving facades was the word "*Ustaše*" or the big black letter "**U**" – pure Croat nationalist bile.

Venturing from the pavement to explore would have meant certain maiming, if not death. Many structures were no doubt booby-trapped; the gardens and ditches mined to ensure that if the enemy ever tried returning, they and their families would pay dearly.

With the peace throbbing in Justin's ears, he tried to peer back at how it must have been when the fighting erupted. Calm daily routines shattered as hordes descended on their town – noise, screaming, confusion and blind anticipation most frightening. People desperately grasping to understand what had gone awry. But they had done nothing wrong. Rage had arrived. People cowering to protect themselves and their families as neighbours screamed and begged – no escape. Who is next? Is there any mercy? So much blindness everywhere – blind fear and blind rage. Those clutching frantically in the darkness trying to hide and those advancing sightlessly, slaughtering all before them.

Justin should have known better than to indulge in such painful mental exercise. Yet, some secluded place in his conscience did not care and relished in it anyway. Despite his mind's tricks, Justin still could not even begin to measure such a quantity of agony. The smoke had long since wafted away and so too had the hamlet's essence. The rubble and graffiti were now just allusions to the past violence. What did Justin know? He was an outsider who had missed the main event. The debris that remained stood as perverse monuments to mankind's savagery – trophies to the forces of nationalism and religion.

Each house in this simple village had been a universe. Each had had its own orbit around hopes, dreams and aspirations. All lost now. Such a high toll could only be exacted for something far far more glorious than individual dreams.

Amongst the piled fragments and refuse of terrorised neighbours, the occasional house was left unscathed and inhabited. So, the plan had never been to wipe out the entire village. It had been more sinister; only remove the undesirable parts. Remaining now were the lucky ones, the spared ones, who belonged to the right group.

Congratulations, you are free. Neighbours of all these years had to leave because they were different. But it is all right now; it is safe. The surroundings are untainted and you can continue from this glorious beginning. All around you are the fruits of purification. How fucking grand.

Trying to break the uncomfortable hush within, Laura commented nervously, "Those people must be lonely."

No answer came and the silence remained. How much better could their existences be than those departed? While lonely during daylight, the haunting echoes of their neighbour's cries kept the purified ones company every night. They would never be alone.

Amongst the confusing waste of local hatred rested a forgotten outpost of well-intentioned but ill-prepared outsiders. In a cluster of damaged houses, a Jordanian checkpoint marked the other side of the ZOS – beyond it lay Krajina Serb territory. With the trio's arrival, the dozing checkpoint immediately came to life. A soldier propped against a machine gun atop a parked APC stirred from his sun-induced slumber. Heads peaked from doorways. Noticing that one of the vehicle's occupants was a woman, the soldiers stood tall and smart. With a quasi-professional air, some stepped up to get a better view inside the car. At the barrier, the sentry welcomed them with an enthusiastic salute. Behind him, a large portrait of King Hussein adorned a white sandbagged bunker.

As Mik rolled down his window, the guard smiled and asked, "Hello my friend. Where you go?"

Mik smiled back and pointed to the road beyond the barrier.

The sentry looked at Mik questioningly.

"Banja Luka," Mik offered.

Still no comprehension.

Mik pointed to the King's portrait and stated, "Your King, he is a very good man."

The guard gasped. He stepped back and bowed slightly. "Thank you my friend," he sputtered.

He muttered in Arabic to a nearby soldier, who also bowed his head and smiled graciously. The sentry quickly opened the barrier and waved.

Beyond the Hashemite oasis, the abandoned homes revealed a distinctly Serbian air of destruction. Most of the wrecked buildings bore Cyrillic inscriptions and a few with the word "*Četnik.*"

Pointing to a large pained cross with four mirrored "C's" in each corner, Justin asked, "What's that?"

Mik replied, "It's the Serbs' symbol. Each C is a Cyrillic S. They say it stands for something like, 'only unity can save the Serbs.'"

Although the graffiti now advertised the opposite side's perspective, the depths of hatred and stupidity remained unchanged.

The group passed yet more lucky examples of those who happened to be from the right group. Had they lived a couple of kilometres back up the road, they would have suffered the fate of the wrong group.

The aid workers soon entered more heavily populated parts that had been far enough from the frontline to escape the blanketing destruction. Now only the occasional Croat home was pinpointed for razing.

On the main southward road, Cyrillic licence plates confirmed their presence in the Western Slavonia section of the Republika Srpska Krajina.

A large white sign beside a UN checkpoint, housed in an old roadside hotel greeted, "Welcome to Nepal Battalion UNPA West." The handful of Nepalese soldiers manning the post waved and saluted with large friendly grins. A farther smaller white sign simply read, "Thank You."

On a slight bend, a sombre commemorative stone, replete with a dangling steering wheel, stood in remembrance to an unlucky driver.

The route wound south and crossed over the E-70 highway once more. The badly damaged road below resembled a post-apocalyptic wasteland. The centre steel safety barrier lay crumpled in the passing lane. A white UN jeep raced by swerving around gaping potholes and the strewn metal. On the opposite side, a farmer walked his cattle past a heap of grain piled on a vacant patch of highway. A shell hole had punched through a travel-distance road-sign where it read "Belgrade."

Across the Mad Max highway, the three passed the NepBat Headquarters housed in a vast industrial complex. An odd assortment of ancient vehicles - Russian trucks and jeeps, Czech APCs and a few Ferret Scout Cars - filled the compound parking lot. Against the dilapidated factory's communist gloom stood an ornate wooden temple and a main gate crowned with a gleaming archway proclaiming, in red and gold, "Long Live the King and Queen of Nepal."

The empty road meandered past more charred hamlets and a pair of eager NepBat observation posts. Rounding a final sweeping corner, they pulled up to a busy Republika Srpska Krajina checkpoint at the foot of a suspension bridge spanning the Sava River – Croatia and Bosnia's natural boundary. Across it lay the Bosnian Serb territory of Republika Srpska and the town of Bosanska Gradiška.

They waited behind a bus and a couple of small white Fiat-like bubble cars for half an hour before a guard in purplish-blue camouflage coveralls marched up. He looked down at Mik sternly and saluted imperiously. The militiaman took Mik's crossing papers and ID cards over to a nearby rusty shipping container and used a telephone.

Horse-drawn carts and farmers milled by while others in assorted military garb lurked around. Two men sporting fat moustaches that drooped over their lips sat on a shaded bench in front of the container. The shoulder patches on their purple fatigues read, "*Milicija*" in Cyrillic. A third buddy, dressed in brown-green camouflage, had a double-headed eagle and the Cyrillic, "*Vojska RSK*" embroidered on his shoulder.

The centre of their attention was a fourth larger man strutting in brand-new US Army dessert camouflage. It had no tactical value in these parts and stood out more than it concealed. As the dessert rat chatted boisterously and waved his arms dramatically, his comrades kept reaching out enviously to touch the beautiful fabric before them. Their lust to prance in army fatigues brought pathetic and instant self-importance. Maybe it helped exorcise their previously unimportant lives in this communist backwater. War was great for local nobodies; why would they ever want a return to normalcy?

After a quarter of an hour, the phone in the container rang. The Milicija-man returned the documents and bid the three, "*Srećan put.*"

On the bridge, the aid workers wove through a maze of Serb tank barriers, a Nepalese APC - whose crew waved keenly - pedestrians, bicycles and a second set of tank barriers.

They had crossed the Sava once more – but this was a different Sava in another universe. A chubby moustachioed Bosnian Serb wearing the same bluish coveralls as his cross-river counterparts greeted the newcomers. An "RS" Cyrillic badge adorned his shoulder. He saluted lazily, asked for the crossing papers and then disappeared into his police hut.

He returned shortly, pointed to the rear of the car and stated in coarse English, "You take cargo. You find football stadium for search."

Before Mik could protest, the policeman directed him, "Go front, right 200 metres maximum."

He impatiently curled his arm, "*Ajde bre!*"

Parking in a dirt lot beside Gradiška's grim little football stadium, they found a British UNHCR convoy already enduring a meticulous search. Serb militiamen scurried atop the 10 DAF trucks and their trailers, peeling back tarps and probing the cargo. Each was loaded with about 25 tonnes of flour, wheat, potatoes and cooking oil.

The drivers - short gruff ex-military types sporting multiple tattoos on their forearms - hung around chatting, drinking coffee and smoking. Warily, they watched the Serbs but none was particularly intimidated by the militiamen around them.

The UN convoy leader, a clean-cut older Englishman, walked over to Justin and nodded at the Serb guards who were now inserting two-metre long pikes into the sides and tops of the trucks' cargo. "Look at these fools. We haul this stuff from Zagreb each week. And every bloody convoy, they do this to for a couple of hours. All the bloody food is for their own people – Serbs in need.

"They claim they're looking for weapons. Who the hell would we give weapons to in Srpska anyway? The whole place is Serb now. Even if we brought a convoy full of RPG's, they should give us a bloody medal."

One militiaman's pike became stuck and he pressed down on it with his full body-weight. Looking up, three Brits on the ground covered their ears and ran manically behind the convoy leader's armoured Land Rover.

Seeing the commotion, the Serb threw up his arms, flung himself off the truck and scrambled for cover. The three drivers laughed hysterically. One Brit poked his head forward mockingly, bulged his eyes toward the Serb and hoarsely yelled, "Boom!"

Embarrassed, the guard muttered, "*Jebem ti pičku materinu,*" and clambered to retrieve his pike. He then opened the truck's side panel and rammed the rod into the base of the cargo.

Pulling the pike back out, it glistened with liquid. A small thick stream slowly flooded out of the truck's side.

The driver glared at the Serb, "Oih, that's cooking oil mate. Congratulations, a 200-litre drum."

The convoy leader shook his head in dismay, "They fuck themselves even when we try to help. BWA."

"Huh?" Justin wondered.

"You know, Balkans Win Again," the Brit replied bitterly.

Over an hour later, with their search mercifully complete, the UN drivers mounted their cabs. They raced off for Banja Luka with a collective roar leaving the aid workers alone in the dusty parking lot.

Turning their gaze to the MOO Landcruiser, the guards opened the backdoor and pulled out boxes of X-ray powder.

"*Štaje ovo?*" an older militiaman, with a standard slumped greasy moustache, barked.

Mik tried explaining it was for the Banja Luka hospital.

"*Papier?*" the guard simply demanded in response.

Mik smiled innocently, "What, a packing list? *Manifesta?*"

"*Da!*" the Serb nodded.

"*Nema papier. Medicament – Serb bolnica,*" Mik attempted. Flustered, he added in English, "Look it's for your hospital."

The guard scratched his scalp and conferred with his colleagues. They shook their heads and muttered unsure how to proceed. Turning to the trio once more, the guard motioned them to stay put. "Telephone *Meister,*" he announced.

"What's a Meister?" Justin wondered.

Mik shrugged, "Must be calling the boss."

The foreigners and militiamen lingered in limbo. Justin shared cigarettes with the guards hoping to overcome the awkward quiet.

Eventually a stout man with a pudgy face, squeezed beneath Foster Grants and a dark curly mullet, swaggered over. He wore an ill-fitting silver suit jacket over a camouflage T-shirt. His manhood, a shiny police badge, hung from his belt.

"*Meister?*" Justin inquired.

"Ah, *Meister!*" the head guard greeted.

The man grunted. Throwing up his hands, he barked an order at the remaining militiamen. They scurried to retrieve one of the boxes from the MOO Landcruiser.

Holding it up to Mik, the Meister snapped, "*Štaje ovo?*"

"*Medicament…*X-ray powder," Mik murmured.

The Meister raised a sausage finger silencing Mik. He flipped open a large knife and slashed wildly at the box's protective tape. Its dusty contents burst onto his hands. Eying the scattered powder, he stopped and looked up suspiciously.

"Hey, be careful it's toxic," Laura cautioned.

The Meister snarled, "*Mee-amee Vice!*" and licked his forefinger dramatically. He dipped it deep into the powder and then into his mouth.

Laura just shook her head, "It's poisonous you retard…"

She retrieved medical gloves from the cruiser and taped the box shut while eying the Meister cautiously.

With a dry cough, he dismissed the group and sauntered away.

"His mouth'll be full of blisters and his tongue purple by tomorrow," Laura muttered.

"BWA?" Justin queried.

"Unfortunately, yes," Laura replied.

Mik slapped Justin on the back, "Always remember – it's not that you're having a bad day in Bosnia. What's important is that you're in Bosnia having a bad day. It's all about displacement my friend."

"So you're saying a bad day here beats a mediocre day in Toronto," Justin wondered in reply.

"You're learning fast," Mik grinned as he exhaled cigarette smoke.

Accelerating briskly from the parking lot, the trio followed a main road littered with pedestrians, rusty old cargo trucks, cyclists and horse-carts pulling overloaded stacks of hay.

Swerving to avoid a large dog sleeping in the middle of the road, Mik yelled back to Justin, "This is an interesting sport. Here you have to drive as fast as you can and try not hitting any locals. If you stop, some thug will steal your car and make you walk. If you hit a local, you lose. When you lose, sign your will. They hang you from the nearest tree."

Outside Gradiška, they approached an elderly figure on the shoulder wearing a tattered peaked police hat. The man stepped onto the road and waved, giving the cruiser directions to keep travelling straight down the road.

Mik honked and Laura waved. Screwing his forefinger into his temple, Mik explained, "That's the famous 'Srpska traffic cop'. He directs traffic every day. The road only goes one way. There are guys like him all over Bosnia. I'll bet he lives for the UNHCR convoy."

A pair of memorials lined a particularly tight corner. A hubcap and pack of smokes rested atop the first. A bottle of beer kept the second company. The victim engraved on it clearly failed to heed the warning of the first plaque.

Nearing a large blue Cyrillic sign that read something partly recognisable as "Banja Luka," Laura winked, "Welcome to Blue Lagoon. The Bosnian Serbs' pride and largest town."

Mik was quick to add that as a university town, Banja Luka was famous for its pre-war ratio of seven women to each man. "But now it's even better," Mik grinned. "War means mobilisation of males to the front...the ratio's up to 27-1."

Laura groaned and rolled her eyes.

Although the previous MOO team had fled Banja Luka as nervous wrecks months prior, Mik had no such inhibitions. Driving into town, people on the streets looked up, smiled and some waved. The closer Mik got downtown, the larger his smile grew.

"You know I can't stand working in Zagreb. Too much bureaucracy and office bullshit. Nobody there really knows exactly what they're doing to help. Here, this is the place to be," Mik beamed brightly.

In the centre, they parked on a large gravel lot. Laura climbed out and headed across the street to an apartment block to find Sophia, the local office assistant.

Standing beside the car, sharing a hand rolled cigarette with Justin, Mik explained in a hushed tone, "You see this parking lot...there used to be an enormous mosque here. One of Bosnia's oldest and most famous. Serbs dynamited it one morning. Just to be assholes, they dynamited the rubble and then bulldozed it into this.

"If you're lucky you can find a picture of it on an old postcard. This wasn't the only one though. There are at least a dozen others the Serbs destroyed around BL."

Nodding at the apartments across the street, Mik continued, "Sophia lives there. She was sleeping when they blasted it. She said the explosion knocked her out of bed."

Laura returned with Sophia, a stocky woman in her earlier 20s with long black hair. She had a tomboyish and enthusiastic air.

The group continued on to the office on a discrete residential street. It consisted of a large front room, small kitchen and two upstairs bedrooms.

After parking the cruiser in an obscured space behind the MOO house, they settled in the main office room. There was no electricity.

"Don't worry," Laura explained, "it comes back for a couple of hours at 1 a.m. or so. That's when we do the house work."

Nodding toward a side window and the outline of the MOO car beyond, Justin asked, "Is the car safe there. I mean, how do you know you can trust the landlord not to rat you out to the cops or mafia?"

Laura lowed her voice to a hush, "There's a third bedroom here we don't use. The landlord's teenaged son lives there quietly – he's avoiding forced military service. So, we pay the rent and the family protects their son from the war. They don't want the authorities coming around this place."

Sophia and Mik went to the kitchen to prepare a pot of coffee. Laura quietly explained, "This office wouldn't run without Sophia. She is a lot more than just an interpreter. She does all the office work each time MOO flees town. She also calls all the local authorities to get our crossing permissions. She even does a lot of the bookkeeping. She's a great social connection. Through her friends, she tries to spread the word about what MOO really does here. It helps deflect a bit of the paranoia I guess. Anyway, without her we expats couldn't even go out to eat or have a beer in this town.

"It's funny, but back home we're sometimes seen as these brave heroes. You know, all these internationals come to the field thinking they're really important and expert. But we are really nothing and achieve even less without our local staff. When they're good, we look good. It's a simple formula. I don't think too many people are aware of that, though."

Uneasily, Justin asked the heavy and long nagging question - one so simple in any other world - "What is Sophia's background?"

"She's a Serb. But she's twenty-something and too rebellious to give a shit about the propaganda being spread around."

"She hates communists and nationalists alike. She thinks anyone here over 35 is brain-dead. If someone grew up under communism, the system pretty much made them zombies. If you weren't successful under the commies, you probably since latched onto nationalism and are equally brain-dead."

Sophia proudly carried a tray of Turkish coffee from the kitchen. Not having eaten in awhile, Justin received his small cup of elixir gratefully.

Seeing his appreciation, Sophia stated, "It's Banja Luka style coffee."

"What's the secret?" Justin asked. "I had a pretty good cup of Turkish coffee in Zagreb the other morning."

Sophia flicked her head slightly and clucked a "Tsk" sound. "They don't know how to make correct coffee in Zagreb," she asserted. "They don't boil the coffee and sugar together."

Sighing dramatically and revealing some great ignominy, she spat, "The Croats add the sugar after the coffee is prepared. What is that?"

Shaking her head smugly, Sophia concluded, "The Croats never had enough Turkish oppression to make their coffee properly. We had too much, so the Banja Luka method is the best."

That evening Mik called the UNHCR office over his VHF radio and arranged to meet up with, Jason, their field officer. After grabbing a hamburger from a nearby street stand, the four drove by the UNHCR office and picked up Jason, a Filipino wearing a lumberjack jacket who looked to be in his late twenties.

They headed for a bar in the town's old castle – Sophia claimed to be a good friend of the owners.

The crowded bar was built inside the castle's main tower. Outside, a row of tables stretched along the adjacent battlement. At the far end, a DJ's booth supporting strobe lights and a disco ball overlooked a dance floor on the rocky terrace below.

In the packed bar area, the newcomers' presence was acknowledged by no one. All eyes were fixed on the TV set, watching an old cheap Soap Opera. A cluster of patrons threw up their arms dramatically and clucked the same "Tsk" noise Sophia had made. Others shook their heads gravely and muttered, "Yoih," and "Aih."

Sophia whispered to the four, "We must not disturb them. Now is the time they watch the show Santa Barbara."

Sophia discretely waved to the owner behind the bar and motioned toward the tables outside. The ramparts afforded a beautiful view of the local Vrbas River that meandered between soft grassy hills, past the castle and into town. On its banks, couples strolled along paths and fishermen packed up their gear in the fading light. Frolicking children hurled themselves from a nearby bridge. How could any evil lurk in such bucolic calm?

Nodding at the scene below, Sonja recalled with a slight ironic smile, "Before the war the river used to always be covered in think foam from the local factory. Seven years ago, nobody dared fish or go near the river. Since the war, the factory shut and the air and water have never been clearer."

With dusk, new patrons, mostly in army fatigues, filled the parapet's remaining tables. The aid workers drank a local beer called, "*Nectar*." The foul concoction tasted anything but. Printed on one side of their beer glasses was the Nectar brand name. The Serb double-headed eagle motif emblazoned the opposite side.

Justin may as well have been staring at a giant swastika. The shrill nationalist label vaporised the pleasant surroundings leaving a festering core of domination. Everyone here needed to be reminded of their identity – even when enjoying a cold beer.

Strange alphabets, double-headed eagles, nervous dark moustachioed men – Justin had seen this place before. A deluded chest-thumping land, just outside the fringe, that taunted outsiders with its uniqueness and took pride in disregarding other's opinions. This was Syldavia and Borduria, the ever-scheming duplicitous mini-states in Tintin comics.

At the next table, a soldier sat with a puppy in his arms. Both had glazed eyes – his from intoxication, the dog's from illness. He placed the pup on the ground; its shivering frame staggered a little.

Although the creature's unnatural movements were laboured and tentative, curiosity took over and he began exploring the neighbouring tables.

The soldier quickly became irritated with the lack of attention he was receiving, and worse, the greater amounts others were showing the dog. The simple man desperately sought devotion and needed to dominate. With a snarl, he staggered over and grabbed the pup. He shuffled back to his domain and threw the creature to the ground. It whimpered and gazed ahead stunned. The soldier cursed and pointed a menacing finger at the creature. Under communism, domination was the only thing he had ever known. Domination always came from the fat people above. Devotion was always offered by the little ones below. It was not about to change.

Totalitarianism was all they had ever known around here. The new world order and its freedom offered so much promise to settle old scores. Even this dumb peasant could now dominate things.

The drunken master cradled the still bewildered puppy. It did not, however, desire such tenderness. Tensely, the soldier placed the puppy back on its feet. The dog meandered to other parts of the battlement. Again, the soldier staggered over, grabbed the pup and dumped it before his chair. He slapped its snout and yelled a warning. Again, it whimpered in dazed confusion.

Although war made losers and hicks suddenly feel important, this Neanderthal was having trouble advancing even in these diminished circumstances.

As darkness enveloped, it came time to retreat to the discreet safety of the MOO office. The group remained strangers in a tense town; staying out as dusk hardened and the local brandy took hold was not prudent. After dropping Sophia at her apartment, Jason, urged by the promise of Johnny Walker, eagerly returned to the MOO office.

The power was still off and Mik lit a gas lantern in the main room. In the shadowy gloom, they sat smoking and drinking whisky mixed with some generic drink called, "Americola."

A distant explosion echoed somewhere across town.

"One less Muslim house in the morning," Mik muttered grimly.

Jason shook his head and looked at his feet. With a sigh releasing prolonged exhaustion, he slowly raised his head, "Banja Luka is evil and I'm an accomplice."

"What?" Laura exclaimed with a snarl of exasperation. "You're a UNHCR protection officer. You're the only one in this town trying to do the slightest thing to help the minorities. Without you they'd be…"

"Yes, I *am* a protection officer," Jason interrupted. "But I seem to be more use to the Serbs than to the minorities I was sent to protect. There may be no fighting in this town, and it may not be the Omarska and Trnopolje camps, but the war's atrocities still continue here."

Justin's face flushed at mention of the concentration camp names. They were amongst the first images to seep into his docile Canadian life and churn his anger. They had been the first distant glimpse at the perverse torment wrought by the loud weaklings that infested this place.

"Crimes go on in this town," Jason continued. "The locals see enemies they don't know but are certain exist amongst them. The paranoia serves the leaders well and keeps the people loyal.

"Whatever the original composition had been, the population in the Banja Luka region is now exclusively Serb. The pre-war figure of 28 maybe 30,000 Bosniak Muslims has been reduced to 10,000 at the most. And it's still falling. In 91, Muslims and Croats made up a good 40% here. Now the Serbs are at least 90%. The remaining 10 are too scared even to leave their houses. Those Muslims and Croats who stayed are still being driven out of town – a few each day."

Taking a large swig of whisky Jason blurted, "These stats are bullshit man…in the end, those goddamned Serbs are terrorising people that look exactly the same as themselves. They partied with these Muslims and Croats for 40 years and married each other…they even opened businesses together. I mean what the fuck? Didn't any of that mean anything? How the fuck do people just lose their minds?"

"They must have always been fucked in the head, I guess." Justin offered awkwardly.

"No man. They can be a very clever bunch. Like their ethnic cleansing. The methods have become far less obvious now. Families are regularly harassed and threatened by Serbs with weapons. And then there are these mysterious travel agencies that sprang up. The Serb officials refer to them as 'Exchange Commissions.' They offer to bus out any minorities who want to leave. In return, they charge huge admin fees. The travellers have to hand over all rights to their property and belongings here. If they're lucky, they sometimes get to take a couple of bags of personal belongings with them. The local cops often encourage families to pay a visit to these agencies with warning shots and grenades."

"If they aren't killed and can't afford the crazy bus, they run to the UNHCR or Red Cross begging for help. The only thing I can really do to protect them is bus them out of town. The Serbs figured that one out pretty quick. So now, I'm just their newest ethnic cleanser. The Serbs get an empty undamaged house and nothing appears on CNN.

"And then, these bastards keep robbing and arresting me. You know how many Nissans they've jacked from our office?" Jason's voice finally drifted off to focus on the remains of his drink and the glowing ember in his other hand.

At 11:30, the room flooded with light as the power came back. Mik leapt to life and set about recharging his laptop and printer batteries. He also hooked up a charger to a pair of car batteries that powered the Codan and Capsat radios.

The Capsat was an extremely reliable means of sending text messages to Zagreb or even Amsterdam. The only problem was that the messages took a good half-hour to bounce between the satellite and its base station somewhere in Denmark and then onward to the intended recipient. The high frequency Codan radio could transmit in real-time anywhere in the world – in theory. Australians however designed the radio for farmers in the outback. It worked great over vast flat distances; it did not always excel in the mountainous Balkans.

With the Johnny Walker virtually empty and all the house chores done, the four called it a night. Not wanting to face any extra police harassment, Jason stretched out on the office couch.

The following morning the four went over to the MOO warehouse located in the basement of a three-story office building that used to house a computer firm. The UNHCR also had its offices upstairs.

In the parking lot, they pulled up beside three white UNHCR Nissan Patrols and a fourth blue Nissan. On the passenger door, the large round outline of the UNHCR decal lingered beneath a coat of cheap blue paint. The car's heavy-duty tires were stripped bare.

Nodding at the blue vehicle, Mik commented, "Wow, I can't believe you actually got one of your cars back from the Milicija."

Jason shrugged, "Yeah, this way they'll steal it back again after we service it and put new tires on. I've been car-jacked twice this month by these assholes."

Jason headed upstairs to check in with his office. The aid workers drove to the rear loading doors. Near the entrance, three weathered older men in dirty overalls sat amongst the carcasses of a stripped-down engine and chassis. Beside the mess, a Bosnian Serb Army jeep awaited repairs. Sharing a bottle of hooch, the men appeared to be interested only in talking about automobiles.

They paused to leer and made licking sounds as Laura walked by.

Maintaining a male-melting smile, Laura cheerily responded, "Classy...you are a real tribute to your people."

The men resumed chatting boisterously, adding women to their conversation.

As Mik piled boxes into Laura's outstretched arms, Justin eyed the neo-socialist building. The Serb four-C's emblem was etched into the cheap brick facade. Below it, another local artist had scrawled, in red paint, "UNHCR FOOK YOU ASSHOOL."

In a storage room at the basement's far end, the three dropped off the boxes and met an elderly man with a fantastic mane of silver hair. Seeing Mik and Laura, he smiled. He eyes remained attentively wide advertising perpetual nervousness.

"Zlatco," Laura greeted enthusiastically. "How are you?"

His face brightened briefly out of relief at seeing Mik and Laura. He then shook his head and slumped in a chair. Looking toward the door, in a soft tone he said, "Last night the police came and took away three men from my apartment building.

"Who were they? Where did they take them?" Mik inquired with a blank expression.

"Two were Croats and the other Muslim. About my age." Zlatco shrugged, "They are taking many minorities south from Banja Luka to dig trenches by the front of Glamoč. On the television last night, they had pictures of dead men in the trenches. They were old men too; I recognised one. I think I am the only one left in my building."

Mik and Laura stepped out to the UNHCR office to make travel inquiries. Justin smoked uncomfortably; he did not know what to say to Zlatco.

Zlatco broke the impasse, asking with a kind smile, "So where are you from?"

"Canada."

"Ah, it is very nice there. I have two sons living in Sweden. I think it is a lot like Canada."

Justin nodded, "Have you ever visited them?"

"Yes, a few years ago," Zlatco's gaze drifted recalling happier times. "But I always returned here. My family has lived in Banja Luka for four generations. I am 65. My heart and history is in this town."

Anticipating Justin's next question, Zlatco continued, "What would I do if I went to Sweden now anyway? I used to work as a computer programmer in this building for 25 years until the war began. Then I lost my job. Local Serb leaders said I was not Serb enough.

"My father was Muslim and my mother Croat." With oft-practised frustration, he raised his eyebrows and frowned briefly, "I am an ethnic Yugoslav. To the Serbs that means you are not totally Serb. To the Croats and Muslims it means you are Serb."

With an ironic grin he added, "I am multi-minority here."

To whom could an honest man who worked hard, had a gentle demeanour and bore no grudges be a threat?

Back at the MOO office that evening, Mik explained to Justin, "I really don't know what to do about Zlatco. I am worried for him, but he refuses to leave Banja Luka. And especially not without his wife. He's even got a brother in Zagreb and we could sneak him out no problem. Zlatco is very clever and careful. But I'm sure that, one day, he just won't come to work."

The following morning Mik, Laura and Justin headed back for Zagreb; Mik and Laura needed to have more discussions planning MOO's activities in Republika Srpska. Justin also needed to get to work on trying to enter Krajina and Bihać to make his deliveries.

The three faced no problems or delays at any of the Serb checkpoints along the way. Passing through the narrow back road into Croatia, they encountered the same Jordanian sentry. He happily and eagerly shook Mik's hand. The soldier chattered excitedly but Mik could not understand anything. In the string of words, Justin heard "caj" repeated a few times.

"He wants us to have tea with him," Justin told Mik.

With a wide smile, Mik informed the trooper, "I would love some caj."

Mik pulled behind the Jordanian's APC and the three climbed out. A captain greeted and guided them to their tea garden – a set of stools in the shade of a charred house.

The officer spoke no English, other than, "I am Captain Ikman."

Justin introduced himself to the captain and then shook hands with a pair of corporals and a sergeant. The private who invited then seemed to be the only one who could speak even a handful of English words. The M-16 he cradled also appeared to be the detachment's only available weapon. The sentry's duties at the barrier were supplanted by the cardinal task of hosting visitors.

Mik took his cue and introduced himself. All responded dutifully.

Eagerly, all eyes turned in silent anticipation to the last guest.

Laura snapped their spell stating, "Hi, I am Laura."

The soldiers all sat up, smiled and in unison hummed, "Ahh, Laura!"

A very young soldier arrived with a large steaming aluminum pot and served a magnificent ginger flavoured tea sweetened with honey. The guests complimented the captain on the tea. He graciously accepted the accolade with a sweep of his arm.

Pandemonium broke out amongst the other lounging soldiers as a vehicle approached the checkpoint – shouts emanated from the defenceless sandbag bunker. The private with the weapon simply leaned back in his seat and yelled over his shoulder. Slowly, he lifted his rifle and got to his feat. A white UN truck driven by a Jordanian comrade raced under the open barrier. The driver honked his horn wildly and hung out his window waving. All at the checkpoint yelped greetings and waved back.

Calm returned and the group sat a while longer enjoying a second cup of tea. The language barrier however, made conversation extremely limited and disjointed.

As Mik, Laura, and Justin thanked their hosts and prepared to leave, the rifle carrying private clapped Justin's shoulder. Weaving together his longest English phrase, he said, "My friend, we are brothers working for peace."

A pocket camera was produced and Mik posed for a snap with the captain. The rest of the soldiers clamoured to squeeze into a photograph with Laura.

Chapter 3

For more than a week, Justin waited to make his first medical delivery to the Krajina. His predecessor had made a loose delivery schedule and standardised packing list before departing the mission; there was really not a lot to prepare.

Justin dropped by the warehouse hoping to familiarize himself with the medical stocks he had to deliver. He had no idea what most of the supplies did. With the exception of a few painkillers and sedatives, it remained a lot of gibberish.

Inside the warehouse, there was nobody in sight and Justin quickly became bored of scouring the medical supplies. He made his way to the small darkened office at the back of the building. In the gloom, the glowing ember of a joint bobbed between three figures. Embarrassed, they looked up.

"Oh, sorry man," one of them coughed. "Things have been pretty slow here. You know with the refugees blocking deliveries."

"We're just relaxing," another added. "Hey, I heard you were in Amsterdam…that's fantastic man."

Turning on a light the three red-eyed warehouse workers - Miroslav, Boban and Cora - introduced themselves.

Miroslav announced, "Justin because you are new here, we must welcome you with something you will see a lot, I am sure."

Beaming, he produced a bottle of milky spirits and poured generous servings into mugs. Offering one to Justin he said, "*Šljivovica*," with a mischievous smile.

Glancing politely to Boban and Cora, Justin offered to share his mug. Both quickly declined with amused looks.

Together Miroslav and Justin toasted, "*Živili*," and took a large gulp.

Justin choked on the noxious liquid that blistered down his throat and into his stomach.

Cringing at Justin's agony, Miroslav apologized, "Yes, it was bought in the shop. It is not the best kind." On an optimistic note, he added, "The best is in the villages. I have a friend, something like a cousin, who lives near Sarajevo, in Kiseljak…oh, he makes a *Šljivo* that makes you cry. You can taste and smell the plums. It is something very special. You cannot imagine how good it is…"

Still grinning at Justin's expense, Boban explained quietly, "It's a drink for old people."

Cora nodded in agreement, "Me, I prefer smoking dope."

Miroslav laughed, "Yes, but this will get you fuck up and costs nothing."

Miroslav was a wiry guy of medium height in his mid-twenties with a military brush cut. Boban, was slightly more hushed than his colleagues, had long stringy black hair and was also in his twenties. He played drums in a local band and already had two young children. Cora had a shaved head and stocky build. He spent most of his time running errands around town and was always in and out of the MOO office and warehouse. In his spare time, he DJed at Zagreb discos. He had built up enough of a fan following to claim minor celebrity. He had a perpetual mischievous glow in his eyes and, with canny street sense, was always devising plans either to avoid military service or to help MOO avoid Croatian bureaucracy. In a country still technically at war, the warehouse boys were all prime fighting age.

Of the three, Miroslav had had the most fortune in staying out of the Croatian army. Due to an administrative oversight, the Croatian military had long since deemed him undesirable for service. Miroslav recounted tales from his days of compulsory military service with the old Yugoslav People's Army - the JNA - in 1990. He had been posted to a mountain regiment in Slovenia where he spent most of his time either deserting or being incarcerated for desertion. JNA service was supposed to have been the coming of age for all 18-year-olds in big happy socialist Yugoslavia. After a year of upholding Tito's ideals and defending Yugoslavia from imperialism, you could finally call yourself a man and grow a fat drooping greasy moustache.

"Who wants to grow a big hairy ass on their face? What girl kisses that? No thanks man," Miroslav stated.

With no future desire to grow archaic facial hair and no worries about the imperialists invading, Miroslav would sneak away from of his military camp on a dare or simply to attend friends' parties in Zagreb. Often, too afraid to turn himself back in after deserting, he would just stay away even longer. When he finally did return to barracks, he was invariably imprisoned for weeks at a stretch. To Miroslav this time was actually rather relaxing and preferred to endless drill sessions. When his term of conscription mercifully ended, the Yugoslav authorities put a note in his dossier stressing that Miroslav's behaviour was evidence that he was unreliable, a poor socialist and mentally unsound.

When Croatia subsequently went to war against the JNA over the Krajina, the newly declared state needed to raise an army. Going through the old JNA lists of Croatian youths, the Zagreb authorities searched for eligible men. Coming across Miroslav's name, the recruitment officers excluded him from service due to his mental imbalances. He had not been approached by the military police at any time during the Croatian conflict.

Smirking, Miroslav explained, "Just like in the JNA, the officers in the new army are totally stupid. This whole place is run by idiot people."

Cora was a Bosnian Croat and had done his service in the JNA a little later than Miroslav. Based near the Croatian town of Vukovar in 1991, he too had experienced considerable good fortune as his tour of service ended a week before the JNA began its three-month siege of the city. At that point, the JNA briefly remained a multi-ethnic army. The bloody irony was that many of Cora's Croat friends, those who had yet to complete their JNA service or flee to almost independent Croatia, remained and had to take part in besieging and levelling a Croatian city. Massive casualties were inflicted on both sides and the Croatian defenders of the city in turn killed many of Cora's friends.

As the Croatian army was now eager to retake the Krajina Serb controlled territories the JNA had originally helped seize, the authorities were rebuilding their army and looking for Cora to do some national duty. Cora's street smarts so far kept him a couple of steps ahead of the military police.

"I stay with friends. I live in five different houses," he said with an almost overconfident grin. "I even hide with gypsies."

Boban's luck lay in the simple fact that he was still alive. After finishing his JNA service in 1991, the new Croatian army, the HV, grabbed him and sent him to fight against the Serbs in the Krajina.

With a despairing shrug Boban explained, "I don't know which army was more fucked up. The old one or the new one..."

Two years after his first stint in the Croatian Army, the HV was getting closer to finding Boban for a second tour. Having a wife and kids made it harder for him to stay mobile and avoid the authorities.

Shaking his head, Boban asked, "How many fucking armies and fucking wars do I have to fight in?"

When he ran out of work to invent at the office, Justin would hang out with the boys in the warehouse. They joked, compared adolescent tales and taught Justin Croatian obscenities. These guys were the same age as Justin. He enjoyed having the odd beer with them after work. In his world, they would have been good buddies. The guys were happy to work for a foreign aid group – it paid hard currency wages in a sputtering war economy. It also shielded them somewhat from military service. They were able to work discreetly without either declaring their place of employment or their salary to the authorities.

They also made no objections to working for an organisation providing part of its medical aid to the Serbs.

Boban was still a big fan of Serb rock music and asked Justin to keep his eyes open for a number of their cassettes next time he was in Banja Luka.

They also did not care for President Tudjman's chest thumping antics. A poster of the Pope hung on the warehouse office wall. A drooping moustache had been drawn on it and coins taped over the Pontiff's eyes. Happy to be free of the previous socialist regime, they felt no sudden need to assert their long suppressed Catholic identity.

"It's all bullshit man," Boban announced. "First they tell us Communism is the only religion. You know, everything is about brotherhood and unity and self-management. Then one day these old dinosaurs tell me I must be a good Catholic. Justin, what's your religion?"

Before Justin could reply, Cora interrupted, "My religion is simple...*piva, Marka, pička.*"

"In that order?" Miroslav wondered.

"OK, *pička, piva, Marka,*" Cora admitted.

Leaning toward Justin, Boban translated, "He says, 'pussy, beer, Deutsche Marks.'"

When not in the warehouse, Justin periodically visited the UN Military Observers at the downtown UN HQ for updates on the situation in Krajina and Bihać. Usually a French or Danish officer would sit him in front of a large wall map and explain the changes to the region's frontlines.

Justin would also stop in at the UN map depot where the entire Former Yugoslavia was put on paper in every imaginable scale. Justin simply pointed to a guide grid on the wall for the map size or region he wanted. In addition, the UN produced a weekly overview map of the entire conflict marking all recent frontline changes and army movements.

Back at the office, Justin re-studied these maps trying to memorize the routes he would need to follow to Knin. He reviewed reams of his predecessor's notes trying to make rough travel itineraries. The first trip would be pretty straightforward and all he had to do was deliver a truck full of cargo to a hospital in the town of Udbina before carrying on to the central pharmacy and main hospital in Knin. The Knin pharmacy was supposed to distribute Justin's supplies onward amongst regional clinics and ambulance stations. To get to Knin, he had to cross into Sector North at the village of Turanj. The few entry points into UNPA North were also not immune to the Croatian protestors though.

The other problem Justin faced was that he needed someone to accompany him. As a matter of safety, MOO workers always tried to travel in pairs. While Justin drove the truck, somebody followed in the Landcruiser. The second car offered an escape in case Justin got hurt or had vehicle trouble.

Normally, a MOO doctor or nurse would have been good company; but none was available. Laura was busy in Banja Luka and most of the project's other medical staff had been whisked away, a couple of weeks prior, to help with the refugee catastrophe in Zaire. The remaining MOO expats in the region were already consumed with their own tasks.

Using local staff was not feasible because of their ethnic backgrounds. Boban and Cora were familiar with the Krajina from their army days. Neither dared revisit that place under any conditions. The Croatian police viewed any Croat's motives for travelling to the Serb-held regions as treasonous. Even if they got by the Croatian police checkpoint, the Serb militiamen would regard a Croat with extreme suspicion too. The warehouse staff was already doing their utmost to lay low. None wanted to give the HV any excuse to pressgang them into the next Croatian military offensive.

Cora did however, have a friend, Demitri, studying at the University in Zagreb. He was Macedonian and might consider the work. There were really no insurmountable language barriers between Macedonian, Croatian and Serbian. Only Albania, Bulgaria and Greece had problems with Macedonia. Greece refused even to acknowledge the country's existence. They could not bear to utter its name and bullied their allies to refer to it as FYROM – the Former Yugoslav Republic of Macedonia. For the time being, the key was that neither the Serbs nor Croats had any grievances with that distant state.

Justin called Demitri for a chat to see how willing he was to drive and interpret in the Krajina.

Demitri a short, stocky fellow with dark eyes and thick eyebrows had his hair cut in a short nondescript style.

Shaking Justin's hand he stated, "My name is Demitri, you call me Dimi." His entire leg shuddered as he nervously tapped his heal.

Jumping to the core issue at hand, Justin explained, "I need a partner to help me make medical deliveries in the Krajina."

"Sure," Demitri shrugged unfazed.

"I need somebody on a casual basis who can accompany me for safety reasons and also to interpret into English."

"I'm that man," Demitri shrugged again.

"You are aware of the dangers that exist for a Yugoslav to travel into a disputed territory like the Krajina?" Justin emphasised.

"Hey," Demitri declared triumphantly tapping his leg faster than ever, "I'm a football goalie. I'm not scared of anything."

Justin was starting to fear that if he could not enter the Krajina soon, MOO might just give up on him and take it all away. He had not truly started doing his work, and until he did, a sliver of doubt lingered that he was not really in this region or its war.

The UN negotiators had made no advances in talks with the elderly Croat protesters and there was no sign of the blockades being lifted. No supplies or aid was getting across. With the exception of the back road to Banja Luka, nobody knew of any open crossings into the Krajina.

Justin struggled with his Toronto-bred uncertainties. There were going to be no guaranties in this place. But why should all this uncertainty work against him? The only given was that he had to change his perspective in these volatile lands.

Justin had breached one hurdle; he had found a willing interpreter. So, why not just go to the blockades and see how far he could get? Anything was possible. This world was not fraught with cold regulations and merit; human spirit governed here. Some of this unpredictability had to work in his favour at some point. Justin had no expectations and nothing to lose. The only advantage he had at his disposal was patience.

Early two mornings later, Dimi and Justin attempted their first trip into UNPA Sectors North and South. Justin had been faxed all appropriate crossing papers by the Croatian and Krajina Serb authorities and the truck and Landcruiser had long since been loaded and fuelled.

In spite of animated insistences that he was fine, Demitri appeared agitated when they arrived at the warehouse. Dimi gazed in awe at the Landcruiser he had to drive and, with exaggerated assurance, promised Justin he could handle such a vehicle – no problem.

To reach the Turanj crossing they raced south from Zagreb on a sparse four-lane highway. While Justin hummed along in his truck,

Dimi fought to master his car as it repeatedly lurched forward and veered from side to side in his lane. On long sweeping corners, Dimi swung too wide and compensated with long applications of the brakes.

In three-quarters of an hour, they approached the major industrial centre of Karlovac. A few kilometres outside the city, the road came to an abrupt end at a T-intersection on a quiet country lane. A crossing barrier and a Croatian policeman reading a newspaper barred the route. Behind him, two other cops engaged in a mock Karate duel inside a converted steel shipping container.

As the MOO vehicles pulled up, the officer reading the paper called to his sparring colleagues. One emerged adjusting his peaked hat. He stared at Dimi with a blank expression. Justin handed him a permission fax stamped and signed by numerous Croatian ministries. The cop took the sheet and read off a string of numbers into his hand-held radio. Before re-entering the shipping hut, he raised an arm ordering the two to stay put.

While birds sang, the odd horse-drawn cart and bicyclist drifted along the rural crossroad. The dull shift the policemen had expected soon became irritatingly busy as a motorcycle with German license plates approached.

The bike bore a hulking red-bearded rider with stuffed saddlebags and a bedroll. The still reading cop glanced up. Not wanting to deal with the unusual scene before him, he buried his head deeper in his reading.

The original policeman exited the hut briskly and demanded the biker's purpose.

The rider answered with shrug of incomprehension.

"What you doing? Where you going?" the cop tried in English.

Looking up innocently, the biker produced a road map. He spread it over his fuel tank and pointed to towns he wished to visit in Serb Krajina.

The cop shook his head in astonishment and told the biker in Croatian that it was impossible to go there. The biker stared in bewilderment.

"English? You speak English?" the cop asked impatiently.

"*Deutsche*," the rider replied apologetically.

Frustrated, the cop pointed beyond the red, white and blue-striped barrier and explained, "*Četnici!*"

The biker nodded, "*Ya, Ya, dar.*" He pointed to his map in emphasis.

Exasperated, the policeman threw his arms in the air and yelled, "War...Serbs...danger...no go there...war!"

Sensing the negativity, the biker started to grasp the message. Shaking his head slightly, he restarted his motorcycle, turned and drove away.

The cop took a deep breath, walked up to Justin and asked for a cigarette. As Justin obliged, the cop nodded toward the departed biker and muttered, "Fucking tourist."

Justin had not normally been much of a smoker back in Canada. Suddenly the habit had such incredible value in easing barriers of tension, time and language.

Demitri climbed out of the Landcruiser and asked for a toilet. The cop pointed to the ditch and, as Dimi hurried over, warned him not to step off the pavement; the area was mined. Dimi stopped in his tracks and relieved himself from the asphalt.

Midway through the cigarette, the cop shrugged and expressed his need to return to work. Pointing to the truck's rear, he asked, "What is in back? Grenades, automatic, bomba?"

The question sounded funny and Justin began to grin good-humouredly. His gut seized the seriousness of circumstance and forced Justin to make a straight face. He calmly managed, "No, medicine."

Nodding toward the rear, the Croat ordered Justin to open his truck. Peering up at the cargo, the cop became disinclined to look thoroughly. He hastily ordered Justin to close up again.

The cop turned to Dimi and, in Croatian, asked questions about Macedonia. They sounded general and made out of curiosity. He did not seem overly interested that Dimi was trying to enter the Krajina.

The radio crackled minutes later and the policeman returned the crossing paper to Justin.

An awkward silence ensued and Justin finally asked bluntly, "Can we go?"

The cop raised his shoulders and replied, "Sure." Pointing at the elderly blockade 50 metres away, he added, "Here, yes. There, who knows?" He gave a flicker of a salute, raised the crossing boom and went back to his hut.

Dimi and Justin drove the short distance to the crowd of protesters and halted. In the moment it took for Justin to walk from his truck to Dimi's Landcruiser, a crowd had converged. A younger well-dressed woman fought her way from the throng and greeted Justin in flawless English.

Justin presented her with a copy of the Croatian paper Mik had produced earlier at the Novska blockade. She read the document and did not circulate it to the others.

"Where would you like to go?" she asked.

Unable to think of a useful lie, Justin answered, "Knin."

She frowned and after a moment asked, "You have permission from the Serbs to enter?"

Justin nodded.

The lady asserted, "You know we also have many problems in Croatia. Why don't you help us?"

Pointing to the information paper in her hand, Justin said, "We do, we're working everywhere."

The sight of the paper jogged her memory and she nodded slightly. Glancing suspiciously at Dimi she asked, "And where are you from?"

"Macedonia," Dimi replied quietly.

"Ah," the woman smiled, "you are welcome. I love Macedonia. Lake Ohrid is so beautiful. I spent so many holidays there. Such good memories." Weighing the situation, she lapsed into thought.

An elderly woman pressed forward and proudly presented a tray of steaming pastry before Justin.

"*Burek*," she pronounced slowly as if introducing a beloved child.

Justin was hungry and gratefully took a piece of the layered cheese pie. After serving Dimi, the lady returned to Justin and forced a second generous offering. Justin's protest that he already had a piece was futile and the woman pressed the extra slab into his free hand.

The English-speaking woman turned to Justin looking perturbed. "You inform the Croatian and Serb police that you will be crossing their barriers. But why don't you inform us?" she inquired sternly.

"We're terribly sorry but we don't know how to reach you here," Justin replied trying to sound empathetic.

"Well, we do have a fax machine," the woman scolded.

"If you give us the number, I promise you we'll inform you of our travel plans next time," Justin replied sensing hope.

"Yes, but next time you must give us at least 48 hours notice," the woman replied authoritatively. "You must also inform us of when you plan to come here on the return journey."

She jotted the number down on a scrap and said, "You are free to continue." As Justin reached to shake her hand, she appealed, "You will please remember us, OK?"

Justin nodded sincerely and, balancing the part-eaten pile of *burek*, turned to his truck. Dimi and Justin inched their vehicles through the crowd and around obstacles strewn across the road. On one side, a five-metre long outline of a crucifix had been made with candle lanterns.

They crossed a short bridge and approached a small checkpoint manned by a Polish peacekeeper sporting a light blue helmet and enormous bulletproof vest that almost covered his knees. The guard demanded Justin and Dimi's UN issued ID cards. Justin flashed his but Dimi had not been issued one yet.

Demitri tried to explain that his card was still at the UN headquarters in Zagreb but the Pole understood neither English nor Croatian. The guard waved his finger insisting that Dimi could not pass and must go back. Dimi tried arguing further but the guard raised his arm; he had thought of something.

The Pole stooped to enter his sandbagged bunker. He emerged with his partner trooper who was clad only in a tight pair of red bikini briefs and his dog tags.

Dimi coughed in shock and attempted to argue with the half-naked soldier. He understood even less than the first guard. Shivering, the scantily clad trooper impatiently waved the MOO workers through the checkpoint.

Dimi flung his arms in exasperation and screeched away. On the VHF radio, he called to Justin, "What the fuck was that?"

In Turanj, a whole new set of wrecked and abandoned houses cluttered the street. Their sectioned-off gardens lay behind barbed wire erected by UN engineers. The existence of the UN installed fencing led Justin to assume the road had likely been cleared of mines. He still tried to avoid the potholes and debris scattered across the town's main street. By VHF, he warned Dimi to do the same.

Red metal triangles marked "Mines" hung at intervals from the barbed wire. The homes' yards, no doubt, remained heavily booby-trapped – neither side wanted the other to return without suffering.

Turanj now lay in the middle of the demilitarized Zone of Separation. Nearby industrial Karlovac had been the main objective for both sides. The Serbs had wanted to take it, the Croats to keep it. Instead, Turanj fell victim as it was wrecked and its neighbours made to flee in opposite directions.

Justin could not tell if the damaged houses were the result of actual combat or attacks aimed just at driving out the undesirables. Or had there ever been a difference? Regardless, the evildoers' perverted desires had come to be. The town was now a ghost and all had left their homes. This suited the opposing loud minorities just fine.

Justin took in the view with the same curiosity he might a fresh leg gash. He meant no malintent but the pull to poke an inquisitive finger in the wound was too great.

Justin tried peering into the passing houses – beyond the smashed doors and windows. He tried imagining the buildings in individual terms, as homes where families had once lived, not just the collective of a wrecked community. He strained to find something special, something human, about the people who had lived there. But all he could see were more smashed universes.

A red, blue, white striped crossing boom abruptly halted Justin's musings. After the lonely Polish bunker down the road, a wooden hut beside this barrier was the only sign of inhabitation in this town.

Justin climbed down from his truck and shared a smoke with Dimi.

"So this is Krajina," Demitri exclaimed with a look of astonishment and triumph. The realisation that no locals in Zagreb saw what he was seeing had set in.

After a silent moment though, he shook his head and muttered, "Tsk, tsk, tsk," in condescension and condolence. It was not clear whom he was pitying and who admonishing, though.

Two pretty girls, in their late teens and clad in purple camouflage, eventually exited the hut. One had long black hair that hung halfway down her back. The other had shorter brown hair and sported a beret tilted fashionably on the back of her head.

A little embarrassed, they smiled and greeted, "*Dobar dan.*"

Dimi was unable to muster a response and Justin simply handed over the crossing papers. This was so far from the toothless bearded warriors with large knives Justin had expected. All in Zagreb had told him Krajina was Ex-Yugoslavia's land of Slavic-hillbillies – a place famous for severe body odour and incest.

As the militia-girls studiously entered the newcomer's names in a logbook, Dimi regained a morsel of composure. He attempted a flirtatious grin and spoke in Croatian.

The longhaired guard smiled and answered good-humouredly.

Dimi shook his head and turned to Justin reiterating, "I asked them if all Serb checkpoints are guarded by cute women. She tells me four beautiful girls work here."

Dimi responded to a query from the guard and then said in English, "She asked where you are from and when I told her, Canada, she said we could marry any of them."

Dimi turned once more to answer another question from the guard. His smile dropped as he replied, "Zagreb."

The guard grinned mischievously and barked a last reply. Her bereted colleague gave a friendly salute and lifted the crossing barrier.

Climbing back into his vehicle Dimi sighed, "When I told her where I live, she said we cannot marry any of them."

Dimi reached out his window, waved to the girls, clapped his hand on the car's roof and drove into the territory of the Republika Srpska Krajina.

The agrarian plains that had surrounded Karlovac morphed into rolling farm hills south of Turanj.

The scattered inhabited villages that followed were devoid of war's external scars. People walked along the roadside and a few tractors pulled bulging loads of hay. The aid workers raced by roadside restaurants and cafes that appeared still in business yet had empty parking lots.

The road itself was in decent condition and almost empty of traffic. Occasionally, a large BMW or Mercedes, with RSK licence plates, raced past. No doubt, the only people able to acquire scarce gasoline were wealthy and crafty enough to possess fast cars – local warlords, politicians or mobsters.

UNPA Sectors North and South of the Serb-occupied Krajina were of great importance to Croatia because the road Justin now travelled was the main and most direct route connecting Zagreb with the coast. Prior to the war, the trip would have taken about six hours. Now it took the average Croat over 13 on narrow, congested and winding roads that bypassed the Krajina. The main train lines to the coast also traversed the occupied region. The Krajina Serbs' capital, Knin, had once been one of Former Yugoslavia's major rail hubs.

A natural gas pipeline crossed the region as well. Serb Krajina covered almost one third of what Croatia held as sovereign. To Zagreb, RSK was a monumental black eye that emaciated the narrow and awkwardly shaped Croatian state.

Although Demitri's demeanour had calmed somewhat since chatting with the girl guards, his driving had not. On sharper corners, the Landcruiser veered dangerously into the opposite lane. On straight sections, Dimi threw up clouds of dirt and gravel as he meandered onto the shoulder. In one village, Dimi cheated mortal catastrophe when he braked centimetres short of a pig wandering the road.

Within a couple of hours, the once lush hills became increasingly desolate. Rocky agriculture was now the region's sole activity.

They passed Slunj, a pleasant town with a small waterfall and picturesque old stone houses lining the river. The town centre was teaming with military activity. Trucks roared by pulling cannons and mortars. On the outskirts, an old T-54 tank sat on one side of the road.

Drawing from his own JNA military experience, Dimi explained over the VHF, "There's a large military training paragon here. They also have some very big missiles...pointed at Zagreb of course."

From Slunj they climbed still more long steep hills for another hour. The landscape grew wooded and convoys of plodding logging trucks slowed progress.

Within the forested tranquility signs of conflict soon emerged. Clusters of burned-out hotels and restaurants again lined the road. Beside the overturned hulk of a charred and shredded sedan in a ditch, a friendly wooden sign welcomed visitors to the Plitvice National Park. A larger hoarding pointed to nearby hotels, campsites and information offices.

Deeper in the park, Justin and Dimi pulled into a treed lot partly obscured from the road. At its edge, a small stone observation point overlooked the park.

Justin lit a long anticipated smoke and gazed down at the view of forest embracing long lakes that fed into each other and dangled by waterfalls. Their turquoise waters were as soft and comforting as the eyes of a girlfriend.

Surveying the view, Dimi muttered, "*Kako...*" in admiration. "This is the first time I've seen these lakes. Incredible." Reciting some long lost school lesson, he added, "There are 16 different lakes. Every year before the war, a million people came from all over the world to see this."

Justin had read about the park in his in-flight magazine on Croatian Airlines. The magazine revelled at the lakes' eternal colour, its glorious natural symphony and surprising first-place spectacle. One could not begin to imagine its beauty until they had drunk the waters and held it to their bosom. Plitvice had to be visited without delay; a trip to Croatia could not be complete without seeing the lakes. The magazine neglected to mention whose possession the lakes were presently in and the obstacles faced trying to visit them.

The only sounds in the refuge now were birds chirping and waterfalls trickling in blissful oblivion. For a moment, Justin also let himself forget he was in a land at war.

The tourists would one day flock back to the many empty roadside buildings and infest them with their obnoxious petty demands. The tour buses would again obscure. But today, Justin was one of two people who got to see the park in its truest intended beauty – a privilege that even the richest traveller could never buy. War had finally brought peace to Plitvice.

Justin set a tablet stove from a French Army ration box on his truck bumper and heated a couple of cans of pork and lentils.

Sitting on the backend of the Landcruiser drinking instant coffee, Demitri sighed, "You know, I must be the only person left where Tito's Yugoslavia still exists." He gazed distantly into the surrounding trees with a melancholy, yet ironic, expression.

From Plitvice, Justin and Dimi descended and climbed for another half-hour. Negotiating a high plain stretching northwest, they passed a large military airfield and climbed a steep winding incline into the town of Udbina. A blue road sign read *"Bolnica"* directing visitors to the local hospital.

Off the main road, they parked beside a simple two-story building. The surprisingly small facility had undoubtedly grown in importance with the war.

In the lobby, Dimi approached two men in white lab coats and asked to meet the hospital director. They were pointed to a room upstairs.

From the office window, the plains below spread toward the horizon. To the right, the airfield stretched in full view. A pair of aging fighter jets rested idle on an apron.

A lone white armoured personnel carrier sat in an observation post, built on an outcrop below the hospital, watching the airfield in case the aircraft ever tried to breach the UN's resolve.

The director and his wife entered the room. She was tall with short reddish hair and an enormous warty growth protruding from her left cheekbone. She spoke some English. The director was a short frail man with glasses and a pasty complexion. He spoke no English.

"Welcome. This is Director Mihailović and I am Radmila, his wife. I am also a doctor. A skin doctor. But I do many other things right now," she stated. "Can we offer you coffee?"

While Justin eagerly accepted, Dimi used the opportunity to find the hospital's toilet. Dimi excused himself and Justin showed the doctors the packing list of supplies he had brought.

The two hunched over the desk scrutinizing the list. The director soon began nodding.

His wife looked up and said, "This is very good. We are very grateful."

According to instructions he had received in Zagreb, Justin asked, "Are there any other medicines you need that aren't on the list?"

Taking a deep breath, the director's wife muttered, "*Kako*...there are too many medicines we need. The biggest need is for intravenous fluids. We treat many soldiers from the Bosnian fightings. We also need more sedatives – Diazepam. You have brought some today but we need five times more. And please not tablets, we need infusions."

As Justin diligently took notes, Dimi returned with a nurse bearing a tray of coffee.

The director and his wife eyed Justin expectantly as he drank his coffee. Seeing his obvious pleasure, Radmila asked, "You like our coffee. It is good no?"

Justin nodded and she continued, "It is the best because it is made the Udbina style."

Leaning forward, as if revealing a family secret she added, "You must boil the water three times with the sugar before you add the coffee."

The director rose and produced a label-less bottle of spirits from a medical cabinet.

"Šljivovica," he proclaimed proudly.

"Do you know this drink where you come from?" Radmila asked Justin. "It's a speciality of this region. We make it in our house."

The director found four glasses in the cabinet and filled them generously. The liquid sunk surprisingly smoothly. Justin's right cheek twitched slightly as acute plum flavour clung to his mouth and warmth consumed his stomach.

"We have another big problem here," Radmila continued in a businesslike voice. "We have no diesel for our ambulances. The UN promises us some every month but it is never enough for the needs of our patients. If we do not get more diesel, patients could be in great danger."

Justin made a note and answered diplomatically, "I will ask in Zagreb but I don't know what we can do. We are a medical aid organisation."

Justin knew he had no fuel to spare. The load in his truck's extra tank would be just enough for himself and the Landcruiser to get to Knin and back.

The Radmila stood up and announced, "We would like it very much if you joined us for a big lunch in our hospital cantina."

Pointing to his watch, Justin declined politely. The day was getting on and they really needed to keep travelling if they were to get to Knin before dark.

Radmila sighed disappointedly and said she would find some workers to help unload the delivery.

Justin climbed into the back of his truck and handed boxes down to a pair of orderlies. It only took a few minutes to unload Udbina Hospital's two and a half pallets.

The director and his wife approached. Shaking Justin's hand, Radmila said, "Thank you again for your help. I am afraid we must go home now. We look forward to seeing you again next month."

Justin gave the pair his copy of the packing list and asked the director for his signature. With the signed document, he presented Justin one of his label-less bottles of Šljivovica.

"This is a special gift from our home," Radmila stated. She and the director waved, climbed into a car belonging to the hospital and drove away.

Walking to his cab, Justin raised the Slivo for Dimi to see. A fly floated blissfully in the bottle.

"Tough drink," Justin joked.

"Tough people," Dimi shrugged.

Chapter 4

The terrain beyond Udbina became even more infertile and rocky. The only residents of these windswept lands were passing sheep herds and long stacked stone fences.

For two hours, Justin and Dimi climbed steep and winding roads. The diesel engine and cargo in Justin's truck forced him to inch up each recurring hill. Abundant sharp corners allowed few opportunities to build any momentum for each new ascent. Justin could only shift down to the lowest gear and climb patiently. A large portion his cargo was intravenous fluids. With the truck's every lurch and turn, the liquids shifted awkwardly a split second later – akin to driving an upside down boat with the water overhead.

The countless mountains eventually bore a barren plateau that funnelled into a high, windy and curving viaduct. The road dropped into a series of steep hairpin turns. A medieval fortress, perched two hundred metres atop a crag, came into view – Knin, Republika Srpska Krajina's mighty capital.

At the hill's foot, Justin used the VHF radio and notes from Zagreb to guide Dimi in town. They drove cautiously along crowded streets filled with men in camouflage. The town below the impressive fortress sat grey and grim. Those on the streets wore nervous expressions. Empty shops lined streets woven amongst socialist industrial buildings and a sleeping train yard.

Approaching the town's edge, the pair pulled up to the gates of the UN base. Fading red stars and the letters "JNA" sandwiched a newer white sign with the UN logo and stencilled words, "UNPROFOR HQ Sector South." From a hut behind the gate, three black soldiers, sporting Kenyan flags on British style army fatigues, ran out to greet the vehicles.

Rolling down his window, an enormous smile welcomed Justin. "*Jambo!*" the guard called.

"Hi," Justin replied and reached down to shake hands. He gave him his UN ID card and the soldier copied its details and the truck's license number into a logbook. Holding up the blue ID card, the guard pointed questioningly to Dimi's vehicle.

"Yeah, yeah, it's in Zagreb. It's OK, he's with me – my guest," Justin stated quickly, trying to sound authoritative. Pulling out a flimsy cardboard, hand-typed MOO ID card, Justin added, "He's got one of these."

Unsure, the guard paused, scratched his head and took a deep breath. He walked up to the Landcruiser and copied down the information on Dimi's homemade MOO ID card. The guard stepped back, shone another wide smile and waved the two though the gate. "OK, good-bye," he called.

The remaining guards also smiled and waved enthusiastically as the vehicles entered the compound. They parked in front of the compound's main four-story building and entered in search of the UNHCR office.

The UNHCR was in charge of co-ordinating the international humanitarian relief effort in Croatia and Bosnia. In Justin's case, representatives from the UNHCR office in Knin personally submitted his crossing requests to the local Serb authorities. As regular phone lines between Knin and Zagreb had long been cut, Justin faxed his requests to the UNHCR in Knin via the UN's satellite phone network. The faxed requests were then carried to the Serb ministry in town and any positive replies were relayed back to Justin in Zagreb. Justin's predecessor had established a good relationship with the Knin UNHCR office and they were happy to help MOO.

On the third floor, Justin stuck his head in an office door with a UNHCR sticker. "Hi," he called tentatively to a middle-aged woman with thick brown plastic glasses sitting at the nearest desk, "I'm from MOO and I'm looking for Jadranka."

"Justin, right?" she replied. "I'm Jadranka. Pleased to meet you after all those faxes." She stood up and shook Justin and Dimi's hands.

Pointing to the two other men in the room, Jadranka introduced Sinisha, the driver, and Dragan, a logistics officer. The rest of the office staff was away in the field.

It was almost 5 p.m. – too late to unload the truck at the Knin Central Pharmacy and Hospital. Jadranka promised to call both places in the morning.

Looking eagerly at the wall clock and then at Justin and Dimi, Dragan asked, "So are you guys hungry? Let's get some food and drink."

Jadranka declined due to unfinished work. "Maybe later," she called as the four left the office.

Outside the group crossed the base parking lot and entered a wooden deck area with thatched savannah decor – the Kenyan Bar. Mounted into the patio's wooden roof were a handful of TV sets tuned to MTV and CNN. The four found a large table and ordered beer and pizza.

As they ate, Dragan, a portly man with a round face and fat drooping moustache, did most of the talking. Overly amicable, he was the loudest and most exaggerated voice in the bar. As Dragan spoke, Dimi devoured his pizza without a word and Justin kept an eye tuned to events on CNN. Sinisha, a tall man with a long face and thin drooping moustache, listened quietly. His expression was thoughtful.

With one arm perpetually raised, Dragan explained, "You see I'm a Serb from Gospić. It's a town in Croatia now. When there was fighting, my house was burned and now I am a refugee. I don't hate the Croats so much. I just miss the good times.

"I used to have a restaurant there. Life was pretty good. I always had enough money to take two vacations each year – one in winter, one in summer." Taking a deep breath, he flexed his hand and savoured a memory. Winking, he went on, "You know, a little sun, drinks, some women…eh?"

Swinging both arms upwards, Dragan continued, "aigh…oww, one time I even went down to a Club Med on the Dalmatian Coast. That was something you cannot imagine." Glancing over his shoulder and leaning forward, he explained in a lower tone, "Try to imagine the biggest orgy in the worst porno movie you ever saw…well Club Med was even better than that!"

Dragan fell silent as he contemplated the magnitude of his superlative description. Dimi and Sinisha grinned; it was uncertain if they were more impressed by the events described or the description of events. Also amused, Justin quietly drank his beer and gazed at the view.

The inhospitable windswept mount glared westward as it rose from the town centre. Atop it, a grey battlemented fortress lorded over the dwellings below. A scattering of square red-roofed houses crept up the shelter of the rock's treed leeward face. From the hard summit, a large, white, red and blue Serbian flag fluttered in windward defiance.

A group of Kenyan soldiers ran across the parking lot laughing and joking. Dragan nodded in their direction. Maintaining the same jovial facade, he explained, "When the war started the UN said they would send peacekeepers here. So we agreed, thinking, 'OK, Swedish or English, maybe French soldiers, no problem.' But they send us Africans! I have nothing against blacks but this is Europe! We're not barbarians you know."

Dragan droned on, "…and friends of mine at the local hospital tell me that before the war there was no Aids in Yugoslavia. You look in town and you'll see a lot of black babies now."

Dragan drifted into another brief contemplative silence. Looking at Justin he blurted, almost pleading, "What do our girls see in these guys?"

Leaning forward, Sinisha interrupted asking Justin and Dimi, "Do you have a place to stay tonight?"

He explained, "Right now it is probably too late to check into the guest house across town. But I know a place that's only 20 Marks. You can leave your vehicles here overnight so nobody steals the diesel. We'll go into town together and I show you the place. In the morning a UNHCR car will come pick you up."

The group lingered a while longer until the light started to fade. Justin bought two more beers for the road and went to the parking lot to catch the UN shuttle bus into town. The van was intended for the base's civilian UN staff that lived in Knin. Only military personnel lived on the base itself.

"There is a new regulation on the base," Sinisha explained. "There have been a lot of hijackings of UN cars in town. So now, all UN staff have to be escorted into Knin by an armed guard."

"Yeah," Dragan interjected, "the only problem is that the guard isn't allowed to have a firing pin in his weapon. They think it's too dangerous for the Jambo Boys and for us!"

While the others waited, Justin jumped in the Landcruiser and made a quick call on the Codan radio informing Zagreb of their safe arrival.

The group of four climbed aboard a Toyota minivan with another 10 UN personnel. Riding shotgun in front was a Kenyan guard armed with an old Sterling submachine-gun. As the van approached the main gate, the guards waved from within their hut – none was eager to leave its warmth. Only one soldier, wearing a thick jacket and wool balaclava emerged unenthusiastically to open the gate.

"Wait till it snows," Dragan muttered sardonically.

Following a circuit of the UN staff's respective dwellings, the van pulled up at an apartment block. Three passengers leaned out of their seats and hunched forward to descend. Fumbling with his weapon the guard had trouble opening the side door.

Dragan sighed loudly and threw up his arm in disbelief. From his seat, he pushed open the van's sliding door. The trio climbed out, waved and slammed the door shut.

Two stops farther, the van pulled into a parking lot surrounded ominously by six or seven stark concrete apartment blocks. Sinisha gestured that this was their stop. The guard, eager to make amends, leapt from his seat and slid open the door with a big smile.

The three bid the guard and Dragan goodnight and the van raced into the Knin darkness. Sinisha guided the two through the unlit parking lot to one of the apartment buildings. He produced a penlight and by its needle beam, they inched up three stories of damp, smelly, graffiti filled stairwell.

As Sinisha opened a door, the penlight's ray outlined a fully furnished and lived-in dwelling. Sinisha found a candle; its illumination revealed a haphazard and panicked mess in the two-room apartment. Clothes were piled in the hallway beside two empty suitcases. Justin's mouth became dry with fear and suspicion.

Turning to Sinisha, he asked slowly, "This isn't your place is it?"

Closing the front door behind him, Sinisha shook his head and replied quietly, "No, it isn't…it is a friend's."

An awkward silence followed. With an embarrassed tone, he continued, "They…had to go away suddenly. But please don't worry; I am taking care of it for them while they are gone."

Justin's suspicions did not subside easily. He wanted desperately to believe what Sinisha was saying. Sinisha seemed like a nice guy. It would have been harder to believe coming from Dragan. But how could he be absolutely sure? What choice did he have at this point anyway?

Paying up the 20 Deutsche Marks for the night, Justin convinced himself that the money would eventually reach its rightful hands. A few decent people must still exist in Knin; war could not have destroyed every friendship.

Sinisha confirmed that a UNHCR car would pick them up in the morning by 7:30 and slipped into the stairwell's depths.

Dimi took the candle and fumbled down the hall looking for the toilet. With his cigarette lighter, Justin inched forward in search of another candle. He found a wax stub atop the refrigerator. In the bouncing glow, crinkled notes and kid's artwork hung from the fridge door. A daily calendar rested at January 4, 1992. Glancing in the cupboard the reek of slimy jars and furry containers pounced at Justin.

Dimi returned from the washroom and stumbled into the main room. They sat awkwardly in an easy chair and couch – neither wanting to become comfortable. They opened the beers and drank in shadowed silence. Dimi gazed ahead at the diminishing candle – Justin at the ember of his cigarette.

Justin broke the silence, "Do you think Sinisha's a good guy? Will the owners get their money?"

Dimi shrugged, "I don't know. He's a Serb."

"Did everyone lose their minds here," Justin pondered.

"There is wide madness, yes," Dimi allowed.

He fell silent and their last candle burned itself out. Dimi's cracking voice broke from the darkness, slowly adding, "You know, suddenly I am a stranger in lands that I was always taught were my home."

Justin leaned back, almost involuntarily, into the recess of his chair and drifted into a tense guarded slumber.

Sunlight poked Justin from his rigid sleep. The flat's main room was crammed with a coffee table, bookshelves, wardrobe closets and chairs. The new day's merciless light illuminated all the wishful ambiguities of the previous night's shadows.

Justin had just paid somebody else to sleep in the abandoned dwelling of a displaced family. And now, he was en route to deliver aid to those people who had forced this family to leave.

As Justin pressed past the furniture to wash his face in the bathroom, faithful items lingered amongst the clutter. Shoes and boots lined beside the front door. Fishing rods and a tackle box waited in the hallway. A souvenir plate of the Zagreb Cathedral hung on the wall. A shopping list was taped to the kitchen door. In the haste to flee with their lives, the owners had left their life behind.

At exactly 7:30, a UNHCR Land Rover arrived in the complex's parking lot. Sinisha was at the wheel; Jadranka and Dragan were already in the back.

In the UNHCR office, Justin showed his packing lists to Jadranka. Scanning them, she nodded and said, "Ah excellent. I see you've brought a health kit from the UN World Health Organisation. They are excellent. I know that the hospital really needs this."

Jadranka drew a sketch of Knin with directions to the central pharmacy and hospital. A confusing series of one-way streets led to the central pharmacy in the town centre. The hospital sat on the far edge of town and was more straightforward.

Before heading out to make the deliveries, Justin and Dimi went down to the Kenyan bar for a quick breakfast. In the patio's shade, they enjoyed a cappuccino along with cheese and tomato toast. The cool morning air was warming as the rising sun bathed the surrounding mountains. In the calm of the new day, Justin's mind lapsed almost forgetting the circumstances around him. One glance at the patio's CNN television reminded him of reality though.

Dimi and Justin found the central pharmacy without much difficulty. Stopping on the street, Dimi hopped from the truck's passenger seat and walked up to the facility's gate. He craned through the entrance, then looked back at Justin and nodded for him to enter. Justin squeezed past the gate and into a courtyard normally used for parking cars. A handful of workers were trying to build an additional floor onto a five-story building.

Half the parking area was filled with bricks, piles of dirt, assorted tools and a contingent of workers standing about yelling orders at their rooftop colleagues.

Dimi shrugged and called up to Justin's cab, "Sorry, not much room." Pointing to an entrance a good 50 feet away, Dimi added, "That's the pharmacy door. You drive there. I will find pharmacy staff to help offload."

Dimi disappeared and Justin drove forward as far as possible. He then tried to back the truck around the various parked communist-built Fiat knock-offs and scattered construction material.

As Justin worked to turn his vehicle, three of the construction supervisors decided the truck was more interesting and tried to guide it through the lot.

One worker stood directly in front of Justin's cab and gave directions to go backwards. In his left mirror, Justin found another man giving different arm directions. In the right-hand mirror, the third man gave another set of orders.

Aggravated by Justin's lack of attention, the front man yelled and waved angrily.

A fourth younger man wearing an army beret jumped onto the truck's doorstep and thrust his hand into the open window. Obliging, Justin shook it.

"Hello my friend," the soldier said. "Would you like me to buy some of your diesel?"

"Uhh, no…" Justin stammered. Not wanting to appear rude, he replied, "But thanks for asking."

"Ah, come on. I buy from the Kenyans all the time, is no problem. I give you a good deal. Deutsche Marks. How much you sell it for?"

"I don't know. I need all my diesel for travelling," Justin replied.

Pointing to the truck's spare tank, "You have too much. You can sell me some." The diesel dealer's smile began to fade and his expression became aggressive.

Shouts came from the truck's rear complaining of Justin's slow progress. The man in the right mirror yelled at the front man for not knowing how to guide vehicles properly.

The front man shook a fist. He yelled back, "*Pička materina!*" and a detailed defence of his traffic guiding abilities.

Taking the confused opportunity, Justin revved his engine and lurched abruptly backward. The diesel man made a chopping motion with his wrist, shook his head and jumped down from the side of the truck. He marched to the parking lot exit. From this strategic point, he lit a smoke and waited. The haggling was far from complete.

Avoiding the remaining obstacles, Justin found Dimi at the building doorway happily chatting with a middle-aged woman in a white lab coat.

Dimi pointed to three unshaven dishevelled figures at the bottom of the entrance stairs and explained, "Here are the men they have found to help with the truck."

The trio radiated great tiredness. Their heavy eyes stared at the ground in complete resignation. Their faces hosted mountainous patches of sores and bruises.

Moving closer to Dimi, Justin asked quietly, "Those men don't work in the pharmacy do they?"

Dimi gave a negative cluck and raised his eyebrows toward the third large building in the courtyard. Wincing a little, he murmured, "They are staying in that building."

Instead of glass, thick rusted metal bars filled the building's windows. Faint murmurs emanated as arms reached out from a couple of main floor openings. "Eh, cigarette," their hoarse voices called.

"It's the jail," Dimi whispered. "I don't think they are there for robbing banks..."

Were they more fortunate than the abandoned flat's owner? At some point, these residents had become unworthy of the fortress' protection. Their isolation somehow made Knin a safer place.

Justin climbed into the back of his truck and began handing boxes of medicine down to the three inmates. Wordlessly and without the slightest indication of emotion, they shuffled the cargo into the pharmacy.

The hovering prisoners unloaded the three pallets of cargo in minutes. Turning to Dimi, Justin asked, "Can you go in and get the head pharmacist to count the boxes and sign the packing list? I'll stay out here and close up."

"Sure."

Justin moved beside his truck, out of view of the jail and obscured partially from the pharmacy. He lit a smoke and offered the pack to the three helpers. They maintained a distance from Justin but accepted the token without hesitation.

Dimi raced down the stairs panting, "They say they won't sign anything until you have coffee with them."

"OK, just a second. I still have to close up," Justin replied.

Hurriedly, Justin tied down the cargo flap and locked the truck's doors. Glancing around, he pulled the remainder of his pack of Marlboro's and handed them to the nearest inmate.

A rough dirty hand instantly transferred them to the pocket of his smelly blue coveralls. Justin looked into the man's sunken eyes for the first time. The empty inhuman pits frightened Justin and he glanced away. Nodding at the other two inmates, Justin said, "Cigarette, for you and *colleaga*. OK."

The inmate gave half a downward nod and hobbled, with the others, toward the jail's entrance.

After a couple of coffees and Slivo's with the pharmacy's director, Justin and Dimi emerged from the building somewhat dazed. Puddles filled with clumps of paper rested just past the entrance stairs. Bending down, Justin picked up 10,000 and 100,000 denominations of money.

"Those are old Republika Srpska Krajina Dinars…better than Deutsche Marks," Dimi said with a wink. Slapping Justin on the back, he added, "It's not hard to be the richest man in Knin."

Jumping in the truck, the pair roared out of the lot. The still waiting diesel dealer tried to step in front of the truck but at the last second, though better of it and waved a menacing fist as Justin passed.

Following the main road northward, Justin slowed to enter a busy traffic circle. An elderly pedestrian stomped up to the white truck and brandished his walking cane. He yelled, "UNPROFOR *Pička materina!*" repeatedly before spitting a large glob of slimy mucus on the truck's windshield.

Inching into the circle, Justin shook his head in disbelief and muttered, "Hey man, all this stuff is for you…"

The hospital was perched atop an austere rise at the town's northern edge. Justin backed easily into the hospital's ample receiving area and ventured inside to find its director. Meandering in basement corridors, they eventually found the head nurse – a woman in her 40s with red frizzy hair, knee-high boots and pudgy fingers covered in cheap gold rings. She took Justin and Dimi to the director's office on the second floor.

The director, a round man with receding hair and dazed sunken eyes, was talking on the phone. Seeing the new visitors, he hung up in mid-sentence and leapt to his feet.

Enthusiastically, he reached forward and welcomed the outsiders. "Quick, coffee," he ordered the head nurse.

As Dimi began introducing himself in Serbian, the director raised an arm. His face grew suspicious. Leaning forward, he asked in halting English, "Where are you from?"

"Macedonia...Kumanovo," Dimi replied nervously.

The director smiled a little and raised his eyebrows at Justin, "And he?"

"Canada."

The director's smile grew wider, "Good then!"

He reached into his desk drawer and pulled out a bottle of Šljivovica. The director swaggered to a small table below a calendar with pictures of General Ratko Mladić in heroic pose – squinting into the distance while holding binoculars, waving soldiers forward with a Beretta machine pistol, listening thoughtfully to compliments from an old lady. The director picked up a silver tray bearing matching shot glasses etched with double-headed eagles. He poured generous servings for his guests.

Justin was starting to look forward to the burning throat, warm stomach and twitching cheek that followed each shot of Slivo.

The nurse entered the room smiling and carrying a tray of coffee.

Nodding toward her, the director stated to Justin, "You will like this coffee. She makes the best coffee in the whole Yugoslavia. People used to say before the war, you haven't tasted a coffee until you have tasted Knin coffee."

Midway through the beverages, the director slammed his hand on his desk and barked, "So, what have you brought me?"

Justin handed over the packing list for the final five pallets in his truck.

"Ah, *dobro*," the director stated noting the list's generous length. "You know, you are the best organisation. I never receive anything from the UN or International Red Cross. But you are good, you bring me things."

The nurse and director pored over the inventory for at least five minutes. Looking up and pointing at a separate list of medical material, the director gruffly inquired, "What is this?"

Justin explained that it was the manifest for the WHO health kit he was delivering as a favour to the UN.

"Yes, but what is this?" Pointing angrily at three specific medicines on the list, he growled, "These are drugs for malaria. We do not have malaria in Yugoslavia! Why do you give us these drugs? This is not Africa!" The director threw the paper across his desk in exasperation.

Justin tried to explain that the WHO kits were standard sets prepared by the UN for distribution all over the world and therefore contained many different types of medicines for many different circumstances. The explanation had no effect and the director sourly continued looking at the packing list.

Eventually, Justin hesitantly asked the director if he had any other adjustments for next month's delivery.

"Overall, there are some good things here," he allowed. "I always need more Diazepam...infusions. And these surgical gloves. You have delivered many sizes. It would be better if you send us more of the larger sizes. Our hands are much bigger here."

The director read the list once more and signed where Justin instructed. To certify the process, he ordered the nurse to find his official ink stamp.

She frantically searched his desk and found it deep in his bottom drawer. She presented the rubber stamp and inkpad as a deacon would a vestment. With the papers legitimised, Justin and Dimi went down to unload the truck.

In a basement corridor, two orderlies emerging from a storeroom stacked with boxes emblazoned with red crosses and UN crests.

With the orderlies' help, the truck was unloaded in no time. Dimi and Justin drove back to the UN base to say goodbye to the UNHCR staff and grab a pizza before hitting the road to Zagreb.

Now familiar with the route home, the pair made excellent time. The empty truck climbed the mountains with greater ease and Dimi enjoyed the opportunity to drive faster. This of course caused his car to veer farther and harder on corners.

In a little more than four hours, they approached Turanj. At the Serb checkpoint, the two girls came out of the hut again, took down the vehicles' registration numbers, joked with Dimi and then pleasantly waved the foreigners along.

Justin was a little anxious approaching the elderly blockade. While calling Zagreb on the Codan the night before, he had mentioned the need to fax the blockade before his return trip. He prayed that the fax had gone through.

As they drove up to the crowd, a few cheered and one beaming man waved a fax adorned with the MOO letterhead. They had been expecting MOO's arrival and were ecstatic to now be part of the Balkan's vast bureaucratic loop.

MOO's fax had unwittingly done more to acknowledge the existence and legitimacy of the protesters than any other statement from the UN or Croatian government.

After parking the truck in the Zagreb warehouse an hour and a half later, Justin and Dimi headed for the office to stash their body armour and maps.

In the kitchen, Justin passed Rolf.

"So how was it?" he inquired. "No problems finding everything?"

"No, it all went pretty smoothly," Justin replied. "I even scored a bottle of Slivo."

Rolf rolled his eyes and quipped, "Let me guess, Udbina hospital. I have a whole shelf of the crap."

"Incidentally," Justin continued, "the directors in Udbina and Knin said we don't deliver enough Diazepam."

"Yes of course," Rolf replied dryly, "more infusions of hard-core sedatives. Even if we delivered nothing but trucks full of Diazepam everyday of the week, they still would not be happy. They're setting the stage for a whole bunch of junkies."

"The Knin director also said their hands are too big for the surgical gloves we send them," Justin added.

Cora walked past and, overhearing the comment, chimed with a mischievous grin, "Big hands I don't know, but small heads definitely."

Chapter 5

In mid-August, the elderly representatives from the Union of Forced Displaced Persons of Croatia (UFDPC for short) lifted their blockades. They vowed to return if their demands were not met by mid-September.

Within a week, Velika Kladuša, the remnant capital of the Autonomous Province of Western Bosnia, fell to a final Fifth Corps push from the south of the Bihać Pocket. The actions and threats of the UFDPC evaporated as APWB President, Fikret Abdić, fled his fiefdom and took along a good 30,000 followers. While Abdić reportedly found refuge in the northern RSK town of Vojnić, his flock split between two locations. One group moved into a massive Agrokomerc complex of chicken coops in Batnoga - a hamlet no more than seven kilometres across the border from Velika Kladuša - and the other to Turanj. While Batnoga residents contended with a lack of privacy and the indignity of living in poultry facilities, the Turanj arrivals faced mines and booby traps lacing most of the town's abandoned buildings. Those who went to Turanj did so with their own cars and tractors or were ferried the 50 km in Agrokomerc busses.

Fearing the deluge ultimately had farther aims, the Croatian authorities raced 1,000 men and armoured vehicles to seal off the border around Turanj. Croatia already had enough trouble dealing with their own displaced persons and had absolutely no desire to accommodate more from Velika Kladuša.

The UN dispatched the local Polish Battalion to park two APCs between the Croatian police and the refugees.

Now displaced Bosnians supplanted displaced Croats in blocking Justin's entry to Krajina. The only route Justin could now take to make his deliveries was via a second crossing point 60 km east in the town of Sisak. This posed a minor inconvenience, as trips to Krajina now involved travelling a couple extra hours on a slower stretch of secondary road. If this was the only obstacle Justin faced bringing aid to the people, things still remained comparatively easy.

Although Justin's priority now became addressing the medical situation in the two new refugee camps, he chose to go ahead with a large delivery he had planned for Sector North two weeks earlier. Justin already had crossing permission from the Knin Serbs and to try changing it at the last moment would have caused yet more delays.

The elderly Croat blockaders had forced at least a month's delay in Justin's planned trip to Sector North. Justin also figured the Serbs would take offence if MOO suddenly postponed that delivery in favour of providing medical aid to the new Bosnian Muslims residing in RSK. Although these Muslims followed a leader to whom the RSK had been selling military support, Abdić was by no means a trusted ally of the Krajina Serbs. In the end, the Serbs were not enthusiastic to host Abdić's people on their territory for any extended period and preferred if they either went onward to Croatia or returned to Velika Kladuša.

Rolf called Laura in from Banja Luka to do a medical assessment of the camps' needs. It would take at least a day before she could get to Zagreb. Justin decided the most pragmatic move would be to make the Sector North delivery in the mean time.

To cover the immediate needs of the refugees, Laura sent Justin a list of basic emergency medicines by Capsat. At least that way, Laura and Justin would not arrive at the camps empty-handed asking lots of questions and making vague promises. There were more than enough people doing that in these lands already.

Early the next morning, Dimi and Justin headed for Sisak in their respective vehicles. Although it was 6 a.m., the road was already clogged and its many curves and village defiles made overtaking difficult. An assortment of UN trucks, tractors, hay wagons and East European clunkers masquerading as cars filled the road.

Of all the delays they encountered, the small white, Yugoslav built, Zastava Fića was the most overwhelmingly infuriating. These wheeled sardine cans appeared easy enough to pass. However, all Fića owners believed that their proud carriage deserved the same full lane of respect granted to Western cars.

Whenever Dimi or Justin tried to squeeze around the sputtering Fica's, their drivers invariably veered to the road's centre or accelerated insolently in affirmation of their car's existence on European roads. Justin watched Dimi's silhouette ahead, waving in exasperation, threat and exclamation at the goddamned Fića drivers.

Without the Fića showdowns though, the trip to Sisak would have been incredibly boring. The landscape was flat and agrarian. It was not Krajina. It was not a forbidden land and, to Justin, it did not hold the same allure as Sectors North and South. The locals on the Sisak road were pursuing normal daily existences. An eagerness to be where only a privileged few could go and where unpredictability laid in abundance spawned Justin's anxiety.

Driving into Sisak, the town's oil refining infrastructure immediately overwhelmed. Like Karlovac, Sisak was an industrial centre that had been a key objective for both warring sides. Although large battles were fought in the vicinity and the Krajina frontier ran dangerously close to Sisak, the town's core did not display much evidence of carnage.

Turning onto a wide bridge, Justin spanned yet another universe of the Sava River. Across it, they traversed a gradual incline that brought them near the town's edge. Signs of combat damage began to appear – smatterings of shrapnel blasts spread over walls, pavement flower impressions from shell impacts, splintered timbers propped against houses.

A thick fog hung at the bottom of the hill. A few hundred metres farther the pair stopped at a Croatian checkpoint set up on a railroad crossing. The police were not expecting rail traffic any time soon.

A policeman took the MOO crossing papers. He radioed in their particulars and received confirmation within five minutes. From his seat in his hut, he waved the MOO vehicles along.

Dimi and Justin drove slowly for a couple more kilometres and passed a last village sporting an exceptionally large red, white and blue Croatian flag from a roadside pole. Without expression, a final Croatian policeman raised his crossing barrier.

They wove through a string of white concrete blocks and under the raised barrier of a Danish UN checkpoint. The pair of blond Danes manning the adjacent sandbag bunker were too busy dealing with the flirtatious advances of a couple of local girls to notice the aid workers.

Beyond the UN checkpoint, a disused factory housed the Danish soldiers. In the haze, Justin made out a couple of football fields across from the complex. Wire fences with red triangle landmine warnings blocked out the recreational area.

A kilometre farther, they overtook a line of waiting French UN trucks and APCs attempting to resupply their bases in Bihać. Meandering past another set of white concrete tank barriers and a Danish bunker, Dimi and Justin pulled into a lip next to a Serb militia hut. Three Serbs in purple fatigues and two French officers milled, looking bored, beside the closed red, blue, white crossing barrier.

Justin and Dimi's arrival aroused the Serbs' attention. The militiamen pored over their crossing papers for a few minutes and then examined Dimi and Justin's blue UN ID cards meticulously. The guards grew suspicious of Dimi's Balkan origins and demanded to see his Macedonian passport. Viewing it, they did not know what to do next. One guard went into the hut and made a phone call.

Dimi nervously asked what the problem was.

The guard pointed to another line of 10 UN Jeeps and Landcruisers backed up on the Serb side of the barrier and replied that the local commander had ordered no vehicles to cross until he personally arrived.

Where was the commander?

The guard shrugged dramatically – who knows.

Dimi asked if he could use the toilet. The Serb directed him to a fly infested, shattered, concrete bungalow behind the guard hut.

The head guard bummed a smoke from Justin. Together they wordlessly surveyed the international scene before them. Across the barrier, a group of Portuguese, Kenyan and Spanish officers waited patiently. Another cluster of two civilian UN employees and a Royal Canadian Mounted Police officer chatted nearby.

On the other side of the road from the militia hut, a group of eight young men, in a variety of combat attire, were constructing a second hut. A short stout soldier sporting Serb army camouflage and a maroon paratrooper beret guided them.

Noticing Justin's gaze at the work scene, the smoking guard nodded in its direction and, feeling a need to distinguish his hut from the new one, said, "*Militaire.*"

Trying to break the boredom, the guard asked to see Justin's packing list. He peered in at the cargo through a slit in the truck's rear. Feeling no enthusiasm to do a thorough search, he simply nodded.

The waiting international congregation scattered suddenly as a UN Jeep Cherokee screeched up to the barrier. Two Serb guards burst from their hut and into the arms of a Jordanian officer climbing from his vehicle. The guards hugged the officer and yelled greetings to the other Jordanian's in the car. As they laughed and exchanged pleasantries, a giant Toblerone chocolate bar and two cartons of Marlboros appeared from the Jeep's front seat. One guard ferried the loot to the hut and another raised the crossing barrier. The Jeep squealed away with its occupants waving wildly. The barrier came straight back down and the rest resumed waiting.

As Dimi returned from the toilet, the smoking guard waved and shouted, "*Hej, Makedonac! Dodji vamo!*"

Dimi turned pale and advanced tentatively.

Moving toward the construction workers, the guard beckoned Dimi and Justin. The labourers stopped and gathered around their new visitors.

Pointing at one worker, the guard introduced Dimi.

Turning to Justin, Dimi interpreted, "This guy is also from Macedonia."

Chatting with his ethnic kin, Dimi performed the global introductory dance of seeing whom they knew common.

Dimi turned to Justin and explained, "We are from almost the same area of Macedonia. He is very unlucky. He came, a couple years ago, to visit a relative in Glina and stayed to work. Now he is stuck here.

"They are a type of war objectors. They don't want to fight. So they are locked up in Petrinja for a few months. The commander did not know what to do with them. So now they build a new army house for the checkpoint." Nodding at the Macedonian, Dimi continued, "He said it is not so bad, another group in Glina dig trenches beside mine fields."

A tall blond in the group stepped up to Dimi and thrust a half-empty bottle of Šljivovica in his face. The man had coarse eyes displaying no recognisable emotion. He wore grey coveralls with a black skull and crossbones patch on the left sleeve.

Dimi obliged and then the blond roughly offered Justin a serving. Justin took a tentative swig. The blond snarled and held the bottle centimetres from Justin's nose. Justin took a larger pull that caused him to cough. The blond flashed a sardonic toothless smile. Nodding at Justin, he mumbled a question to Dimi.

Translating, Dimi said, "He wants to know if you liked the Sljivo."

"It was not as bad as I expected," Justin replied.

As Dimi interpreted the blond stared right through Justin and mumbled some more.

Dimi explained in English, "He says there is no bad Sljivo."

Looking at the blond and smiling, Justin said, "I had some from a store in Zagreb a few days ago."

"Zagreb... *pushie kurac*!" the blond snarled and spat at the ground.

Diligently, Dimi continued translating, "He says Zagreb...suck my dick..."

"Yeah, yeah I caught that," Justin interjected impressed with his growing knowledge of Serb and Croat profanity.

Dimi and Justin waited for another hour and were encouraged to finish the workers' remaining Slivo. To avoid any new bottles, the pair moved back to the militia hut and smoked with the Serb guards.

Without warning or explanation, the hut's phone rang and a guard opened the crossing barrier allowing all passage. Not wanting to be stuck behind the French convoy on Krajina's narrow roads, Dimi and Justin jumped frantically in their vehicles and were first through the gate.

About a kilometre later, they approached the shattered dwellings of Petrinja's outskirts. On their right, the desolate hulking silos of an industrial plant stood idle.

Over the VHF Dimi called, "Wow, that is a very famous factory. It was once the biggest sausage producer in the region."

Farther into town, tree-lined streets housed faded baroque buildings. The slowly lifting fog and proximity of smashed homes along the tight streets completely exorcised any whiff of pleasantness Petrinja might have once offered.

The pair wove through vacant one-way streets and followed signs to the town's hospital. At an old building marked "*Psihijatrijska Bolnica*" they parked in a small lot to its rear.

Pointing at the sign and crossing his eyes, Dimi whispered, "It is a place for crazy people."

As their footsteps echoed along the tiled hallway, Justin asked, "Then why is this place so empty?"

Inside an office with a doorplate reading "Dr. Radovan," they found the director.

The director, a short thin old man, served Dimi and Justin coffee and gave a brief explanation of the hospital's specialisation.

Justin apologised that he was not a medical person but, in the near future, would return with a nurse who could review the institution's needs properly. In the mean time though, he had brought a delivery of essential medicines.

The director smiled appreciatively and glanced at the packing list. He nodded tentatively at its contents and then, through Dimi, explained, "I know you're not a doctor but in the future, we need more sedative infusions."

Outside, Dimi and Justin peeled the shrink-wrap off the two pallets for Petrinja Hospital. Four elderly men wearing faded pyjamas and rough expressions came to help unload. Slouching, with their heads held low or to the side, they moved with a slow, yet awkward, fluidity. None spoke a word.

When finished breaking down the hospital's pallets, one of the helpers came forward and looked up at Justin. He made a scissors motion with his fingers. Justin reached into his pocket and offered a pack of smokes. Pointing to the other three now standing by a wall and looking at the ground, the man slowly pried a handful of cigarettes from the pack.

At the far end of the treed town square, a fresh pig roasted slowly in a restaurant's street-front grill. Following signs for Glina, they crossed a UN-erected Bailey Bridge and left Petrinja. On a tight bend of a winding hill, the shredded hulk of a crashed Croatian Mig-21 jet fighter rested proudly as a roadside trophy.

Yet more wrecked and abandoned homes spotted the surrounding rolling pastoral lands. Some now served as army installations and command posts. Serb nationalist slogans adorned most facades.

Vegetation crowded and partially covered the empty buildings. Indomitable nature was attempting to shroud mankind's artificial disgraces and live over the death.

A Ukrainian peacekeeping post nestled behind the ruins of a small ancient monastery. It was hard to determine which army, in which century had caused that building's damage.

Approaching the edge of Glina, Dimi and Justin passed the Ukrainian Battalion's main base. A Ukrainian soldier tried to thumb a ride into town. Glancing in his rear-view mirror, Justin saw a local white Fića stop to give the trooper a lift.

Just off the town's park-square, the gutted shell of what had once been a large church hung in agony. Its entire facade had vanished and it now resembled a cutaway picture from an anatomy textbook. The remaining building framed the core of what was once a proud and glorious structure.

A row of darkened gloomy shop-fronts lined the street's far side. The few still operating offered nothing more than the odd article of dusty clothing and shoes; things no one in town had the means or inclination to purchase. Farther along, two Ukrainian soldiers, laden with plastic shopping bags, window-shopped contentedly.

Following a hand-scribbled map from Rolf, Justin guided Dimi through Glina's one-way streets. As the map did not really correspond with the objects on the ground, or Dimi with Justin's directions, it took some time to locate the Glina Central Pharmacy tucked on a side street.

Inside the pharmacy, a large elegantly dressed woman in her 40s welcomed the guests in almost flawless English. Her well-appointed office contained a glass-topped meeting table and bulky leather swivel chairs. Resting prominently on the wall behind the director's desk was a portrait of the Bosnian Serb leader, Dr. Radovan Karadzic, gazing thoughtfully into the future – possibly composing lyrics.

The director ordered coffee and produced a sliver tray with tumblers and a bottle of Balantines. She poured generous glasses for the guests and took delight in their surprise at the offering. The coffee arrived almost instantly.

Watching Justin enjoy his beverage, the director said, "I see you like our coffee."

Justin nodded gratefully – partly out of a need to suppress the drunken pangs festering in his empty stomach.

"We make it a special way in Glina. It is the way of the Krajina," the director stated. "Your office is in Zagreb no? I don't know if you know about Turkish Coffee but they do not make it the right way in Zagreb. There most prefer espresso or cappuccino with umm...*schlag*..." Pausing to find the right English word, she scrunched her face and rubbed her forefinger and thumb vigorously as if something disgusting was stuck between them. "What do you call it? Beating cream. That is not right. They think they are Germans."

"So what's the secret?" Justin inquired politely.

Proudly she explained, "The secret is in how many times you boil the coffee. Sometime it takes 15 minutes to make properly. I cannot reveal any more to you though; it's a secret."

Noticing Justin's gaze had settled briefly on her Karadzic portrait, the director explained, "That is our real leader."

"I thought he represented the Bosnian Serbs," Justin pondered.

"Tsk," she corrected flicking her eyebrows. Putting a hand to her bosom, she explained solemnly, "Officially, yes. But in the heart, every Serb is Radovan. He is the only one who cares for us all. Did you know he is a doctor and a poet? If only you understood Serbian, you would see the true beauty of his writings. He is the greatest of all."

Glancing at her desk, the director handed a series of lists and tables to Justin. "This is an accounting for your past medical deliveries that have been distributed each month amongst the pharmacies and *Dom Zdravlja's* throughout this northern region," she explained.

Justin was impressed. The tables detailed the exact quantities each town's medical institution received – down to the last

Paracetamol tablet. The director made a photocopy of the documents on her fax machine. Presenting the stack to Justin, she smiled and said, "It is very important to follow the medicines you have provided us. There are some very crooked people out here."

In return, Justin gave her a copy of the current packing list. Scanning its contents, she looked up and said, "This is very good. Thank you."

"Is there anything specific you need in the future?"

"We need many things," she replied wryly. "But what you have brought is very good and complete. You and the International Red Cross are the only ones who really help us reliably. We get nothing that is promised from the government in Belgrade."

Looking up suddenly she asked, "Do you give medical help to UNPROFOR?"

A little surprised, Justin replied, "No, we only help local hospitals and clinics. UNPROFOR's supposed to have their own medicine."

"Last week two medical officers from the Ukrainian Battalion came here asking if they could buy medicines from our pharmacy because they had none for their own soldiers."

She shook her head and said, with a condescending smile, "The UN says they come here to protect us but maybe it is us who really protect them."

Getting up, the director left the room and returned with three middle-aged female pharmacy workers to help unload the truck.

Departing, the director thanked Justin again and promised to provide more distribution tables next month.

Justin climbed into his cab and grabbed at the contents of a Dutch army ration. He ate a handful of thick crackers with liver *pâté* followed by a roll of hard barely chewable fruit candy.

Looking up from the ground with a slightly bewildered look, Dimi said to Justin, "She seems very efficient and organised but she is totally crazy. She has no logic."

"I'm confused too," Justin frowned. Apparently, it was not just the peasants and hicks who were nationalists, even the educated and professional could contract the seductive disease.

Following signs for the Glina Hospital, they drove across town and into a large seemingly vacant complex. In the main building, the pair bounced between rooms and floors before a nurse eventually directed them to a small bungalow outside.

The annex served as the facility's lab and storage area. Inside, a doctor took the packing list gruffly and, before looking at it, asked, "So, have you brought Diazepam?"

Without awaiting a reply, he signed the bottom of the sheet, handed it back and announced, "Thank you. I must go now." He barked an order to the back room and left the building.

An older kinder looking woman emerged from the back smiling. Four stunningly beautiful nurses in their 20s followed her. The weather remained cool and overcast. Before exiting the building, the nurses donned long blue wool capes over their thin white medical outfits. From the truck, Justin handed boxes down into the nurses' perfectly manicured hands. Laughing incessantly, Dimi eagerly assisted the nurses in carrying boxes.

Looking up and grinning to Justin, Dimi said, "This place is very good but strange. Too many women work in this part of ex-Yugoslavia. What is wrong with Zagreb?"

As they finished unloading the hospital's two pallets and Justin tied down the truck's canopy, the nurses noticed the Landcruiser's mobile phone. Immediately, they asked politely if they could call some relatives and friends in Croatia. Dimi smiled and could think of no way of refusing.

The senior nurse emerged from the building to beckon Justin and Dimi to have coffee. Seeing the available phone, she too asked if she could call an old colleague in Zagreb.

Dimi and Justin stood by and smoked in the parking lot for three quarters of an hour as the nurses took turns chatting. Concerned about the distance they still had to travel, Justin kept glancing at Dimi anxiously. With an enormous grin locked on his face, Dimi simply shrugged.

When all calls were finally completed, the aid workers were ushered into the bungalow and served their obligatory cup of coffee. While Dimi and Justin drank, the nurses crowded the small room, smoking and chatting giddily about what they had learned from their respective calls.

For a series of conversations that could easily have turned ugly or bore bad fortune, all seemed ecstatic and relieved at the news they had gained.

Nodding toward Justin, the head nurse performed the mandatory ritual of asking if her guest enjoyed the coffee.

Through Dimi, Justin obediently replied, "Yes. What's the secret?"

The nurse frowned and Dimi translated, "There's no secret. It is all crap. You boil the water with whatever coffee you can find. It is all good no?"

She abruptly broke off the conversation – she had said too much.

As Dimi and Justin departed to make their next delivery, the senior nurse shook their hands vigorously. Dimi translated repeatedly, "Thank you so much,"

Eventually, she added, "The telephone call was the best…worth more than all the medicines in the world." Pausing, she glanced around suspiciously, as if by reflex, and went on, "This is the only reliable news I have received in a long time. You can't trust anyone here…"

Just outside the hospital, Dimi and Justin crossed a narrow ageing suspension bridge. A flat winding road left Glina and dissected a cluster of damaged homes. Beside them, a string of almost identical newer houses appeared to have been part of a planned suburb. There was little to distinguish the destroyed houses from the unfinished shoddy condominiums.

The road traversed hilly and forested terrain. At times, they drove through bucolic villages, undamaged and oblivious to the circumstances in which they rested. It was almost just an afternoon drive in the countryside. Inevitably, military posts and vehicle lots in subsequent villages quickly dispelled the myth though.

It was well past noon. Trying to line his stomach with something other than caffeine or alcohol, Justin ate more Dutch crackers. The effect was minimal and fleeting.

Dodging a longhaired dog slumbering in their lane, the two pulled into Vojnić about an hour after leaving Glina. Although Vojnić was not a large town, its importance came from its location at the crossroads leading to Velika Kladuša 25 km away. Justin and Dimi had no trouble finding the hospital on the town's main periphery road. The facility was improvised from a small hotel complex.

They stopped in its large empty parking lot and went inside to find the director. Dimi was guided to the emergency room. In what had once been the hotel lobby commotion reigned amongst six medical staff attending to various ailments. A tall young doctor stepped forward in introduction. His English was very good and he motioned enthusiastically for Dimi and Justin to sit at the emergency room's only desk.

Taking the packing list from Justin, the doctor said, "I'm afraid the director is away right now. It is not a problem, I can handle this also."

Looking over the list he said, "This is very good, thank you." Lighting a cigarette, he continued, "The situation in this town has become a little crazy in the last two weeks. This hospital was temporary and originally could handle a maximum of 60-70 patients. With the fighting in Velika Kladuša, we were at first helping a small number of badly wounded soldiers from there. But now Abdić has left his town and the number of people asking for help is high. Last week we treated more than 200 patients."

"What kinds?" Justin asked taking notes.

"A lot of war wounded but also many old people with typical chronic problems. Most we treat and send out the same day."

"What kind of medical facilities existed before in Velika Kladuša?" Justin asked.

Exhaling smoke, the doctor shrugged, "Oh, I don't know. That's in Bosnia. I've never been there in my life."

Pausing for a moment, the doctor went on, "You must please inform your medical colleagues that our work here has doubled because of the new situation. We are the nearest hospital to the Batnoga camp…and also to Turanj."

Justin assured the doctor he would forward the message. He also told the doctor of MOO's plans to provide medical assistance directly to the nearby refugee camps.

At that prospect, the doctor seemed greatly relieved.

A burly 6'3" tall man with a walrus moustache and wearing a camouflage field jacket entered the emergency room.

Looking up, the young doctor explained, "Ah, it is the director."

Justin and Dimi introduced themselves and the group chatted for a few moments. As the director spoke no English, the doctor and Dimi interpreted respectively. When the director found out that the young doctor had already given his approval to the packing list, he invited the group to join him immediately for coffee in the hospital canteen.

The group seated themselves on a large terrace in an adjacent building that had been a restaurant in a previous incarnation. The view was rustic and pleasant. The smell of wood fires wafted through the late afternoon air.

In the distance, yet more hills crowned by deep and rugged forest unfolded exquisitely. What was once a source of pleasure, to behold and savour, now taunted and imprisoned all at its feet. Evil seeds had been planted and atrocities committed in their shadow; no one would ever be free to enjoy or share them peacefully again.

The attachment people had to these resplendent lands made sense. Justin too would have defended such a place if he felt threatened. Yet if they really loved them so much, how could they be willing to destroy, desecrate, maim and poison such beauty for generations to follow. What love was that?

A waiter in a red blazer arrived with a tray of Slivo and coffee. The director distributed the drinks and quietly scrutinised Dimi and Justin. He threw back his Slivo and called to the waiter for another. The director's glazed eyes hinted that he had probably spent much of the day in the restaurant already. Nodding in Justin's direction, the director inquired of his nationality.

Upon hearing Justin's reply, the young doctor leaned forward with a look of delight. "Canada," he said, "That is great. Where in Canada? I have an uncle in Toronto who owns a pizza shop on Queen Street, near Spadina."

Justin coughed in surprise, "I'm from Toronto. I probably ate at that pizzeria a few months ago."

"Ah, Toronto is fantastic," the doctor continued. "I was there visiting over four years ago. I saw the Rolling Stones' Steel Wheels concert at the Skydome. Oh, that was something."

The doctor turned to the director and described the stadium and its retractable roof. The director nodded and seemed slightly impressed.

Recalling a set of free promotional tickets he had won in a university raffle, Justin exclaimed, "I went to that show too. What a small world."

"Especially for those with big hearts," the doctor asserted. "Ah, those were good times."

Looking at the Slivo before him, Justin decided the best strategy would be to drink it in one shot and get it over with fast. Maybe then, its affects would wear off by the time they had to leave. The stuff tasted like turpentine.

Spotting the empty glass, the director yelled to the waiter for another drink for himself and his Canadian guest. Glancing at Dimi, Justin noticed that his glass remained two thirds empty. Dimi smirked knowingly.

Continuing, the doctor asked Justin, "Your main office is in Zagreb no? What part?"

Remembering the only landmark that came to mind, Justin answered, "Near Salata neighbourhood."

The doctor gave a large smile, "Ah, *Šalata*. That is the hospital where I did my medical internship. A great place. I have so many friends there."

Taking a drag of his cigarette, he went on, "I miss Zagreb. I spent some wonderful times there with some very good friends...I think they are still my friends. We have not spoken in a long time...I don't know how they would act if we met now.

"When this whole fight started I did not really have any problems in Zagreb. The people I knew there never made trouble for me. They knew who I was and that I was a Serb. But then it was the people from the countryside and the villages who came into Zagreb who were loud and made shit."

Raising his eyebrows slowly and frowning, he continued, "So eventually I had to leave. Then I was working in one of the best hospitals in the entire country. Now I am a doctor in a *dom zdravlja* that was a restaurant before."

Nodding at a pocked wall on the main building, he explained, "Look, you can see the marks from a couple of rockets fired from Karlovac that landed here a few months ago."

Dimi and Justin finished their drinks and unloaded the truck's two remaining pallets. The director and doctor waved from the parking lot as the MOO vehicles departed. It was almost 4 p.m. and the pair had two hours of driving ahead to get to the Serb checkpoint outside Sisak.

Justin was feeling unpleasantly light-headed. He tried eating more crackers and an old army chocolate bar that was white with age.

As his truck was empty, Justin would be able to make good time. In the shorter days of the coming cold months, they would really have to push themselves to get back to the border before it became completely dark. There had been numerous stories of roadside banditry and car-jackings aimed at the white vehicles driven by foreigners.

Exiting Vojnić, Justin knew he would often have to travel this route inebriated. He needed to etch the road's every nuance, curve, bump and straightaway indelibly in his memory. He would have to drive the road fast, drunk and on an empty stomach without hitting any locals. If he could do this before dark, he won. If he hit a local, he lost. The discipline was a challenging one; it was the Olympic Sport of Krajina.

Dimi and Justin made decent time in lighting that rapidly became flat and grey. On a narrow stretch between Glina and

Petrinja, a UN truck lay on its side in a ditch. A Ukrainian soldier sat on a campstool by its front wheels. Dimi slowed and asked the trooper if he needed help. The soldier raised a large radio from his lap. He waved that he was OK and Dimi sped off.

Pulling into Petrinja at about 6 p.m., the turning pig on the spit was now roasted golden brown and half-eaten. The sight merely increased Justin's anxiety for real food.

At the Serb checkpoint, the guards recognised the approaching vehicles, opened the barrier and waved them through. Dimi stopped just beyond the guard hut and asked if he could use the toilet.

The guard nodded and, in feigned frustration, told him to be quick.

At the Croatian crossing, the two stopped and again flashed their crossing papers from the morning. Although the guards had not changed, they did not appear to recognise the aid workers. Seeing Dimi's passport however, they quickly remembered and made a call on their radio. Dimi looked nervous and Justin shrugged in an attempt to allay his fears. About five minutes later, they were allowed to proceed.

The home stretch was unbearably packed with rush hour Fića's in both directions. Tired and hungry, Justin wanted desperately to finish this part of the journey. The trip's final hour was the day's longest.

After dropping the truck off at the warehouse and Dimi downtown, Justin returned to the office with the Landcruiser. In the kitchen oven, he found welcome dinner warming. Justin grabbed a beer from the fridge and dropped onto the living room couch.

After eight hours of drinking and driving, he felt exhausted but also pumped. The relatively staid environs of Zagreb made him appreciate where he had just been. A selfish contentment simmered knowing that, as the world looked on, he was one of the few who had been to a conflict zone today. He was an elite witness to the core of a place so many had heard about on the news. He had made a small contribution and was now enjoying a cold beer; it felt pretty damn good.

Rolf entered the room proudly carrying a bottle of Single Malt Scotch he had acquired duty-free at the UNPROFOR PX. He slumped on the couch, poured a large tumbler and nodded at the bottle in offering to Justin. Grabbing the TV remote control, Rolf put his feet up on the coffee table and, with an ironic grin, muttered, "Let's see what happened at work today."

Chapter 6

Soon after returning from UNPA North Justin prepared to make a delivery to Turanj's new inhabitants. He managed to fit two pallets of medicine and dressings, like a giant jigsaw puzzle, into the Landcruiser. That afternoon, Laura arrived from Banja Luka and the crossing permission came by fax from both sides. Apparently, the Serbs and Croats were happy to see someone else giving the Velika Kladuša refugees medical assistance.

As there was only room for two in the packed Landcruiser, Dimi could not join the pair. Justin and Laura figured they would find an interpreter somewhere within the refugee camp.

Leaving before dawn the next morning, they arrived in Sisak without much delay. As usual, a thick fog hung on the town's edge. At the Croatian crossing, the police were efficient and allowed passage immediately.

Weaving through the UN checkpoint, Justin waved to the bored Danish soldiers. They barely mustered the enthusiasm to wave back.

There were no other vehicles at the Serb checkpoint and Justin drove straight up to its flimsy red, blue and white striped barrier. The militiamen from the previous trip were on duty and demanded to see Justin's crossing papers.

The military hut across from the militia hut was now operational and the stout soldier, who had overseen its construction, emerged. He too, wanted to perform an inspection of the Landcruiser. The soldier glanced at the vehicle's tightly packed boxes. Impressed with the stacking job, he pointed a finger in recognition to Justin.

Noticing Laura, the guards became self-conscious. The militiamen straightened their uniforms and the soldier gave a crisp salute before viewing Justin's crossing papers.

All tried striking conversations with Laura, but lacking Dimi, were restricted to asking, "Good morning, how you?" and, "Where you from?"

Amused by the spectacle, Laura smiled and answered in the few words of Serbian she knew. This, the guards found flatting to the highest degree.

Realising they still had duties to perform, the guards eventually refocused on Justin and demanded a closer look at the car's cargo. After prying out several boxes and peering in, all they could see were still more tightly packed boxes. They decided it would not be necessary to look farther. Seeing it was all destined for Turanj, the militiamen appeared neither impressed nor offended.

The soldier, who had already returned to Laura's side, pointed to the vehicle's medicines and then motioned that he had head and throat pains.

Interpreting the charade, Laura said, "I think you probably need Aspirin and cough syrup."

"Aspirin. *Da! Da!*" the soldier nodded enthusiastically.

"No problem. I'll bring some next time. Uh…*Drugi put*," Laura replied.

The soldier spread his arms and, with a smile, tilted his head back, "*Ah, hvala lepo Gospodjica.*"

Another militiaman emerged from his hut, yelled, "OK. *Idi breh!*" and waved for Justin to proceed.

Following a now familiar route, Justin made excellent time. After Vojnić, they took the road north and headed back in the direction of Karlovac and Zagreb. Just under two hours after leaving the Sisak crossing, they passed a Polish UN peacekeeping base and climbed a long slope. At the top, a chain hung across the road. A watchful group of Serb militiamen seated in the nearby shade glanced lazily at the white vehicle and lowering the flimsy barrier. The guards were likely more interested in the comings and goings of the town's new residents than foreign aid workers.

Entering Turanj's fringe, a few people walked on the road and a smattering of houses showed signs of habitation. Quickly, the volume of pedestrians grew and the dwellings became more populated.

A few hundred metres into town, Justin found a gravel patch UN engineers had cleared and levelled for a water tanker, two white prefab containers and three military tents bearing red crosses. People lined up patiently behind the truck, waiting to fill buckets and assorted plastic containers. Justin parked and found a French UNHCR officer in one of the prefabs.

Introducing himself, the UN rep said with an wry smile, "Good to see you. Right now, things in this town are rather chaotic. I am sure any assistance you provide will be appreciated very much."

"What's the town's current population?" Justin inquired.

"Ah, the magic question," the UNHCR man replied. "Presently, the UNHCR estimate 12,000 individuals. Of course, Abdić representatives claim there are at least 35,000 in Turanj alone. It is a very touchy issue. Abdić will not let us make any type of headcount and he says that the UN is only trying to underestimate the total so that we don't have to give as much help to his people."

"What's the UNHCR's position on the Turanj refugees?"

"Initially, we felt this was not the best place for the refugees to stay. This is a town in already disputed territory and it is extremely unsafe. The houses are badly damaged and dangerous.

"Believe me, Turanj was not these people's end destination either. This just happens to be the only empty town available and the last one before Croatia. But since they are here now and no side is allowing them to go anywhere else, the UNHCR is doing its best to find a lasting solution to their problem. In the mean time, we're also working so that the inhabitants can have adequate living and hygiene materials while they stay in the two camps."

"What about landmines?" Justin asked.

"One man already lost a leg and another couple were killed when they entered a house with a booby trapped door. UNPROFOR engineers are trying to clear safe areas in town. But this is almost impossible now because the people have moved into all the houses before they could be inspected or made safe."

"What's the medical situation?" Laura inquired.

"The Polish battalion down the road have supplied some tents and medical personnel for now. We're trying to establish a medical facility in town. So far, a doctor and two nurses have been identified amongst the town's population. Anyway, they definitely need all the medical material they can get."

As Justin and Laura continued in search of the new medical facility, a cluster of kids chased after the cruiser and clung playfully from its rear door and bumper. Justin drove slowly and gently applied the brakes a few times to dislodge them. This only seemed to strengthen their resolve. Laura eventually jumped out and hollered at them. They scattered immediately.

Justin drove up to the town's familiar Serb militia checkpoint. It was hard to tell exactly what the barrier now separated as inhabitants lived on either side and walked by freely.

The longhaired militia-girl emerged from her guardhouse, gave a subtle smile of acquaintance and waved. Holding up the logbook, she asked from where Justin and Laura had just come.

"Zagreb," Justin replied.

"Zagreb this," the guard said pointing in the direction they wished to drive. "Where you go?" she asked with a deprecating grin.

Also grinning, Justin pointed at the town beyond.

"*Ciao*," she winked and opened the barrier.

Justin pushed forward into the flowing crowd. Turanj throbbed with life and could not possibly be the same place he had seen a few weeks before. Only the town's name remained unchanged. All dwellings were full and everything seemed much closer together. People moved in every direction busy with tasks of all types. Some pulled felled trees or carried loads of scavenged lumber along the street. Chopped wood sat piled before houses. Ragged clothing hung from lines and balconies. Smoke rose from chimneys and outdoor cooking fires.

Entering the town's core, the already busy street became almost impassable. Justin could only inch forward as humanity swirled and brushed against his vehicle. While many appeared busy with activities of habitat and small commerce, scores more milled about aimlessly. Other small groups hung around languidly on the roadside – sharing in the universal pastime of the displaced.

Elsewhere along the shoulder, a few inhabitants were building or had already set up small stands. People were selling baked goods, cigarettes and bottles of Bell's whisky. Other stalls sold shots of local hooch.

A larger wood hut operated as a café and another as a barber. Kiosks offered mobile phone services – signs outside listed the call rates to European cities.

A Polish soldier armed with a large machinegun stood at the entrance of another levelled gravel patch housing white prefab huts. People and vehicles took no notice of the sentry and entered at will.

Pointing to a line of residents outside one prefab, Laura said, "I bet that's where we'll find a doctor."

Squeezing past the queue, the pair entered the hut and found a fashionably kept middle-aged woman with perfect hair attending to patients. Her nursing assistant spoke a little English and interpreted.

The doctor was from Velika Kladuša and upon hearing of the aid worker's delivery hugged Laura. Glancing quickly through the MOO packing list, she expressed more gratitude and affirmed that the items would more than cover her immediate needs.

Excusing herself from her five patients, the doctor sat down with Laura and explained the medical situation facing Turanj. Bearing expressions of profound confusion, the patients in the crowded 20 foot-long container stared silently at the proceedings.

Justin unloaded his vehicle's cargo in the neighbouring prefab. With the exception of a pallet of International Red Cross boxes, the container was empty.

As Justin had a smoke beside his vehicle, a Danish UNCIVPOL officer approached and asked for a cigarette. Lighting up, the cop nodded at the road's kinetic proceedings and said, "Not bad for a group that arrived a couple of weeks ago, eh?"

"Huh?" Justin asked – unsure what the Dane meant.

"They've already set up more businesses than this town had before the war," the officer explained. "They've even got decent Scotch and cigarettes for sale."

"I saw that. Where'd they get it from?" Justin wondered.

Nodding disdainfully at the town's southern edge, he said, "Our Polish friends down the road. Some UN officers will make a pretty profit from this war. There are even reports of prostitution after dark. Not that you'll find me staying here at that time of day!"

Pausing to savour a drag of his smoke, the Dane continued, "These are real 90s refugees. Many came here with their own vehicles. Supposedly, all their gold and valuables are locked away in special buses parked down the road…to follow them to their afterlife in the West."

From their slightly elevated vantage, a view of Croatia spread beyond the town. Eyeing the neighbouring territory, the police officer added, "They're all getting on the mobile phones and calling their families and friends over there or in Sweden."

Finishing his cigarette, the Dane excused himself and continued his rounds.

A nearby couple, who looked to be in their 40s, zeroed in on Justin. In English, the woman asked for a cigarette. Justin obliged and she took two.

She lit one and gave the other to her husband. With trembling hands, she exclaimed, "Look at us."

Pointing her bony chin at the street proceedings and then shaking her head in self-pity, she added, "This is Europe in the Twentieth Century! And now we must live like animals. This is not Africa. How can this happen?"

With an air of annoyance and surprise, she spat, "We are refugees now. We have rights now. But what does the UN do for us? Nothing. The just want us to go home."

"What would happen if you went home?" Justin asked quietly.

Exasperated at such a naïve question, the woman replied, "We would be killed – massacred. Dudak, the monster of Bihać, he already hung 10 enemies from a crane in Kladuša. They say he makes his enemies eat dog food.

"It is not possible to return now. The whole of Velika Kladuša is destroyed. No, we are refugees now. We must go to the West."

Turning her gaze to the luscious tormenting view of Croatia, she wondered maudlinly, "Why doesn't Croatia help us anymore?"

Abruptly, she shook Justin's hand, said, "Thank you," and entered the street's flow with her partner. Justin simply nodded. He did not know what to say to these people; they seemed utterly bewildered. Somebody had raised their hopes.

Was it Justin's perception that was irreparably obscured and tainted or was everyone else just witnessing a different universe than he?

Laura, the doctor and her assistant emerged from their container. Smiling, the doctor thanked Laura repeatedly and profusely.

"Not at all, not at all. It is my pleasure – it's my job," Laura kept stating.

As they drove out of the compound, Laura explained that in addition to the local doctor, personnel from UNPROFOR and UNICEF were providing children's medical care. MOO would be most helpful by delivering basic medicines on a regular basis.

Frowning, Laura went on, "The doctor's an interesting person. She actually has a visa from the Croats allowing her to move to Rijeka where she has relatives. She could simply leave this place at any time if she wanted. But she feels a duty to stay. Her chance to leave could be revoked at any time by the authorities."

Justin nodded wordlessly. Real heroes seemed so rare.

Instead of turning left and heading back the way they had entered, Justin went to survey the rest of the town. A pair of one-legged young men in tracksuits stood by the road. They gazed silently with their respective stumps propped upon their crutches. Both used their free hands to smoke. A wandering friend, proudly carrying a claymore landmine, waved in greeting.

Justin wanted to try getting through the crossing point at the bottom of town. Having not actually seen what the police situation was at the point, it was worth a shot. If successful, the two could be back in the comfort of the Zagreb office, their day's work complete, in a mere 45 minutes. Otherwise, they faced a good two and a half-hour drive back via the way they came.

The masses of humanity thinned near the bottom of the hill. Even at that point though, not a single house or structure was left unoccupied. A row of Agrokomerc buses were parked along the shoulder. In an adjacent lot, another line of buses parked in a protective circle around a cluster of Zastava's.

Justin drove past the Polish UN checkpoint. Its sentry had simply left the barrier permanently open. He nodded wearily to Justin. It was uncertain what political line this crossing now marked either.

On the other side of the small bridge sat the two UN APCs. Behind them masses of Croatian police buses and armoured vehicles waited ominously. In the new no-man's-land, UN Jeeps idled and a few elderly persons tried to negotiate entry into Croatia. Crossing the bridge, Justin found himself wedged in with no room to turn the vehicle around. The Polish armoured vehicles barring the route did not budge.

As Justin scanned for an exit route, a Canadian RCMP CIVPOL officer walked up and knocked on his window.

"What the hell are you trying to do?" he barked.

"We were hoping to cross here," Laura called.

"Yeah, right. Fat chance pal!" the cop replied and waved for Justin to go straight back. "Not even the sick or elderly get by."

Justin reversed the cruiser slowly for almost 100 metres before finding a space where he could turn.

Crawling back through town, they stopped again at the Serb checkpoint.

With her usual smile, the guard asked, without opening her logbook, "Where you go?"

"Zagreb."

Pointing questioningly, down the road they had just come, she said, "Zagreb that..."

Laughing at the running joke, Laura called across, "Yeah, we know."

In spite of the tedium Justin felt at the extended return journey, seeing the camp doctor's genuine relief at their delivery made it all OK. She had no complaints or games to play; she was just trying to do her bit too.

Chapter 7

The day after returning from Turanj, Justin received Serb travel clearance for Batnoga. To his surprise, the Knin authorities had also given permission to visit Velika Kladuša across the border for a medical meeting of NGO's and UN agencies working in Bihać. Maybe the Serbs granted the permission this time because his request stated that only one car would be travelling and its cargo was destined for the refugees in Srpska Krajina. Maybe he was giving the Serb's too much credit for logical thought. As long as unpredictability remained the norm and things were in his favour, Justin would just keep going along with it.

He was anxious to get his first glimpse of Velika Kladuša and a chance to witness the true situation in northern Bihać.

Batnoga was a hamlet that did not appear on any conventional road maps and Justin's only inkling was that it lay in Krajina, close to the town of Cetingrad – no more than 10 km from Velika Kladuša. In search of the route to the camp, Justin dropped by the UNHQ for advice and topographical maps. At the map depot, Justin bumped into a French UNMO he had met once before.

The officer pointed out the village's location. As Justin traced a hypothetical route along Sector North's main road via Slunj, the UNMO interjected. He knew a more direct back route, just past Vojnić, that branched off the road to Velika Kladuša. The conventional road via Slunj would have taken a good four hours – the back way, about two and a half. The UNMO assured Justin that, although too narrow for trucks, the back road was paved and travelled frequently by UN vehicles.

As Justin rolled up his new maps, the officer mused, "It's funny all these new bandages we must hand out. They never stop thinking of ways to fuck each other over?"

Justin shrugged noncommittally, "Never boring here I guess."

With a dark expression, the officer lowered his voice a notch and said, "Between you and me, it's all a waste of time. We work our asses off trying to fix some problem just a little bit and then they go and screw themselves again – making more trouble for everyone."

Holding up the UNPROFOR ID card dangling from his neck and pointing to its expiry date, the officer continued, "Look at this. I leave this place in three weeks. I'll have been here for one very long year."

"Wasn't it worth it at all?" Justin asked.

"Financially yes, but constructively, the effort was a total waste. I've seen no results for the long hours of working here at the HQ. I'm sure I'm not the only one who feels this way either."

From the UNHQ Justin went over to the MOO warehouse and spent the remainder of the afternoon stacking cargo into the cruiser. He lingered with the warehouse boys, smoking and listening to stories about the bad food in the JNA.

During Cora's conscript service in 1991, all they ever ate in the mess hall was canned sardines. His unit had a running competition to see which soldier received the most expired can. Cora gained brief fame one evening when, to the rapturous applause of his comrades, he took a bite of a fish and read off the can's date – 1961. It was a unit record, most cans only dated back to 1969.

Cora shook his head with a combination of pride and disgust, "That fish was swimming before I was born."

Miroslav had been on a long exercise in the Slovenian mountains. Every night, for weeks, his unit ate foul watery vegetable stew. A train hit one of their pack mules in the night and they suddenly received watery vegetable stew with meat for days thereafter.

The next morning, Justin and Laura headed out at about 5 a.m. to deliver the medicine to the Batnoga camp and then onward to the meeting in Velika Kladuša.

At the Mošćenica crossing outside Sisak, the Serb guards were cheerful. The militiamen asked Justin where he was going and when he replied, Batnoga, they barely glanced at his crossing papers.

Clutching a small Ziploc bag of tablets and a bottle of cough syrup, Laura climbed out of the Landcruiser. Approaching the stout RSK guard, she inquired, "*Kako ste?*"

Taken aback by Laura's concern and use of his native tongue, the guard bowed his head in his best attempt at graciousness. Rocking his hand tentatively, he replied, "*Dobro. Hvala.*"

Having reached the limit of her Serbian vocabulary, Laura held up the small bottle. Making motions to her throat, she said, "I've brought penicillin syrup for your throat. And also some Paracetamol. It's like Aspirin."

The guard nodded with dazed appreciation, "*Ah da, Aspirin. Dobro.*" He quickly called for his comrade to open the crossing barrier.

Laura smirked slightly to Justin. They did not know exactly how or when it would pay off, but the extra attention shown to the guard would go far. Building rapport with one of the belligerents ensured that one of the victims received help.

At the MOO training course in Holland, Justin's Dutch instructors had repeatedly stressed, that under no circumstances, should bribes or preferential treatment be given to any of the warring parties. This was not really a bribe anyway; it was just being human. Justin had yet to decide how far he was willing to go personally to get the aid to the beneficiaries. How many lies would he spin or rules would he break?

The road forked approximately 20 km past Vojnić. Justin followed a very narrow path leading southward. The thin route wound over and about rolling hills as it connected farming hamlets. Although it remained paved, the road became so tight it was barely wide enough for the Landcruiser.

On one farm, two old T-34 and T-54 tanks rested in a barn's shadow. A few kilometres farther, three 105 mm artillery pieces sat in the front yard of a house. Although not in use, the guns still pointed southeastward at Bihać.

Cresting one last hill, an agro-industrial complex came into view below. The facility consisted of two rows of 12 large barns – each building about 100 metres in length. The normally isolated and forgotten compound teemed with humanity.

At the hill's base, they entered Batnoga – little more than a hamlet with a couple of small shops. A Serb militia post sat at the edge of town; its barrier opened automatically when they saw the white Landcruiser.

The road deteriorated into a slimy mud track. Justin's movement was further slowed by the aimless masses milling by in the muck. Most individuals walked with no apparent objective and had expressions identical to those seen in Turanj. The Landcruiser brought a flicker of interest to the day's monotony.

Justin continued for about 50 metres toward an enormous white storage tent on the right of the track. Around it were a number of green modular army tents and UN prefab huts. Rolls of razor wire, stacked five feet high, fenced in the entire area. Halfway along the wire, a Polish UN trooper stood watch with a GPMG. When Justin inched up, the sentry swung a three-metre section of the wire aside like a gate. Justin squeezed past a UN articulated truck whose cargo had just been unloaded into the warehouse tent by local workers. Sliding in the mire, he parked alongside six other Nissans and Land Rovers from various aid groups.

A line of about 20, mostly elderly and mothers with infants, waited patiently at the fence entrance. Periodically, a few were let in and guided to the medical tent for treatment. Along other parts of the perimeter, children paced or stood by listlessly. Some leaned gingerly against the razor wire and wearily viewed the ongoing activities within the compound.

In one module, Laura found a Polish army doctor - an older man with an enormous walrus moustache - chatting with representatives from UNICEF. The doctor explained that, to date, he had only received a small quantity of medicines from the UN. He welcomed Laura and Justin's delivery gratefully.

"There is talk that a Norwegian NGO will build a mobile hospital here. I cannot wait, though. I need medicines right now," the doctor explained.

"How many people do you think are in the camp right now?" Laura inquired.

"We are still trying to count. It is hard to say. The people have stopped arriving. So I hope to know more soon. I think the total in both camps is maybe 30,000."

A lanky Englishman from UNICEF spoke up, "Counting is very difficult. We want to start an immunisation program so all the residents are up-to-date with their shots before the winter. Abdić's people are making it difficult, though. They know we'd have accurate records of the camp's composition if we carried out the immunisations."

As the discussion went on and became heavily medical and technical, Justin slipped out to back the Landcruiser up to the giant warehouse tent. Inside, he found a well-stocked storage area with substantial quantities of basic foodstuffs, building materials and rolls of UNHCR plastic sheeting. Wooden pallets kept everything raised off the moist ground.

A British UNHCR field-worker was taking inventory. The portly man with long thin hair and a balding scalp had the demeanour of a congenial English pub owner. As the pair chatted, the UN worker explained, "This camp is an epidemic just waiting to happen. Those chicken coops haven't been properly washed out. There are probably a good 750 people crammed into each of those buildings. They're begging for Salmonella at the least. We're trying to get electric lighting inside the coops. So far, they've been using open flames. The doctor has been dealing with lots of burn cases already. With that many people living like animals, it's only a matter of time…"

"What's the camp's population?" Justin interjected.

"Right now UNHCR's conservative estimate is about 12,000 in Turanj and 18,000 or so here. Abdić's inner circle keeps blocking anyone from making a headcount. They claim at least 60,000 of his refugees are now in Krajina. Abdić says every resident from Kladuša and its nearby villages fled the massacring legions of the Fifth Corps." Raising an eyebrow cynically, the UN worker added, "The pre-war population of VK was only 35,000 and not all of them left town…it doesn't add up."

"What's the food situation?"

"We've shipped in good quantities of food, sheeting and blankets. We've also been supplying flour to local bakeries so bread can be distributed to the camp residents. It's still reasonably warm right now but winter isn't far off and that's when there will be big problems. Properly winterising this camp is going to be tough.

"The best would be for everybody to go back home. At least winter in their original homes would be safer than being crammed into chicken coops. The Sarajevo and southern Bihać governments have been reasonably receptive to allowing their return to Kladuša and having the UNHCR ensure their protection. There isn't much enthusiasm at Babo's end, though. Right now, these people are the only army he's got. So, they're not going anywhere. Every night the Serb cops seal off the area. No, complaints from Abdić about that. Don't want anyone getting any ideas and walking over the next hill back to Velika."

"What about the folks in Turanj?" Justin wondered.

"The Serbs keep an eye out for them too. But Abdić doesn't worry as much about them trying to sneak back; they can almost see the West from their camp."

As the two exited the tent, a pickup truck towing hole-boring equipment entered the compound. Nodding at the vehicle, the UNHCR officer explained, "Here's another problem we're dealing with. Trying to get clean water into the camp. Trucking stuff in is not realistic."

The pick-up stopped beside the pair. "How you doin' mate?" the driver greeted with a thick Australian accent.

"What's the news?" the UNHCR rep inquired.

"We found a couple of spots for wells in nearby fields. We dug a few holes and hit water pretty quickly. Would have been a reasonable supply for the camp. But then the local farmer comes over and says, 'Thanks for digging the holes. Now how much are you going to pay me for the water?' We told him to get fucked and filled the holes back in."

The UNHCR field officer jumped in the truck and departed in search of solutions to the water supply problem.

Justin deposited the MOO cargo with other UNICEF and WHO boxes. He went back to the cruiser and lit up a smoke. Sure enough, a kid in his mid-teens soon joined Justin. The youth had been helping in the compound earlier. His English was decent and that was probably why he was hired.

As Justin shared his cigarettes, he eyed the spectacle outside the razor wire perimeter.

"Can you imagine such a thing in Europe today?" the teen asked.

Justin shook his head to one side, still not knowing how to respond. Trying to buy time, he took a long drag from his cigarette and hoped the question was rhetorical.

"Before this shit we had a good life in Velika Kladuša. Abdić gave us everything. He built us swimming pools. Everyone had great jobs with Agrokomerc. Did you know that Babo used to find the best medical students in the country and offer them a house in Kladuša and 2,000 Deutsche Marks each month for salary? We had everything."

The teen paused for a moment, possibly to allow Justin to digest these facts. "Look at us now," he continued. "We are refugees but nobody wants to help us. They say we must go home. But Kladuša is now flattened and our homes are totally destroyed. Dogs are eating the dead bodies. If we go back we will all be murdered by Dudak. They say he let all the criminals go free to kill anyone who returns."

Glancing at his watch, the teen made a motion to leave the compound. Thanking Justin for the smoke, he said, "Someday, when this is all finished, you come see me in Kladuša. You are welcome. You stay in my house and I show you a great time. Ah…we'll go to the night clubs and I'll find you so many women…*Ciao*." He waved and headed out into the swarm of camp residents.

A few minutes later Laura emerged. "I just met a couple of medical staff from this Norwegian NGO that'll be building a mobile hospital here next month. They seem pretty well equipped. So we won't have to worry too much about supplying this place. They might need some specific drugs - Insulin and stuff like that. I told them we'd stay in touch."

Looking anxiously from the compound, Laura announced, "Let's go have a look at the camp."

Although, a simmering curiosity had been nagging Justin, the rolls of razor wire had offered convenient insulation. He faced a daunting plunge away from the UN's meagre protection and into the throngs of the misled.

Moving hesitantly past the sentry and crossing the paralysing pressure of the residents' spurning glare, Justin and Laura headed along the mud track. The chicken coops were in rows on a slight incline to their left. To the right, a few family-sized tents and huts, built from scrap wood and UNHCR plastic sheeting, stood in the field. Small cooking fires crackled amongst the scattered dwellings. A cow's carcass stretched drying from a tall wooden rack.

A few stalls and tables had been set up selling simple amenities. The level of commerce was nothing close to that in Turanj, though.

Justin and Laura soon turned back and made their way up the crowded track between the chicken barns.

The UNHCR had established a bread distribution point using a locally hired truck and workers. Two large posters of Abdić's silver-haired head were slapped over the truck's existing UNHCR stickers. At the bottom of the images read the bright inscription, "Babo is here for you!" Resident camp leaders had placed a large distribution table right below the portraits.

As UN field workers did their best to sustain some comfort for this latest tangent of Balkan despair, the refugees' perverted leaders worked to sustain their pain. And, all the while, the international officials that we looked up to for guidance could only offer more discussions on how best to avoid taking action that might offend somebody.

All the drudgery before Justin served to justify his efforts. There in the camp, he saw exactly who was receiving the medical aid he delivered. He wanted desperately not to become yet another talker from the West; one of the many well paid who spent their efforts pontificating in comfort while the suffering of others continued all day. The supplies Justin brought would bring a tangible amount of relief to those in pain. It was a small thing and it railed against the foreign talking heads. Justin would do his best to keep bringing what he could for as long as he could – regardless of any barriers raised by the belligerent or the inept.

Being in the camp was a privilege that brought Justin an uncluttered satisfaction. Folks back home fretted about the ever-increasing price of stupid things like postage stamps and, at the most, watched this abstract suffering on the news each evening. But Justin, stood in the crisis – ankle deep in the shit and history. He shook a mental fist at them all from his miserable world. What the hell are you up to right now?

Justin and Laura walked slowly up the incline amongst the crush ebbing between the rows of coops. The people moved in every direction but most had nothing particular to do.

As the pair reached the top, they bore a new sense of confidence and ventured into the nearest chicken coop. Stepping hesitantly, they squinted into the dimness ahead. An overwhelming stench prevailed – stronger than in the hospitals and less medicinal. Recognisable within the smell of the displaced was the odour of fermenting sweat, damp clothing, human secretion and uncertainty.

From the gloom, a thousand embers of smouldering misery peered out of blank faces. They gazed at the two intruders who had a foreign smell. Such fragrance was now just a distant memory and an even more distant dream.

All the decrees made in far removed international offices about the various motives and loyalties of these people suddenly had no relevance. Nobody was deserving of such an existence.

Families of at least five to six had sectioned off two-metre plots with dangling plastic sheets, bags and mats. Clothes hung but it did not mean they got any cleaner or drier. Each group attempted to make their plot a home. The endless building was packed beyond sight. Nobody smiled and none had reason to hope. All eyes looked no farther ahead than to the intruders.

Quietly, they turned and left, having not ventured more than three metres into the coop. It was farther than most had gone. Not glancing inside would have been worse – a regret that would have followed Justin forever. His intention had not been as a spectator in a sideshow of human wretchedness. He had just wanted the dwellers to know he was different and that no matter what comparative comfort he returned to at day's end he would not forget them. He was dreaming though – he and Laura were still just trespassers.

Back at the razor wire sanctuary, a white Mercedes 4x4 belonging to the European Community Monitoring Mission had arrived. Inside sat three older men in white uniforms. With a colonial air, they gazed upon the large specimen natives living in dwellings fit for poultry.

A fourth monitor beside the vehicle spoke to the British UNHCR officer. The only colour on the monitor's white uniform was a blue sash, bearing the stars of the European Union, hanging from his belt. He took notes and stopped periodically to tap at his pipe. Throughout the conversation, he glanced at the back of his pants for dirt. He tried to stand carefully so that mud did not consume his white leather shoes.

After a few minutes, the monitor climbed back into the white Mercedes and drove away. Its other occupants shook their heads in disbelief at what they were seeing in the heart of Europe in such civilised times.

The monitors were there to watch the savages fight. It was the loudest scorn Europe could level at these lands and their desires for self-determination.

Justin and Laura bid farewell to the British UN worker and promised to return periodically to monitor the camp's situation. Justin headed back toward the Vojnić road. He then turned right in the direction of Velika Kladuša.

This would be the real thing now; Justin was about to cross the front line between Croatia and Bosnia. He was about to enter a bona fide and active war zone. Although the day had been quiet and from Batnoga they had heard no sounds of conflict, Justin remained excited by the simple prospect of seeing a place where combat had recently occurred.

Along a long sweeping corner, a half-dozen T-54 tanks rested in an industrial yard. Within ten minutes, they arrived at Maljevac – the last Krajina Serb town before the Bosnian border. Off the village centre, Polish peacekeepers had based themselves in an old factory. Stopping next to the safety of compound's white sandbagged wall, Justin and Laura climbed out to don their body armour.

They could hear no sounds of shelling but the pair had no idea what to expect from that point onward. Being their first trip in, they zealously played it safe.

With his bulletproof vest strapped firmly in place, Justin felt like an invincible warrior and an exposed target. With all the protection his chest now received, his arms and legs suddenly seemed more vulnerable than ever. If he were the victim of shelling, the shrapnel would not concentrate on just his shielded torso. The body armour also brought new self-consciousness. People wearing these vests drew attention, which in turn usually drew trouble.

In Maljevac, the villagers went about their daily routines without the luxury of body armour. These folks spent much more time in a danger zone than Justin and Laura ever would. Strutting about in expensive Kevlar vests during occasional visits seemed somehow insulting.

At the end of the day though, you covered your ass. Justin would have felt really stupid if he suddenly needed the vest and had not bothered wearing it.

From the Polish base, Justin and Laura drove to a small Serb checkpoint nearby. A UN observation post sat 50 metres beyond. Slowly, they approached the crossing's raised barrier and its empty guard hut. Justin could see no militiamen.

Just off the road, two militiamen in purple camouflage sat on the terrace of a small restaurant drinking coffee in the early afternoon sun. Justin hesitated, unsure how to proceed. One of Serbs waved impatiently for him to continue.

At the UN post, the aid workers wound around a trio of white tank traps and past an old white Soviet-era armoured reconnaissance vehicle parked in the debris-strewn parking lot of a smashed auto shop.

Midway up a steep curving incline, a large blue and white striped crossing boom barred the way. To its right sat a blue metal shipping container painted with the Bosnian *fleurs-de-lis* coat of arms.

A young man in American style camouflage emerged from the container. Seeing the white Landcruiser, he smiled, waved and raised the boom. Where were all the maniacs? Justin wanted to get out and ask if this was actually the right way to Velika Kladuša. Remembering to keep stumbling along for as far as possible, he drove under the barrier.

They climbed the steep embankment for a couple hundred metres more. A small brown suitcase sat fractured on the roadside discarded in what must have been a panic. A few articles of clothing crept from the box's splintered sides. At the peak, the beginnings of Velika Kladuša came into view. The scattered houses at the town's edge looked intact. Only a few buildings bore sporadic bullet pockmarks. Driving through the vacant streets, Justin and Laura passed the occasional pedestrian. Something was definitely wrong with Justin's maps and he wondered how much farther it was to the main Velika Kladuša.

They quickly came upon the town's UNCIVPOL station. Justin and Laura stopped and went inside to confirm their bearings. In the main foyer, they found a short Portuguese police officer sporting brush cut hair.

"Hello," the cop greeted the newcomers warmly.

"Hi," Justin replied. A little embarrassed, he continued, "We're from MOO. We need to go to the NGO meeting at the French Base in Velika Kladuša…I've never been before."

"FreBat is just on the south side of town. You have to keep going straight on the main street, go right around the park square and then follow the sign for Cazin. You won't miss it."

Patting his chest, the cop smiled sympathetically and said, "You know, you really don't need those. Velika Kladuša is dead quiet. No shelling in many days. The Fifth Corps has few big guns to fire – only mortars. This town has not been this quiet in a long time. Those locals that did not flee don't make trouble. Most are old people."

Pausing, the cop asked, "Your organisation is medical isn't it?"

Justin nodded, "Yeah. We're trying to bring deliveries into Bihać but the Serbs won't let us. I'm really surprised we got here today."

Motioning to the rear of the office the cop said, "Come here. Let me show you one of the things we're doing in town."

In a back room, small piles of medicines were laid out on a large worktable. A note rested beneath each pile.

"We've been distributing certain medicines to the needy in Velika Kladuša," the officer explained proudly. "FreBat supply the medicine and we sort them for each person. We deliver them to people who are too old or sick to come pick them up."

Justin and Laura thanked the officer for his help. They headed back to the Landcruiser and peeled off their body armour.

Farther into town, they skirted a long and quiet park square. Atop a treed rise, a dejected medieval fortress looked for its once faithful peons below.

Two-story grey brick and plaster houses crowded the road. They shouted a cold angular functionality imposed by some other heavy-handed overlords. Token trees lined the street. The houses were mostly unscathed. A few young people and a handful of unarmed men in camouflage walked the streets. Some waved to the white car.

There was little evidence of their having been any recent bloody battle. It was a bit anticlimactic. Where was the flaming Velika Kladuša? Where were the rabid murderers? It was all wrong. Yet, Justin could never tell the Batnoga or Turanj refugees any of what he had just seen. They would only accuse him of working for the enemy. Which of this was the truth and which some horrible illusion? Maybe Justin was the victim of some elaborate manipulation.

At the town's southern edge, a vast industrial site appeared just across a bridge. Resting amongst surrounding meadows and wooded hills, the compound sat on a lot the size of at least five football fields. A colossal warehouse consumed almost a third of the complex. The remainder consisted of a central two-story administration building and a labyrinth of while prefab containers behind walls of sandbags. French military trucks, APCs, two-man armoured reconnaissance cars, and light tanks filled the parking area.

At the main gate, Justin met a gruff French private. They presented their blue UN ID cards and mentioned the meeting. The soldier bent into his sandbagged bunker and spoke into a field phone. Five minutes later, he emerged, asked Justin to sign a logbook and allowed entry.

A UNICEF Landcruiser and a Care Canada Land Rover were already parked in front of the two-story building. As Justin gathered his clipboard, he glanced over at Laura who remained seated. Concentrating in the sun-visor's mirror, she ran her finger's through her hair a few times and squinted to touch-up her eye makeup.

"What are you doing?" Justin exclaimed with amusement. "This is Velika, not downtown Zagreb."

"Hey, just making sure I'm presentable," Laura replied calmly.

"Ah...it's the French isn't it?" Justin pressed.

"Hey, they do look good in their uniforms," Laura allowed. "Even their combat pants are tapered. They're the handsomest men in this part of the world...they make women aware of themselves. I mean, look at the Canadians...they look like slobs in those green potato sacks for pants."

"I always thought the Canadian troops looked pretty sharp," Justin protested.

"Take it from a woman; beside French soldiers, the rest are hicks," Laura stated hopping out of the vehicle.

Unsure where to go next, they asked a French corporal for directions. He shrugged and pointed them down a long hallway in the main building. At the end of the passage, they entered a large auditorium filled with benches and long tables. A few soldiers sat dining at one. Justin and Laura entered the adjacent kitchen area hoping to find someone helpful.

The cooks were too busy preparing massive pots of spaghetti, potatoes and tomato sauce to notice the two intruders.

"Looks good," Laura mused as they exited the kitchen by a service door.

Outside, a truck was being unloaded under the supervision of a soldier with lots of gold braid and insignia on his uniform. Laura guessed he was important.

As cases of Bordeaux and Burgundy wine were hauled from the truck, Justin and Laura asked the decorated soldier, in their best high school French, for directions to the meeting.

Pointing a thumb at the doorway, the soldier replied in English, "That is the officers' mess. But past it is the medical area."

Inside an auditorium where medical tents had been erected, a small group of people sat a long table chatting. Justin and Laura introduced themselves to the UNHCR officer convening the meeting. After making introductions to the others, Justin helped himself to instant coffee and Madeleine cakes.

In attendance were representatives from UNICEF, WHO, a British woman's health organisation, the International Red Cross and Care. The directors of the Cazin and Bihać hospitals, along with the newly installed head of the Velika Kladuša facility, were also present.

The meeting began quickly and, as it centred on medical issues, Justin's mind tuned out almost immediately. He fought to stay awake by eating more Madeleines and doodling in his notepad. Laura gave a brief description of the types of medical supplies MOO was planning to deliver throughout the Bihać Pocket. Thereafter, she had little else to say and soon found the debate that emerged tiresome as well.

The other organisations followed by detailing their own plans and all that they had or had not done in the region.

As the discussion was in two different languages, everyone could only speak in half-sentence fragments so that the interpreters had time to translate. This doubled the length and monotony of the dialogue. All matters of depth were compressed into five word sound bites. The discussions never achieved any level of substance.

In response to plodding descriptions given by the aid organisations, the local doctors reciprocated with long superlative filled statements. Each hospital director repeated that the foreigners working in Bihać were great people and that the Serbs were bad. The doctors all needed more of everything and nothing was being done by any other foreign organisations. Inevitably, each director's presentation came to focus on their critical interest in how the UN would supply diesel for their own vehicles.

Relentlessly, the directors turned every facet of the conversation to the topic of diesel. Eventually, the UNHCR rep had enough. She stated bluntly that she had come to discuss medicine and would end the meeting if the topic of diesel came up again.

The local directors apologised profusely and then asked when exactly they could expect diesel deliveries in the Bihać Pocket.

The UNHCR rep dropped her head in despair.

The discussion floundered for about an hour and a half until Laura interrupted, explaining that she and Justin had to leave because of the lengthy drive back to Zagreb.

Justin grabbed the last Madeleines and slipped away from the futile forum. As the pair departed, the remaining organisations discussed when and where to hold another meeting to clarify the Bihać situation further.

As Justin departed the FreBat base and headed back through Velika Kladuša, a few people still strolled the quiet streets. The castle on the hill sat silhouetted in the warmth of the falling sun. The portrait could easily have hung on the wall of any tourist office.

At the Fifth Corps crossing, the guard opened the gate and waved casually.

At the Serb crossing, the barrier remained open and its guards still comfortably lodged on the nearby café patio.

Three hours later, Justin walked into the Zagreb office. Rolf approached holding a report with the European Union logo. With a sardonic smirk, he said, "Just got the latest sitrep from the ECMM Milk Monitors. Thought you might like some toilet reading."

The monthly report was 15 pages long and consisted almost entirely of one-paragraph snippets from ECMM monitors in the field reporting on the situation in the entire Former Yugoslavia. With the exception of a very brief one page executive overview, the remainder had no logical order, and contained no analysis or interpretation – simply raw data collected by spotless spies.

In a section mentioning Batnoga, a three-line segment stated that Monitor YYX had been told by reliable sources that the fields surrounding the camp were definitely mined.

Monitor XXZ stated two pages later, that a person in a neighbouring village told him that there were most certainly no landmines around the camp. A line in the report's executive overview suggested that the nearby Slovak Engineering Battalion use its mine clearance vehicles - T-55 tanks with rotating chain flails - on the land in question - unharvested fields - and verify the issue once and for all. At the most, this would only cost the local peasants half their year's crop.

Chapter 8

As Justin settled into a delivery schedule that kept him in the field for at least three to four days each week, the next two months became rather routine. On top of his deliveries to the main medical facilities in Sectors North and South, Justin also made monitoring trips with Laura to the smaller *dom zdravljas* and *ambulantas* in the outlying villages. They wanted to ensure that the remote facilities were actually receiving their cut of the deliveries Justin made to the central pharmacies in Knin and Glina.

Shifts in the frontlines in Bosnia often caused new sick and wounded to show up at these distant clinics along the border in Serb Krajina.

As time allowed, Justin also made overnight trips with a full truck to Banja Luka. When not on the road, he sorted out and juggled the various permissions needed to go anywhere. Things were generally humming along nicely.

As Justin was making regular deliveries, the warehouse boys kept themselves relatively busy too. They did not mind and often put in extra hours to deal with last minute delivery changes. There were often times when Justin received his travel permission from the Serbs or Croats the afternoon before he wanted to travel. He would race over and drop off a hastily prepared packing list with Boban and Miroslav. By day's end, they had faithfully sorted and loaded the cargo. As Justin carried out other office tasks as well, he rarely had time to hang around the warehouse checking on their work. Justin placed a great deal of trust in the guys and they never let him down.

In October, Justin received calls from representatives of yet another nebulous branch of the international community – the Sanctions Assistance Mission. Every phone call to Justin was with an air of great importance. As a joint European Union and Organisation for Security and Co-operation in Europe effort, it was their mandate to verify that all embargoes against the Serbs were obeyed and that the Serbs did not receive anything they did not deserve. The SAM monitors spent their days visiting UN and NGO warehouses in Zagreb.

One morning, as the boys prepared a delivery for Sector North, SAM announced that they would be auditing MOO's facilities and the organisation's loading procedures.

Moments after Justin arrived at the warehouse, a brand new Ford 4x4 pulled up. A man and woman emerged sporting blue windbreakers with the bright letters "SAM" stencilled across the back. With the enthusiasm of FBI agents on a drug bust, they glanced at the surrounding buildings, as if searching for rooftop snipers.

"Good morning. I am Frederika Johansen and this is my partner Lars Olafsen. We are here to review your facilities."

Justin led the way into the storage area. Thankfully, Miroslav and Boban were still busy sorting pallets and not relaxing in the dark office. Both looked up, waved to Justin and continued working.

Lars scribbled notes. Frederika eyed the boys with a suspicious squint. "You deliver medicines to the Serbs right?" she asked.

"Yes," Justin slowly answered wondering why that seemed such a strange thing. Pausing, he added, "We work with all sides of the conflict."

"Are you always present to monitor how exactly your local staff are loading your trucks?" Frederika asked. After a moment, she rephrased the question, "How do you ensure no contraband reaches the Serbs?"

Justin simply lied, "Yes of course, I am always present."

Both SAM reps nodded and Lars scribbled more notes. Justin was a bit put off. Why were they asking such facile questions? And worse, why were they actually taking his word for it?

The warehouse boys were reliable and had long ago been loading trucks of meds for the Serbs without incident. The guys' reasons for working with MOO were varied. Altruism towards the Serbs was not one of them though.

They were also in no hurry to help their enemy's war effort. The notion that any of the guys would break the UN embargo by loading Justin's truck with contraband or weapons for their enemy was laughable.

The SAM monitors poked around a little longer and then walked back to their vehicle.

Shaking hands, Frederika said, "Thank you for your co-operation. Everything appears to be in order here. You must keep in mind that it is important to always be present when the truck is being loaded."

The pair climbed back into their 4x4 and raced off to enforce the international community's iron will.

As the majority of Justin's journeys were day trips, he rapidly grew tired of the Zagreb-Sisak road. The route's monotony, its artificial speed limits and arrogantly driven vehicles all clogged his desire to get across the border into to the zone.

Most of all, Justin grew to truly despise the little white Fića's that persistently got in his way. His hatred became nearly pathological. Instead of passing, he fantasised about driving his truck right over the curves of the sputtering little mechanical rodents that refused to make way.

With time, the guards at the checkpoints grew to recognise Justin and his destinations; they let him and Dimi through with relative ease.

Once in the Krajina, Justin drove with a great sense of freedom. He had become intimate with every dip and curve in the region's roads. At night, he would lull himself to sleep retracing every bend and incline, every gearshift and application of brakes along Krajina's empty roads from Mošćenica to Knin.

It was a driver's dream and it was a survival tool – especially when having to drive home in the dark half-drunk. He remembered a sign jokingly posted on the UNHCR's bulletin board in Knin. It read, "Krajina Rules of the Road – If a Serb driver hits you, it's your fault. If you hit a Serb, it's your fault. If you hit a Croat, go to the nearest police station to claim your prize…"

Justin also made small deliveries to the Turanj and Batnoga camps as needs arose. In those instances, Justin would hop in the Landcruiser, often by himself and even without crossing permission. Familiarity and his rapport with the border guards were starting to make Justin complacent.

Through September, the refugee camps settled and gained an air of semi-permanency. With the winter nearing, the UNHCR abandoned efforts to convince the refugees to return to Velika Kladuša. At this point, staying put until the spring became the safest option. Accordingly, the UN field staff shifted to winterising the camps so the inhabitants had a fair shot at surviving the looming cold months.

The UNHCR worked diligently to distribute extra plastic sheeting, cooking stoves, fuel, blankets, children's clothing, and footwear. Latrines were constructed. In Batnoga, they installed electric generators and lighting for the chicken coops. The promised 50-bed Norwegian mobile hospital was also up and running. As September closed, there was a sense of modest accomplishment amongst the foreign aid workers.

However, for all of Justin's consistent and honest work helping Serb institutions in Krajina, the Batnoga camp was as close to Bihać as he could get. Justin repeatedly asked the Serbs for permission to go to the Bihać Pocket but his requests were all blocked.

When Justin pressed Jadranka at the UNHCR for an explanation, she would reply that the local Serb minister answered, "You do know that Bihać is in Bosnia and we are at war and that the Muslims and Serbs are enemies?"

That was fine. At least they were being straight and Justin knew where he stood. On other occasions though, the authorities in Knin approved Justin's travel request but warned that there was a new directive. Justin would also need permission from the local RSK military commanders in the regions he would be crossing en route to Bihać.

How many military districts were there between Mošćenica and Maljevac? And how would he get hold of those commanders? The authorities in Knin had no idea; they were just civilian representatives and had no dealings with the military.

The UNHCR faced similar difficulties trying to distribute aid to Bihać. As a larger more prominent organisation trying to provide basic food to tens of thousands in the Pocket, the UNHCR was prone to far greater political manipulation by all sides in the conflict. MOO was far smaller and had avoided the same machinations. Medicine did not have the same weight as food. Halting food deliveries had become yet another accepted implement of war. The Serbs were in no hurry to see the enemy they were blockading receive food so they could keep surviving the siege. Although no sides were making any delivery easy, Justin sensed he still had a slim chance of eventually breaking the siege.

With winter closing in, the Serbs clung ever more fervently to their siege of the Bihać Pocket. Since the end of May, only a dozen UNHCR convoys, out of 150 attempts, had managed to pass Krajina Serb checkpoints into Bihać. For the 180,000 inhabitants of the Pocket, these deliveries were their only real source of sustenance.

As the situation became increasingly desperate, the UNHCR arranged airdrops of food over the Pocket from Hercules aircraft. It looked dramatic on TV. In reality, they could only drop a fraction of the region's needs and that was if it landed on target – which it rarely did. When the pallets hit the ground, the UNHCR had no way of ensuring the relief supplies ended up in the right hands.

To make matters worse, Serb forces surrounding the Pocket began targeting the aircraft with shoulder-launched missiles. These easily concealed weapons could bring down a slow moving Hercules with little difficulty. The Serbs only had to lock their radar targeting devices onto the relief planes a few times before the UN abandoned the operation.

Towards the end of October, the French government pulled its peacekeeping battalion out of the Bihać Pocket as part of a previously scheduled force reduction. The Serbs were becoming masters at smelling the slightest whiff of international community indecision.

From the Pocket that nothing was allowed to leave, the Serbs happily gave departing passage to the only army better equipped than their own. All the nations that indignantly condemned the conflict's belligerents remained silent when asked to contribute to the new peacekeeping needs in Bihać. Only a brave few stepped forward offering troops to fill the French void. In the end, 1,200 Bangladeshi troops, lacking both the firepower and political clout available to their predecessors, were tossed hurriedly into the Bosnian cold.

While making his deliveries in Krajina, Justin got caught behind convoys of earnest yet trepid-faced soldiers snaking slowly in the direction of Bihać. Rusting BTR-60 APCs escorted the long procession of trucks. Young faces peered out nervously and dutifully from the vehicles' rear openings. At sharp corners and intersections, the whole caravan became stuck, as the wide-bodied BTR-60s could not negotiate the turns without shifting back and forth.

The Bangladeshi soldiers wore ill-fitting cumbersome East German winter fatigues and flimsy wellington boots that appeared neither insulated nor waterproof. For a people unaccustomed to winter, these soldiers were doubly cold. Their appearance did little to portray a menacing image to the Serbs or the residents of Bihać.

Into the region that virtually nothing was allowed entry, the Serbs happily granted admission to the Bangladeshi Battalion. The Serbs then slammed the door tightly and added them to their starvation list.

As the UN appeared to spiral deeper into confusion, the conservative military minds dominating the ECMM decided, to take firm grasp of the situation. In their executive summary of an early November report, they recommended the immediate use of NATO fighter jet escorts to protect the UN airdrops. This brave WWII era idea would have worked better in times before shoulder-launched missiles; it provided neither real protection for the cargo planes nor hope for Bihać's starving inhabitants.

As the international community stammered and gave forceful apologies for its inaction, the Bosnian Serbs and Krajina Serbs pressed for greater advantage. With each weak response and lowering of international determination, the Serbs squeezed the Bihać pocket a little bit more.

On October 26, however, the Fifth Corps punched back. Relying heavily on his experienced and desperately motivated light infantry,

General Dudaković launched a series of attacks against the more heavily armed but less mobile Bosnian Serb Army in the Northeast and East of the Pocket. Facing incredible odds, the Fifth Corps then broke out of the Pocket in the Southeast around Bihać town. Dudaković led his forces to take almost 150 sq km of terrain. Most importantly, the Fifth Corps grabbed control of the Grabez Plateau from where the Bosnian Serbs had been shelling Bihać town with complete ease. In this push, they also managed to capture precious pieces of Serb artillery and a few tanks.

Although stunned, the Bosnian Serbs regained their vicious senses, regrouped and counterattacked on all fronts with mighty vengeance. Within a week, the Serbs had regained most of what they had lost and pushed to within a few hundred metres of Bihać town.

Ever watchful for new opportunities, Abdić hired Serb troops and artillery and raised an army of volunteers from his two camps in mid-November. These volunteers then beat those that did not volunteer until they too wanted to join. Both refugee camps emptied of fighting age males. An estimated 5,000 Bosnian Muslim youths were volunteered to fight alongside hired Bosnian Serbs against other Bosnian Muslims and distant family members. With his new army, Abdić took advantage of the heavily distracted Fifth Corps and pushed into Velika Kladuša to regain his kingdom.

Into this full-fledged battle, the ill-equipped and underfed Bangladeshis tried to acclimatise themselves.

Sustained Serb artillery and missile attacks pounded all fronts. The lightly armed Fifth Corps stretched beyond their limits as they frantically defended Bihać town, the Pocket's eastern flank and Velika Kladuša at the same time.

Krajina Serb jets took off from Udbina to assist their Bosnian Serb brethren in the attack. Initially, the jets skirted the Bosnia no-fly zone by firing missiles at Bihać while remaining in Krajina airspace. Soon they just flew straight into Bosnia to drop cluster bombs and napalm on Cazin and Bihać town.

The United Nations expressed displeasure at such violations of international borders and the no-fly zone. On November 21, UN leadership grudgingly took action. In NATO's first air raid since the Second World War, alliance planes attacked the Udbina airfield. The political leaders ensured that NATO did not go too far though. The jets avoided hitting Serb warplanes or equipment. Instead, they carried out a high precision strike of the runway – leaving deep holes in the large tarmac target. Undeterred, the Serbs filled in the craters by week's end and continued squeezing the Pocket.

On November 23, Bosnian Serb forces east of the Bihać Pocket targeted NATO jets with surface to air missiles. In self-defence, NATO bypassed their obstructive political overlords and attacked Serb radar installations in the area. In turn, the Serbs took 250 UNPROFOR personnel in Bosnia hostage. The Serbs forced their international human shields to sit in weapons sites and military installations to ward off NATO airstrikes.

In Banja Luka, the Serbs dragged the three UNMO's based there out to the local airfield. They were made to lie on the tarmac beside their white vehicles for days on end. One UNMO, with an existing heart condition, became extremely ill. A local Bosnian Serb doctor even recommended his evacuation. When a pair of UN officers came to retrieve the stricken soldier, they too were taken hostage by the Serbs. The international community had been well and truly emasculated.

Out of desperation, the UNHCR began making public threats that, if they did not gain entry to the Bihać Pocket, they would freeze their regular food shipments to Serb Krajina. It was a bold move but the Serbs knew that bureaucratic and political influences within the UN would still delay any real action on the ground.

Justin took note and placed his own personal medical embargo on the Serbs in Krajina. He made no bold statements or defiant stands. He simply stopped delivering to the hospitals in RSK. Justin had only wanted to help those in need fairly. This was not fair; he could not keep working like this. Justin also had a hunch that given his consistent deliveries to the Serb hospitals, it would not take long for word to get to the top that they were not getting their free stuff.

Still playing games, the Serb relented and allowed UNHCR food convoys to pass RSK en route to Bihać. The catch was that all convoys had to travel via Velika Kladuša. With fighting raging in and around the town, the Serbs knew that no vehicles would be getting through there any time soon.

Chapter 9

As Justin focused solely on getting to Bihać, he spent much of his days discussing strategies with, Rolf, Laura and Mik. Under Kees' guidance they, measured the progress made so far, made new plans to gain permission and mapped what they would do if they got into the Bihać Pocket. In Justin's mind, the only logical approach to follow was simply to keep trying until all options were exhausted. The group decided that, as the southern, non-Abdić, portion of the Pocket had been blockaded for so long it would be their priority. MOO's initial delivery would be to the busiest institutions in the south – in Bihać town and Cazin. Bihać hospital was the obvious first choice due its size and location in the Pocket's population centre. The *dom zdravlja* in Cazin was a much smaller facility but it was located in the middle of the Pocket and almost certainly faced high numbers of wounded from both the northern and eastern fronts.

They earmarked smaller quantities of supplies for the villages of Pištaline and Bužim. Pištaline was a speck on the map that had a clinic. However, the eastern front lines were now a few hundred metres away and its importance as the first stop for wounded surpassed its size exponentially. Bužim was a larger town but its proximity as the first major population centre near the northern front lines gave it a similar importance to Pištaline. They only had one available truck and many people to heal; this was the best they could do.

After dropping off that load, they planned to assess the situation in the north, around Velika Kladuša, and then deliver what they needed on their very next trip.

Based on existing medical notes and MOO reports on the region, Laura made her best measurement of the population and the essential medicines and materials they would need in an emergency. The medicine itself did not take up a lot of space in the truck. The bandages and intravenous fluids filled the most volume. When there is fighting, these simple items were the ones that would save the most lives. Medicines were not much use if the patients bled out.

The situation around Velika Kladuša had become extremely dangerous. Abdić's army and his hired guns attacked the town steadily as they moved closer by the day.

There was a road, farther south, into the Pocket that avoided all the combat in the north. However, the Serbs were letting no one use it. Anyone going to the Bihać Pocket was going to Velika Kladuša first. Where they went after that was between them and Abdić to sort out.

That was the weak part in the MOO plan. Even if the aid workers did enter Velika Kladuša, they still had to get permission from Abdić's people to deliver the entire cargo to their enemies in the south.

Yet, the situation was new and unstable and any number of things could happen in fleeting instants. Justin wanted to make sure they were nearby when those moments occurred. Who knew what could happen? In the end, they would just have to go there and see how far they could get.

While the warehouse boys hurriedly prepared and sorted the emergency shipment, Justin set about organising the other logistical matters. He gathered sleeping bags, ground mats, water and 10 days worth of Dutch and French combat rations in case they became stranded. He swung by the UNPROFOR PX and bought a few bottles of scotch and cognac.

By coincidence, MOO headquarters in Amsterdam had recently ordered a custom-built armoured Landcruiser. It was intended for ongoing MOO operations in Central Bosnia and Sarajevo – places where armoured vehicles were essential. Considering the raging situation around Velika Kladuša and the shifting front lines, Rolf asked that the vehicle be used, for the time being, in the Bihać area.

Upon arrival in Zagreb, the vehicle became the instant focus of all male affections. Mik, Rolf and Justin clamoured to have their photos taken with the fancy new wheels and jockeyed anxiously to drive it out around the block. The warehouse boys also fawned over the car and ensuring it remained washed and waxed.

The Landcruiser cost MOO over 150,000 Deutsche Marks and was customised by a German company that specialised in fitting cars with low profile armour. It had been MOO's experience in Bosnia that when bored gunners and snipers saw vehicles that clearly looked armoured, they fired on them just to see what happened. In this case, the metal plates were built from the inside of the vehicle. Although the new Landcruiser weighed three and a half tonnes and handled more like a boat than a car, it did not look armoured to the naked eye.

Unfortunately, protection came at the cost of functionality. The extra bulletproof plating made the Landcruiser's normally spacious interior rather cramped and dark. It also made the vehicle almost completely soundproof. This Landcruiser had smaller fuel tanks and a larger engine to deal with the extra weight. To compensate for the car's reduced range, Justin strapped four Jerry cans in the rear of its narrow interior.

As the truck driver, Justin would not have much armour, other than his bulletproof vest and Kevlar helmet, for the journey to Bihać.

By the first week of December Abdić's army had firmly surrounded Velika Kladuša. All UN staff and Bangladeshi peacekeepers in Velika Kladuša were stranded on the former FreBat compound. They could offer few details of the location of any front lines. The only information they could give was what they could see from their base.

The poorly motivated youths pressed from the refugee camps into Abdić's army were a highly unpredictable bunch. MOO decided that, under such circumstances, the safest way to travel would be as part of a UN convoy. That way if it all went bad, Justin, Mik and Laura would at least have access to medical or mechanical assistance from the convoy.

While eating lunch, Justin watched a Sky TV News report from Bihać. Sky News was the only network that had a reporter inside the Pocket. Their correspondent, Aernout Van Linden, showed footage of Bangladeshi peacekeepers fighting with a broken down APC in front of the Bihać Hospital. Van Linden interviewed the hospital director, a lanky man whose eyes begged for help and sleep free of fear.

He stared straight at Justin – he said he was waiting for help; he was really waiting for Justin. They had never met, but now Justin knew for whom he was risking it all.

The living room phone suddenly rang. Rarely receiving calls, Justin shuddered and answered with a tentative, "Hello."

"Justin, I think you should take this call," the office receptionist explained calmly from the basement before putting him on hold.

"Hello," Justin called into the unknown.

He was greeted by his own echo and then by a desperate and broken woman's voice, "Hello, this is the Cazin *Dom Zdravlja*."

The voice spat almost incomprehensibly, "You must help us fast, we have no other chances. We have 500 patients each week and not any medicaments. The Chetniks are shelling even the hospital. We are rewashing our bandages."

Not sure how to respond, Justin stammered, "We are trying our best right now to…"

"Yes but…" the voice echoed back. The line went dead.

Justin continued holding the phone to his ear not knowing what to do or think. How did they manage to call him anyway?

Putting down the receiver, he gazed at the topographic map on the wall. As the crow flew, Cazin could not have been more than 90 km from Zagreb. Numbers failed to describe the distance now.

A nagging anxiety grew in Justin's feet. He tapped them and tried stretching in his seat to relax. A tense sense of urgency lingered, though. This was not like the Krajina. The desperation in that voice made the requests of the Krajina hospitals sound like those of vacation resorts.

He stood up and stuck his head into Rolf's office.

"I just got a call from the Cazin hospital."

"Really," Rolf replied a little bemused. "I wonder how they managed that."

"They claim they're treating 500 patients a week," Justin reiterated.

Nodding and digesting the figure, Rolf explained, "Cazin is the biggest and most central facility after Bihać. It was originally just a *dom zdravlja* that was upgraded to a hospital because of the war. Normally, it only has the capacity to deal with 60-80 patients, though."

Justin called Jadranka at the UNHCR in Knin. She was still having problems getting permission from the Serbs. The Knin civilian authorities claimed the UNHCR was free to go to Bihać immediately. However, the Serb military commander in Sector North claimed that he was concerned because he could not guarantee the safety of any convoys travelling through his region. Other than the Serb commander, there were no other sources of danger in Sector North.

Jadranka promised to keep trying to include Justin, Mik and Laura names with any future UNHCR convoys. She would call as soon something occurred.

To hedge his bets, Justin also approached UNPROFOR to see if he could join one of their resupply convoys for the peacekeepers in the Pocket. He was directed to Lieutenant Colonel Lysandier - a congenial aristocratic gentleman who took pleasure in practising his English. He liked Justin's enthusiasm and found romance in the idea of helping deliver medical assistance to the needy in the Bihać Pocket. He promised personally to help Justin fight through the UN's military bureaucracy. Nevertheless, the colonel added, he would need five days notice for any future permission requests Justin submitted.

The colonel stated that there was a convoy attempting to cross the Krajina in the morning. It was too late to tag along but there would be a subsequent convoy five days later.

Justin raced across town to prepare the necessary documents that same afternoon. The next day Justin phoned the UN HQ to enquire about the status of the previous day's convoy. Eventually, one of the colonel's subordinates stated that the convoy sat blocked all day at the Serb crossing in Mošćenica. The convoy returned to Zagreb that evening and tried crossing again the next day.

The second afternoon, Justin tuned the office Motorola radio into UNPROFOR's frequency to monitor the convoy's progress. The transmissions were relayed through a series of UN repeater units. Conversations were heard clearly from as far away as the Velika Kladuša and Knin.

For much of the afternoon, discussions on many unrelated topics took place between people with many different call signs and accents. Eventually in the late afternoon, the call sign, "Lima Yankee," came over the air with a very distinct and familiar French accent.

The resupply convoy had been waiting at Mošćenica since early morning. Lima Yankee was calling an officer at Camp Pleso in Zagreb. Although Lima Yankee possessed the proper authorisations from the civil and military authorities in Knin, the Serbs at the Mošćenica checkpoint claimed that their commander had not informed them of the convoy's arrival. The local commander was unavailable and nobody had any idea when he would become available. The Serb guards stated that they had orders that all convoys must register with their commander. However, in order to enter Krajina to register, the UN would first need a specific special permission from Knin. In addition, the guards noted that the convoy's route would be crossing territory controlled by a second local commander and they were expected to register there as well.

Eventually the call sign, Papa Echo, joined the conversation. Papa Echo appeared to be a liaison officer at the Sector South HQ in Knin. Colonel Lysandier tried confirming his understanding of the day's regulations from his vantage at the checkpoint.

"Papa Echo this is Lima Yankee. Let me get this straight. I have permission to cross Mošćenica today but I need another kind of permission, which I personally have to acquire, but in order to do this I need another kind of permission that the Serbs will only give tomorrow when the permission I have today will have expired. Correct? Over."

"Not exactly. I will talk to the Serb authorities here in Knin and see what needs to be done. It really does not look good today, though. Over."

"OK. I will be here waiting," the colonel replied. "This is a very funny joke."

"Roger that. Standby."

"Lima Yankee," the voice from Camp Pleso broke in, "If there is anything else we can do at this end let me know. Over."

"Yes," Lima Yankee shot back, "You can get me a Mil 24."

"Say again...?"

"It's an attack helicopter...forget it. I was making a joke."

Three mornings later Justin, Mik and Laura attempted to cross with yet another French convoy. As directed by the colonel, the trio headed to Mošćenica to meet up with the waiting line of UN vehicles. In the no-man's-land leading up to the Serb checkpoint, the MOO truck and armoured Landcruiser squeezed past a line of 13 white cargo trucks parked in the right-hand lane. Stopping in the usual space to the side of the Serb barrier, Mik got out of the cruiser, approached the Serb militia hut and showed the guard a photocopy of the convoy's crossing papers. The guard shrugged, pointed at the parked line of trucks and told Mik to keep waiting.

Climbing down from his truck cab, Justin approached the Peugeot jeep at the head of the convoy. Crouching beside the vehicle, Lysandier was cooking a ration meal. The colonel gazed toward the barrier with great amusement.

A Danish major was trying frantically to gain the attention of any guard who would listen to his pleas. The major had set an open briefcase on the ground and was extracting various official papers. He waved each new sheet at the guards who calmly took no notice of the stressed Scandinavian officer.

Seeing Justin, the colonel smiled and greeted him with a warm handshake. Nodding at the Dane, Lysandier said, "I don't know what he's thinking. We will not get in today."

The group continued waiting at the crossing point until late in the afternoon. The Dane had long since retreated, drained and exhausted, to the sanctuary of his Nissan Patrol. At strategic times throughout the day, the colonel made enquiries with the Serb guards. However, he was unable to get any definitive answers that would untangle the day's crossing regulations.

At about 5:30 p.m., the colonel called it a day. With a handshake and a smile, Lysandier told the Serb guards, "I will see you in the morning." He then turned the entire convoy round and headed back to Zagreb.

To join the next UNPROFOR convoy, Justin would have to submit another formal request that would take a few days to trickle through the UN HQ's network. With each new UNPROFOR request, Justin also had to make sure his concurrent UNHCR convoy requests stayed in order. Any changes in those convoy dates meant revisions to his requests to the Serbs and Croats as well.

Justin, Mik and Laura attempted to cross with three more convoys – two UNPROFOR and one UNHCR. Each time, the convoys were barred entry at Mošćenica and eventually returned to Zagreb. The trio tried joining a fourth UNHCR convoy but when they arrived at Mošćenica, the checkpoint was empty of all vehicles.

The Serb guards shook their heads when asked if they had seen any UNHCR convoys that morning.

With hand motions one guard attempted to explain, "Today, *nema papira. Nema telefona za komandant Knina. Ništa.* Sorry." It seemed that the guards were not expecting a convoy that day. Of course, they had been saying this every time there had been a convoy there as well.

With the Codan, Justin called Rolf in Zagreb and asked him to call the UNHCR to find out what happened to their convoy.

In the cold quiet morning, the trio shared cigarettes and thermos coffee with the guards. The Serbs accepted eagerly and repeatedly said, "*Hvala...ah, Dobro,*" as they savoured the rare nectar.

Rolf called back on the Codan an hour later. "I called HCR Knin and they said that they had cancelled the convoy late last night. The Serbs only gave crossing permission to four of the 10 trucks. The UNHCR told them to get stuffed and called the whole thing off. The Head of Office in Knin is very pissed off. Over."

"Wish they would have told us. Over" Justin called back.

"What can you do? Here's something interesting though. The head of office down there said that your old friend Lysandier managed to get a resupply convoy though to Bihać somehow. She says he went into Bosnia through the Maljevac crossing. She did not know any other details though. I also called the UNPROFOR liaison officer in Knin. He said the colonel went into Bihać through a crossing point near Bosanska Bojna in the south of the pocket. Something isn't making sense. Anyway, your work is done for today, come on back. We'll have a few beers and try to figure this out later. Out."

As Justin, Mik and Laura waved good-bye to the guards and prepared to turn their vehicles around, a lone French Peugeot jeep approached the checkpoint from the Serb side. The guards waved it past the barrier. Justin recognised the passenger and waved the car to a halt.

Colonel Lysandier climbed out and walked over to Justin. They shook hands and he smiled over to Mik and Laura.

Nodding at the MOO vehicles, the colonel said, "So, no luck yet I see."

"No," Justin shook his head. "We were hoping to cross with a UNHCR convoy but they cancelled. I hear you entered Bihać the other day, though."

"Yes it is true. It was not easy but I had no choice. The Bangladeshis were getting desperate for food. They had no water or fuel either."

"What route did you take to get there?" Justin inquired eagerly.

"I crossed in Cicici."

"Where's that?" Justin asked, more confused than ever. "I've never heard of that crossing point."

"It's in the Northeast of the pocket." Raising an eyebrow cryptically, the colonel added, "I avoided the front-lines that way. It is not really a crossing point – just a small bridge."

"The UNHCR thinks you went through Maljevac and UNPROFOR thinks Bosanska Bojna," Justin explained.

With the slightest grin, the colonel said, "Those crossings are closed. It is impossible to go through Maljevac with all the fighting in Velika Kladuša. And the Serbs would never allow us to go through Bos Bojna. Anyway, it is better that the UN keeps believing that."

Pausing for a second, the colonel revealed, "I was able to cross only through local arrangements I made with the Serbs." Winking, he went on, "But that route is extremely dangerous. The road is bad. Full of mines. And the Serbs there are complete psychopaths. Their eyes are totally blank. Except when they fired their AK's at our vehicles...they thought that was very funny."

Nodding at Justin's truck, Lysandier reached up and flicked his forefinger against the door a couple of times. "This is very soft. You'll need something a bit thicker if you go that way." Eyeing the armoured MOO cruiser, he exclaimed, "Yes, something like that...*Bon chance*." He waved and jumped back in his jeep.

In the following days, the UNHCR in Knin applied their most sustained effort to get permission and the Serb authorities finally relented. They gave unconditional permission for convoys to enter Bihać later that week. As this was an unprecedented move by the Serbs, the UNHCR Head of Office in Knin personally asked Justin to wait and join the subsequent convoy. As this would be the first UNHCR convoy since the beginning of October, she was desperate to see it succeed. She did not want to complicate matters and offer any variables that the Serbs could use to cancel the event.

After facing two days of stoppages and searches from Serb militiamen at every possible point along the way, the UNHCR convoy arrived in Cazin on December 9.

While closing in on Velika Kladuša, Abdić and his Serb gunners pounded the area with random heavy artillery. Abdić's undisciplined forces even fired a rocket at a BanBat APC as it was parking in the UN compound – wounding five Bangladeshis.

When the UN tried to evacuate one particular soldier, who was blinded and had his hands blown off, Serb militiamen obstructed the ambulance's departure. Unable to get immediate treatment, the trooper later died at the UNPROFOR mobile hospital in Zagreb.

On December 15, a second UNHCR convoy managed to enter the Pocket. Justin was unable to attach himself to it because, this time, the Krajina Serbs, refused, without explanation, to give him crossing permission. Just outside Velika Kladuša, the convoy came under shellfire and one truck driver suffered face and eye injuries from flying glass.

Over the weekend of December 17, Abdić finally occupied Velika Kladuša. All approaches into the town were in control of the Krajina Serbs and Abdić's men. His forces continued fighting for more territory east and south of the town.

In the final week of December, as Justin thought continuously about the attack on the Bangladeshi APC, he began to question his abilities. United Nations compounds - places Justin believed offered sanctuary - were no longer safe. It had always been an illusion though. No matter how many precautions he took, Justin had to face the danger just like everybody else.

As he, Mik and Laura tried to think of new options to pursue, MOO suddenly received permission from Knin. Without warning or explanation, they were to join a Bihać-bound UNHCR convoy leaving Zagreb on December 30.

Getting away from Zagreb was the only way to fight the fear. Just get out and do the job – then there would be no time for the frivolity of thought.

Now that Velika Kladuša sat firmly in Abdić's grasp, he had more control over who entered the pocket. The town's new stability brought one more layer of bureaucracy. The danger really had not diminished; it had only moved a few kilometres away from the town. Eventually, the trio would still have to cross that danger, though. At least now, Justin could get one step higher in the climb.

Justin also had no way of informing the Fifth Corps of his intended movements. There was a possibility that the people he worked so hard to help could in turn open fire on the MOO team while trying to cross the Pocket's internal front-line.

At this point though, such musings were academic. Justin knew he had come too far and stood too close. Once more, he had to keep going and see how far he could get. While the authorities had all the power and position, he still clutched the advantage of patience. It was not much, but it was the one thing so many others had discarded.

As long as the rules changed by the day, on the spot, it would have to shift, if even for a moment, in his favour. There was only one way to find out.

Chapter 10

At 8 a.m. on December 30, Mik, Laura and Justin arrived at the Croatian checkpoint outside Sisak and waited for the UNHCR convoy to pass. At the police booth on the railway track, the Croatian cop looked at the crossing papers. Seeing the intended destination, he smirked, "Good luck."

Parking just beyond the crossing, they met a German woman, Gretel, also awaiting the convoy. She worked for a British NGO, the Women's International Health Group - WIHG. Her Land Rover Discovery was crammed with supplies she hoped to deliver to the organisation's field office in Bihać town.

During MOO's attempts to enter Bihać, Justin had decided not to bring Dimi along. The situation was now far trickier than it had ever been during the Krajina deliveries. Trying to get a Macedonian-Croat past the Croats, Krajina Serbs, Abdić's anti-Sarajevo (sometimes pro-Serb) Muslims, and the pro-Izetbegovic Muslims was more than a long shot. His presence would likely hinder the already slim chance of success. More importantly, it placed Dimi in thoroughly unreasonable danger.

Justin had a hunch that crossing the checkpoints might be easier without an interpreter anyway. When Dimi was present, the guards could ask anything they wanted. The inability to give detailed explanations could help the aid workers bluff their way to Bihać.

Within 15 minutes, the 10-truck UNHCR convoy passed and the waiting group tagged along. Meandering through the UN checkpoint before Mošćenica, the convoy squeezed past a dozen French UNPROFOR trucks already waiting in a long string.

The MOO and UNHCR vehicles found enough space to halt just in front of the French trucks. Blockaded relief supplies stretched over a few hundred metres of road.

Justin dismounted and walked up to the crossing barrier where Mik and Laura waited in the armoured Landcruiser. A Serb militia guard was explaining the rules to the UNHCR team leader – the same Englishman from the convoy search at the Gradiška football stadium. Apparently, the local military commander was not informed of the convoy's plans to cross. They would have to wait for the commander's arrival before anything could happen. As was the norm, the guard had no idea of his commander's whereabouts.

A growing frustration ebbed through Justin; this all sounded so ominously familiar and he held little hope of crossing that morning.

Having nothing better to do though, he just kept waiting with the others.

As Laura stepped out of the cruiser, one of the guards smiled and waved in recognition.

"*Kako ste*?" Laura called back.

Shaking his head, the guard cringed, "*Nije dobro*." Massaging his temples and rubbing his throat, he muttered, "*Puno problema*."

"This guy's always ill," Laura mumbled to Justin. She crawled into the back of the cruiser and emerged with a small bag of tablets.

Handing it to the guard, she explained, "Paracetamol."

"*Da, Da. Hvala*," the guard smiled patting her shoulder.

While the group lingered smoking and chatting idly with the guards, a red Renault 4 with Slovenian plates squeezed up to the barrier. Two Americans climbed out and tried speaking to the Serb guards. The pair were journalists trying to reach Knin; they presented UN press passes and crossing papers. The guards did not know what to do and told them to wait for the local commander with the rest of the gaggle.

Asking Justin for a light, one of the journalists inquired, "You been waiting long?"

"We've been trying to get to Bihać for three months," Justin replied.

"We're trying to get there too actually. Not too many reporters in the Pocket right now. Hoping to head down to Knin first and then wing something from there."

"The only stuff I've seen was from Aernout Van Linden on Sky News," Justin stated. "Would love to know how he got in."

Conspiratorially, the journalist lowered his voice, "Rumour has it Sky paid the Croat Army thirty grand to fly Van Linden in on a chopper at night."

"I guess the hard part now is getting out."

The American winked, "Hey, for good journalists, getting out is nothing compared to getting the story."

Pointing to Justin's outfit, the other journalist joked, "Nice vest." Tapping his own grey vest filled with camera parts and rolls of film, he added, "Got mine at a hunting store in the Detroit."

"Same here. But in Toronto," Justin laughed.

With a sly but slightly bitter grin, the journalist concluded, "You know a country's gone to shit when the guys in fishing vests show up."

Almost an hour and a half passed before a white Lada sedan pulled up to the Serb side of the crossing. An elderly man with slicked-back silver hair and clean fatigues stepped out. He carried a Magnum .45 in a large leather holster encrusted with a long row of polished bullets. The man looked more like a gun-toting physics professor than a hardened warrior. The guards saluted immediately and tried to resemble disciplined soldiers before that hitherto mythical creature known as the local commander.

The commander nodded questioningly at the two Americans. "Who are you?" he asked in accented English.

Examining their papers, he dismissed them with a flick of the wrist. "You have no permission from my high commander. You will not cross here."

Before the pair could protest, the old man turned and entered the guard hut. He sat beside its wood stove, lit a cigarette and called for the UN convoy leader.

After a few minutes quiet conversation, the Englishman emerged and announced simply, "OK. We can cross, I guess."

The journalists tried to appeal but the guards blocked access to their leader with growls and brandished AK-47s. The journalists squeezed a retreat between the UN trucks.

As each UN vehicle approached the crossing, guards climbed on top and pulled back corners of the tarp. Peering in at the nearest boxes and sacks, the Serbs poked pikes into a few before waving the next truck forward.

To everyone's relief, the convoy advanced with surprising methodical ease. The UNHCR convoy two weeks earlier had been sent down the road to an abandoned bus depot. There, every single box and sack of its 100 tonne payload was offloaded and matched against the cargo manifest. This procedure took more than a day. The convoy was later subjected to the same crucible twice more along the road to Velika Kladuša.

When Justin's turn at the barrier came, the guard with the headache motioned tiredly to the truck's rear. Justin lifted the canopy and the Serb craned to look up at the cargo.

Turning to Justin, he asked in his best English, "You pack truck? You?"

"Yes, of course," Justin lied.

The guard peered at the cargo once more and took a breath. "OK. *Srećan put*," he said shaking Justin's hand.

Being last in line, Justin started his engine and raced to catch up with the already departed caravan. Immensely relieved, he sparked up a smoke. Justin had fully expected to endure a ruthless search of his entire cargo that morning. The hint of trust exhibited by the ailing guard was touching. The rapport Justin and Laura had built with the militiamen over the past few months seemed to have paid off at the instant they needed it most. Regardless, trepidation still lingered and, by the end of his cigarette, Justin remained unconvinced that they would get much farther. There were still too many game-playing commanders waiting along the route. To this point, it had all been too easy.

Justin caught up with the convoy in the twisting streets of nearby Petrinja. The procession drove rhythmically for a good three-quarters of an hour before approaching the Topusko intersection. The crossing barrier - normally open - sat closed; Serb soldiers stood before it poised for another search.

The convoy halted and sat in expectant silence. From his vantage, Justin could see none of the proceedings at the convoy's head. Mik and Laura also sat tight awaiting word from the convoy leader.

The Motorola under Justin's jacket came to life. "Sorry guys, looks like another search," the convoy leader announced.

Visibly annoyed UNHCR drivers clambered down into a callous ice drizzle.

Justin polished off three smokes and was soaked to the bone with sleet by the time a pair of Serb soldiers arrived. One sported a trim beard, aviator sunglasses and a professionally moulded maroon beret. His pressed camouflage fatigues bore paratrooper jump-wings over the breast. He was obviously in charge of the searching detachment. His younger partner wore an equally crisp uniform, black beret and a few days fashionable stubble – not exactly the panoply of Chetnik rabble.

Looking up at the MOO truck and then at Justin, the Serb commander asked, in flawless unaccented English, "Where are you from?"

Surprised by the total absence of Slavic drawl, Justin stammered, "Uh…Canada."

"Canadian eh?" the Serb taunted, "I must compliment you on your English. It is good but you stutter at little."

Unsure how to respond safely, Justin just smiled dumbly.

Pointing to the truck's rear, the chief ordered, "OK. Let's look in the back."

The younger officer hooked an arm around Justin's in an oddly intimate fashion. His hand then slid down brushing the Motorola under Justin's jacket.

The Serbs coveted VHF handsets greatly – especially those pre-programmed with UNPROFOR's frequencies. Finally catching on, Justin's temples pounded anticipating the radio's confiscation – or worse.

Staring at Justin, the younger officer asked, in only slightly accented English, "So what is this?" Pulling the jacket aside, the Serb announced knowingly, "Ah, your Motorola. Very good."

Looking to his chief, the soldier asked, "What shall we do with him?"

Staring blankly at Justin, the chief paused and finally said sardonically, "We'll let him go...this time."

Untying the rear canopy, the younger officer climbed into the truck and began searching. Justin remained on the ground trying to keep one eye on the front cab. He did not put it past these Serbs to try planting something incriminating in his truck – no doubt to be found during a subsequent search.

Hovering behind Justin's right ear, the older officer whispered hoarsely, "So you are helping our Muslim friends. They really don't need help. Why don't you help us sometime?"

Before Justin could think of a suitably diplomatic reply, the junior officer had grown tired of examining abstract medical materials. He nodded to his chief and jumped down.

As Justin retied the canopy, the junior officer announced, "You will now continue to the Polish Battalion in Maljevac where you will stay tonight...This is the phantom convoy." Pointing to the procession, he asked Justin slyly, "Do you know what phantom convoy means?"

Justin guessed, "It does not exist?"

The officer nodded, "It's not going anywhere..."

Justin glanced at the chief for confirmation.

A sadistic growl emanated from the chief's whisker and sunglass shrouded face, "Get the fuck out of here."

Climbing aboard, Justin lurched onward with the other trucks. So, they could get as far as Maljevac – just outside Velika Kladuša. That was as far as the Serb games would let them go.

So much was beyond Justin's control. All he could do was persevere. Let the locals keep acting stupid; eventually they would stumble and do something convenient.

In the grey downpour, the convoy plodded into Vojnić. Turning onto the southeasterly road out of town, the route became completely clogged.

An unending line of tired and dirty families inched along in packs of six or seven. All manner of horse and tractor-drawn carts were stacked with wood, possessions, provisions and family members. Some had improvised covers with wood and UNHCR plastic sheeting snatched from their previous abodes. The passengers transmitted a misery matched only by the unrelenting weather.

Now, upon the glorious recapture of Velika Kladuša, Abdić had called his flock back. Abdić had fought the UN all this time. He told his people the UN only wanted them to die under the Fifth Corps invaders. He had pushed his people to attack UNHCR staff when they dared mention the idea of going home in the warm months.

As conquered lands are worthless without bodies to fill them, the manipulated residents from Turanj and Batnoga were uprooted once more. They had travelled 30 km from Turanj and faced another 25 to Velika Kladuša.

The winding road layered in frozen slime slowed the convoy to a crawl; overtaking the clusters of refugees made that crawl disjointed. The convoy's rhythm vanished and its trucks soon scattered over a couple of kilometres.

Deadened eyes peered sullenly at Justin as he pushed past the slower traffic. The sight of white UN vehicles was supposed to mean that help, however small, had arrived. The eyes locked on Justin bore no such illusions. These confused souls had ingested too many lies to be that naïve. White vehicles only brought relief to one's enemies.

The supplies Justin and his accomplices hauled would not ease this group's anguish. He just had to tune out and concentrate on the goal. Otherwise, he would end up helping nobody.

Hours passed as they inched amongst the displaced. The sad grey daylight yielded its tentative grasp to wet growing darkness.

On the sweeping curve before Maljevac the Serb tank compound now sat empty – its contents intended for somebody else.

At dusk, the convoy squeezed into Maljevac. Just beyond town lay the steep approach into promised Velika Kladuša. The procession of the miserable backed up into town – their carts surging forward only occasionally.

The aid convoy pulled into the factory yard of the Polish Battalion's base. The facility sat at the town's edge, no less than a couple hundred metres from the Krajina Serb checkpoint and the Bosnian frontier on the hill. The compound housed a company of peacekeepers in a handful of buildings, a warehouse and a few prefab containers. There was just enough space in its parking area to fit the convoy.

The base's sentry closed the compound gates and blocked out the din of Abdić's bottlenecked flock. Justin typed a Capsat message to the Zagreb office confirming their location. The base commander appeared and invited Mik, Laura, Gretel and the convoy leader to join his officers for dinner.

The UNHCR drivers stayed put and prepared rations in the comfort of their heated sleeper births.

Justin transmitted his message and went to join the others. Crossing the yard, he passed a lone BRDM armoured vehicle; its 7.62 mm turret gun was the only bastion standing between the peacekeepers and the full fury of Bosnia's onslaught.

In the dining prefab, Justin found his colleagues seated at a long table with a group of Polish officers. As Justin moved to sit, the officer in the next seat jumped to his feet.

The Pole had a round weathered face, red nose and completely glazed eyes. He reached to shake Justin's hand; his clasp was rough and grip inordinately long.

"It is so very nice to meet you…" the officer growled in a low demonic tone, his stare focussed thousands of metres away. "I am the base doctor," he eventually revealed.

When Justin took his seat, the doctor grabbed a mug and violently poured a cup of tea. The steaming liquid surged over the rim and onto Justin's lap.

Before Justin could protest, the doctor muttered, "I am so very sorry…" and sat back in his chair. He waved and cursed in Polish for the cooks to clean up the mess.

The doctor then turned his attention to Laura and Gretel's conversation. He quickly dominated all subsequent discussions and refused to let anyone leave the dining table.

He preambled each incoherent diatribe with, "I am very sorry but!" and, "I must let you know that…" or, "No! Let me tell you this…" The babble that followed was unintelligible in English and Polish.

Wolfing down their dinner of watery goulash, the guests contemplated their escape. Turning to the base commander, Laura raised the topic of the night's sleeping arrangements. Mik innocently offered to sleep in the Landcruiser.

The doctor slammed his fist on the table. Shaking his head, he bellowed, "I am a doctor in the Polish Special Forces and I can swim 50 metres with my boots on…my men will sleep in the snow and you will sleep in their beds tonight!"

From the table's far end, the base commander quietly and soberly told the two women that he would vacate his quarters for them.

Taking the initiative, the doctor guided the women to the commander's room in the main building. He then turned to Mik and Justin and roared, "Now, you come with me."

He took the pair down a corridor to a large auditorium. Young soldiers in varying states of undress lounged on cots scattered across the chamber.

"You will stay with them tonight," the doctor ordered.

Justin glanced at Mik in fright.

Mik mumbled, "Uhm...I've got to get my stuff out of the car."

Darting blindly for the parking lot, Justin called hoarsely to Mik, "I don't know about you but I'm going against the good doctor's orders. I'm sleeping in my truck tonight."

"Fucking right," Mik muttered in agreement. "Except for the commander, I don't trust any of the men in this place..."

As Justin inflated his air mattress and laid a sleeping bag across his cab, Mik grabbed his bag from the cruiser and skulked back to the commander's room.

In the warmth of his down bedding, Justin was lulled to sleep by the clawing and scraping of Abdić's caravan metres from his head.

Chapter 11

Justin awoke to a dull dawn. His frozen breath shrouded the cab's interior. Wiping a strip of condensation from the windshield, he peered out. Ice rain still fell and Abdić's caravan continued plodding past the compound gates.

A methodical thump, preceded occasionally by a tearing flash, came from the next hills. Thud upon thud, the ground shook. Shelling! At last! Justin's excitement grew with each impact. Shelling brought validity to his efforts; there really was a war and he really was in Bosnia. Shelling meant there were people truly in need of his medicines. Shelling meant history was occurring. Shelling meant the complacent world was watching from the outside. Shelling made Justin special.

Following the initial thrill of arrival, Zagreb had quickly become rather staid for Justin. Even after the euphoric breaching of forbidden Krajina, his repeated trips there had ebbing into the mundane. Those places were tourist zones, mere memorials to a war Justin had missed.

But this was real; there was war – just up the road. Now Justin could say, in almost good conscience, that he really had seen the war! Each impact brought stimulus; it was the ultimate motivation to keep trying.

Conveniently, the exhilarating blasts stayed just beyond reach. It was still someone else getting maimed – someone else's dreams erased. Standing tall was easy when the bravery was of your own choosing.

The UNHCR drivers were already awake and seated in their dry climate-controlled cabs. Steam from dashboard coffee cups climbed their windows. New Years' Eve balloons and streamers hung festively in a few windshields. Not wishing to leave their cabs' comfort, the drivers chatted amongst themselves over the VHF. Some squirmed to don body armour.

Justin started up his engine and ate a cold can of cheese macaroni. As the cab heated and the roof thawed, water dripped all over his equipment and papers.

Mik and Laura emerged from the main building to stow their overnight bags in the Landcruiser. The UNHCR convoy leader started up his Land Rover and headed for the gate. His drivers confirmed their readiness over the radio and waited with engines revving. The MOO and WIHG cars followed the convoy leader from the compound. At the nearby Serb crossing, the group began ascertaining the day's crossing procedures.

Justin soon received a radio update. The Serb guards claimed that going into Velika Kladuša was no problem. The entire convoy could enter and then make arrangements with Abdić's authorities to continue southwards.

Mik called Justin over to the crossing. The UNHCR convoy leader, however, told his trucks to stay put. He was not bringing his convoy into Velika Kladuša without prior guaranties that he could travel unhindered to the south.

Justin arrived at the checkpoint to find a heated discussion had erupted between the Serb guards and a French woman from the UNHCR office in Velika Kladuša. She expressed severe reservations that, once the convoy entered Velika Kladuša, it would be at the mercy of Abdić's demands. There would be no recourse for escape if the UN refused to comply with the Velika Kladuša authorities' whimsical desires.

Disavowing all knowledge of the politics within Velika Kladuša, one Serb militiaman pointed across the barrier and shrugged, "That Bosnia. This Srpska Krajina."

Justin, Mik and Laura agreed to take a shot at talking their way past Abdić. Gretel only had one car and decided to join the MOO team to Velika Kladuša.

Exiting RSK, the three vehicles halted at the blue and white striped barrier midway up the steep approach. A middle-aged man and two youths in pinstriped East German camouflage emerged from their steel shipping container. The box's Bosnian white lily crest had been painted over hastily with blue paint.

The thud and crack of gunfire, no more than a kilometre away, did little to stop Abdić's flock from clawing their way into town. One guard held the crossing boom half open for the carts and tractors to pass. Occasionally, he would wave or nod to a familiar face in the procession. None returned the greeting.

Devoid of any method, the man and two youths searched Justin's cargo for a good hour. Ambling from corner to corner, they randomly grabbed and pulled open boxes. They quickly became confused and found themselves looking through the same items repeatedly.

Climbing down, the guards ordered Justin to open the truck's side flaps. From this angle, they poked at the cargo for another half-hour. They then climbed back in the rear and rummaged some more.

As Justin watched the trio of ransackers from the ground, a third youth, in a US Army boonie hat and rain poncho, approached. He appeared a little brighter than his three colleagues and told Justin, in fair English, that he needed to search the truck's cab.

Climbing up into to the cab, the soldier looked down at Justin and asked, "Where are you from?"

"Canada."

"Canada. OK," the soldier nodded. "Well, welcome to hell. What kind of music do you like?"

Justin shrugged, "Hard rock...Led Zeppelin, AC DC, Van Halen..."

"Ah, rock music," the soldier replied. "Good you didn't say techno because I hate that shit. They play it every night at Café Playboy."

The three soldiers quietly moved to the MOO Landcruiser. There, they waited listlessly and smoked Mik's cigarettes.

A blue Jeep Cherokee raced up the hill as horse carts tried desperately to get out of its path. The three smoking troops jumped to attention and saluted. A Serb officer inside the vehicle returned the salute before disappearing into town.

With a smile of admiration, the ponchoed soldier sighed, "Jeep Cherokee...do you have a Jeep in Canada?"

To Justin's negative reply, the youth explained, "We have many in Kladuša." Pausing, he added wistfully, "There are too many Jeeps in my country now."

Sifting carefully through the cab, the soldier soon came across the bottle of Johnny Walker stowed in the food box.

Holding it up, he demanded, "What the fuck is this?"

Putting two fingers to his head and pulling a fictitious trigger, the soldier stated, "This is forbidden. We are Muslim and my commander will kill me if he finds this."

Stashing the contraband under his poncho and returning to the metal hut, he added, "I must keep it."

He then ordered his semi-retarded underlings to search the Landcruiser.

With a triumphant yell, they soon extracted their own bottle of cognac.

With a toothless grin, the middle-aged soldier cradled his prize and looked toward his boss. The ponchoed youth shook his head. "Do you have more alcohol?" he yelled.

Mik nodded tentatively, "One more."

"Where the fuck is it?"

Mik reached into another food box and produced the remaining Cognac bottle.

"You call that a hiding place?" the soldier exclaimed grabbing the bottle. Walking to the passenger side, he opened the glove compartment, threw its contents on the seat, squeezed the bottle in and shut the flap.

Still grinning, the toothless soldier carried his loot back to the hut.

"*Živeli. Srećan nova godina,*" Laura called in her best Bosno-Serbian.

The guard raised the bottle to return the toast and corrected Laura's enemy dialect, "*Živeli. Sretna nova godina.*"

Watching the returning residents struggle up the hill in the unceasing downpour, Justin sank into a mild miserable daydream.

He was aroused violently as the English-speaking soldier punched him in the chest. Impressed with Justin's body-armour, the guard nodded, "Strong." Firing more rounds from his fictitious pistol, he joked, "Stops bullets."

Trying to catch his breath, Justin coughed dumbly, "I hope so...*Inshallah.*"

A white Lada Niva swerved down the hill and skidded to the barrier.

Motioning at the car, the head guard explained, "He will take you to Bangladesh Battalion."

With tires squealing and only occasionally finding traction, the foreign vehicles inched up the slope. The abandoned old suitcase from the summer's exodus still lay cracked open in the road – untouched and unwanted.

In Velika Kladuša, confused families scuttled between the town's charred and wrecked houses. Those buildings still standing gave precious little protection from the encompassing conspiracy of man and nature.

The Lada escorted the aid workers past the town's southern edge to the facility that previously housed the French Battalion. Decay emanated from the complex; a few white vehicles sat in the vast frozen lot surrounded by empty white hills. Three crows sat atop a rusted building crane that loomed at the compound's edge.

The massive parking lot, once bristling with modern French armour, now held a handful of old trucks and Russian BTR-60s. In an attempt at reassurance, a blue UN flag and a green and red Bangladeshi flag fluttered defiantly from the main building.

At the gate, the Lada peeled back to town and a Bangladeshi soldier in green East German fatigues emerged from a sandbagged bunker. Smiling broadly, he jotted down the aid workers' ID-card numbers. Without further delay, he waved them into the strange oasis of blockaded foreigners.

The vehicles parked in front of the complex's main building. A private immediately ran out and beckoned them to follow.

Weaving through the sandbagged maze lining the building's interior, they entered a dark chamber marked "Duty Room." Two officers sat on the room's sole desk intently watching a fuzzy TV. One, a major, jumped to his feet, welcomed the group and searched for chairs.

"So you want to go to the south," the officer began. He picked up a field phone receiver and spoke quickly in Bangla. Shaking his head, he explained, "I'm afraid that will be very problematic today. Fighting on the ICL is too fierce at the moment. You will have to wait.

"It is not a problem, though. You are welcome here for as long as is necessary. Can I offer you coffee?"

The group nodded and the officer yelled toward the door. It flew open and a private stood at attention. The officer barked in Bangla and the trooper disappeared without a word.

The room's other officer looked up from the TV and explained, "You are very lucky to have come this far. Our re-supply convoy is still stranded at Mošćenica. It really is a shame because we had ordered some special treats to help the men celebrate the New Year tonight. But the Serbs have stopped it and will not let it pass."

Laura nodded, "Yes, we saw the convoy waiting yesterday morning."

The major added, "I believe our interpreters have organised something for us tonight, though. You are very welcome to join us.

A third officer, wearing naval insignia, entered the room and greeted the new visitors with warm handshakes. "Welcome, I am Commander Jahangir, BanBat liaison officer."

Hearing of the group's desire to head south, he nodded, "There was heavy fighting this morning but it could die down tomorrow. To cross the internal confrontation line, you will first need permission from the local authorities. If you acquire that, we will give you an armoured escort to the front-line."

The door opened again and the private carried in a tray of steaming coffee. Motioning to the beverages the naval officer said,

"After your coffee, I will take you into town and help arrange a meeting with the authorities."

Outside, a tinny white Volkswagen 4x4, bearing a driver and two armed Bangladeshis, waited with its engine running. The commander tightened his camouflaged flak vest, hopped into the passenger side and headed out the compound gates. The MOO trio and Gretel followed in their vehicles.

They were stopped at an internal checkpoint on Velika Kladuša's edge. The young guard on duty motioned aggressively at the Volkswagen's occupants. Commander Jahangir dismounted and yelled at the youth. The Abdić rabble pointed repeatedly at the aid workers' vehicles and shook his head. Jahangir stood his ground until the guard relented and waved the group through.

The three vehicles circled the town's main park and pulled up to an officious grey building – one of only a few still relatively unscathed. Timbers and large concrete slabs were propped against the building's side to protect the windows from shell blasts. The four-story office throbbed with people carrying boxes and crates.

The commander nodded vaguely toward the troublesome checkpoint and explained to the four newcomers, "That guard wanted crossing papers for your vehicles to enter town. He would not believe that you had just arrived and could not possibly have such permission. We will have to ask for something from this office."

Jahangir led the group up two flights and into a small waiting area. In the gloom, an elderly secretary shivered behind a small desk.

Smiling to the woman, the commander knocked on a leather-covered door and entered the adjacent room. Cracks of light squeezing between the timbers outside were the only illumination in the large freezing chamber. Workers came in and out piling boxes of files and books everywhere. Another team hammered a large wood stove in place.

A tall, undernourished and balding man sat behind a glass-covered conference table consumed by a labyrinth of cracks. He looked up from reams of papers and let out a tired sigh. In a few forced words of German, the thin man explained that he was Mr. Doric, the regional president in charge of authorisations. He motioned toward a set of low chairs across the table.

On the wall facing Justin, a hastily hung portrait of the silver-haired Abdić dangled crookedly. The faded outline of a forgotten predecessor's portrait crept from under the new image.

Beneath the picture, an aged white-bearded man sat at a table sorting through yet more stacks of paper. A leather belt and suspenders held up his ancient green wool Partisan uniform. Perched atop his head was a JNA wedge hat; a cloth patch of the People's Defence Force of the Autonomous Province of Western Bosnia was stitched where a red star cap badge once sat prominently. The man seemed to be simultaneously aware and oblivious of the room's proceedings.

Doric began speaking in Bosnian. His preamble was interspersed by snoring as the old soldier drifting in and out of nap.

Commander Jahangir translated, "Mr. Doric says that new procedures have just come into effect for acquiring permission to travel south. To go, you will need approval from both Mr Djedovic, Abdić's Military Minister, and from Mr. Hirkic, the Interior Minister."

Leaning forward, Mik asked Doric, "Why can't you give us permission directly?"

The commander translated the question in Bosnian.

Doric looked a little shocked at the query and replied through Jahangir, "But I am not a minister, I am only a president."

Doric allowed the magnitude of his statement to sink in before adding, "Mr. Djedovic and Hirkic will require at least two days notice of your intentions. Before they will give you permission, the ministers will probably demand that you leave a portion of your cargo in Velika Kladuša to accommodate this town's needs."

"How much do you think they'll ask for?" Laura inquired.

With a shrug, Doric answered, "Who knows? Maybe 40-60%."

As Mik and Laura shook their heads, Justin inquired, "Why can't we make another independent delivery just to this town instead of leaving a portion here now?"

"Right now, our needs are greater than in the south. We are the priority," Doric replied sourly.

"But the population of Velika Kladuša is 35,000," Justin protested.

Doric raised a finger and shook his head slightly. Offended by Justin's assertion, he explained, "We have just re-conquered more territory, our population is now 70,000."

Laura interjected, "Look, I am a medical officer. What MOO is offering is this. I would like to make an official survey of your hospital's needs. We also wish to make a delivery to the south. As soon as we go to the south, we can return to Zagreb and prepare a delivery for Velika Kladuša according to the investigation I will make here."

Doric nodded silently and appeared on the verge of taking in what Laura had explained. He did not allow the information to sink in long enough, though. Stifling any hint of conscience that may have lurked in his bowels, he replied blankly, "Yes, but we need guaranties."

"We will perform an analysis of the Velika Kladuša hospital with its director and then we will provide exactly what you need," Laura paused and, before Doric could rebut, added "Come on, just handing over half our cargo now is no use to us or to your hospital."

Slightly flustered, Doric pleaded, "Yes, but you are offering no guaranties that you will not just go to the south and nowhere else after."

Silence followed, as no one knew how to respond.

Eventually, Doric shrugged, "I will have to talk to the ministers. Maybe if the hospital director gives us a written recommendation saying that you have made an agreement with him, then the ministers might agree to let you pass to the south sooner."

Pausing, Doric added one further stipulation, "But first you must make a formal written request according to the new regulations."

"Where can we find these ministers to give them the formal request?" Justin asked.

Doric made a face, "Who knows? They are both out of town."

"To whom do we address this permission request?" Justin inquired.

Dismayed that the group would ask such an obvious question, Doric replied curtly, "To the Liberated Territory of the Autonomous Province of Western Bosnia."

"OK," Laura announced, "in the mean time we will go to the hospital and have a meeting with the director."

"He is also out of town. Maybe tomorrow," Doric revealed.

Unsure of her status in the current procedures, Gretel spoke up explaining that she was not with MOO.

A little confused, Doric asked, "What organisation are you with?"

"Women's International Health Group - WIHG," Gretel stated, "I don't have any cargo to deliver to the south, though."

Doric's eyes narrowed and his face grew severe, "WIHG. You are the one working with women and giving them abortions. You are not welcome in this town. You give help to women when it is the men who are fighting and being wounded. You threw a party here months ago and danced while we buried three of our brave men."

Appalled, Gretel sputtered, "But she worked for our office in Velika Kladuša and it was her birthday. We meant nothing else..."

Shaking his head gravely, Doric stated, "No, for you there will be no hope of any permission to travel anywhere. You are an enemy of Velika Kladuša."

"Maybe I can discuss this with one of the ministers."

Doric let out a contemptuous half-laugh, "You can try. I do not know where they are." He then stood up, indicating the meeting's conclusion.

Mik suddenly remembered to ask Doric for authorisation to travel between Velika Kladuša and the BanBat base.

Doric nodded impatiently and reached across his desk for a scrap of paper. He glanced at its contents, crossed out the original name at its head, "ICRC" scribbled "MOO" on top and handed it to Justin.

The big negotiating game with Abdić's peons had officially begun. Although the end was nowhere in view, the impediments were not completely insurmountable. At least for now, they had some kind of permission to show the agitated, drunken kids at the internal checkpoint. It was a small step.

As the group returned to their vehicles, Justin asked Commander Jahangir the question they had been dying to know. "Where did you learn Bosnian so well?"

Smiling at the oft-asked inquiry, he replied, "About a decade ago I trained with the Yugoslav Navy for almost five years. It was part of a Non-Aligned Movement exchange program. I never thought I would need to use Serbo-Croatian after I finished the training though."

Holding up the permission scrap, Justin asked Jahangir to translate.

"It says that, MOO has permission to travel between BanBat and the municipal offices, the hospital and a place called Café Playboy...I'm afraid I'm not familiar with that establishment."

Back at BanBat, the group returned to the duty room. Recounting their discussions with Doric, Mik asked for a printer to make a formal crossing request.

They were directed upstairs to the UNMO's office – an exposed room with large windows overlooking the base parking lot. A stout Portuguese officer surveyed the landscape through binoculars while a short Malaysian officer sat with his feet on a desk.

Seeing the new guests, the Malaysian waved, "Hi, I'm Major Yaser." Speaking in quick bursts, interjected with laughter, he added,

"I hope you're having a fun New Years' Eve. That is Major Ricardo. Our job is counting shells."

Ricardo, slightly taller and heavier set than Yaser, bore a calmer demeanour but still laughed with all his partner's jokes. "Today has not been too bad," he explained, "Yaser and I counted about 200 impacts so far. Since Abdić restricted our movements, we can't leave the base to observe the situation around town. So all we do is count shells."

Donning a camouflage jacket and mesh scarf, Ricardo continued, "I have to go into town right now to talk to Abdić's Liaison Officer about letting us patrol outside the base again."

Straightening his light blue beret, Ricardo said, "Yaser can help you with whatever you need. See you later."

Ricardo' beret was missing its UN cap badge. As he turned to leave, Yaser pointed chuckling, "Look, there goes the new recruit; he's got no cap badge." Roaring with laughter, Yaser added, "He managed to loose it last week."

Shaking his head and muttering, "It was stolen," Ricardo departed.

Yaser hooked up MOO's laptop to his ink-jet printer. Within minutes, the trio had created a signed and stamped crossing request, on MOO letterhead, addressed to the appropriate leaders of the LTAPWB.

Mik, Laura and Justin returned downstairs to the duty room where Gretel was sullenly drinking coffee and watching the fuzzy TV. The Bangladeshi major explained, "I have arranged a container for the four of you. You can stay in it for as long as is necessary. One of our men will show you the way a little later."

A tall bespectacled officer entered the room; all proceedings stopped.

The major jumped to his feet and introduced the officer to the aid workers, "Ah please, this is Colonel Salim. Our base commander."

The colonel graciously shook the guests' hands and explained, "You are very welcome to stay with us. If there is any assistance we can provide, please let me know. These are very difficult times for us but we will do our best. In fact, we would be honoured to help you however possible because this battalion's priority is to assist the local population. As you are also here to assist the local population, we must help you to succeed."

Glancing at his watch, the colonel added, "You are also more than welcome to dine with us in the officers' mess. You are our guests. These are hard times but we are touched that you have chosen to share them with us."

Colonel Salim guided the group down more sandbagged corridors to the mess hall. It contained a long dining table and cluster of chairs placed before three TV sets and a ghetto blaster. A good 15 officers were already seated chatting excitedly amongst themselves.

The cavernous chamber's only source of heat was a lone overwhelmed electric radiator. All present dined in their winter coats and a few even kept their flak jackets on for extra insulation.

Two orderlies, also in winter coats, brought out heaping plates of rice, vegetables, meat, flat bread and potatoes.

A young Bangladeshi Lieutenant sat beside Justin. Nodding at the feast, he explained, "This is a very special meal for the New Year. You probably know about the convoy that did not arrive. The cooks have been saving supplies for this night. When the French departed, all they left us were emergency combat rations. It has been so desperate lately that we were forced to eat them. Unfortunately, half the French meals contain pork and the rest are a little too rich for our palate."

Eager to impress their new guests, the Bangladeshis offered generous portions of each dish. Mik was particularly hungry and ate two full plates of the spicy feast. The officers beamed with pride as they watched him inhale the food. Pointing to each dish, Mik inquired about their preparation and made comparisons with Indonesian equivalents. Endeared to no end, the Bangladeshis clamoured to proffer their deepest cooking secrets.

As dinner wound down, two lieutenants jumped up and put a techno-dance cassette in the ghetto blaster. Chuckling, they danced around the room and soon drew a handful of other junior officers into their midst.

Three younger women, the battalion's local interpreters, entered the mess to announce that they had organised a New Year's Eve party in the UNMO's office.

As the senior officers moved to sit in front of the TV sets, one pulled Justin aside. "Please allow me to introduce myself. I am Major Abdul. The base doctor." In a hushed tone, he continued hesitantly, "Between the two of us, I was wondering if you had possibly brought any alcoholic beverages with you. I...and a couple of other officers have a slight fondness for spirits on special occasions."

Before Justin could reply, the officer added nervously, "Please don't take this the wrong way, I don't want to you to think I am a habitual drinker. But this *is* New Years'...I find it also helps steady the nerves a bit."

Justin nodded and told the doctor to visit his container later if he wanted.

A private appeared and guided the four guests to their sleeping quarters. At the edge of the compound parking lot, they were led along a row of prefab huts. The thin metal huts' only protection from the hostile hills, a hundred metres beyond, was a long eight-foot high wall of white sandbags. The private pointed wordlessly to a door at the defile's far end. He smiled humbly and returned to the main building.

Inside the freezing box, the group found two bunk beds and a pile of wool blankets. Justin switched on the room's neon light and electric radiator. Hoping to keep both the heat in and the light from seeping out, Justin hung blankets over door and window.

He then went to his truck to let the Zagreb office know of their whereabouts. With frozen fingers, Justin strained to press the membrane keypad of the dashboard Capsat. In the six lines allowed, he keyed,

> *Bihać Team safely in VK. Must stay to negotiate ICL crossing. Shelling along ICL intermittent. Abdić wants big part of cargo. UNHCR convoy stranded in Maljevac. We will stay at BanBat for now. Mik likes the food. We are in good hands.*

After ferrying their overnight kit from the vehicles, the four aid workers made their way up to the UNMO's office. For the New Year's Eve festivities, BanBat's interpreters had set out a table filled with instant coffee packets, soft drinks and a selection of candy hoarded from countless French combat rations.

As the night progressed, music blared from a ghetto blaster and the officers took turns dancing with themselves and the room's five women. The aid workers eventually slipped out discreetly for a festive drink.

They were immediately accosted, by the Lieutenant Justin had dined beside. He quietly asked if he could join the group, explaining, "You know I was schooled in Britain. I acquired a number of local tastes there...I would really enjoy a small glass of alcohol this evening."

Once seated on their prefab's bunks, Mik poured generous offerings of the precious Cognac into plastic cups.

The Lieutenant took a slow sip and held his breath. Momentarily relieved, he revealed, "The last few weeks have been quite hard for us. When the French left at the end of October, the UN deployed us rather hastily. Our government was the only one that had offered enough troops to fill the void at the time.

"Unfortunately, the ship transporting most of our rifles, section weapons and mortars was delayed. It had problems passing Suez. The UN deployed us here before we had even our basic defensive weapons. Of course, at the time, the Serbs let us enter the Pocket no problem. But now they are pressing us to the limit."

Taking another long pull of his drink, he glanced around and asked shyly, "Do you happen to have any cigarettes?"

Justin tossed over a pack. The officer lit up and took a drag as soulful as his first sip of Cognac. Staring at the glowing ember, he stated, "This is wonderful luxury. Cigarettes are in very short supply lately. We are at the point where, each day, five of my men have to share a single cigarette. Of course, even this is not as bad as what the civilian population is facing. And we like to smoke almost as much as the Bosnians..."

The Lieutenant slipped into an entranced joy, his attention consumed by the smouldering tobacco in his hand. The others watched him anxiously awaiting further details of his battalion's difficulties.

Eventually, the soldier looked up apologetically and continued, "Between the 1,200 Bangladeshi troops in the Bihać Pocket, we have a mere 120 Kalashnikovs to defend ourselves.

"You know, I have actual combat experience. Many of my men have already served on other peacekeeping missions.

"Two weeks ago Abdić's forces fired a wire-guided missile from a nearby hill at one of our APCs. They actually shot at our vehicle while it was in the parking area outside. The APC was destroyed. Four of our men were wounded and one died after being blinded and loosing both hands."

Drawing on his smoke, he waved hypothetically, "Normally, I could have launched a counterattack...but here, what with?...Look at our old APCs! And that's another story altogether...because our government could only spare the men for this deployment, the UN promised to provide us with adequate vehicular equipment for the mission. So, when our battalion arrived in Zagreb, we found that the UN had purchased the rustiest most ancient BTR-60s we'd ever seen.

These machines, these Cold War relics, must have been 10 minutes away from the scrap yard. We had never even seen such things in Bangladesh. What choice did we have at that point though?

"Then, as we also had no proper winter combat wear in our possession, the UN purchased discarded East German field jackets and these leather wellington boots. My men's feet are frozen solid and now Abdić is complaining that we are wearing the same uniforms as his army."

Finishing his drink, the Lieutenant smiled and stood up, "I must be boring you." Letting himself out of the container, he turned, "Thank you again for the drink. Please be assured we are doing our very best. Happy New Year."

The aid workers returned to the party room a few minutes later to find the celebration still in full swing.

Seeing Laura and Gretel, the base commander smiled and called "Where have you been? I'm getting sick of dancing with my adjutants!"

As the women vanished into the dance abyss, Ricardo flashed a drunken smile and handed Justin and Mik two plastic cups.

Taking a swig, Justin cringed, "What is this shit? It tastes like distilled honey."

Still smiling, Ricardo raised a bottle labelled "Bison Port." Refilling his own cup, he shrugged, "It's all I could find here."

While the party raged on, Mik and Justin rebuffed Ricardo' repeated attempts to finish the Port. As midnight neared, Justin quietly left the room and went downstairs to the building's entrance. A sentry stepped forward, opened the main door and stood at attention as Justin passed. A little embarrassed, Justin pleaded that he was not an officer. Not understanding English, the guard remained erect.

Lighting a smoke, Justin offered the guard his pack. Although curious about the civilian before him, the sentry remained hesitant. Having seen Justin associate openly with the battalion's officers, the guard held him in a different caste. After an awkward moment though, he glanced nervously down the main hallway and shyly took a cigarette.

From behind the entrance's sandbagged shelter, the pair gazed at the peaceful crisp sky beyond the base's fence. The day's shelling had long since ceased and clean moonlight now spread over the neighbouring pastoral hills.

Through sign language, the two attempted to describe their respective homes, families and favourite cigarette brands.

At exactly midnight, bursts of small-arms fire grabbed their attention. Weapons cracked from unseen points around the compound. The crackle graduated to heavy machine-gun and mortar fire, then, grew further, to cannon blasts of every calibre. Tracer rounds flew in all directions above and beside and behind. The horizons beyond every hill lit up and slow moving shells passed overhead like comets. Heavy machine-gunners tried firing with musical rhythms. There was no target to the gunfire, just pure celebratory mayhem.

Pointing to the guard's Kalashnikov, Justin jokingly motioned for him to join the festivity. Aghast, the guard recoiled and shook his head in horror.

Chapter 12

As the year's first rays cast warmth on the surrounding snow-covered hills, Justin was roused by the Call of the Faithful emanating from the base's PA system. The only commotion outside came from Bangladeshi soldiers scurrying to prayer in light fatigues and sandals. Šljivovica induced hangovers would delay the destructive activities of the area's other Muslims for a few hours.

In the officers' mess, Mik, Laura and Justin joined Yaser for a bowl of Corn Flakes. Ricardo was still asleep. Yaser was in high spirits and laughed incessantly throughout the meal. Upon hearing that the MOO workers planned to find the hospital director and perform a medical assessment, Yaser offered Suada, his interpreter, to assist them.

Suada was in her early 20s and had been studying at the university in Banja Luka when the war started. She had thick straight brown hair that fell just above her shoulders. Her round face likely once made her appear younger. She had a cheerful demeanour but drooping facial features betrayed chronic worry and insomnia.

Driving out through the base gates, Mik halted to allow a slow line of about 80 gaunt and filthy elderly men shuffle past. Shredded footwear, flimsy shirts and tattered pants were all that protected the group from the winter. A handful of unenthusiastic young men with old rifles guarded the string of slouched prisoners.

"Those are the people who did not leave Velika Kladuša when Abdić ordered us to Batnoga and Turanj," Suada explained. "Abdić says they are Dudaković fifth columnists."

"Abdić's war criminals," Mik muttered in disgust.

"What about you? Did you go too?" Justin asked.

"No, I stayed and worked for FreBat. But most of my family went to the Batnoga camp."

"What about the Fifth Corps? Didn't you feel danger when they controlled Velika?" Justin pried.

"Tsk," Suada shrugged. "The Fifth Corps made no problem for us or UNPROFOR. I have uncles and aunts from the south also. Who doesn't in Bihać? It is such a small place."

Nodding at the passing prisoners, Suada continued, "I am like them. Because I stayed, many people now say I am a southern collaborator and traitor to Babo. My prison is BanBat...is a little more comfortable than the chicken farm."

Smiling cynically, she added, "I think the truth is that I am a traitor because I stayed and earned Deutsche Marks, they left and earned nothing. We don't have many choices…"

The journey into town was treacherous as the overweight armoured cruiser slid erratically from side to side on the icy road.

The local kids from Abdić's Army manning the internal checkpoint wore ill-fitting fatigues and brandished WW2-style submachine guns. Looming behind them were three older men with modern equipment. They had purple fatigues, Cyrillic shoulder patches that read "*Milicija*" and a distinctly murderous air. They watched both the passers-by and the young troops with the same intimidating glare.

A schoolhouse sat beside the barrier. A shell had blown the bottom corner away. A smattering of older locals passed, with their heads down, as they tried to carry water and food home before the noon curfew.

After close scrutiny of their crossing paper and an explanation by Suada, the guards allowed the aid workers to proceed into the town centre.

At the hospital, Mik squeezed the cruiser into the busy lot separating the facility's three buildings. It was cramped with the war's losers. Dazed soldiers, with metal surgical rods jutting from shattered limbs, hobbled on crutches. Mothers staggered clutching infants. Recycled medical supplies from the Batnoga camp - some still bearing MOO stickers - were being unloaded from a dented van. A cluster of stooped old men, avoiding all eye contact, swept the grounds and chopped wood. At the yard's far end, a heap of medical refuse, used bandages and human tissue smouldered. Entranced dogs scrounged hungrily through the purest by-product of the region's hate.

Inside the main building's emergency area, medical staff worked frantically. The sickly stench of cooked cabbage, old dressings, rotting clothing and dirty water greeted Justin and clung indelibly to his memory.

No matter how many false smiles and brave faces were attempted, the smell always told the truth. It always transmitted the deepest hopelessness and despair and fear within.

The buildings, the colours, the weather, the sounds – all could be described one day with a degree of justice. Capturing the smells' essence and passing it to the world outside would be an impossibility. This was to be the great frustration and the gem held precious by those who were there. To those who never had a choice, the smell was the curse. To those who volunteered, it was the prize – a reward that made them elite and outcast simultaneously.

Dumped against walls, humbled young men sprawled in soiled fatigues and dripping bandaging. Some clutched lifeless limbs. A few groaned at the ceiling. Most were too dazed to cry. The stench clung to them all. This was so far from the glory they were promised.

Deep in the second building, the aid workers found the director, Dr. Tabaric. The middle-aged doctor had soupy eyes that made his long moustache droop even farther. He welcomed the group to sit at the long glass-covered conference table in his office. Behind the table stood a cabinet crammed with all order of trophies and plaques.

Noticing Justin's gaze, the director stated, through Suada, "We used to play many football and water polo tournaments against the Bihać and Cazin hospitals. We always won. We were the best."

Laura nodded politely. She then explained the group's circumstances and need for permission to travel south.

Dr. Tabaric's congeniality dissolved with Laura's words. "Why do you want to help the south? What is wrong with us?" he demanded.

"Nothing is wrong." Laura replied calmly. "We have every intention of assisting you according to your needs. We do not discriminate. MOO has delivered medicines to you regularly when you were in Batnoga."

Glancing at Justin, the doctor gave a nod of recognition and conceded, "That is true, you did. But we are in the worst situation right now. Today we have 70,000 people we must take care of."

"How can that be?" Mik protested. "There were only 30,000 people in the two refugee camps."

"Tsk," the doctor twitched his eyebrow and raised his voice, "Those are UNPROFOR numbers! They are lies. There were many more people than that in the camps. Besides, in the past two days we have retaken a lot of new territory. Thousands of people are fleeing to safety here from the south of Bihać.

"Right now this hospital needs more attention because we have just returned. We have to make many new preparations. We need the most attention right now.

"With the liberation of our territory, we have too much work to do. When Babo defeated the Fifth Corps, we were so happy because we knew we could go home again."

The director's eyes narrowed, "But then the UNHCR told us that we should not return home. They wanted us to stay in the camps like prisoners. They would not help us to go to our homes.

"So Abdić arranged all our transportation back to Velika Kladuša. Look at the town now. After the Fifth Corps left, everything is destroyed."

Pointing a thick finger into the table, he concluded, "Here it is the worst. We need the most."

Unruffled, Laura replied, "We regularly supplied you medicines at the camps and we know you have moved those medicines here now. We have not managed to go to the south of Bihać in months and we are trying to do that now. We want to do an assessment of your hospital's medical needs and then, once we have made our delivery in the south, we will go back to Zagreb and deliver to you exactly what you need."

Nodding, the director replied, "I will help you make your assessment but it is up to our ministers to decide if you go to the south."

"Yes, but the ministers have said we need your agreement first."

Shrugging dramatically, the doctor said, "It is not in my control."

For the next hour, Laura interviewed the director on details of Velika Kladuša's medical situation. The director claimed there were only three other doctors and two auxiliary staff at the hospital. Rubble and broken glass needed to be cleared from most rooms before they could be used again. The hospital was treating a good 50 patients daily. Owing to a shortage of beds, the majority were released the same day. The most serious cases were taken for treatment at Krajina Serb hospitals in Vojnić or Glina.

The only heating came from a handful of wood stoves. The few existing in-patients did have enough blankets and received a simple daily meal of bread and soup.

After rushing the group through a cursory tour of the facility, Dr. Tabaric bid them goodbye. Shaking Justin's hand, the doctor assured, "I will inform Mr. Doric, that you have made an assessment of my hospital."

Hesitating, he added, "If you do make it to the south give my regards to Dr. Balic in Bihać hospital. We go back far. Tell him I am still smoking Marlboros...is an old joke."

Glancing around as they exited the building, Laura gasped, "Where the hell is Mik?"

They found him already in the yard sharing cigarettes with one of the old men cutting wood. Neither Justin nor Laura had noticed Mik disengage from the guided tour and had no idea how long he had been away. As Mik spoke quietly, the woodcutter looked down nervously from fear of association with the outsider.

Laura marched up to Mik, grabbed his elbow and muttered sternly, "What are you doing? Do you want to throw away our slight chance of getting south?"

Mik remained silent until they were back in the cruiser heading for Doric's office. "That old man was a prisoner," Mik revealed. "He was one of the ones who didn't leave when Abdić told them all to flee in the summer.

"The man said there are a few hundred others being held in a chicken farm just past BanBat. He said he was lucky because he only has to chop wood. Others were forced to dig trenches along minefields and the ICL…often during combat.

"Something needs to be done. That's not right," Mik closed with a troubled tone.

"I hear you," Laura replied. Triaging the situation, she continued, "But right now there are too many people counting on us to get our truck through to the south."

In Doric's dark waiting area, a newly installed wood-stove glowed beside the secretary's desk. Without a word, she ushered the group into the larger and colder adjacent office. Composed and serene, Doric sat at the far end of the conference table. Across from him, sat a flustered Gretel begging, in German, to be able to meet with any of the ministers.

In stunted German, Doric replied that all the ministers remained away indefinitely and even when they did get back, they would still never be available to speak with her.

Doric quickly shifted his attention to the MOO team and welcomed them to sit. Gretel lingered in her seat, ignored, but refusing to give up.

"So, what did the doctor say?" Doric asked wryly through Suada.

"We performed a comprehensive survey of the hospital, have noted its needs and will deliver them as soon as possible," Laura replied.

"That is good. I will now need Dr. Tabaric's authorisation before I can ask the ministers to consider allowing you to go south," Doric explained.

"But the doctor said he'll inform you of our visit," Justin interjected.

"Yes, well then I will still need you to submit a formal written request for permission."

Mik handed the document he had printed earlier to a visibly surprised Doric. Startled that such a professional document could be produced in Velika Kladuša, he eyed the red letterhead, justified text and MOO stamp over Justin's signature. After reading the letter carefully, he paused. He appeared on the verge of revealing yet another new travel regulation when the office door flew open.

A stern man marched in. "Ah, Gretel, I thought I'd find you here!" he greeted with a thick German accent.

Somewhat shaken by the interruption, Doric glanced at Mik. "I will submit this document and see what happens," he said quietly.

"We'll come back tomorrow to see what news there is," Mik replied.

"Alright," Doric shrugged.

Outside the office, Gretel explained her situation to the older newcomer. In German, she nervously recounted how the local authorities were not allowing her to cross to the south because they alleged she had been working against Abdić.

"That is preposterous!" the man shouted in English. "You are representing a European Union funded organisation. They must allow you to continue. They simply must!" Eyeing Mik, Laura and Justin, he asked Gretel, "And who are these people?"

"They are from MOO."

"Well hello. I am Claude Von Steinburger of the European Community Task Force. I don't know if you know it but my office gives your group a lot of money. What is it you are doing now?"

"We're negotiating to cross to the south," Mik answered quietly.

"That is very good. What we need amongst European NGO's is communication," Von Steinburger preached. "We need communication and co-ordination so that we can travel together as one united group and show everybody the correct way. European method and communication!" He wheezed and braced himself to continue.

"We haven't completely lost hope yet," Justin broke in. "We're going to keep negotiating for as long as we can with the authorities here."

"That is good but I think you should wait until there are more European representatives here. We must work as one."

"Well, I don't see too many other EU types in town right now," Justin asserted. "The people of Bihać can't wait for the EU's bureaucracy. So we'll keep negotiating by ourselves."

Steinburger's eyes bulged, "That is piracy! You will work according to the EU standard. You cannot just do whatever you feel like. This is still Europe not Africa. I will be speaking with your superiors about this ill discipline and amateurism. This is humanitarian piracy. This is wholly unacceptable!"

The German's rage simmered a moment longer allowing malicious motivation to ferment. "Maybe your director needs to be reminded of who funds MOO's operations here…and of how easily we can take that money away…"

The four slid away awkwardly to their Landcruiser leaving a frothing Von Steinburger and a disconsolate Gretel stammering in the building foyer.

As Mik started the car, Suada timidly addressed Laura. "This is my first time off the base since everybody returned from Batnoga…could I please stop by my home for two minutes to pick up some things?"

Nodding, Laura tapped Mik's shoulder to alter course. Suada guided the vehicle to a once quiet residential street just off the town centre and ran up to a two-story house. Blatantly astray from their approved path, the aid workers immediately felt their white vehicle, glowing out of place and attracting all surrounding suspicions.

The tree-lined street was writhing – alive yet bleak and oppressive. Young soldiers roamed menacingly and civilians shuffled under bloated parcels. Just as they had in Turanj, the returning residents were moving into any available dwelling they could find. And once again, they had to make foreign, damaged buildings inhabitable.

Suada's home had no windows but it still had most of its roof intact. The walls bore only scattered shrapnel marks. One neighbour's front wall jutted out at a 45-degree angle. The other neighbour's charred roof had caved in.

"Welcome home…" Mik muttered grimly.

Could this possibly be the same town that Justin had visited with Laura a couple of months earlier? The once empty streets were now filled with the miserable and the empty houses with strangers.

Fears expressed by those in the camps had all come true. Their homes *were* shattered and smouldering.

So, whose eyes were telling the truth now?

Why had they been so certain of what had happened? Why was the rest of the world so certain of what had not? And why was Justin so uncertain of what he saw now?

In the camps, the refugees had been so insistent in their descriptions of Velika Kladuša's ruin; they could only have been telling the purest truth. It was Justin, and all the other outsiders, who must have been lying. How could Justin's perception of what he saw ever stand against such defiant portrayal?

Justin had never come here seeking to mislead. Yet, in the end, it mattered little what Justin knew or thought he had seen. He had obviously been deceived and was now trying to deceive others. Nothing could ever dispel present reality and the fruition of the residents' original fears.

The only ones who might still try telling the people otherwise were the UN and the criminals locked safely away in the chicken farm. The UN always told lies and always worked for the enemy. The cooped criminals were Abdić' foes and Fifth Corps collaborators.

It was really no use trying to express any of what Justin had once seen to the returning residents. How would it help them now? Justin was fighting to avoid the lattice of lies and illusions inflicted by all sides. Regardless of all he did though, he too had already joined that web.

In the end, Abdić was the only one who really knew the truth. That was why the town was wrecked, the hospital reeked, inhabitants were freezing, youths were bleeding and old men were marched shoeless in the snow. Abdić was deceiving them all. And the more he deceived, the more they called him a saviour.

Suada returned after five minutes clutching a plastic bag and small cardboard box.

"That was my family's house before. Three families I do not know are living there now. They were nice enough to leave some of my things. I found my university records..." she trailed off distantly.

Burning in Justin, Laura and Mik was the question of Suada's family's whereabouts. None dared asked.

Only Suada croaking, "Thanks" broke the silence.

Back at BanBat, Gretel approached Justin while he smoked alone outside his container.

"It appears I have no option but to return to Zagreb. The ministers still refuse to talk to me. I have hit a wall," Gretel explained ruefully. "I was wondering if you could help me with something."

Justin remained noncommittal awaiting details.

"If you make it to the south," Gretel continued, "I was wondering if you'd transport the medicine and food in my car to our office in Bihać. I also have 10,000 Deutsche Marks to pay for our field office's rent."

"Who do I give it to?"

"My interpreter, Dragan, is now working for the UNMO's in Ćoralići," Gretel explained. "If you can give it to him, he'll take care of the rest."

"Sure, not a problem," Justin replied.

"I also have some personal letters for my local staff from friends and family in other parts of the country," Gretel added.

Justin nodded – also a simple request. Carrying mail was a small act that meant so much to both its authors and recipients. Justin was eager to take the mail. Each personal letter delivered tore at the war's highest barrier. Each word of condolence, tale of birth, expression of regret, utterance of reassurance, reminiscence of friendship and each granule of truth between the separated ripped a chink in the wall. This was Justin's way of thwarting the feeble deceivers. At the end of it all, this might well be his only effective deed against the war's efforts.

Anxiously, Gretel blurted, "There's one more thing. My previous interpreter, Dragan, is 19 years old and a Croat. I managed to help him apply for a scholarship in America. On his behalf, I also applied for a passport in Zagreb. He's a bright young man but won't be able to study without documents...would you bring him his passport?"

Without weighing the request, Justin nodded. He did not need to think about it. Fuck all these people and their small-mindedness – their restrictions and their limited mandates.

From her jacket pocket, Gretel handed Justin a blue Croatian passport.

This went well beyond ferrying personal mail. This booklet, emblazoned with a checkerboard shield, meant so many different things.

In one man's possession, it meant a fair shot at a new life and fulfilling his potential. If that one person escaped this confinement of others, then the deceivers had truly failed.

In Justin's possession, the chequered pamphlet meant personal harm if discovered by the wrong people. Worse, Justin was irresponsibly jeopardising his partners' safety and the success of MOO's mission. If the mission failed, the medicines would not get to those in bodily need. The potential cost of carrying this leaflet in his pocket was exorbitant.

And for what exactly? For some abstract romantic ideal that would not heal the wounded or bring hope to the sick? Yes.

Justin relished the risk; the reward was neither tangible nor numeric. Too many had abandoned all principles of right and justice in the name of impartiality and detachment. The outside world's strongest resolve was in skirting its basic moral imperative. The globe's pontificators spouted indignation galore but risked little in its defence. This would be Justin's revolt against all the leaders who spewed defeatist diarrhoea to avoid the inconvenience of settling a war. Justin would risk it all to poke a stick in the eye of the belligerents and the apologists.

Justin was placing many in danger for a person he had never met. No thoughts of glory or heroism passed Justin's mind. All that throbbed in his forehead was a grim desire to fight the evil ones and beat them at their own game. He wanted to breach the walls that imprisoned these people because of whom their parents were or who they were told their parents were.

Even if one person made it out of the crucible then Justin knew he had fought them all. He would have foiled total victory because one had escaped the warmongers' reach.

Croat, Muslim, Serb – Justin did not care. He would have done this for anyone of them. He despised these fences that stopped friends and decent people from speaking. Relatives passed away and children were born without relatives knowing. Justin despised this confinement of living spirit as much as all the killing and destruction.

In his truck, Justin slid the passport behind the rear ceramic plate of his body armour. Shrouded beneath his jacket and fishing vest he figured this would be a decent hiding place. For now, the best thing he could do was act normal and forget he even carried the document.

Justin returned to the container where Mik and Laura were helping Gretel carry boxes from her Land Rover. Pointing to the stack, Gretel explained, "I'm off to Zagreb now."

Defeated, Gretel shook the MOO workers' hands and turned to leave. "Thank you. Please don't give up trying."

In the ensuing boredom, Mik and Laura soon fell into nap on their cots. Justin read a novel for a while. Light sporadic shelling fell on the surrounding hills and eventually soothed Justin to nap too.

Fighting the temptation of deep slumber, Justin forced himself up and went outside to bring some order to his ransacked cargo. Guided by the false conviction that the shells were targeted elsewhere, Justin felt invincible walking beneath the incendiaries arcing overhead.

In his truck cab, Justin composed a Capsat message updating Zagreb of their progress. There was little news to offer. He simply stated that they were still safe and would keep trying.

Justin then re-stacked the medical boxes and bandages until his hands were numb with cold.

He headed indoors to the UNMO's office. There, Ricardo was scanning the nearby hills through the room's panoramic window. Every few moments he lowered his binoculars and reviewed a wall map marking gun emplacements and targets. Yaser was typing at his laptop and keeping a running tally of every shell impact Ricardo noted.

Both smiled to welcome the visitor.

"How's the day been?" Justin inquired.

"Not too bad. A few hundred shells. Nothing too heavy," Yaser explained in characteristic bursts. "There are no major offensives going on, if that's what you were wondering...haven't been for a few days now. When one does start there should be at least 1000 shells."

"Abdić's folks claim that the Velika Kladuša population is now a good 70,000. They say they took new territory and the population rose," Justin stated seeking a response.

"Yeah OK," Ricardo laughed. "If that's true they must have taken over at least half of the Bihać Pocket in the last few days without us or the UNMO's in Ćoralići noticing."

"You guys have been in Velika for a while," Justin pondered. "Why wasn't the town destroyed when the Fifth Corps took it in August?"

"What? You mean I'm not the only one who noticed something odd about VK lately?" Yaser chuckled. "Ask Ricardo, he's the gunner. He's been here longer than me."

Pausing for a moment, Ricardo explained straight-faced, "The Fifth Corps barely have any heavy guns. Light infantry is their strength. Yaser, what was the shell count yesterday?"

From his notepad, Yaser tallied, "Oh, about 500 detonations fired from positions under Abdić's control. Everything from mortars to 76's to 105 mil. The Fifth Corps fired maybe 200...almost entirely mortar rounds."

"So who wrecked the town?" Justin asked still unclear.

Shrugging sarcastically, Ricardo said, "I would not know." Pointing to the wall map and tapping a finger quietly against RSK territory, he asked, "Who has the biggest guns in this neighbourhood? And then, who has the money to hire them?"

Yaser laughed more, "But what do we know? We're here only to spread lies, right?"

Down in the TV room, Justin found Mik, Laura, the colonel and a handful of other officers pouring over an instruction booklet.

"Ah, just in time," Colonel Salim greeted. "The French left us a satellite TV receiver but we need to direct the dish at the right satellite."

Handing Justin a compass and Motorola, the colonel requested, "Could you please go with this captain and try pointing the antenna in the correct direction?"

Outside, Justin climbed a ladder to the building's roof. The young captain remained on the ground with the Motorola. Stretching from the top of the ladder, Justin tried to wrench the satellite dish's frozen support pole in line with co-ordinates radioed by the colonel. The captain called back on the Motorola to check if they had any reception in the TV room.

Nothing.

Justin fought to adjust the dish's horizontal angle.

Still nothing.

The colonel radioed a string of co-ordinate variants but none worked.

As new shells flew over the base into nearby hills, Justin tried turning the dish in the opposite direction.

Again nothing.

Justin's bare hands turned numb and he tried to put them in his pockets while hooking an arm though a ladder rung. He had run out of ideas. The captain looked up with a smile and shrugged.

Colonel Salim appeared and called up, "Come here and warm up your hands."

Justin clambered down and buried his hands under his armpits. The colonel scrambled effortlessly up the ladder. Without referring to the compass, he shifted the antenna violently in all directions.

The captain's radio quickly came to life cheering, "Yes, Yes, Colonel that is it!"

The colonel hopped down beside the captain who beamed in admiration. Brushing his hands on his pants, Salim announced, "That's why they call me the base commander." Slapping Justin on the back, he added, "Come, let's see what's on television."

In the mess area, three TV sets, tuned to different channels, (one Serb, one Croat, one satellite) blared simultaneously. A smiling orderly offered Justin a fresh cup of coffee. Over the echoing cacophony, the colonel barked questions in Bangla. When no response came, he shouted them once more. Fixated to the two local televisions, all ignored the new satellite TV. The colonel was about to utter an order when he was silenced decisively by his subordinates. Santa Barbara had just begun.

Chapter 13

A cluster of BanBat officers greeted Justin, Mik and Laura enthusiastically as they entered the mess for breakfast. From the table's head, Colonel Salim called, "So my friends, how is your quest for crossing permission?"

The aid workers shook their heads.

"I think Abdić is asking for too much *baksheesh*," the colonel laughed. "You know our priority is to assist the humanitarian effort. Please let me know how we can help."

"Thanks," Laura replied. "For now we really just need to borrow an interpreter for a few more hours."

From the other end, Ricardo called, "Feel free to use Suada again. We still have no freedom of movement, so we don't have much work for our interpreters."

As Suada and the MOO team left the mess, the base doctor, Major Abdul, approached. "When you have a little time today, I was wondering if I could show you my medical facilities. It is not just for our own soldiers. During non-curfew hours, many local residents come for treatment. In fact, I'm seeing more people everyday. At first, the locals were very hesitant about visiting us. But word is spreading and they seem to trust me now. "

"We'll drop by in the afternoon after we've met with Doric," Laura promised.

At the internal checkpoint, the young lethargic guards were nowhere in sight. Instead, three towering and heavily armed soldiers in purple fatigues guarded the barrier.

Leaning out to speak to one of the guards, Suada strained to open the cruiser's heavy door.

After a short discussion, she turned to Mik and explained, "The guard says access to the town is completely restricted this morning. But it is OK for us to go in and try to maybe arrange some meeting for later in the afternoon."

"Alright," Mik shrugged and craned to smile dumbly to the guard.

As they pulled away, Justin hunched forward from the back seat and asked, "Those were Serbs, right?"

"Oh yes," Suada replied, "but not from Bosnia. His accent was from Belgrade."

With the exception of small robotic squads of soldiers gathered tactically at corners and intersections, Velika Kladuša's streets were devoid of life. The area directly before the municipal office had the largest concentration of military activity. Soldiers stood on the roof, on balconies, in windows and all over the steps. A BOV armoured personnel carrier sat on the street outside.

As the Landcruiser neared the building, a soldier in a black wool hat and full combat gear stepped forward. He ordered the car to stop with a large raised fist.

Through Suada, the soldier explained gruffly that "somebody very important" was in town for meetings all morning. He estimated the gathering would last at least another hour; the aid workers could wait in the cruiser if they wanted.

Parked in the town square, the four sat in the cramped Toyota for an hour eating chocolate and smoking. None spoke. In the ominous silence, the town's lone white vehicle glowed once again in the midst of so many edgy soldiers. Even behind the vehicle's armour plating, the aid workers felt every tense eye and trigger-finger.

Mik turned on the vehicle's intercom speaker to listen outside their insulated pod. Only the sound of combat boots pacing crisply through the streets pierced the blanketing silence.

Small teams of Serbs patrolled the streets smoothly; their well co-ordinated movements choreographed by hand signals. Their uniforms were smart and all were bedecked with the latest weaponry and webbing.

As the second hour dragged on, Mik announced, "I'm going to find out if there's any news." Nodding at the municipal building's entrance, he added, "Let's see if I can talk to one of those guys covered in hand grenades."

They knew the answer already but Mik could not get past the mulish desire to ask anyway. Not wanting to let Mik be reckless alone, Justin crawled out the car's rear to accompany him.

The pair advanced tentatively while trying to act as if they were making a perfectly normal inquiry – every rooftop gun-sight trained on their heads.

As Mik climbed building's first step, a giant finger poked into his chest.

A Slavic beast plastered with explosives, pistols and knives growled something sounding like a question.

Looking up, Mik politely presented MOO's internal travel permission and, in a mix of German, Serbian and English, tried to explain that he had a meeting with Doric.

With no regard for the paper, other equally large predators gathered around.

"No. Not possible," one snarled.

Mik again tried to make his case but nothing was absorbed. He was attempting to hold a discussion with leashed evil – their only reason for existence was intimidation and suffering.

For the first time, Justin stood before beings he was absolutely certain had killed and maimed with brutality and efficiency.

Motioning to his watch, Justin tried to determine what time the ongoing meetings would end. Again, it was a thoroughly pointless question but he thought it important to show these creatures that he was not afraid. None of the guards likely noticed or cared; any could have killed Mik and Justin where they stood without even missing a drag of their cigarette.

"No today."

"OK. Thank You," Justin smiled.

The soldiers remained blank-faced but were likely growing annoyed with the two civilians before them. One subtle twitch could well have been the only precursor to the infliction of great pain. While their expression stayed unchanged, Mik and Justin took the opportunity to retreat politely.

With a big friendly wave, Mik turned for the car. Once out of earshot he whispered to Justin, "Let's get out of here before they cut our throats."

The entire exercise had been monumentally futile but time and options were growing scarce.

Returning to BanBat's hospitable environs, Mik, Laura and Justin found Major Abdul working in a corner of the factory's auditorium.

"Ah, thank you so much for coming," the major greeted. "Today has been rather slow. I've actually seen nobody."

"Somebody important was in town." Justin explained.

"During the past week I've seen an average of 20 patients each day. Mostly for minor ailments. No war injuries," the base doctor explained. "I see mainly infants and elderly. They cannot get into town and back before noon curfew, so they come see me. Unfortunately, I'm running low on medicine and I'm expecting my daily number of patients to grow to 30 shortly."

Pointing to storage shelves, the doctor noted, "We're running out of most things. Before we had a quantity of medicine left behind by the French. We also received a few new stocks with the re-supply convoys. But, as you know, the Serbs continue to block them."

"It's not a lot but we have some surplus medicines in our vehicle," Justin offered.

Laura and Mik nodded in concurrence.

A couple of Bengali troopers helped carry Gretel's boxes in from the MOO Landcruiser.

With Major Abdul's rising number of patients, the medicines would do the most good in his hands. Justin felt guilty that the supplies would not reach the WHIG office in Bihać town. They still had no idea when they would reach the south. What if the trio never made it at all? Everybody around here was in need. So, you helped the ones you could and that was how you lived with your conscience.

"This is marvellous," the doctor exclaimed poking through the stack of boxes. "These are many of the basics I require each day. Thank you."

Shaking the aid workers' hands, the doctor kept repeating thanks. Finally, he added, "These are very hard times. I assure you this help will be put to good use."

Laura returned to the container to read and make notes for her medical report. Justin and Mik dropped by the UNMO's room to check on surrounding developments.

As usual, Ricardo was straining at the terrain through his binoculars. "Come here quick," he beckoned. "Want to see something interesting?"

Handing the binoculars to Mik, he pointed to a small mosque on a hill about a kilometre away.

"Watch closely. See how each new shell crawls up to the target." Ricardo explained technically.

They were near enough to see the shells impact. Silent flashes of blinding light were followed by a momentarily belated thunderous blast. The room shuddered as this invisible force pounded their ears and temples. A few short metres were the difference that turned the once distant exhilarating wumpf into an indiscriminate explosion – blistering and lacerating without prejudice.

Artillery duels picked up from points all around the base. New explosions came unseen from hills farther away. Ricardo paused estimating where to mark each on his wall-map.

Yaser simply chuckled from his seat.

"So which shells are incoming and outgoing?" Justin inquired trying to make sense of Ricardo's map-scratchings.

"It's not so easy to say. The confrontation line twists and turns a lot. Both armies have positions in some very strange places. Shelling comes from every possible angle. We seem to be in the middle of it all today." Pointing up, Ricardo continued, "You hear that? It's a slow moving shell; you can hear its trail...that's a 76 mil."

Keeping an ear skyward, Ricardo called out other gun types and calibres as subsequent shells arced outside.

Still keeping a tally on his notepad, Yaser grinned, "Ah, he's just showing off."

Three trucks, pulling short-barrelled cannons, raced south past the base's perimeter. Grabbing the binoculars, Ricardo yelled "Yaser! Yaser! Quick look at this!"

Leaping to the window, Yaser caught a glimpse and chortled, "Excellent! Mountain guns. Three!"

The next morning Mik, Laura, Justin and Suada returned the municipal offices once more. They passed yet another strand of Abdić's decrepit enemies shuffling into town for daily toil. With gnawing frustration, Mik muttered hoarsely, "I'm sorry guys. I wish I could help you."

At the municipal building UNHCR and ICRC vehicles already waited on the street. In the dark waiting foyer, the secretary ordered the four to wait; Doric was busy.

An expressionless man and woman sat in the waiting area – large International Red Cross badges dangled from their breast pockets. They seemed to be ignoring a third younger man seated beside them. The cynical smirk beneath his UNHCR ball cap parted only to pull on a hand rolled cigarette.

"Hi, I'm Peter – UNHCR. Welcome to the wait," he blurted to the MOO team.

The ICRC duo remained silent and only glanced at the new arrivals to size up their perceived competition.

"How goes your effort to pass through the Newly Liberated Banana Republic?" the UNHCR rep asked.

"No luck yet. But we haven't quite given up hope. How about you?" Justin replied.

"You're a few steps behind us then. You still have hope. Things are not good," Peter sighed. "Our trucks are still parked at PolBat in Maljevac. Apparently big Babo has personally decided to keep screwing with the UNHCR and make my life miserable."

"Where's your partner?" Mik inquired.

"Francesca's busy yelling at some other clown in charge of the local police station."

In the ensuing silence that descended over the room, Laura glanced at the Red Cross pair and asked amicably, "So, how are your negotiations going?"

With a French accent, the woman answered curtly, "They are going well."

Trying to keep the conversation alive, Laura continued, "What types of medical supplies are you delivering to the south?"

Staring back, the woman eventually replied, "ICRC provides assistance to the war wounded and prisoners. We already have staff in the south. Their stocks are running low."

"So what's the overall supply situation like down there for you and the UN right now?" Laura pressed.

"We do not operate with the UN. The Red Cross has its own network in Bosnia."

After another uncomfortable pause, the ICRC woman stated, "We also do not pay bribes. You are from MOO, no?"

To Laura's nod, the woman added, "I think we will be the first to get to the south."

Doric stuck his head around his office door, greeted the Red Cross workers and welcomed them into his room. Half an hour later, Doric re-emerged. The ICRC duo departed without a word.

Lingering in the hall, Doric addressed the UNHCR rep through Suada. "I am very disappointed with you. Right now I have nothing to say to you."

Slumped in a chair disrespectfully, the UNHCR officer yawned, "I'm very sorry to hear that."

"Your partner, the French woman, she is very rude and has been treating me in a very unprofessional way," Doric continued.

"I am sorry you feel that way."

"I will be writing a formal complaint about her to your superiors in Geneva," Doric barked sternly.

"Well, that's your right I guess."

Doric returned to his office.

"Good luck trying to find a fucking post office," the UN rep called toward the closed door. "See what I'm up against here?" he said to the MOO workers.

Glancing at his watch, the UNCHR officer added, "I guess I'll go find my rude French partner. See you guys at dinner."

Pausing, he added, "Hey, I'm a bad example. Don't give up yet. You've probably still got a better chance of succeeding than the UN does."

Although MOO worked near the UN and they helped each other out when in need, MOO remained an independent relief organisation. Medicine seemed to be something abstract to most – magic understood only by a well-trained and respected elite. In a conflict where all flagrantly flouted almost every Geneva Convention written, medicine still held a notional point of honour. Blockading food had long since become another of the war's base implements. No side made it easy for medicine to reach the other. Yet none had obstructed its delivery with the same ruthlessness as they had food. All sides were willing to starve their enemy but were less inclined to let them bleed to a slow death.

The aid workers continued waiting and eventually asked the secretary when they could see Doric. She shrugged and showed no inclination to inquire.

Out of desperation, Justin knocked on the office door and peered through. Doric looked up from the conference table questioningly.

Not hearing any order to leave the room, Justin continued forward smiling innocently. Seizing the chance, his colleagues followed on his heels.

Through Suada, Justin stated, "We need to know if there have been any discussions with the ministers or if you have spoken to the hospital director."

"No I have not," Doric replied.

"When will Ministers Djedovic or Hirkic be making a decision?" Justin pressed.

"They have been very busy. I do not know."

"When will it be possible for us to meet with them?" Justin inquired.

Shaking his head, Doric explained, "They are out of town today. Nobody knows when they will return."

Hearing nothing forthcoming from Mik or Laura and unsure what else to say, Justin announced, "OK, then we'll come back tomorrow to see if the ministers are available."

Frowning, Doric replied in English, "Sure."

"That was fruitful," Justin muttered as the group returned to the cruiser.

Following lunch at BanBat, Mik and Justin attempted to put snow chains on the Landcruiser and truck. The weather was growing steadily colder and the roads icier.

As the afternoon progressed, the shelling around the base increased further. A Capsat arrived from Zagreb anxiously inquiring about the team's situation. Justin had little information to offer and asked them to remain patient. After getting so close, Zagreb could easily order the team back it they saw no more progress.

Justin believed that, in spite of Doric's continued evasiveness, they had not reached that waiting wall of total impasse. Doric had yet to reject MOO's requests outright. Although the group had still not met with the mythical ministers, they had not been denied outright.

Doric was just stalling. MOO had not yet spoken to anybody who claimed to be in a decision-making capacity – assuming such a person actually existed in Bosnia at all. Justin wanted to keep hammering at least until they met somebody one step higher than Doric. They just had to keep waiting for that right moment.

Even though all efforts focused on reaching that next meeting, it was also a point Justin dreaded. When and if the instant came, the group would have to make a critical decision – would they offer a portion of the cargo to Abdić in return for passage? Justin was undecided whether this was something he was willing to do. Succumbing to the bribe was a precedent he did not want to establish. He was not above paying bribes to deliver relief. But in this case, he and MOO never had any intention other than to bring Velika Kladuša exactly what it needed anyway. In a place so consumed by the lies of circumstance, it was the sincere people the locals feared the most.

If Abdić forced MOO to either release a portion or all of its cargo, the organisation would likely not return to Velika Kladuša anytime soon. This would mean additional hardship for Velika Kladuša's inhabitants and, under present conditions, would prolong the suffering for those in Fifth Corps territory too.

The alternative, leaving Velika Kladuša and returning to Zagreb without giving anyone the cargo, troubled Justin as deeply. This course brought no help to anyone. To abandon all sides, no matter how much their representatives extorted and connived, was a crime to the masses.

In reality, the Velika Kladuša authorities would likely never allow the MOO trio to return to Zagreb with an entire truckload of medicine. This was precisely why the UNHCR had left their trucks across the border in Serb Krajina.

Both choices were terrible and Justin could scarcely stomach toying with either. Pushing the debate away, he would simply continue forward quietly and see how far he could go.

Mik and Laura had grown somewhat more anxious and had a lower threshold of patience. They agreed with Justin's views but only for the very immediate time being.

At dinner, the three ran into Commander Jahangir. He too was unable to speak with any person of importance in the municipality. He had hoped to raise the issue of MOO's delivery with whomever he could find.

Francesca and Peter from the UNHCR soon arrived. They both looked tired but Peter remained defiantly cynical. Sitting next to Justin, he asked, "Any luck?"

"No, all ministers disappeared indefinitely. How about you?"

"We are at the beginning," Francesca interjected. "The convoy is still in Maljevac. I am sending it back to Zagreb. Abdić is acting totally unreasonable. Of the 10 trucks, he wants six to stay in Velika Kladuša before the remainder can go south. Four trucks of food for 160,000 people! The trucks are too much of a liability staying so close to Velika. I had absolutely no choice but to order them back. So now we are nowhere."

After a pause, she strained to add, "And now Abdić sits in comfort in his castle and he will again tell his people that the UN wants only to starve them. He is a war criminal and some day he will fucking pay."

Francesca lit up a smoke and continued as the whole table sat in attentive silence. "I came here to help these people and after all this incredible bullshit, I end up prolonging their suffering."

Tapping the cigarette ash on the edge of her dinner plate, she continued, "What can I do though? We can't reward Abdić with food while he lets the rest of the Pocket keep starving."

The following morning Laura visited the base doctor seeking more details on the numbers and types of patients he treated.

The UNMO's and Suada ventured into town to talk with Abdić's liaison officer about the continued restrictions on their movement. Rumour also had it that an UNPROFOR re-supply convoy had crossed into RSK a day or two earlier and was due to enter Velika Kladuša soon. The UNMO's were eager to find out when it might reach BanBat.

Without any available interpreters, Mik and Justin decided to visit Doric and try their luck alone.

Finding nobody in the municipal offices, the pair stood in the empty hall for almost half an hour before Doric mysteriously emerged from his office. He appeared startled but managed to recover and greet the MOO workers calmly.

"Is there any news from the ministers?" Mik struggled in his best German.

"No, nothing," Doric replied in equally limited German.

"Have you spoken with Dr. Tabaric?"

Doric hesitated, then nodded and raised a finger for the two to wait. He returned from his office shortly with a copy of the MOO packing list.

Stammering for the right words, Doric stated, "The doctor looked at the list and asked for this."

In pencil, Dr. Tabaric had marked the quantities he desired beside almost every item on the list. He demanded roughly 60% of the medicines and dressings in Justin's truck.

The knot of inevitability tightened in Justin's stomach. He shook his head and protested in his best kindergarten German, "...That not what we spoke..."

"That is what the doctor wants," Doric shrugged.

With a wry smile, Mik stabbed at the list. "This is not possible. You know what this means don't you?...We could give you this now, but these are conditions we cannot work under..."

Justin cringed realising that they were no more than two words away from becoming another of the war's weapons. They verged on the same point as the UNHCR – ordering their food convoy back to Zagreb.

A thunderous silence welled. Doric stared blankly at Mik. Justin's jaws bit down furiously begging for a reply – anything, just let them know their fate. Finally, Doric licked his lower lip, made a half-downward nod and croaked, "Minister Hirkic is in my office right now...wait," and disappeared.

In the dark silence, Mik and Justin did not know what to think. What the hell was Doric doing? Their fate was still unclear. Did Doric understand that MOO truly wanted to provide Velika Kladuša with its rightful medical needs? The aid workers would get no more chances to make their case. Doric could have a sizeable shipment of cargo right now, fulfil the whimsical delusions of his superiors and then never see MOO in town again. Or he could allow the MOO truck to continue south and then receive a fair and proper delivery in his town a few days later. Unfortunately, the only collateral MOO offered was their word. And in return, they demanded the most valuable, most abused and rarest of commodities – Doric's trust.

Mik and Justin fretted wordlessly in the cold for another half-hour. Neither dared speak nor reveal a flinched feeling. Mercifully, Doric emerged and with a dark timorous look announced, "I spoke with Minister Hirkic. Tomorrow morning early, you come to this office for your permission to travel.

"You must wait for the next UNPROFOR convoy. You join it and deliver all your medicine in Bihać. Then you return to Zagreb and make a delivery to Velika Kladuša quickly."

Mik and Justin held their breath for the final unreasonable caveat Doric must have been about to add. Maybe they had not understood his German correctly – so simple a scenario must have been a set up.

Pre-empting the rub he was certain would still appear, Justin smiled and reached to shake Doric's hand. Making eye contact, Justin replied, "Thank you…all medicine to Bihać?"

"*Ya*"

"Tomorrow morning?"

"*Ya*"

Doric's tense expression clung. It was he who gambled the most by placing a morsel of faith in these young foreigners.

Walking back to the Landcruiser, Justin risked the slightest celebration and chimed, "Who needs an interpreter anyway?"

Still bewildered and sceptical at the encounter's eventual outcome, Mik revealed, "I don't speak much German. But when I get angry I speak it quite well."

Mik, Justin and Laura returned to the municipal office the next morning to see if Doric's words were true or just another Balkan ruse.

The ICRC couple was already waiting in front of Doric's door. The Red Cross woman glanced at the MOO workers and smiled smugly, "Still trying to get permission to go to Bihać?"

Mik shrugged noncommittally, "And you?"

"Yes, we think things are going well. We believe we will be successful soon."

Doric opened his door. He smiled quickly and shook Mik's hand. He muttered a request to his secretary who began typing on a flimsy half-sheet.

Doric gingerly pinched the holey strip, stamped it with the latest official NLTAPWB seal and signed the bottom. He handed the threadbare scrap to Mik; some of the typewriter keys had punched through and Doric's signature had slashed the bottom of the priceless agreement. Doric had given his word and put it on paper. He was offering MOO exactly what they requested; yet, they still stood in Velika Kladuša, far from their goal.

Quiet resentment ebbed from the Red Cross reps toward the upstart aid workers. The petty hierarchy in their world of altruism was askew. For the MOO trio, the Red Cross's ire was pure icing.

Mik smiled innocently in their direction.

The ICRC woman smiled back tersely and stammered, "Well, good luck…"

Doric then confirmed that an UNPROFOR convoy had arrived in town the previous night and would be travelling to Ćoralići soon.

Mik, Laura and Justin all pressed to shake Doric's hand. "We see you soon," Justin promised.

Doric nodded – were these words true or just a foreign ruse?

Returning to base, the MOO trio passed the fabled UN re-supply convoy parked along a curb. A ring of Abdić's men trained RPG's and machineguns at the trucks' French soldiers. Parked alongside the dozen trucks was a pair of white Jeep Cherokees and a Peugeot Sedan. The UN troops toiled to offload their cargo onto the snowy ground. Abdić's men cut open boxes and sifted through sacks of rice while trying to match each article with the convoy's manifest.

At the far edge stood two elderly officers, a Russian and a Dane, frozen with stern disapproving scowls. Ricardo and Yaser were patiently trying to calm them. Seeing the passing aid workers, the UNMO's grinned sarcastically.

At BanBat, Mik, Laura and Justin sorted through the cruiser and truck once more to make sure all was in order. Justin also checked the vehicles' chains, engine, fuel and oil. This was the one time in his life he could not afford engine problems.

The three squeezed into the truck cab and ceremoniously sent a Capsat to Zagreb. Although excited they had made it this far, Justin remained nervous and still wished not to gloat prematurely. The gods always frowned on such displays and always conspired to alter circumstance.

Justin kept the message short and devoid of sentiment. He ended the four-line statement with, "Will keep you posted," hoping this was ambiguous enough to avoid jinxing themselves.

Shelling continued at a moderate rate and it remained uncertain whether they would be allowed to travel at all that day. Any delays now could reset all promises.

The UNMO's reappeared at the base and called the MOO trio up to their office. Hearing of their success, Yaser chuckled, "Well done. Very well done. That really is something."

"You're in luck. You saw the convoy. It arrived last night," Ricardo confirmed. "For the past two days, the Serbs at Mošćenica, Vojnić and Maljevac searched it, each time, right down to the last grain of rice. And now Abdić's boys are doing the same."

"Yeah," Yaser chimed, "and they've got a senile Danish general and a drunken Russian colonel leading them. Last night when Abdić's men forced the soldiers to sleep in their trucks, the two officers demanded to sleep in proper beds. Abdić's men told the two to fuck off and forced them to sleep in their Peugeot."

Beaming mischievously, Yaser added, "They are not taking it well. They are extra grumpy today."

"What happens after the search? Will the convoy be overnighting here?" Justin inquired.

"No, they have to keep going straight to Ćoralići," Ricardo explained. "They have no fuel there. The base is in complete darkness and can barely communicate right now."

"What about the shelling today? Will they travel if there's fighting?"

"Ah, it's not that bad. There's been worse," Yaser smiled. Eyeing the wall map, he added seriously, "As far as we can tell fighting is not so heavy along the road and ICL. It should be alright to cross for now." Laughing suddenly, he howled, "But there are no guarantees in Bosnia!"

"We've tried to arrange a short cease-fire so both sides will let the convoy through." Ricardo explained. "But it's hard when there are no phone lines and you don't really know when the convoy will be crossing."

Pointing at the map's squiggles, Justin wondered about the ICL's present location.

Still grinning, Yaser shrugged, "We're not exactly sure anymore. It's probably about 10 kilometres south of Velika, just past Mala Kladuša. But the front could have shifted anywhere up to four clicks in the last few days. We're not allowed out of town so we're hoping the convoy leader will give us some intelligence once he gets through. If you get to Pecigrad, you're OK. That's definitely in Fifth Corps' hands."

Still eyeing the map, Justin spotted a large red "S" marked on a curve just outside Velika Kladuša and asked what it was.

"Abdić's sniper," Yaser replied. "Just south of town, the road passes the foot of a steep hill with a cemetery. The sniper hides on top behind the gravestones. He doesn't like the UN. He shouldn't be too much trouble if Abdić's officers tell him not to shoot at the convoy."

"Does he usually listen?"

"He also has no telephone," Yaser laughed.

"Don't worry," Ricardo tried to reassure the three. "We'll give you a shout as soon as they finish searching the convoy. Just be ready to leave immediately."

Chapter 14

The afternoon passed with slow anxiety. The aid workers dared not stray more than a few metres from their vehicles or the main building's entrance. With darkness descending, MOO's primary safety directive loomed overhead – never travel after dark.

As the aid workers made the disappointing decision to call it a day, Ricardo burst outside wearing his unadorned beret and British camouflage smock and scarf. Yaser raced in his shadow.

"They've finished the search. The convoy will be here any minute." Ricardo sputtered breathlessly as he and his partner hopped in their Landcruiser and sped into town.

Darkness instantly ceased to be a concern. Besides, Justin rationalised, daytime could be just as inhospitable and unpredictable as night. Silently, the three strapped on their body armour and helmets and climbed into their vehicles. Even a single word could jinx it all.

Justin rolled down his cab windows. Not having the luxury of an armoured vehicle, he hoped to reduce the chance of getting a face full of glass if hostile projectiles where generous enough to avoid hitting him.

Beside Justin, an old Bengali APC bellowed smoke as it awoke from a frozen slumber.

Everything around Justin accelerated well beyond abstractions. They had finally surged past all the speculative posturing and hurtled toward giving southward passage a real shot. Justin started his engine, checked the lights and tuned his radios. He typed a quick Capsat note to Zagreb office telling them of the team's impending departure. He did not hit the send key though.

As Justin awaited the next step, realisation of what he was getting into finally surfaced. How had he lapsed so far from the tranquillity of Toronto, beyond the Amsterdam train station and outside Zagreb's pretend danger? Justin had to suppress these thoughts if he was ever going to get anything done. Bravery was little more than self-deception of surrounding reality.

As a string of slow-moving headlights glimmered beyond the compound's far end, Justin's UNPROFOR Motorola pierced the darkness. "All stations. Please be advised, we have mortar impacts – 200 metres from the convoy." The prosaic voice continued with a slight hint of concern, "UNMO's, where's that cease-fire you promised?"

"We're still working on confirmation." Yaser replied from parts unknown.

The convoy had not even left town and was already under attack. It all would definitely be called off now. Each long minute allowed the danger to become ever more conspicuous.

A white Peugeot sedan raced into the compound and skidded to a sidelong halt near the building entrance. Commander Jahangir, in a flak-vest and blue beret strode forward with confidence worthy of TV coverage. He handed a package to the vehicle's occupants. The commander then squeezed into a waiting Volkswagen 4x4 loaded with a pair of armed Bengali troopers.

A Bangladeshi captain poked his helmeted head from the APCs hatch and led a smoky advance out the base gate. He stopped on the roadside followed by Commander Jahangir, a French Jeep and two UN Toyotas. The Peugot had trouble finding its feet on the icy ground but eventually also slipped into the file.

This was a good sign. The next step should be near. The flash of uncertainty from the Amsterdam train platform tried once more to leap from Justin's bowels. This was it – the danger that had always awaited Justin.

He still had no time to dwell; he had to keep moving forward as far as he could go. There were too many people counting on at least that. His conscience would forgive nothing less.

Justin and Mik advanced to the gate as the beautiful, battered French trucks emerged into view. The convoy queued behind the waiting UN vehicles and Mik and Justin pulled up at their rear.

"All stations, we're just waiting for a local escort from Abdić's people," Yaser assured over the radio.

With Abdić's history of fickle cease-fire commitments, the local escort would serve as a shaky hostage helping ensure safe passage to the front line. In the end though, this likely had as much value to Abdić as any other promises he made not to attack the UN.

Justin caught a glimpse of his watch's fading luminous hands resting at 5 p.m. More vehicle motion glimmered in Justin's rear-view mirror. A young Abdić soldier charged up to Justin's door brandishing his AK-47.

"*Jebem ti sunce! Tko si ti, pička ti materina!*" he screamed almost in one breath.

The warehouse boys had taught Justin well on those many idle afternoons. From the soldier's Bosnian rant, Justin picked out the phrases, "Fucking sunshine" and, "Fuck your mother's pussy."

Jumping down, Justin was not sure how he should go about showing the soldier MOO's crossing permission. Mik had all the papers.

"*Medicinska*," Justin offered, trying to define his cargo.

Hopping as the soldier's rifle jabbed his side, Justin hurried to the back and lifted a corner of the tarp.

The soldier growled to open the cover completely. Peering up at the cargo, he swore some more and yanked at a few nearby boxes.

Four French tanker trucks pulled up behind Justin and revved their engines impatiently.

The soldier ripped open a box and found disposable Bic razors. Before he could continue, the UNMO's Landcruiser sped past honking its horn. Justin caught a glimpse of Yaser grinning and waving. The local Lada Niva escort followed in their snowy wake. The vehicles disappeared to the head of the column and the procession ground forward. Clutching a handful of plastic razors, the soldier stepped aside.

"*Jebi se!*" he dismissed Justin.

Justin had no trouble catching up with the departing convoy. Although the caravan inched along at 10 km/h, it was now truly moving. Justin finally dared hit the Capsat's transmit button.

The road was a total sheet of black ice but the truck's chains kept Justin on the verge of control. His only reference came from the bobbing red lights of the vehicles ahead.

"Everything OK?" Mik radioed back to Justin. "Just wondering if you've still got your helmet and BP on." His voiced tinted with humour, as Laura giggled in the background of their armoured interior.

"Funny one, asshole. Everything's fine," Justin called back.

Small arms crackled nearby. Justin could hear everything. Mik and Laura were isolated from the cold and sound. It was hard to tell which was better.

Houses became less frequent as the caravan plodded beyond Velika Kladuša. Entering the outline of sloped farmlands, the convoy halted abruptly. They waited breathlessly in clear night warmed only by the moon. A lit farmhouse sat no more than 20 metres from the road. With Justin's forward sight obstructed by the trucks ahead, he sat in a void with no clear view of what had caused the stoppage.

Led by Commander Jahangir, his Bangladeshi guards and two Abdić soldiers scoured the road's edge.

"Oh, hello," Jahangir greeted passing Justin's door. "Just a small problem. There seems to be a low hanging electrical cable leading to that farmhouse. Our lead cars passed under without noticing. But the first truck came within millimetres of severing it. We shan't be too long now." He smiled and turned to bark an order in Bangla.

A small group of kids converged and ran from vehicle to vehicle. In their best French, they asked, "Eh, bon joor. Bon bon. Hey you. Goomy goomy."

Mik's door opened and he handed out a pack of caramels.

A Bangladeshi raced past holding a long tree branch aloft. With it, he raised the aberrant cable high enough for the trucks to pass beneath. The convoy advanced, bit-by-bit, as another Bangladeshi climbed atop each truck to ensure the cable scraped over without snagging any corners or rivets.

Resuming its slow pace, the procession pressed ahead into the slippery darkness. The foot of large hills rose to Justin's left and, to his right, flat open expanse and sky.

The road wound through sharp turns. Justin could pick out stones of the Muslim cemetery sloped on a steep incline. All remained still except for red taillights drifting around the hill's base. Justin held his breath as he and the vehicles in his mirror floated past without incident as well.

A warming but uncertain thump beat from under Justin's ceramic breastplate. The loudest sound was his own breathing as it made up for lost time. So far so good – they had passed one more obstacle. There were many more still. Just keep going; keep pressing.

Sporadic gunfire coughed in the periphery as they delved deeper. The terrain spread open again and they rolled through farmlands. Shells landed in the fields ahead; their searing shards' chaotic reach fell just short of the convoy. The trucks crawled through darkened and shredded Mala Kladuša. They were closing in on that most elusive confrontation line. If they kept going, they had to find it soon.

At the edge of town, Justin passed the UNMO's Toyota and the local Lada Niva backed into a farm driveway. A little farther, at a rural bus stop, sat the BanBat APC. Without escort, UNMO's or armament, they entered the void of confrontation. They were on their own but they were still moving.

On a thoroughly desolate stretch, well beyond town, they curved past a lone general store. Slivers from the shop's large window-front glittered in jagged beauty. The moon hinted to a bullet-pocked store sign and a charred doorway. The internal front line had passed unsympathetically over this rural meeting point. In a few violent moments, more attention had been bestowed upon this tiny location than some of the world's busiest metropolises.

The store quickly became one more memory passed as wooded slopes again enveloped the procession. Creeping ever closer to the heart of combat, tracer rounds blipped from the forest hills and occasionally skipped over the convoy. Justin's heart quickened further with each glowing trail. His hearing verged on clairvoyance. As breath entered and left with unfamiliar smoothness, he attained the clearest awareness of his own existence.

With every passing footfall and weapon's crack, Justin strained to peer deeper into the shroud outside. Hearing took supreme precedence relegating sight to the dullest of his senses. His ears became so keen that he extrapolated the sonic crack of rounds impacting into his cab. Where would they hit first? What glass and metal would splinter? Which bones would shatter?

A jeopardy-fuelled narcotic slowly overwhelmed Justin. As apprehension slipped into recess, Justin rose to a calm plane where reality's reference points were long abandoned.

Although he had relished a little adventure in his life, Justin had always set conservative barriers to avoid uncomfortable situations. Those barriers had evaporated; all his original fears had been misplaced. All the waiting was worth this. This was war – or at least, as close as he would get prostituting himself for scraps of its exhilaration.

He was still just a perverse tourist – a visitor sneaking peaks at a most sacred happening. An event concocted by cowards and relished by fools – always performed and endured by people far braver than any outsider.

It was the other youths, in the forests and the hills, in sodden stinging clothing, different only in the fate of their birthplace, who now cowered to avoid the exhilaration's ruthless glare. Amongst the undiscriminating explosions and shattered limbs, the only warmth found was beneath charred skin. These youths dug into holes and squeezed beneath unyielding rocks, always naked to laceration. None had ever volunteered to be here.

From Justin's cushioned seat, the war was seductive beauty. He could not hear the individual screams or paralysing terror that besieged. Beyond the shell impacts and weapon bursts he so scientifically counted, there sat a cold foundation of malicious noise and eternal confusion. Within the trees wafted callous bloody forces that pushed young men maniacally. For them, to stop going forward was to die.

Replying to his queries on this forbidden universe, Justin's clairvoyance attempted to create a nightmare. Yet no matter how vivid and spooled the dream, he would never know the truth of such experience. Justin pitied those within for the terror borne and envied them for the pure truth gained.

In his heightened awareness, Justin's handset spit to life, "All call-signs, convoy halting. Lead car just hit a dog…"

What?

Squinting at the line of vehicles curved on the road ahead, Justin made out the first car – its unflattering blue flag illuminated by the vehicle behind. Its headlights revealed two French officers crouching to scan the ground. Satisfied, they lifted a long heavy object and dumped it on the road's edge. Jumping back in their Toyota, they continued into the void.

Straining to harness the moon's glow, Justin stared at his watch. It appeared to read 7:55 but time had lost all relevance.

Moving through the bend, Justin glanced at the discarded inanimate obstacle. It was actually a log – a log with a police traffic lollipop wedged into it. Was this one side's interpretation of today's front line? And if so, who put the log there anyway?

Justin still refused to digest what it could represent. He had to avoid even a glimmer of misplaced hope. One just does not drive up to a front line, push aside a log and carry on. They were not there yet. Anything could happen still. He just kept going.

They passed smatterings of farmhouses and clusters of dwellings. All sat darkened; none revealed even a hint of inhabitation or allegiance. Circumstance had demanded they change their affiliation too many times already. There were no sounds of combat – whose territory where they in?

The snaking route entered a prolonged climb that slowed the convoy to a pained crawl. As the slope became treacherously steep, the convoy pulled up in an unlit town. Armed men lingered in its shadows.

"Pecigrad," Mik radioed triumphantly, his enormous smile transmitted for miles throughout the darkness.

This was supposed to be a Fifth Corps town but Justin still clung to the conviction that they had not yet arrived. They had come too far and too close to throw it all away with false optimism.

A flashlight bobbed along the truck line ahead. Stopping periodically, it grew gradually brighter. Reaching the truck in front of Mik, Justin made out the nervous Danish major he had seen previously with Colonel Lysander at Mošćenica. The Dane, a Bosnian officer and two armed men reviewed a list.

Peering up from the sheet at the truck, the Dane confirmed to the Bosnian, "Yes, this is another of my vehicles."

Stopping at Mik's cruiser, the Dane asked, "Ah, and who is this? MOO..." After scanning the manifest, he looked questioningly at Mik and uttered, "But you are not from UNPROFOR."

"I'm afraid the Fifth Corps did not know you were coming," the Dane continued. "They will need to register you with their commander before you can proceed."

The Dane spoke into his Motorola ushering the UN trucks onward up the slope. Panic washed through Justin as his security blanket departed.

"What? Wait a minute...what's happening to the convoy," Mik pleaded with similar anxiety.

"Oh, it's alright. This is Fifth Corps territory," the Dane announced. "You're safe with them."

"Why can't we just register later once we get to Ćoralići?" Justin asked.

"It's just a formality. You know how it is out here. Don't worry, I'll stay. They know me," the Dane explained while reaching in the front flap of his flak vest. He pulled out a 9 mm automatic and slid the breach to unload it.

Slipping the handgun back into the pocket, he sighed, "Well, my day's work is about done."

The Bosnian officer asked Mik for official documents. Mik passed a sheet simply bearing MOO letterhead, the Zagreb office address, and the registration numbers of both vehicles. Most importantly, it was stamped and signed by Rolf. Jabbing appreciatively at the paper's signature, the officer walked to a nearby hut with the officious tablet.

Slithering from the dark periphery, a gaggle of unshaven Bosnian troopers, in American-style fatigues and black wool caps, surrounded the novel guests. Aside from boredom and curiosity, their main ambition was cigarettes. To their glee, Justin produced a pack.

After ravenously grabbing the smokes, the soldiers demanded to inspect Justin's cargo. Peering through the rear hatch, their eyes fell upon the already open box. The group's leader held up a handful of Bic razors and muttered to his comrades.

"Razors, yeah," Justin nodded making a cutting motion along his own stubbly cheeks. "You guys could certainly use a few," he added motioning for them to keep the handful.

The leader hesitated, unsure and suspicious. He was overruled as his comrades reached around him at the box. Chuckling, the troops made a group charade pretending to shave and shower in distant luxury.

A bespectacled soldier called to Justin in flawless English, "Hey, thank you very much. One day we'll use these properly."

Mik inquired ambiguously, "So, is the town quiet right now?"

Glancing around at the darkened buildings, the soldier replied, "Well...there are no bars or discos open right now."

Laughing quietly, Mik continued, "So, what do you do for fun then?"

"We just sit around and smoke grass."

"Really," Mik wondered, "where do you get it?"

"We have a couple of farms down by the Una River...Why do you think the Chetniks try to capture our side of the river?"

The Bosnian officer exited his hut and spoke to the aid workers through the bespectacled trooper.

After absorbing the officer's speech, the soldier explained, "OK, he says, he spoke with his commander. Your papers are in order. You are allowed to pass but for one small price."

"And what is that?" Laura inquired impatiently.

The soldier smiled sheepishly, "Well, his wife is pregnant and really needs a special kind of medicine."

The officer shrugged and shyly produced a baggie with a medical label.

"Look, I don't have time to go through our cargo," Laura replied firmly. "I think we have something like that but he's going to have to go down to Cazin or Bihać to get it."

The officer made a pleading face.

"And if that doesn't work," Laura said trying to assuage the sceptical officer, "come to the UNHCR office in Ćoralići. I'll make sure you get it. OK?"

A UN Landcruiser drove down from atop the slope and stopped near the Dane.

"I must return to the convoy," he explained. "Just follow the road up. It's the only way to Ćoralići."

Once back in their own vehicles, Mik and Justin pushed up the long incline carefully following the convoy's vague tire tracks. Through turns and dips, they clawed up the mount until they entered another small town. The hamlet was alive. Shards of light broke from a few houses and the smell of burning wood wafted through the air.

Here the convoy stood attempting to breach yet another new administrative barrier. Children ran around calling, "Hello. Hey yoo! Goomy goomy!"

Local inhabitants peered from windows and balconies at the rare sight lining their street.

Without warning, the procession lurched ahead and down a long hill. To keep control, the heavy UN trucks stayed in first-gear crawling even slower than on the ascent. It took an anxious eternity to reach the bottom of what was little over a six kilometre decent.

A dark hulking industrial complex rested at the slope's foot. The caravan pulled into the facility and peeled into a large parking area. Mik continued along the facility's perimeter looking for a suitable place to halt. He eventually came upon a cluster of prefabs with four armoured UNHCR Land Rovers at the side. Mik's headlights caught a handful of civilians standing in the doorway of a lantern-lit container.

One rushed forward waving. He slapped Mik's car door and then ran up to Justin's cab. "Well done! Well done in deed!" he called reaching up to shake Justin's hand.

"The local hospitals were getting desperate. You're just in time," he announced excitedly. "Hi, Isaac Jaco, UNHCR field rep down here. We really didn't think anyone would make it past Abdić."

After parking beside the UNHCR vehicles, Mik and Laura disappeared into the compound searching for accommodation. Justin removed his body armour and reached beneath its rear flap. Relishing his success as a smuggler, Justin slid the passport from its hiding place and transferred it to his breast pocket. He then composed a Capsat message confirming the team's safe arrival in Ćoralići at 2300 hours, January 5, 1995.

Stretching and relaxing to a truck-side cigarette, Justin awaited his colleagues' return. The base teemed with activity guided by dozens of flashlights, lanterns and headlights. Soldiers scurried in all directions and trucks roared into offloading areas. Tanker trucks circled past and engineers fought to restart a long row of diesel generators.

A lone Bangladeshi approached Justin grasping a large aluminum pot. The soldier timidly held up a steaming mug in offering.

Startled, Justin took the cup and swallowed a mouthful of the most fragrant tea he would ever taste.

"Thank you," he murmured as the soldier waited patiently for the teacup.

Smiling, the soldier whispered, "*Asalaam wailaikhum*."

Justin finally allowed himself to believe he had arrived.

Chapter 15

Awaking from the deepest slumber, Justin needed a few moments to regain his bearings. Large diesel generators hummed outside. Unfortunately, the room's lone electric radiator had done little to warm the frozen air.

Aside from the aid workers' air mattresses and sleeping bags, the only other furnishings in the stark aluminum container were a cot frame, an empty metal locker and an intravenous drip stand. A strip of tape with "Isolation Ward" scrawled across it, stuck to the door.

Mik's sleeping bag already lay empty. The container door soon opened and he entered rubbing a towel over his wet curls.

"Morning," Mik greeted Justin, "They actually have hot showers in this place."

Not needing further prompting, Justin pulled on his T-shirt, jeans and boots. He wove through sandbagged passages to a prefab outfitted with heated toilet stalls and washing facilities.

After a long celebratory shower, Justin returned to the isolation ward where Mik and Laura were already making breakfast. Canned pork and beans sizzled atop a pile of sandbags outside the container's entrance.

As the tablet stove's flame danced beneath the bubbling army ration, a concerned Bangladeshi corporal approached. "What are you doing?" he asked pointing to meal.

"Please, you must have breakfast with the officers. Please come," he beckoned.

The trio followed the corporal past other sandbagged prefabs and piles of cement pipes and sewer fixtures.

In the parking area, a section of Bengalis stood in rank. Justin smiled to the troops and greeted, "Hi."

All faces remained stern, staring straight ahead.

Mik called, "*Asalaam wailaikhum.*"

The troops broke into a collective toothy smile and clamoured to respond, "W*ailaikhum asalaam!*"

"Where are you from?" the corporal asked Laura.

"Winnipeg."

"What is that?"

"It's in Canada," Laura replied.

"Canada! Do you know our base commander? He is from Canada. His name is Colonel Lem-ee-ucks. He is a very good man."

"What's his name?" Laura pried.

"Lem-ee-ucks. A very very good man indeed."

They passed trucks being unloaded into the compound's warehouse. Both of the convoy's lead Toyotas were parked to the side. Apparently, not all of the mesmerising tracer rounds from the previous night had passed harmlessly overhead. Some had found one of the vehicles and shred its hood like a knife-wielding psycho.

The corporal halted at the door to the compound's main two-story building. "Please, this is the Officers' Mess. Please enter."

Timidly poking their heads in, the trio found Isaac Jaco at a nearby table.

"Good morning," he waved, "Come on in."

An orderly raced across the room calling, "Yes please? Coffee, tea, breakfast?"

"Thanks. Coffee and breakfast please," Laura replied.

The orderly smiled shyly and disappeared.

Nodding to the table's other occupants, Jaco began, "May I present the base commander, Colonel Lemieux, and the civil affairs officer, Commander Winston."

"Gentlemen, this trio is with MOO. They actually made it past Abdić in last night's convoy," Jaco explained.

The colonel, a greying man with a politician's jovial expression, smiled. "Outstanding. With the increased fighting and shelling of late, the hospitals have been dealing with vastly elevated numbers of casualties. They are definitely in need of your supplies."

A hulking moustachioed Canadian soldier approached the table cradling a compact assault rifle. Bedecked in full combat webbing with a large fighting knife strapped to his chest and a 9 mm automatic in a shoulder holster, he came to attention snapping, "Sir, your vehicle is ready and waiting."

"Very good." The colonel rose clutching his blue beret.

"It's been good talking to you. I hope we can meet again," the base commander said as he left the auditorium. In the doorway, a second squat soldier, with wool hat and wire spectacles, waited with his assault rifle at the ready.

Leaning forward, Commander Winston announced, "I guess I better get going too. I've got a meeting with my Fifth Corps counterpart. Should be a long day."

The orderly arrived with a tray of coffee, corn flakes and boiled eggs.

In animated bursts, Jaco explained, "The Serb blockade of the Pocket is really beginning to pay off. This is exactly like warfare in the Middle Ages. The UNHCR needs to do something dramatic soon or it will just be standing by helplessly – watching people starve and freeze to death.

"The food situation is terrible. Thanks to you know who in the North, we've had only a few convoys get through. In December, three made it in and we distributed about 280 Tonnes of basic food to a population of 160,000.

"Before that we had no convoys arrive since October. And there wasn't a good harvest this year. It's not like they had lots of seed and fertiliser to plant in the first place. They can barely even distribute what they did grow because there's no fuel.

"When flour is available, it sells for 10 Deutsche Marks a kilo. Cooking oil is up to 45 Marks a litre. And life's biggest commodity, cigarettes, go for 20 Marks a pack – sometimes as much as 30 for Marlboros. People have even been smoking what they call Green Ronhills."

"What's that?" Laura queried.

"Grass," Isaac explained. "And not marijuana…what cows eat."

"I've been given orders to hoard the little diesel we have for our UNHCR cars," he continued bitterly. "I'm told that if I distribute it to the locals, I could jeopardise my impartiality. The fuel will only be misused – helping the army or making the Mafia stronger. But as I sit here with Jerry Cans of fuel, I commit a crime of complicity against each patient who doesn't get to hospital when there's no ambulance!

"Water and electricity are almost non-existent. The Serbs captured most of pumping stations south of Bihać town. They prioritise the little available electricity for the hospitals. But that's hardly anything. For heating, they've been using wood. They can't use generators because they need diesel.

"ICRC has plans to work on repairing the water supply. Unfortunately, they have yet to get their supplies past Abdić. We're really hoping they get through this week. Blocking humanitarian aid is a crime against humanity…"

Adding an advisory footnote, Isaac stated slowly, "I do not know how soon you'll be able to get back out of here safely. Look how long it took you to get in…just so you know, the UNPROFOR convoy finishes unloading today and will likely head back to Zagreb early afternoon the next day."

While Mik and Laura went to stow their overnight kit and remove the vehicles' snow chains, Justin dropped by the UNMO's office. Next to the UNHCR office, Justin passed a small covered alcove filled with a vast collection of shrapnel, shell casings, rocket fins and even a cluster-bomb cover. Peering through the adjacent prefab door, Justin found a hefty New Zealand Air Force officer chatting over a Turkish coffee with his interpreter.

"Can I help you?" he asked Justin.

"I arrived with the convoy last night and need to make a delivery down in Bihać. I was wondering what the safest route was," Justin explained.

"There are two main routes. One a little better than the other," he explained twisting the waxed tips of his pointed moustache. "You definitely don't want to take the road that goes south parallel to Krajina; it's pretty volatile. There the Serbs have pushed eastward into the Pocket and are four to five clicks from the road...closer to Bihać town they're within two clicks. By squeezing the south, the RSK forces split Dudaković's Fifth Corps and helps Abdić's army in the north. Chances are pretty good you'll get shot on that road."

"What's the other route?" Justin asked turning to the office wall map for guidance.

"On the eastern side of the Pocket, the Bosnian Serbs have pressed right up to the Una River. They've even crossed the river near Pištaline. There the front is rather active and maybe only three clicks from the town," the Kiwi continued. "South of there the front is fairly static until you hit Bekovica...about where the Cazin road bisects the Una and heads south to Bihać. There the front is relatively active but for now, the Fifth Corps still holds the east bank, the road and train tracks. That doesn't mean the Serbs can't shell the road. I'd say this is the safer way to take though..."

Justin was about to comment when the interpreter interrupted, "Did you travel in with Gretel?"

"Yes, but she was not allowed past VK. They said she was a traitor," Justin replied.

"Everyone's a traitor to someone here..." the interpreter shrugged.

"Are you Dragan?" Justin inquired.

"Yes."

"Gretel mentioned you ..."

"You smoke?" Dragan asked stepping out the prefab door.

Taking the hint, Justin nodded, called thanks to the UNMO and followed Dragan outside.

In the war trinket foyer, they lit up.

"Gretel asked me to pass on some mail and rent for the office," Justin explained producing a small stack of envelopes.

Glancing around, he reached into his breast pocket and handed the diminutive and priceless pamphlet to Dragan. "She also asked me to give you this," Justin added as he saw chunks smash from the surrounding walls of ignorance.

Unflustered, Dragan accepted the document and placed it in his own pocket. "Thank you, I will put this in a very very safe place," he said quietly. His words barely hinted at the document's enormity and betrayed even less adulation. Justin had to remind himself that it was actions that remained paramount not the ensuing fanfare.

Returning to the isolation container, Justin found Mik and Laura engaged in heated discussion. At the core was disagreement over how long they should stay in the region. Mik wanted to perform a thorough investigation of the local situation before leaving – no matter how long it took. Laura worried that MOO would be of help to no one if the trio were stranded in the Pocket for any extended period. Hijacking the argument, Justin threw his lot with Laura. Aware that they had no time to get into a full debate, the aid workers agreed to make their deliveries in Cazin and Bihać immediately and then review events at day's end.

With the morning sun fighting through patches in the cloud cover the frozen ground began to loosen. With the vehicles free of snow chains, the trio rolled through the base gates and headed south on the main road to Cazin.

As Justin rumbled along, the melting snow crunched triumphantly beneath his truck's confident wheels. From his elevated vantage, everything was so clear. They approached Cazin victorious. They had finally prevailed over all the forces that had sought failure.

From farmyards and driveways, children ran up to the road cheering enthusiastically. Clusters jumped and jigged playfully as the two white vehicles raced past.

A father holding a toddler waved and whispered in his child's ear – one soul who would grow up recalling his Dad's faded tale of the day someone outside actually cared. The value of the passing vehicles was apparent to all. No suspicions were borne. The motives of the vehicles' occupants were universally appreciated.

Justin, Mik and Laura had burrowed into the planet's most isolated dead-end. History and the world watched helplessly from the side. The trio were inside and doing a little. Yes, they were inside!

Justin had it all figured out. It was all so clear.

Cresting a rise on Cazin's outskirts, yet another boy and girl waved from their yard fence. Justin coasted into town as a good-intentioned conqueror that had breached the evildoers' barriers. It would not get any better that this. He had history by the throat.

Today, Cazin sat on the perverse pedestal of the world's attention. To strangers, it was a place in need of pity and feigned indignation – a far abstraction where wretched people starved. Yet sweeping before Justin was the truth in all its sharp beauty – a view afforded only to a most precious few and a privilege of such delicacy, most would never realise it existed.

This was exactly what he had wanted all along. This was what had ached in his Canadian complacency.

He felt no shame, seeing the truth and entering its misery. He was a bit more than just a witness; he was doing something and making his own contribution. It was all worth it. The troubles and risks endured were so completely minimal. He would have paid far more if required.

Regardless of future successes his life may bear, Justin knew this moment of youthful naiveté would always stand as his greatest achievement. In the solace of a lonely café, the tedium of a crowded bus, the banality of office meetings, this moment was the gem he could always unwrap to caress and savour with the purest pleasure. It was his deed, his war.

The aid workers found the hospital on a steep slope in the town centre. Entering the single story facility, they followed a hall around its courtyard. They passed a packed waiting area and headed down a passage marked "*Recepcija*." On the wall hung a panoramic photo of the joyous crowd at the opening ceremony to the 1984 Sarajevo Olympics.

At the hall's end, the trio peered into a secretarial office. A slender woman sat aimlessly behind a barren desk. Seeing the aid workers, she grimaced with instant relief.

"We have been waiting for so long for you," she pronounced before the trio could introduce themselves.

Transfixed, Justin stared at the face of the desperate voice he already knew from the telephone. Her eyes gave clues to her real age but the wrinkles and bags beneath overwhelmed the truth. She had fought to maintain an attractive air through dress and cosmetics. But it was no match for the circumstances that forced her to age with unfair acceleration.

"My name is Elmira," she continued. "I am the director's receptionist. The director, Doctor Marović, is in the next room."

Elmira brought the group through a leather-covered door to the adjacent office. At the head of a long glass-covered meeting table sat a man with youthful looks. His straight dusty hair cropped on the sides and long at the back, bore a misguided attempt at male fashion.

He sat before a glass cabinet crammed with medical tomes and sports trophies. As he looked up from a stack of papers, the receptionist explained, "*Direktor. Medicinska Pomoć.* MOO."

The director said nothing. He stared blankly at the space occupied by the newcomers.

Elmira motioned to the trio, "Please. Please sit."

She took a seat facing the group.

Silence ensued.

Awkwardly, Justin fumbled through his folder, produced the packing list and placed it before the director.

The director lit a Marlboro and took a thoroughly soulful pull. He exhaled with even greater exorcism. In Bosnian, he spoke quietly to Elmira.

Translating she explained, "The situation is very difficult here. This facility was only a *Dom Zdravlja* before and because of the fighting was promoted to hospital. In the past month, we treated over 400 patients each week. Everything has run out.

"Even the director was loosing hope. He is not allowed to loose hope. He is the only one."

Dr. Marović laboured to pick up the packing list and peer at its contents. He continued talking quietly.

While he paused to take a drag of his smoke, Elmira translated. "The director's brother was shot in the back by a fragmenting bullet. It was very bad; there was nothing to treat him properly. But now, the director thinks there is a small chance for his brother and others."

Looking up at the trio, the director blinked eyes about to glisten. He swallowed and, in his best English said, "Thank you."

Every difficulty and danger evaporated deeper into Justin's memory. There really had been no obstacles getting to Cazin. Nothing compared to what the others faced.

While the director resumed his scrutiny of the packing list, a short, elderly man entered the room and nodded to Justin, Mik and Laura.

"This is the Chief Pharmacist," Elmira explained.

The pharmacist joined Dr. Marović and, as they progressed through the list, their spirits grew.

Standing up, Elmira announced, "I must make coffee."

The director lit another cigarette and offered his pack to Justin and Mik. As he continued surveying the list, the pharmacist looked up anxiously.

"OK?" Laura inquired.

"*Da, Da*," the pharmacist replied. "Diazepam *dobro*...very good. Mannitol...bring plus Mannitol."

Justin glanced questioningly at Laura.

"To reduce swelling from head injuries," she explained.

So much dehumanising puss oozed from the war's apologists and commentators. They spat terms so empty, so utterly meaningless, that they were moral insults to the victims within and the witnesses without – safe areas, beleaguered enclaves, ethnic cleansing, morass of warring factions, territorial integrity, tactical disadvantage, conditions conductive to security, militarily advantageous encirclement. On and on the pompous taunts came. But these were nothing more than lands where the most common ailment was brain swelling; where life's reciprocal purpose was inflicting swollen heads on others.

The pharmacist's calm demeanour alarmed Justin. How could a man act so placidly facing hundreds of shattered patients in an institution built for no more than 80? So many head wounds in such overwhelmed conditions were supposed to incite sheer panic. Yet, in Cazin, head wounds were as routine as ankle sprains.

And if it was not Mannitol, it was Diazepam. If they managed to reduce the swelling, then the doctors doped up the patients with painkillers. It was all they could do until the fighting ended and the new drug-induced lunacy of peace became the norm. That day however, was too far off for even the most optimistic to fathom.

Elmira returned proudly balancing a steaming copper coffee set. With great care and ceremony, she poured each cup from a separate copper pot. All eyes locked reverently on the ritual.

Expectantly, Elmira watched the guests take their first sip of her coffee.

"The coffee is good no?" she queried without awaiting comment. "It is the best in Bosnia. Much better than in Croatia."

"Ah, delicious," Laura remarked.

"Yes, this is excellent." Justin concurred. For the sake of discussion, he added, "I've had so much good coffee in the former Yugoslavia."

Frowning, Elmira dismissed such suggestion, "Maybe for you the coffee is good in those other places. But ours is still the best."

"I could drink this all day," Mik chimed.

"But of course," Elmira continued. "We make it properly here because the Ottomans taught us. Even Chetniks in Krajina will tell you this. And Croats cannot possibly know the good coffee."

Pausing and shaking her head smugly she added, "You see they do not boil the coffee and sugar together. They drink their coffee like Czechs and Slovenes…we all know how bad that is…"

The pharmacist and director snickered. Justin nodded pretending to understand the joke.

The director's face faded back to seriousness and Elmira resumed translating matters concerning his hospital. "As you know, the situation is hard. We have almost no medicines and diesel is finished. Our ambulances cannot run anymore and we are using horse wagons to bring people to hospital.

"Here is not the biggest hospital but it is the most central. Refugees and wounded come to Cazin from everywhere. The hospital is totally full. We have 120 patients sleeping here. Most are in the corridor. There are 35 more sleeping in a kindergarten. Most patients are sent home the same day."

The director eyed Laura scribbling notes and, through Elmira, said, "If you do not believe me, you can check our register…I wish I was exaggerating."

Laura nodded, "Sadly, I believe you."

Elmira continued translating, "We have two surgeons making 20 surgeries in a day. We do not have enough medical staff for our needs. We have taken medical students who did not finish school. We give them training here to work as nursing assistants."

Smirking, she added, "Here they get a better practical education.

"Also we are washing old gloves and bandages two or three times. But now we do not have even detergent anymore. Bed sheets and clothes cannot be washed either.

"Our storeroom is almost empty. What you brought will save many lives but will not last long."

Laura explained, "It is our intention to continue bringing medicine to your hospital for as long as possible."

Nodding, Elmira continued, "Food is also a very big problem. The UNHCR cannot enter for a long time. Before, we collected food donations from local families so we could feed the patients. But now nobody has any food anywhere."

Standing up, the director donned a blue wool cape and motioned the group to follow on a tour of the facility. Trailing his flowing robe, the procession was led along generally clean corridors. Large gashes gaped from dented walls and UNHCR plastic sheeting patched smashed windows. Wounded men slept on cots and mattresses in any available hallway space.

Yet, for all the valiant efforts at tidiness, the odour of exhausted and wounded humanity still lingered. Ensuring it would not fade from memory, the odour bit deeper at Justin's core. It clutched desperately to remind him always – never forget the smell of the maimed.

Periodically the director stopped to explain details and conditions. He was eager to reveal how tirelessly his facility worked under strained conditions. With each explanation, his pride grew.

The first room – likely intended for no more than three patients - bore at least 15 wounded. The chamber was little more than a pile of quiet resignation – missing limbs, swollen heads, disfigured faces and collapsed torsos consumed the portrait.

Ward after ward, the director described the ailments suffered by each room's occupants. Pulling blankets from prostrate patients, Dr. Marović detailed the actions taken to address their wounds. At the same time, he also managed to offer each patient a moment's undivided attention – giving words of support and querying how they were faring.

Man upon man lay helpless beneath sections of missing flesh, jagged lacerations threatening testicles, bruises consuming more tissue than available. The doctor pointed to fresh amputations bandaged with stale dressings and sucking chest wounds patched with plastic bags. Throughout, Laura took notes professionally. She was the only one seemingly detached enough to do so.

What the hell was Justin doing here? He was no doctor. This land's heroic marching youth had just awoken as stars in an international freak show. Was turning a self-righteous head worse though? That is what the world was doing. Justin just nodded and whispered thanks to those he intruded upon; he did not know what else to offer.

An elderly patient mumbled inquiringly toward the visitors.

Trying to transmit a morsel of optimism Marović explained, "*Medicinska Pomoć.*" The old man smiled weakly and turned his head to resume his desperate resting.

Stumps attached to men no older than Justin kept reaching and pointing at him. Where was their promised glory? Somebody had lied to them all. Were there any causes worth a young man's arm? Justin could think of none. They had all been screwed. In the end, we would all be too if we allowed it. Our countries, our communities, our neighbours, our religions, our heroes, our gods – all would not flinch at screwing us if ever expedient. The good causes were few and they certainly were not the ones our leaders urged.

Justin's wellbeing brought throbbing embarrassment. Little more than a blink of fate set him apart from the wounded. Men, supposed to be in their most confident epoch, now lay in shame and confusion – their adventures forever over. Their futures obscured. Their youth robbed so blatantly by loud nobodies.

Justin finally made a retreat. Mik was right behind him.

Finding a section of corridor free of sleeping patients, Mik leaned against the wall and lit a cigarette. He reached into his jacket and handed Justin a second crooked smoke.

Justin had no words to utter and just stared stupidly at Mik.

Staring back blankly, Mik managed to mutter, "War" and then peered aimlessly at his feet.

This was war. This was truth. Pure truth extracted at the vilest cost. A truth clear only to the maimed and those who loved them.

How Justin wished others – all others – could see this, for but one fleeting instant. He wished it upon those in living rooms pronouncing sweeping dismissals and those at conference tables passing complacent judgement bathed in convenient oversimplification. The leaders, the sheep, the preachers, the followers – this was what came from their all-knowing diarrhoea. There were no simple solutions, just dismembered youth.

The remainder of the procession emerged a long moment later and continued toward the next ward. A young man, with tired exasperation etched in his brow, toiled along the corridor trying to master new crutches. Marović broke from his tour to greet the patient with a warm smile and strong hug.

Grabbing the youth's upper arm, the doctor inquired, "How are you doing?"

The boy shrugged.

The doctor shifted on his heel to transmit a deep stare - an injection of hope and perseverance - and then patted him on the back.

The attention appeared to improve the young man's spirit and he bravely continued on the wooden props replacing his missing leg. Compassion seemed to be the only commodity Dr. Marović still had in any abundance.

The tour became a blur of unending laceration interjected with the director's optimism and pride. The group followed the director through every room around the facility's courtyard. They viewed the empty pharmacy, the full emergency room and the exhausted surgery theatre that overflowed into an adjacent hallway.

The same tantalising truth that had once been such an invigorating prospect began to weigh heavy. The director winked and beckoned the group to enter one last room. In it, nurses were washing and bundling a newborn while his mother lay dazed on a nearby bench.

As Mik, Justin and the pharmacist went to unload the cargo, Laura stayed to review the facility's medical records and talk to the surgeons. Justin parked his truck by a garage at the compound's edge and drew an instant mob of children crying "Hello, Goomy, Goomy!"

Hopping from his cab and into the clutches of the excited kids, Justin called, "OK. OK. Wait a second." Pointing to the back of the truck, he added, "You guys help me first. OK?"

By the time Justin reached the rear flap, the kids were already fighting to offload the cargo.

As Justin hacked and tugged at the shrink-wrap protecting the tall pallets, the pharmacist asked to keep the disposable plastic sheets. He had already thought of countless uses for the wrap.

Justin handed the cargo down and the kids raced it into the storage garage. As Mik moved forward to help, the kids brushed him aside. The Cazin supplies were unloaded in mere minutes. The pharmacist pointed to the empty pallets that remained; their wooden slats represented yet another priceless commodity in this besieged land.

As Justin passed the pallets down, the children demanded fair payment for their services. Engulfed, he and Mik fought a path back to the truck's cab. They pried as many candies as possible from their army rations. Small hands immediately grabbed at the caramels and chocolate bars. The pair then resorted to tearing open the ration boxes and just handing over whatever was inside – canned macaroni, powdered milk and instant coffee. To the kids' unquenched pleas, Mik and Justin locked the vehicle and retreated.

At the main building, Justin dropped off a Styrofoam cooler box of sensitive meds in the pharmacy. Returning to the Landcruiser, he found both of his colleagues standing beside the vehicle.

Leaning to put the cooler back in the Toyota, Justin bumped against two empty jerry cans.

"Hey, weren't these Jerry's full this morning?" he called out.

Laura grinned, "I know nothing...must have gone to a good cause."

"I hope so, there aren't many left these days..."

Chapter 16

From Cazin, the trio crossed a snowy plateau on top of the world. Mothers and children walked along tire tracks left on the white road. Small clusters of young men in fatigues marched with Kalashnikovs and rucksacks slung. They looked up at the passing white vehicles. Some even waved.

An old fortress with tiled spires loomed at the plateau's eastern edge. Serb shells, from across the valley, had damaged most of its old cupolas. Emblazoned on the last undamaged steeple was the Bosnian coat of arms. The aid workers passed the castle and inching down a steep winding slope. The majestic curtain that unfurled beyond beset Justin. Bosnia's mountains, her invincible defenders, overwhelmed all senses and stood in far greater defiance than any painted heraldry.

Squelching all momentum, Justin reined his truck into lowest gear. Tugged by the view at every turn, it was increasingly difficult to concentrate on the unfamiliar icy road. Each hairpin gave Justin an ever so fleeting glimpse at the tantalising peaks.

Bosnia was so beautiful. Her pinnacles rose accentuated by shadows, snowcaps, mists, clouds and haze. Each august row was backed by greater grandeur beyond – eternal summits whose aspect begged the purest love.

Shafts of light pierced the clouds to illuminate portions of land below. The heavenly spotlights brought Justin deeper warmth and amour. Long simmering yet unconscious feelings now manifested with unquestionable clarity and grasped at his very core. Justin doubted few outside this realm could understand such sensation. Similar emotions might well have awoken in his colleagues – forever held in common yet impossible to explain.

At the valley's foot, they passed a vast hotel resort – its tennis courts empty and unwanted. Spanning yet another vein that slashed so many universes, the trio crossed the Una River.

The Bosnian Serbs were not supposed to control this section of the river. It was unclear though, how much of the adjacent hills were actually in Fifth Corps possession and how much of the road remained vulnerable to shelling.

Mik, Laura and Justin strapped on their body armour and sped along the riverside. Despite the foreigner's zealousness, locals with no protection still walked along the route – most halted to gaze at the passing rarity. They were really the best experts on military activity.

Menacing hills and crags towered above the road's only vehicles. Had Justin's directions to the Kiwi UNMO been clear enough? Had they discussed the same route? Which heights squinted down at the tantalising white target through Serb crosshairs?

The road meandered beside a rusting railway track that disappeared periodically into jagged tunnels. In the ravine below, the Una churned and smashed through rapids with unadulterated force. Tranquil snow-padded pasture and hilly forest rose from the far banks. Pristine rock and wood blended without dispute. Scattered farmhouses cowered under timber lean-tos that offered small shield from the south and east. Wood, invaluable as fuel, had become more vital as blast protection.

Amidst the morass of their elders' idiocy, kids still ran out of passing homes waving and cheering.

On the outskirts of Bihać town, the trio entered an exaggerated expanse of dark factories, warehouses and apartments lingering in cold socialist gregariousness. From their maps, the trio knew the hospital rested precariously at the southern edge of a town on the southern edge of a siege. Nearing Bihać's heart, its older narrower streets began to bear more individuality and more humanity.

Led astray by the lack of street signs, Mik was forced to stop periodically and lean out his heavy door asking, *"Bolnica? Bolnica?"*

All responded with vague waves southward.

Backtracking and turning and reversing and u-turning, the newcomers began passing women clutching bundled children and men with arms in slings and legs held together by metal rods.

Staying the course, the aid workers pulled into the quiet treed compound of a multi-building complex. A strange calm emanated from the grounds. Amongst the stumps of trunks hacked for fuel and the surviving trees, a few people milled – some smoked, others just lingered and one collected litter.

In the yard, an orderly pointed the newcomers to a damaged single-story wing stating, *"Direktor."* According to the UN and news reports, the hills resting a few hundred metres beyond the hospital were in Bosnian Serb Army hands. Attempting to stay out of more Serb gun sights, Mik and Justin parked as close to the building as possible. In the end though, safety really remained just as much fluke as common sense.

Exploring the building's murky, rubble-strewn passages, the trio suspected they had been misinformed. However, at the darkest end of the main corridor, a tall sinister man emerged from what must have been the only functioning office.

Justin slowly recognised the vaguely familiar sunken face. It was the hospital director who a manic journalist had interviewed during the past manic weeks. Sadly, television had conspired against the director; he now looked worse than he had on Sky News.

"*Gospodine Direktor*," Justin greeted in his best bastardised Bosnian. "*Ja sam Medesinki Pomoc.* MOO."

With a faint smile, the director held out an arm and guided the visitors into his office. From the frozen unlit hallway, they were welcomed by the pleasant blast of wood-fuelled heat on their faces. A haphazardly installed iron stove crackled in the corner with complete friendliness.

A bulky desk, with three telephones and a mobile unit, consumed the room's wood-panelled southern wall. Behind, a large white Bosnian flag draped from a flagstaff.

A mounted mortar shell, with the inscription "*Armija R BiH – V Korpus*" rested proudly on a huge conference table.

The director ushered the guests to the meeting table. He offered coffee and then, through waving, clapping and fluttering, conveyed his narrow English ability.

Taking a seat behind his desk, the director tried to make a phone call. His initial attempts were unsuccessful and he repeatedly bashed the phone receiver against its base. When he did connect, he had to yell into the handset.

Replacing it calmly, he smiled to his guests. Pausing, he held up a forefinger and repeated, "Ah, *nema* English…Moment."

On a different phone, he resumed the violent calling process.

A few minutes later, an elderly secretary brought coffee and the four sat in silent enjoyment of the warm panacea.

As the group wondered how they would ever communicate, a young woman, not over 20, entered the room. She was elegantly kept in a light blazer, wore simple makeup and had unbleached hair. Mik and Justin viewed her with identical fascinated surprise.

"Hello. I am Alemka. I am here to help you," she explained with youthful enthusiasm.

As Mik and Justin continued smiling dumbly, the director began speaking to Alemka in Bosnian.

Pointing to her chest, Alemka translated, "The director, Dr. Balic, welcomes you but says you will not need these in his hospital." The trio glanced at the body armour that remained in place equally for warmth and confidence.

Smiling proudly, the director continued speaking and pointed to a savage hole that had splintered at head level behind his desk.

Alemka translated, "Dr. Balic says a Serb shell hit the wall one week ago when he was giving an interview to a journalist from Sky News."

The newcomers nodded. Far from reassured, they politely removed their Kevlar vests.

As Laura began describing the contents of their delivery, the director's mobile phone rang. Breaking away, he yelled once more into the receiver.

Returning to his guests, Dr. Balic explained that his hospital had an 800-bed capacity but claimed there were currently over 1200 patients in his care. He expressed deep gratitude that MOO had finally arrived. He said that nobody had helped them; the UNHCR had ignored all their requests and the International Red Cross had not delivered a single bandage in months. He added that cases of malnutrition were imminent if significant amounts of food were not delivered and distributed soon.

As the interview dragged along, the director glanced at his watch and asked the group to be his guest for a large hot lunch in the hospital canteen.

Laura quickly declined and asked if she could have a tour of the facility instead.

Hesitantly, the director agreed but said it would have to be quick, as he was very busy.

Balic guided the group to a large chamber at the building's opposite end. Inside, natural light spread randomly across a small group of hunched orderlies. Shovelling and sifting through rubble, ice, and glass, the workers occasionally plucked at salvageable items.

Dr. Balic spoke to Alemka in a low brittle tone.

"The hospital was shelled by the Serbs this morning," Alemka translated as her wood-fuelled rosy cheeks turned pale. "This room was hit directly."

As the aid workers stood mesmerised, trying to comprehend the mess before them, none noticed Alemka abruptly flee the room.

Justin's eyes followed the contours of the ceiling's holes where the blast had entered. Metal bars jutted downward severed and bent. Concrete gashes chiselled in beautiful jagged angles. Light shafts pierced through the roof casting warmth on the wall's fissures and flower impressions. Purplish and red shadows splashed across the coarse surface. What force could do these things? Such effort would take human hands ages to accomplish.

Thankfully, Justin could find no signs of casualties in the room; the hospital had been lucky. Justin caught a whiff of an appealing aroma emanating from the cold air and frozen dirt. It massaged hunger pangs deep in his empty stomach. His conscience had been an instant too slow though and nausea overwhelmed him.

An orderly pried a running shoe from the tangled slop of brick, sheet metal and bedding. Justin strained to focus on the article and, as he did, he found a bloody slimy ankle attached. What vile creature found cooked human flesh appetising?

A co-worker extracted a mess of dark string dangling from a flattened face. Human faces were not supposed to do that – this mask had to be part of some grotesque hoax. And where was the skull that provided its human traits?

With his eyes cruelly adjusted to the lighting, Justin distinguished a soft mass to his side. Some of it was recognisable as human. But which part? What the fuck did something like this? What power changed people into such unrecognisable monsters?

A pasty sickly man lay a little farther away. The shredded scraps of his hospital gown hung open. Parts of swollen scrotum protruded from his bloody briefs. The murder of a hospitalised man had not been enough; he had been condemned to vicious humiliation as well.

A panicked glance to another corner confirmed that this force did not discriminate. It had ripped an entire set of intestines from a woman's once fertile abdomen and dumped them in a pile beside her.

A step away, the same force had decapitated a man but had not touched his best Sunday suit. The red and grey mush bubbling from his neck was the only hint of his head. An entire vault of personality and its dearest dreams had evaporated somewhere in this room.

The human mind was not meant to absorb such perversity. Dehumanising and debasing, smashing skulls and smearing entrails – that was the bomber's real design.

Alemka re-entered the chamber that had triggered some deep personal horror. "I'm sorry," she croaked to Justin. Attempting to restore the Herculean composure that was virtually a national trait, she took a sobbing breath. "Last week, my two brothers were killed by mortar bombs in Velika Kladuša."

Justin reeled. "I'm Sorry"? Or, "Now, now, don't worry"? Or, "It'll be OK"? How the hell do you respond? Once again, the only decent thing to do was swallow and just look stupid.

Impatiently, the director marched the group over to the hospital's cavernous main building. Inside, they found virtually no patients sleeping in the hallways; almost all were squeezed into wards. Bihać hospital had four times as many patients as Cazin yet the expansive building seemed less crowded. Although Laura inquired repeatedly, she was unable to clarify how many of Dr. Balic's 1200 stated cases were actually in-patients and how many were treated and sent home the same day.

On the upper floors, the south-facing wards contained only mounds of plaster chunks and glass shards. Poking his head through a splintered doorframe, the director held up a finger of warning. Pointing to the paneless windows, he hissed, "*Snajper.*"

Dr. Balic ushered the group downstairs to lower north-facing environs. Passing through improvised basement operating theatres, he grew increasingly edgy and reticent to Laura's continued queries.

Climbing a flight of stairs, Justin glanced through a storeroom door left ajar. He caught a glimpse of UNICEF and WHO health kits and a few pallets bearing red crosses.

The agitated director urged the trio to keep following him.

The place was under siege but the director was playing games. What was he hoping to gain? The hospital's stores were far from abundant. Even daily medical deliveries would not address present needs. Yet, things did not jive. Why all the duplicity and ambiguity? As much as the aid workers tried to avoid it, they had become fixtures of Bosnia and her war. And in such acceptance, all now deemed them worthy of deceit and manipulation.

Regardless of the director's nebulosity, the hospital still needed help. Holes in buildings and shattered humanity stood as far clearer illustration than any of the doctor's embellishments.

Escorting the aid workers to the parking lot, the director shook their hands and, through Alemka, stated tersely, "I thank you for your assistance. As you can see, we are in very great need. I must go now. I am expecting a very important meeting with Colonel Lemieux. You can unload your cargo on the other side of this building."

He twitched his heals and bowed his head slightly in an oddly servile manner. In English, he added, "Thank you. Good bye," and disappeared into his building.

The trio lingered in the parking area and asked Alemka if she was willing to translate for the remainder of the day. A white UNPROFOR Iltis jeep raced up to the building and the large moustachioed Canadian soldier leapt from the passenger seat in full battle mufti. He wore Wayfarers, a radio earpiece and a microphone that choked his throat. Hunching beside the front wheel-well, he aimed his assault rifle and scanned the surroundings.

A few moments passed before he rose tensely and beckoned, "OK Colonel. All clear."

Glancing at the captivated MOO team, the soldier barked, "Hey, how you guys doin?"

The colonel emerged from the vehicle smiling and approached the group. "Good to see you again," he called sounding more the politician than soldier. "So you've already seen the good director? Outstanding. Well, keep up the good work."

As the colonel walked to the building, his bodyguard followed muttering into his choker. With each robotic step, the soldier trained his weapon on a new target. At the entrance he hunched, rifle at the ready, still muttering.

On the hospital's south side, Justin backed his truck up to a doorway filled with waiting orderlies and nurses. Like the empty wards upstairs, the facility's receiving area sat exposed to the Bosnian Serb Army. The Serb-held hills loomed to Justin's left – just beyond a parking lot and 300 metres of open plains. Conveniently high above, unseen NATO jets broke the silence while enforcing the no-fly zone.

The only defiance standing between the hospital and the Serbs was a BanBat armoured personnel carrier parked behind a wall of white sandbags at the parking lot's edge. In the ballsiest act of determination, two Bangladeshis with a rifle and a rusty APC stared down Europe's most battle hardened and ruthless army.

The hospital staff did not loiter. As soon as Justin opened the truck's tarp, they piled MOO's boxes onto a pair of bloodstained gurneys and rolled them to the storeroom.

Standing safely inside the doorway, one nurse turned to Laura and, half-joking asked, "Where are you going after Bihać?"

"Zagreb," Laura replied and immediately regretted uttering the name.

"I wish I could go back to Zagreb in your truck," the nurse said wistfully.

Knots wound in the aid workers' stomachs obscuring whatever light intent the comment may have had.

"I wish I could take you," Laura mumbled.

Justin swallowed and looked dumb yet again. He glanced at the NATO jets roaring above as they offered just as little help bringing these people to safety.

After unloading and sharing a smoke with the medical staff, Alemka directed the trio across town to the policlinic. Although MOO had nothing to deliver to the policlinic, Laura had read mention of the place in her predecessor's notes and wanted to learn more. From the truck's passenger seat, Alemka guided the group through the town's old core and shopping district. Almost every building bore scarred façades and shattered windows. Pointing to the neighbourhood's pervasive shelling damage, she explained. "We call this part of Bihać, 'Vukovar Street' because it is so badly destroyed."

Slashing through the town's centre, the Una swirled through frothing rapids and around forested islets. Once wooded parks flanked the riverbanks. The pleasant shaded summer meeting spaces stood barren and spread apart – the victim of desperate saws and hatchets.

Across the river, in the town's suburban southeastern corner, they drove up to an ostentatious glass and aluminum building. Sandwiched between a set of neo-socialist apartment towers, train tracks and a fuel depot's massive storage tanks, the policlinic bore the subtlety of a child's dabblings in futuristic architecture. Long scraps of aluminum siding and tarpaper dangled from the hulking dark residential blocks. Behind them, the usurped enemy hills stood as close as ever.

"This is a special part of town," Alemka explained. "These were new buildings built just before the war. The most comfortable and fashionable."

Entering the hypermodern vision, the group's footsteps echoed through the tiled foyer. The building bore a clinical lack of character and had none of the suffering of the Cazin or Bihać hospitals. The place was simply forgotten.

From the end of a long adjacent hallway, a round bald man rushed toward the group. Surprised at seeing visitors, he nervously demanded their business.

As Alemka explained, the man's demeanour turned welcoming and even jolly. He was, in fact, the policlinic's director. Eagerly, he pressed the group into a spartan office containing a smattering of bland aluminum furniture.

Still excited, the director sputtered about how few drugs and patients he had at his facility. The patients he did receive came from the surrounding neighbourhood. Owing to an almost total lack of drugs though, most cases went directly to the main hospital. Shrugging despairingly, he said the little medicine that did come to Bihać always wound up at that hospital.

Hoping to alleviate some strain from the main hospital, Laura offered to bring a few basic items in future deliveries. The director shook his head and frowned thankfully but he had heard many promises before.

When asked for a tour of the clinic, the director leapt to his feet and excitedly raced through its halls. He steered the group away from the main stairwell and took them up a narrow set on the north side. Shelling had long since blown out the opaque glass lining the main staircase. On the second floor, they passed through wide halls encased by tall panoramic windows. Biting winter wind funnelled between the neighbouring apartment towers and surged through the empty windows.

On an old table lay a stack of deposed Tito portraits – multiple framed poses and uniforms looking up through a film of dust and grime.

In spite of all the damage and piles of debris, the director remained fiercely proud of his facility and wished to show the group every cranny.

Stepping carefully on shards of littered glass, the director explained, through Alemka, "I worked for eight years building this clinic. It is my child. Only under the old socialist Yugoslavia could we build such places."

"When did you finish building?" Justin asked.

Recalling the date, he murmured, "1991," and trailed off, no longer wishing to exhume the zenith of his clinic's birth.

Departing, Laura again apologised for having nothing to offer the director.

He shrugged, "I am not the only hospital in need. But you have brought me hope."

The afternoon was getting on and the light becoming flat. Justin offered Alemka a lift home.

Reaffirming her availability for future translation work, she stated, "Next time you are in Bihać you can find me at the Hotel Lipovača. My uncle is the owner."

Heading down a main street, Justin dropped Alemka off at the hotel. He thanked her and paid 50 Marks for the day's help.

Struck by his rumbling stomach, Justin asked, "Hey, I'm getting really hungry. Does your hotel serve food?"

Shaking her head with a dismissive laugh, Alemka replied, "No. Not for a long time. But I think there is one restaurant on this road that does."

The trio continued along slowly, stopping periodically to peer at shop and café-fronts. None appeared open.

A familiar UN officer dashed out in front of the MOO vehicles. With a big dazed smile, Commander Winston waved to Mik.

"Food? You're looking for a restaurant?" he half-shouted glancing up and down the street. Hoping to conjure the answer, the commander continued, "Uh...I've been in that restaurant there for six hours with my Bosnian Army counterpart. I don't know about food. But they have tonnes of Slivo..."

"Do you need a ride?" Mik asked

"I'm OK. I left my car around here somewhere. Have you seen it?" the officer asked.

Mik shook his head.

"OK, well good luck. And stay away from the Slivo," the commander bid while attempting a salute that missed his temple.

A little farther, the trio found an establishment that appeared operational. Inside, the restaurant was busy but nobody was eating. All eyes were riveted to the TV set.

"Oh shit," Justin muttered. "Guess what's on..."

"Shhhhhhh!" he was instantly rebuked.

The aid workers looked for a free table as far from the TV as possible. Ignored by all, the newcomers soon succumbed to boredom and gazed at the spectacle of angst and affluence that united the Balkans every evening at five. When Santa Barbara's closing credits finally rolled, patrons uttered solutions to the complex dilemmas just witnessed. Some problems were easier to solve than others.

A young man emerged from the cacophony of soap operatic discourse. Spotting obvious foreigners, he asked in English, "How can I help you?"

Slightly embarrassed, Laura asked, "Do you have food?"

"Yes, of course. This is a restaurant," he replied dryly. "How many portions? Three?"

The trio nodded.

"Yes, of course," the waiter confirmed.

After initial reverberations of surprise from the kitchen, the meal arrived shortly. The aid workers received a serving of potatoes and meat fried in translucent batter.

Although bland, they consumed the feast hungrily and gratefully.

When finished, the waiter returned and asked, "How was the meal?"

"Great," Mik replied with a smile. Maintaining a naïve demeanour he asked, "How did you get the meat?"

Dropping his tone, but not the pride of resourcefulness, the waiter replied, "We buy it from special places...from the Serbs."

In a final personal coup, the waiter scribbled the meal's cost on a scrap of paper. Not entirely surprised by the tally, Justin paid the 180 Marks without hesitation.

Outside, it had become too dark to attempt travelling back too Ćoralići. At this point, a pair of headlights moving along the Una would have been magnets for trouble.

Instead, the trio decided to see if they could spend the night with BanBat. Turning north off the main street, they wove toward the only illuminated part of town. They soon found a floodlit compound beyond a weathered sign bearing a boy and girl running and the inscription "*Škola.*" A perimeter of stacked razor wire protected a crammed parking lot and a three-story pyramid-shaped building.

At the front gate, a flock of at least 10 kids called playfully to the Bangladeshi sentries for bonbons. They had none to offer and simply waved in reply. The guards spoke no English and appeared utterly confused by the arrival of the MOO vehicles. One sentry jabbered into a field phone and a young Bangladeshi captain soon appeared.

"Good evening. How can I be off assistance?" he asked the new arrivals in refined English.

Upon hearing the trio's predicament, the captain replied, "Of course. We would be happy to have you as our guests. Do not worry. I will find you some accommodation." Pointing to a row of parked BTR-60s, he added, "Please park there while I will find you a place to sleep."

The captain re-emerged from the main building a few minutes later. Pointing to a lone prefab near the perimeter, he said apologetically, "I am afraid, that is the only space I can offer tonight."

A handful of soldiers scurried in and out of the container removing a miscellany of medical lockers, drip stands and chairs. They left only a few health charts and an electric radiator. Turning on the heater the captain said, "While this warms up, please make yourselves at home. You are welcome to the officers' room. Watch TV. Have tea. Breakfast is served with the officers on the main floor, just to the right of the entrance. Washing facilities are in the containers behind the school building. I hope this is alright."

"This is fine," Laura smiled. "Thank you."

"Then good night," the captain said and disappeared into the school building.

Justin, Mik, Laura and a few Bangladeshis spent the next couple of hours watching TV in a large draughty room with boarded-up windows. One soldier, who had commandeered the remote control, flipped between Sky News and the movie, "Back to the Future" airing on a Serbian channel.

Upon returning to their warmed container, Justin produced the surviving bottle of Cognac. Reclining on their air mattresses, the trio reviewed their plans over plastic cups of brandy.

It was clear that fully assessing the Bihać Pocket's medical conditions would require much more than a few short discussions between Laura and the hospital directors. Far too many factors needed detailed scrutiny. Interviews with epidemiologists, water specialists and surgical experts, amongst others, would be required in any in-depth appraisal. However, from this short trip alone, Laura could make a fair determination of the region's immediate needs.

Justin and Laura maintained that the best thing MOO could do to address the dire circumstances was help replenish local medical stocks – basic drugs, dressings and hygienic materials. In Laura's opinion, accomplishing this involved making a concise assessment of the main institutions and then returning immediately to Zagreb to prepare the promised delivery for Velika Kladuša. The shipment MOO had promised Doric was key to maintaining any access to the south. Lingering in Bihać and searching for undiscovered institutions and political figures would defeat all such purpose. Ensuring good will on all sides was the only way they would be able to keep helping.

Facing the medical needs of the weak and wounded amongst 160,000 inhabitants in the south and 40,000 in the north, the MOO truck's eight-pallet capacity was really very little. The Bihać Hospital alone would require half a truckload of any given delivery.

Mik however, was not convinced and still wanted to make a thorough investigation, starting with medical staff in Bihać town, municipal and regional leadership and even General Dudaković. It had taken a long time to get to Bihać and he wanted to make the most of it.

What Bihać needed was pretty obvious; delivering aid was always more use than performing research. The vote again went 2-1 in favour of leaving the next day. The group agreed to head for Bužim and Pištaline in the morning, make their deliveries and have quick consultations with the staff at these locations.

They would then get back to Ćoralići and join the empty UNPROFOR convoy to Zagreb. As soon as the Serbs and Croats granted new crossing permission, they would load up a new delivery specifically for the Velika Kladuša Hospital. From then on, only a combination of decorum, tact and blatant deceit would help the people of the Bihać Pocket fairly and adequately.

They were, of course, getting carried away. By now, the trio should have known all too well that planning for the future was a most perilous exercise in these lands. Their success to date was the result of stubborn stumblings based on the slimmest of plans.

Justin crawled into his sleeping bag and settled to the escape of a cheep espionage novel. Mik flipped though a Dutch magazine with panoramic scenes of celebrities in St. Tropez. Fuelled by another mug of Cognac, Laura typed the outline of a medical report into her laptop.

Around midnight, Justin began to doze beneath his novel. A man yelling in Bosnian broke the night's silence. His shrill voice grew alarmingly close to the container. The hollering was finally emphasised by piercing bursts from a Kalashnikov.

Without warning, three short salvos thumped from the 14.5 mm turret gun of a Bengali APC.

Quiet returned to Bihać and remained for the rest of the night. Justin rolled over in his sleeping bag. He fell into slumber, his well-being assured in the hands of the East Bengal Regiment.

Chapter 17

Early the following morning, the trio joined a British Marine Commando and Belgian Army officer in the mess area for Corn Flakes and a boiled egg.

The officers' chirping Motorola's resonated through the cavernous foyer. The mechanical babbling of aged cynics erased the echoes of naïve cacophony that once brimmed the school's halls.

The British officer rose muttering, "Time for work. Off to pick up shell fragments along the Una."

The Belgian winked and followed his partner to the parking lot.

Finishing their meal and thanking the beaming orderly, the aid workers headed outside to load their vehicles. In the cold morning, Bangladeshis, bundled to their chins in ill-fitting Warsaw Pact fatigues, tinkered with a row of ill-equipped APCs. In discomfort to which they would never acclimatise, the soldiers stomped their feet and rubbed their hands.

The captain appeared. "I hope all was comfortable last night."

In gratitude, Mik presented the officer with a MOO T-shirt.

Slightly embarrassed, the Bangladeshi managed a smile, "This is far too kind. Most unnecessary." Nodding, he took the gift, "But thank you. Thank you very much."

The captain waved goodbye as the MOO vehicles exited the compound. Behind him, a few rusty BTR-60s coughed black smoky phlegm.

Inching toward its highest vantage, the sun fought to clear the grey sky. Its beauty soon shone beyond the discomfort of winter's lingering elements.

The Una's environs remained as seductive as the day before. Realising that the vision had not been some wishful apparition, Justin's emotional attachment grew ever more. Despite its fortune in madness and idiocy, falling for this land was not difficult. Through the winding journey along the seething river, ardour simmered gently within Justin – to linger into the morrow and many stormy days after.

The slow icy climb to the Cazin plateau proffered a longer view of Justin's Balkan mistress. As he lumbered around each hairpin, the supreme mountains, with features most delicate, arced through Justin's horizon – a universe that allured and distorted rational thought. Its bosom was so inviting it bore no evidence of those entrapped within. And while it beckoned unceasingly, it still held the clutching world at bay.

She was a temptation Justin had to fight without compromise. Such creations only spawned the deepest jealousies and caused men to commit the most bestial acts in her name. Yet, with even the fiercest resolve to cast her asunder, the mistress' long clutch would newer fully relinquish.

Atop the plateau Mik and Justin followed the main route back to Cazin before pealing east onto a lightly paved road. Slicing through rolling farmland, the track gradually deteriorated as pedestrians and dwellings became increasingly sparse.

They entered Pištaline 15 rocky kilometres farther. Little more than a handful of houses perched amongst open meadows, the settlement sat nearly six kilometres west of the Una. Unfortunately, the Serbs had breached this section of the river. The front-line actually stood less than three kilometres away.

Pištaline's generations had contented themselves to a lot of pastoral insignificance. And then one heinous dawn, without preamble, Bosnian fate wrought unimaginable importance upon them. Pištaline's clinic, now minutes from its eastern enemy, was the first stop for Fifth Corps wounded.

Amongst the cluster of dwellings, the aid workers found a two-story home; a bed sheet painted with a red cross hung from its balcony. In a small farmhouse next-door, they located the clinic director.

A serene stocky man with thinning ashen hair, the director smiled warmly to the guests and began his introduction in Bosnian. Although he spoke no English, his secretary spoke it passably.

"I am very happy to see you," the secretary translated. "We have been waiting for so much time for help. I stopped expecting. So, now you are here. It is a happy surprise."

The director resumed his preamble and pointed beyond the medical house.

"You arrived at a good time," the secretary continued interpreting. "Twenty minutes before, Chetnik bombs blasted in that field."

"We are also very glad to be here," Justin replied handing over the packing list. "Please understand that we have been trying for a long time to bring you these medicines, pain killers, dressings."

"We will try to keep delivering here," Laura added. "But to be more effective, I need to discuss the medical situation with you."

Still smiling, the director nodded and, through his secretary, replied, "Thank you very much. I will use these things immediately."

"Where are you from?" the director asked abruptly.

"Me? Canada," Laura replied a little thrown off. "And he's also Canadian and he's Dutch."

"Ah, this is very good," the secretary translated as the director beamed at his good fortune. "Now, I am two times happy you came. My sister is right now in Slovenia. She is going to Canada as refugee."

"But I am worried for her," the secretary continued. "When she gets to Canada. What will happen? She is a nurse but will she find a good job in Canada?"

"I think with some training it is very possible for her to one day find work as a nurse," Laura explained diplomatically. "But she'll also need to learn English very well. Don't worry, the government helps new refugees."

"But nurses, is it a good job in Canada? Will she survive?" the director pressed.

"Yes, it's a good job. She'll be OK."

Laura's vaguely optimistic responses were not enough, though. The director inquired about average wages, housing prospects, cost of living, weather and education possibilities for her children.

With the pressing lack of time, Laura grew increasingly impatient and stressed her need for medical data.

The director leaned back to digest all he had just heard. A hint of relief emerged and he appeared tentatively sanguine that his sister would be fine.

While Laura continued her inquires, Justin and Mik retreated to unload the truck. The director dispatched an aged orderly to help carry the supplies to the storeroom.

Entering the darkened entranceway next-door, the stench of sour rot was excruciating. The first unwitting hit stung Justin's throat. He wanted to cough but was afraid to breathe; the slightest gasp could unleash decay within. Who the hell could work under such putridity?

In what would have been the living room, nurses hand-washed stained sheets and bandages in milky basins atop a wood stove. Above, pairs of old surgical gloves dangled drying. Plastic sheets suspended from the ceiling sectioned off tables bearing dazed men begging for relief from fresh wounds.

The screams of those receiving attention blended with the groans of those waiting. Succumbing to agony some moaned through bravely clamped jaws. All pleaded for narcotic's sweat delusion.

The elderly assistant guided the aid workers to the kitchen and pointed to a corner. He did not intend to carry the cargo. Instead, he pretended to putter around the empty room while Mik and Justin lugged the tall pallet from the truck.

A visibly frustrated Laura and the chatty director emerged a few minutes later. The doctor thanked Laura profusely for the visit. She promised to return as soon as possible.

Without awaiting the guests' departure, the director ducked into the medical house to attend his weeping wounded.

Climbing into the Landcruiser, Laura announced, "OK, Bužim next."

Nodding affirmation, Justin called, "Hey, did you get any useful info from the director?"

"A little," Laura scowled. "When he wasn't asking about Canada, he mentioned they're completely exposed to Bosnian Serb forces. When there's combat, they get a good 50 patients a day. They can't do anything complicated though. Just lots of amputations. Bad cases go to Cazin by horse cart…if they make it. Most freeze or bleed to death on the way."

From Pištaline, the trio returned to Cazin and then followed another meandering road north for almost 20 km. Skirting yet another rampart of Bosnia's periphery, the route wound past mountains and wove through valleys. Within an hour, the trio had retreated safely from the eastern Bosnian Serb front and advanced perilously toward the northern Abdić-sponsored front. In this impoverished place, armies and frontlines appeared the principal measure of wealth.

Pressing through a vein between rolling wood-speckled hills, the trio entered Bužim. Higher mountains lay in wait farther to the south and east. Downtown, decrepit cafes and kiosks adorned a small artificial lake as they loitered in flaked and rusted abandonment.

The ruins of an old stone fortress rested peacefully on a slope above. Along other ridges, a small mining facility and factory slumped in dark impotent gloom.

Ignoring the blemishes of industrial brutality, Bužim was likely once a very pleasant getaway for Bihać and Velika Kladuša residents.

Through the deserted streets, the trio found the *Dom Zdravlja* in the town centre. The isolated settlement was virtually devoid of life. The only bastion not relenting against the trend was the narrow two-story medical facility.

Bužim was no more than a couple of mountain peaks east of Pecigrad and maybe 10 km south of the confrontation line.

Inside, a nurse guided the group to an ill-lit cellar room. A tall man, possibly in his late 30s, sat at a desk conversing with four older female staff.

In thickly accented English he said, "Welcome. Please..." and pointed to a cluster of wooden chairs. "I am the director of this house of health."

Laura explained that they had a delivery and a few questions.

"Yes of course. Thank you," the director replied. "I must first say that you are welcome here always. We are most grateful. You are the best of all aid groups."

Smiling wryly, he added, "You must excuse my office. I have a better office on the top but yesterday afternoon it was destroyed by shelling."

As Laura presented the packing list, the staff immediately engulfed it. She began asking about the general situation at the facility but was interrupted by a ringing telephone.

Finishing the short phone call, the director explained, "Today this *Dom Zdravlja* is quiet. We send many patients home. Others go to Cazin. When there is new fighting and Abdić attacks, we are busy again. We treat many war wounds but..."

The phone rang once more and the director chatted into the receiver.

A tall black staff member peered into the office inquiringly. Seeing the guests, he boomed with a large smile, "Ah, foreigners. Well hello. We get so few able-bodied visitors these days. Where are you from?"

Reaching to shake hands, Mik replied, "Me, Holland. They're Canadian."

"Great."

"You're not from Bosnia are you?" Mik pried.

"How did you guess? It's the accent right?" With a deep chuckle, the black staffer explained, "Nah, I'm from Zambia! I was studying in Yugoslavia a few years ago, on a kind of Non-Aligned medical exchange programme. I was finishing my practical studies when the war started. So, I'm stuck here."

Shrugging philosophically, he added, "But this is my calling. It's what I swore to do...it doesn't really matter where I practice, does it?"

Justin felt visceral relief for all those who had fled and found a getaway from this war. He would have done the same. Yet, this group before him stayed and fought the evil forces without ever raising a weapon. Each day tested their oath to help the ailing and dying beyond all reason.

If war had any heroes, it was these men and women toiling with defiant dignity – bereft of glory yet resplendent in decency.

They plodded on under such dismal prospects – a collection of the land's brightest gems of interminable stamina. Affluent industrialised states could only dream of having workers of such dedication and resourcefulness. But here they languished, wasted and targeted. This realm had vision only to nurture its wealth of destroyers and takers.

Replacing the receiver, the director apologised to his visitors.

Glancing at her watch and realising the session could easily take longer than desired, Laura explained, "We plan to make more regular trips to the Bihać Pocket if possible. I know the delivery today is small but it is all we could carry this time. For the future deliveries, I will need more information on this clinic's needs."

The phone rang again. The director grimaced; raising a finger, he suspended his answer.

Increasingly agitated, Laura looked at her watch again. It was nearing noon and the trio had to hit the road soon.

Finishing the call, the director apologised deeply.

Laura stated, "We really need to leave in a few minutes. Do you have any statistics available on paper that we could take back to Zagreb?"

"Yes, I have a medical list," the director replied. Frowning he added, "But it is in Bosnian."

"That's not a problem." Laura prompted anxiously, "The medicine's in Latin. We can use it for now and talk more next delivery."

"OK. *Dobro*," the director smiled and muttered instructions to the head nurse.

She returned moments later with a flimsy typed list.

As the director's office now occupied the facility's storeroom, the staff descended into argument over where to stow the delivery. Mik and Justin unpacked the last of the truck's pallets and simply stacked the boxes in the main hallway.

The director slipped away from the fray to express further gratitude to the aid workers.

Racing out of Bužim, the valleys and virgin rivers passed Justin in a tragic blur. The pristine sights screamed for appreciation but he could offer none. Instead, he strained to stay on the road and near the wake of Mik's squealing tires.

A smattering of white plaster homes nestled amongst green hills came into view as they approached Cazin. The road became progressively more crowded as people wandered past busy roadside commerce. Black-market cigarettes and candy bars were spread on cardboard boxes. Plastic Coke bottles, filled with pink fuel few could afford, stood in pyramids along the curb.

Leaving town, kids appeared faithfully from the outlying houses and farms. Running furiously to the road's edge, they jumped and waved to the white vehicles. Justin had yearned for them all morning. In spite of the hate and lies the elders had fed these children, in the haze of the moment, they remained unfettered. They yelled without prejudice and adult stupidity; they yelled because they were kids. Grownups would call them immature and tell them to be quiet.

The young were fighting a war too – one to protect childhoods the elderly so desperately tried to steal. For, they were ripe pastures begging to be poisoned. If the evil seeds took, the hate could flourish in at least one more generation.

These kids screamed to the outsiders, "Look at us please! We don't believe all the old ones told us, you'll see…"

In that flash, Justin forgot all the futility around him – that of his own actions, of the barriers, of the hate, of the murderous graffiti, of the vengeance. For the most fleeting of moments, it all faded and he knew there was still hope.

Pulling up to the Coralići base, just after one o'clock, Mik and Justin parked inside the front gate. A line of UNPROFOR trucks coiled expectantly through the compound. At the head, a French Lieutenant gave instructions to a rank of men. Beside them sat two UNHCR Land Rovers. Isaac Jaco chatted with their drivers.

Seeing the MOO vehicles, he waved and ran over. Shaking his head and smiling, Jaco called, "You guys are just in time. Some of the UN trucks had a few problems unloading. Their departure was delayed a bit. Lucky for you. We're just waiting for them to come up from Bihać town. As soon as they arrive, the convoy leaves."

Nodding toward the French Lieutenant, Jaco stated, "You better let the convoy leader know you'll be joining."

Jaco led Mik to the Lieutenant. Laura climbed back into the Landcruiser to radio Zagreb. Justin lit a smoke and savoured the moment.

Lapping the midday rays lavished upon him, Justin drew upon the contentment of accomplishment. He caught a glimpse of his own reflection in the Landcruiser window. Unshaven, he sported a grimy baseball cap and a red and black chequered jacket covering body armour and a hunting vest – he looked damn cool that afternoon.

United Nations military jargon crackled from the Motorola clipped to his belt. A Land Rover, driven by the Royal Marine from breakfast, pulled up to the gate. He nodded in recognition to Justin and entered the compound.

The radio on Justin's hip was really his membership badge to this isolated, elite fellowship. The passing nod was the secret handshake of acceptance into this strange club. He really was part of something big and momentous. It would all fade, as the next emergency arose and lives moved on, but it felt so magnificent to belong on this sunny day.

The old Danish general appeared and strode toward his white Peugeot sedan followed by a slouching Russian colonel.

"These delays are outrageous," the cantankerous general yelled at his Russian underling, "I have meetings in Zagreb. We must move now. I cannot wait here."

The Russian nodded nonchalantly and handed a flak jacket to his superior.

The general squirmed and hunched awkwardly but could only get one arm though. Swinging the vest to the ground in infantile frustration, he growled, "Help me put this damn thing on!"

Mik and Jaco returned. "The Bihać trucks arrive in five minutes," Mik announced. "The French trucks here will leave first, followed by the Bihać trucks. We can follow at the back."

Jaco patted Mik on the back and shook Justin's hand. "Good luck. Keep up the good work. I really hope to see you guys again soon."

The French drivers climbed aboard their trucks and revved the engines eagerly. One soldier tossed his comrade a disposable camera and leapt in front of his parked vehicle for a last war souvenir.

Five UN trucks soon pulled up on the road from Bihać town. The lead Bangladeshi jeep raced into the compound. The French Lieutenant waved to his waiting trucks and hopped into a Peugeot jeep. He pulled out of the base, followed by a collection of French transport trucks, BanBat jeeps, UNMO and UNHCR cars and the fuming general in his sedan.

The remaining trucks fell into the wheeled millipede and lurched collectively up the first long snowy hill. Justin put on his uncool Kevlar helmet and followed Mik at the procession's fringe.

Chapter 18

As the caravan lurched up the glistening slope, an untainted layer of snow made the accent progressively difficult. The now empty trucks had even less traction then when they arrived.

Tires spun and engines howled. The convoy advanced in starts and stops, straining to grasp the next slight patch of asphalt. At the uneasy peak, the drivers' weak knees and dry mouths found little redress. Descending toward Pecigrad, they needed one last gasp to tap their sharpest fear and concentration. Justin's engine screamed as momentum tried to overwhelm the restraining low gear. Mik battled with his brakes while ice and gravity amplified the Landcruiser's buoyant tendencies.

The crisp sun beaming on the bucolic surroundings remained a fierce distraction as well. Justin could not totally resist and pried hungry glimpses of these most precious lands.

Midway down the pass, the elongated tanker before Mik encountered severe handling trouble. The ageing 18-wheeler groaned perilously along the road's edge as its rear wheels seized and refused to unlock.

The more frantically its driver applied the brakes, the more uncontrollably it tugged at the precipice. The truck skidded diagonally into a sweeping curve and its rear-end shot straight for the cliff's edge. The air brakes shrilled desperately against the awaiting finality. Mercifully, the vehicle creaked to a halt at the ravine's threshold.

Mik and Justin halted safely behind the stricken French truck. The vehicles ahead stopped in zigs and zags as word was radioed along the line.

The truck's two crewmembers clambered out through the driver's side. One paced and stared over the taunting ravine. The other muttered agitatedly as he chocked the wheels and peered at the undercarriage. A second pair of French soldiers ran up the hill lugging a large toolbox.

Taking advantage of the bonus moment, Justin hopped from his cab, stretched his legs and lit a smoke. They had stopped just past a village, not more than two kilometres up the hill from Pecigrad. Justin stole another last gaze at the calling valleys and slopes beyond; it was such a peaceful view. Cocking his head northward, the air was free of war's reverberation. It was just another weekend afternoon in the country.

The most immediate sound was of children's laughter and feet stampeding down the road. It had not taken the village kids long to realise the wealth that had just arrived. Weaving meticulously through the vehicles, the short mob leapfrogged along – smiling, jumping, yelling.

To calls of, *"Bon joor.* Hey you. *Goomy Goomy!"* drivers handed the remains of their rations down to outstretched hands.

Mik opened his door and tried to distribute the contents of a ration box. Clawing hands shredded the container and Mik yanked his door shut. To their further pleas, he smiled, shook his head and then concentrated on rolling a cigarette. Not wanting to miss any other opportunities, the kids gave up and focused on the remaining vehicles.

A French soldier in combat webbing, his rifle slung, marched up the line. Stopping to talk with each driver, he explained to Mik, "Gear box problems. Maybe 20 minutes more."

A half hour later, the broken truck started up its engine and inched forward testing its grip. The convoy's vehicles coughed to life and slid past the waving, momentarily content, kids.

Pulling into Pecigrad, the convoy leader paused at the final crossing barrier. The absence of shelling and Fifth Corps bureaucracy made the wait no more than cursory.

Plunging into the disputed environs, the road levelled and wound along a river banked by farmland and scattered forest. Hills walled the road's eastern flank. The tunnel of their nocturnal arrival was now a wide rural panorama.

However, with day's sight Justin lost night's hearing. The only noise entering his open window now was a searing winter wind. Nearing the confrontation line, Justin strained to find familiar reference from his earlier journey. There were none. The front lines had likely shifted anyway. Only the fighting men had the slightest clue of the front's real location.

Staggering to a trickle, the convoy passed clusters of Fifth Corps fighters. Armed with AK-47's and wearing mangy fatigues, their faces were filthy and unshaven – they did not feel cool at all.

One combatant looked up at Justin and made a two-fingered request for a cigarette. In any other lifetime or fate, that youth could so easily have been Justin. The soldier's hungry comrades crouched nearby in a ditch on an icy road not of their choosing.

Justin tossed the trooper his Marlboro pack. On a bad day, any of the soldiers could have killed Justin for a smoke. At 30 Marks a pack, one human life was a minor tariff. Justin was having a good day in Bosnia; maybe the smokes would help these guys out a little. Besides, the Fifth Corps had never given him trouble.

The soldier's eyes bulged in disbelief at the red and white box in his hands. He and two comrades glanced at Justin and waved hurried, startled thanks. They leapt back to the cover of their gutter like excited children. As they fumbled to open the pack, other troops emerged from their trenches for a cut of the score.

Justin wove past the tail fin of a spent antitank rocket. Small arms fire became audible. The frontline's log marker had disappeared. A small gunfight, waged in a pasture to the convoy's left, was the front's real indicator.

Justin calmly watched the battle performance less than a hundred metres away. Drivers and peacekeepers had already lost eyes, limbs and lives along this road. The clash was fascinating; its danger seemed minimal and abstract.

Leaving the skirmish behind, the convoy accelerated slightly through more scattered hamlets. Signs of inhabitation began to return the farther north they travelled.

An elderly man stood passively at the edge of a cemetery. He leaned against his cane taking in the view sweeping past – armoured cars, jeeps and trucks, with black "U" and "N" stencilled on them and a few with unfurled blue flags. How many armies and vehicles and people and deeds had passed his vantage through the years? What tale would he tell about those before him now? How did our heroic and cowardly deeds match up with those of the predecessors? Had the world progressed to tell a different tale of imprisonment and destruction? Was this pathetic gaggle as far as we had advanced? Was this impotent offering all that the world had to show for itself? Who would pass next or would this circus be the last?

Had anyone cared to listen, he could have told such wealth.

The convoy did not stop, though. It pressed on and, nearing Mala Kladuša, came to an abrupt stop on a long flat bend.

No explanation came over the VHF and no apparent cause could be seen on the road ahead. Uncertain of the day's unfolding combat or of the Abdić troops' nervous intentions, Justin sat anxiously – his body armour and helmet firmly in place.

It was not long before a handful of Abdić-rabble milled toward the exposed vehicles. Cold and bored, they looked at the vehicles curiously. A few troops plied drivers for smokes.

Three unshaven youths, one carrying a large medical bag, stopped at Justin's cab. The oldest called up for a cigarette. Justin pulled a handful from his last pack and held them out the window. The soldier climbed up on the doorstep and took them gratefully.

Grinning mockingly, the bareheaded trooper tapped Justin's white helmet and asked if he could try it on.

With an unpractised "Tsk," and awkward flick of his head, Justin replied, "Yeah right."

Lingering to peer at the cab's contents, the youth's searching eyes found a pack of Kleenex on the dashboard. Pointing to it, he burst into laughter.

"*Daj mi, daj mi!*" the soldier urged.

Justin handed the pack over good-naturedly.

Hearing their buddy laugh, his colleagues stepped closer. The trooper jumped down, dispensed the smokes and then carefully, with his thumb and forefinger, extracted a single tissue.

With aristocratic pomp, he dabbed at the corner of his caked lips and at a muck-clogged nostril. His comrades howled with gut-wrenching laughter.

As they calmed, the soldier climbed back on the doorstep and wiped the rear-view mirror clean. Breathing against the glass, he buffed it further. He admired his reflection and extended a hand requesting payment.

"Very nice," Justin smirked and handed over more smokes.

The soldier smiled and feigned a bow.

Grinning, he and his comrades ran up to Mik and Laura's car to wipe their mirrors with similar comic enthusiasm. When no payment was forthcoming, the soldier proceeded to the headlights. Eyeing his reflection in the car's front, the soldier called to his buddies for confirmation of his work's lustre.

Before they could extract remuneration, they hastily straightened up. A group of better dressed and shaven soldiers approached.

Three higher-ranking Abdić troops, in Serb fatigues, walked up to Mik's cruiser. Trailing them were the old Dane, a Dutch UNMO and a Bangladeshi officer.

The Dutch officer tried to communicate with a handful of Bosnian words. The excitable Danish general stated emphatically, "Tell these Yugoslavs that I have already said that none of these soldiers have any cameras!"

One of Abdić's men, replied in stunted English, "We see flash. We find camera."

Mik was ordered to exit his vehicle. The Dane thundered defensively, "This vehicle is not with us. We cannot be responsible for it."

The Dutch officer muttered something to Mik, who shrugged and stepped aside. The local officers proceeded to search the Landcruiser for illicit cameras.

Finding nothing, they set their sights on Justin's truck. The scrutiny was wasted; they came up empty there too.

While the cluster continued arguing with the Dane, two other Abdić soldiers ran up from the convoy's front. They proudly presented their commander with a pair of disposable Kodak's and a pocket Minolta camera.

The local officer glared at the UNPROFOR soldiers triumphantly. The general stammered and managed to bellow, "This in outrageous! Pure harassment! I shall have very harsh words for your commanders!"

The Abdić troops shrugged and walked away with their contraband. The Dane stormed back to the comfort of his sedan and the convoy soon continued.

Picking up their lost momentum, they sped through Mala Kladuša. Although the town remained skeletal in daylight, there were a few signs of lives clinging to the last shards of normalcy. A couple of chimneys bellowed smoke and a handful of women lugged freezing buckets of water.

Impatient to cover the final uncertain stretch, the remaining seven kilometres to Velika Kladuša passed with little concern for the surroundings. The convoy pulled up outside the BanBat base and entered the parking lot one at a time. It was almost 3 p.m. and such a long group could not make the last leg to Zagreb before dusk. The convoy would stay overnight in Velika Kladuša.

It was not clear if the Danish general would still push for his important meetings in Zagreb or stay to reap wrath upon the poor soldiers who had sought unauthorised mess hall souvenirs.

The MOO vehicles stood-by outside the UN compound. Mik radioed Justin expressing his desire to make a push for the Zagreb. Without the slow convoy, they could probably make it across the last Krajina Serb crossing around sunset. Laura was also eager to get the Doric and Tabaric delivery loaded and on the road as soon as possible.

Justin concurred without hesitation.

They pulled away from the roadside and squeezed past the remnants of what had been both their protection and hindrance.

At the Velika Kladuša internal checkpoint, Mik presented Doric's permission scrap once more. The soldier glanced at it and waved them along. With curfew well in effect, the town streets were deserted except for roaming soldiers.

The contentment that simmered within Justin evaporated as Velika Kladuša's smouldering wreckage came into view. His empty stomach cramped with pure rancour for this ugly land.

"Let's get out of here," Mik called enthusiastically on the VHF.

Justin cringed at Mik's confidence; it only jinxed their passage through Bihać's final barrier of unpredictability. The absence of the UN convoy's shielding cloak exposed them to any soldiers' whim.

On the Bihać Pocket's final sheer, the aid workers inched down to the closed blue and white barrier. A young man with glazed eyes swaggered from his metal hut brandishing a Kalashnikov – he thought he looked pretty cool.

Mik exited the Landcruiser and tried explaining his desire to depart Bosnia. The soldier pointed his weapon at the car's rear indicating his desire to search it.

Justin hopped from his cab. Mik flipped the unlocking switch on the dashboard and Justin pulled the rear door open.

A second soldier in a black wool hat strutted from the hut. His features were equally glazed. He reeked of many things but particularly of alcohol.

The first guard poked aggressively through the Landcruiser's scattered contents. Shoving the first aid kit aside, he grabbed at the four spare jerry cans. Finding two still bearing diesel, he turned to Justin and demanded, "*Staja ovo?*"

"*Benzin,*" Justin replied. "Uh…it's leftover."

The guard understood no English. "*Nema benzina,*" he growled.

Wondering how to explain that they had originally brought the fuel in without a problem and should therefore be able to bring it out as well, Justin tried, "It's old…*stari.*" With hand motions, he continued, "Entering Velika Kladuša *nema problema.*"

The guard spat at Justin's feet. The second soldier stepped up and, inches from Justin's face, said, "*Benzin, veliki problem.*"

Mik re-emerged from his seat and moved to enter the dispute. The first guard raised his weapon warning Mik to stay put.

Justin caught Mik's concerned expression and motioned reassuringly, "It's OK."

Unsure what to do, Mik stood his ground nervously.

The first guard again spat at the ground, shook his head vigorously and growled, "*Veliki problem.*"

Trying to appear as apologetic as possible, Justin replied, "Sorry…*oprostite.*"

The guard held up two fingers, "*Dva benzina maksimum.*"

"Next time…*drugi put samo dva,*" learning Bosnian, Justin tried optimistically. "*Nema problema.*"

Brandishing his weapon, the guard corrected Justin, "*Ne. Veliki problem. Imaš čhetri benzin. Papier. Ti.*" Making a writing motion, the guard tried to convey that Justin had four jerry cans instead of the two allowed that day. He would need some kind of written permission to continue.

"*Nema papier. Kolega. Nema problema,*" Justin tried vainly.

"OK. *Maximum dva,*" the guard replied. Pointing to himself he added, "*Ima chetri. Daj mi dva benzin.*"

It was the hook Justin had been expecting – the guard's move to gain the remaining fuel. Justin had little intention, at this point, of handing it over. He wanted to try and get through with the diesel. UNPROFOR might have become Bosnia's grab bag but Justin was fed up and tired of these people, he wanted to make a last futile point to them.

Shaking his head, feigning ignorance, Justin pointed to the two full Jerry's and said simply, "*Dva diesel*. OK."

The guard shook his head and again demanded, "*Dva* OK *drugi put. Danas nije dobro. Daj mi tvoj benzin.*"

Rage flared and the soldier's weapon stabbed at Justin's chest. The jagged muzzle glanced off the ceramic plate, caught his shoulder and nicked his chin. Shards of pain shrieked down Justin's neck and arm. He tried to collect his bearings and appear calm. Had the soldier's fury peaked or would he just pull the trigger? This was the big exam – all lessons led to this mortal quiz. Display confidence or fear; this is where Justin won or lost – no prize.

Justin strained to deceive himself of danger's truth once more. He did not want to hand over the diesel. This was his choice and he continued haggling with a dumb nod. "*Ne razumijem.* I don't understand."

Silence followed; anger ebbed. Seeking guidance, the guard muttered to his colleague.

No advice was forthcoming. Warped silence remained; the guard glared at Justin. He lifted his arm slightly and then jerked it upward in exasperation.

"OK. *Pićka materina. Idite breh,*" he snapped at Justin and swung his weapon for the two vehicles to get lost.

He stomped over to the barrier and flung it open angrily.

Still trying not to look panicked, Mik and Justin quickly got in their vehicles and rolled down the hill.

Beyond the barrier, realisation took hold as Justin's heart thundered and his hands shook. He was never sure about that guard; he had put his odds at 50-50. It could all just as easily have turned bad.

"Good work," Mik called back on the VHF.

Justin fumbled to light a smoke. He took a deep drag that slowly filtered down through his body and spread rewarding tranquillity.

At the hill's foot, Justin advanced toward the Maljevac checkpoint with great relief. The stout middle-aged militiaman at the RSK barrier gave a feeble salute. He grinned impishly and pointed to Justin's chin.

Sweet sweet adrenalin and nicotine had masked the trickle of blood under his jowl. As Justin plucked at his moist crimson neckline, the guard chuckled in his best German, "*Musliman... savage...nicht richtig...*"

The Serb performed a cursory businesslike search of the vehicles. He gave another laboured salute and opened the crossing boom.

The aid workers were still far from Zagreb and anything could happen in the remaining three hours to Mošćenica. Regardless, Justin's tension eased the deeper they drove into Krajina.

Racing along the partially cleared roads, Justin sought to allay his conscience and enjoy a respite from thoughts of Bihać's reality. But before he could assuage himself with a waiting cold beer, hot shower and sleep he had to contend with memories of the caged land he vacated. Sitting silently in his stark cab, kept company by only a droning engine, Justin had few distractions in which to hide. Thoughts of celebration for a job well done were embarrassing. The few threats and inconveniences he received along the way were so trivial compared to those faced by the Pocket's inhabitants.

Many would die during Justin's absence. All the men who asked for smokes and all the kids who clamoured for candy could be maimed and mutilated at any passing instant.

Bihać had long ceased to be an abstraction on a map or a sound coughed from plastic TV personae. Bihać was all the faces that had spoken to Justin and allowed him a precious glimpse into their lives. In the end, all were faces just seeking the same simple pleasures as Justin and anyone else. Faces different only by the criminal conditions in which they pursued those simple desires – adult faces wanting safe homes, young faces wanting a childhood, elderly faces wanting to savour quiet reflection and affection. How was it that these incontestable desires were the most elusive and demanded the most savage cost?

The cold of that waiting beer would be orgasmic and the hot of the shower delicious. Yet, it gave little exorcism and only short sanctuary from the Bihać that would forever peer into Justin's waking and slumbering hours. Even the most tantalising of a journey's gems always came with obscured and dear appendages.

Bihać and other places cursed by historic prominence and aggression and destruction and displacement and panic, bore souls that strove so much harder to be ponds of normalcy. Bihać deserved its unusual punishment no more than anywhere else. Justin was not special and neither was his home. The privilege of birth he bore today could easily be enslavement tomorrow. His actions now meant little. How would he face-up to challenge when it was not of his preference but instead meted by fate.

The places on the news and in the history books had always seemed so extraordinary; their names bore qualities of such higher substance than all elsewhere. Bihać was now one such hallowed name yet its billing disappointed Justin. Nobody there had ever claimed to be special. Exceptional circumstance might have made them different for a moment. Maybe in the future, as in the past, Bihać would be allowed to exist with the same ennui as the happy places in which Justin had lived and grown up.

Outside Vojnić, the trio passed an UNPROFOR truck that had been hauling 2x4's. It lay upturned in a ditch; its cargo scattered in a field. Its driver stood at the road's edge relieving his bladder on the truck's exposed underside.

The aid workers approached Glina's outskirts as daylight faded. In the flat cold, the scattered shells of houses glowered louder than ever – yelling one more reminder at Justin. He should have known better; lands of such exquisite beauty could never exist without equally insidious repulsiveness.

All the world's magnificence would never obscure this truth. No matter how many shrubs grew back to shroud the past's flaws, the charred houses stood in testimonial that little would ever change. These were disgusting lands deserving of the deepest disdain.

And when the last home crumbled to obscurity, there would always be other self-righteous and spiteful loners awaiting the cue to raze the reflections of those who dared to create. These insecure weaklings spewed convictions that offered no good, no food, no freedom and no happiness. These vicious torchbearers stalked those who dared commit the blasphemy of disregarding yore's blood for the dream of a decent future.

The simple houses were mighty shrines to each family's sacrifice and pain. This was the land's true identity – these were monuments as noble as the oldest mosques and tallest cathedrals. The land's strength and beauty were really built on the foundations of each family's labour. They were the symbols of pure hope that marked the insignificant's place in the universe.

These lands had suddenly ceased to care about such things though. For here, the scrawny sheep sought only to destroy tangible optimism for fictitious opiates of the past. These dim determined forces reserved their deepest hatred for the builders.

As the journey's final hour to Mošćenica grew darker, the land's self-inflicted disfigurement faded into the welcome night – the only remaining glimpse pierced back from the edges of the truck's headlights.

The trio arrived in Mošćenica under full darkness. At the Serb checkpoint, below a lone streetlight, the only visible objects were the guard hut and closed crossing boom. The aid workers waited before the barrier, its red, blue and white stripes shimmering in the Landcruiser's headlights.

A guard peered from the warm hut. It was getting late and he did not feel like searching a bunch of empty vehicles. Recognising Laura, he waved and casually stepped out to raise the barrier.

In his cab, lit only by the glowing dashboard, Justin abstractly tried to recall what exactly had brought all these crossing barriers there anyway. He had discussion upon discussion with Mik, Laura, the warehouse boys, UN officials and inhabitants around him. The talks were always long and invariably ended in ambiguity. The problems originated from religion. Or no, they were definitely social in nature. Yet, there were also cultural aspects. A political facet could not be overlooked either. Then there was the philosophical slant on it all. History played a considerable part too. Foreigners lacked the soul to understand the subjective; locals were too biased to see the objective.

Approaching the other side of the no-man's void, the vehicles pulled up to the closed Croatian crossing boom beneath a massive illuminated Croatian flag. The red, white and blue striped barrier radiated in the Landcruiser's headlights.

All discussions of high values and just beliefs meant absolutely nothing. The only reason they were fighting was that each side had wanted to paint their fences and barriers and cloth in colours of their own choosing. It mattered not if they were the same colours, for it was the order that counted – the right order. This reason was as good as all the others they had tried to pawn off on all of us and on themselves.

It was all a fucking waste.

Chapter 19

Past the last Croatian barrier, the MOO vehicles entered the ever-boring home stretch of Zagreb-bound rush-hour traffic.

In just over one long hour, they would be settling into a relaxing dinner. Of course, their rest would be short; the next morning they had to prepare the promised delivery for the Velika Kladuša hospital.

Justin took smug solace in believing that he had nothing to do with all the arguments and theorising about the conflict. He had been neither a belligerent nor an apologist. Justin had not stood by and allowed the feeble deceivers to work unhindered. Their evil work had not completely succeeded everywhere.

While his deeds had done nothing to change the overall situation, Justin felt no disillusionment. He was confident he had done something and he knew exactly whom he had helped. Even if the contribution was minute in the historic scheme around him, a few people had benefited from his efforts. Some now lived with a little less pain and a little more dignity. It would never alleviate the guilt he felt for those he may have neglected or could never help, but it would make waking in the morning tolerable.

Maybe at the very least they had set an example. Maybe one of the young, who received his aid, would do some good one day. Maybe he would dedicate his life to helping others and be a tribute to his people. Maybe such dreams were too lofty to dwell on now though.

In Zagreb, the three strode proudly into the office just after 7 p.m. The place sat dark and silent. In celebration of the trio's entry into Bihać, an empty bottle of champagne and a Roquefort cheese wrapper littered the living room coffee table. A note stated that Rolf and the remaining staff had gone skiing in Slovenia for the day.

No hot food awaited the trio and there were no beverages in the fridge. Justin found a warm beer in the pantry. He split it with Mik and sat down to watch CNN. There was absolutely no mention of Bihać or their deeds.

It did not matter. The best accolades are neither written nor spoken. A patient's smile and a doctor's thankful pull on a cigarette had long since rewarded Justin more than anyone could ever measure.

It is never a waste.

Aubrey Verboven spent most of the 1990s living and travelling in Eastern Europe with his wife. During this time, he worked for various aid groups and international organizations including Médecins Sans Frontières, CARE Canada, the Organization for Security and Cooperation in Europe, the United Nations High Commissioner for Refugees and the International Organization for Migration. He also contributed a number of travel articles to publications such as the Guardian Weekly, Globe & Mail and Central Europe Online.

Today he works as a researcher for the Canadian government and lives with his family in Ottawa. This is Aubrey's first book.

Made in the USA
Charleston, SC
07 November 2011